CODING OF A CONCRETE ANIMAL

The Billy Michaels Story

CODING OF A CONCRETE ANIMAL

The Billy Michaels Story

PAUL KNIGHT

Matador
9 De Montfort Mews
Leicester LE1 7FW, UK
Tel: (+44) 116 255 9311 / 9312
Email: books@troubador.co.uk
Web: www.troubador.co.uk/matador

ISBN 10: 1-905886-41-1
ISBN 13: 978-1905886-418

Typeset in 11pt Stempel Garamond by Troubador Publishing Ltd, Leicester, UK
Printed by The Cromwell Press Ltd, Trowbridge, Wilts, UK

Matador is an imprint of Troubador Publishing Ltd

In memory of

'TIGER'

1971–2005
My friend, my back up, my family

May you have been greeted at the gates
by the others who went untimely before you.

I hope you are raising Hell in Heaven's tranquillity.

To my family
To my extended family
To the family

To all those who encouraged me to actually
finish a project I started.

Special Thanks to...

Denny Cooke, Senay Zeki, Alan Hill and all the family and friends of all the wonderful characters I have met in this life time that are no longer with us but made my memories full of story telling tales.

Plus

A 'nod and a wink' to 'er indoors who helped me design the front cover with a respectful tip of the cap to Frank Miller, who inspired it.

To all those not mentioned, please do not take offence there will be other books that could bear your name in the near future.

I'm open to bribes!

Disclaimer

Any similarity in the characters betrayed in this book and actual figures of the criminal underworld is purely coincidental. Absolutely no disrespect is intended towards these people or their families.

In addition, this novel is in no way a two-fingered gesture to the establishment that was unable to solve certain crimes similar to those that are depicted in this book.

Other factual events are used as a time reference throughout the story that is about to be told and again is in no shape or form an insult to the memories and lives of those that were affected.

I thank you all for your understanding and hope that you enjoy reading this fictional piece of literature that although is based on actual events, it should not be mistaken as a confession or as the missing jigsaw pieces to the puzzle known as the criminal way of life. After all, I am but an honest family man with an over active imagination and not someone who has changed the names of the characters depicted to protect the guilty nor do I endorse the torture and murder of scum who grass, disrespect or steal from their own.

Honest Guv, would I lie to ya?
Regards

Foreword

Dennis Cooke

Billy Michaels is a man that has seen life at the beginning, the middle and the end of life's spectrum. The path he has travelled, from arriving into this world until the present day would have fazed most human beings, but Billy can hardly be described as an ordinary everyday human being.

He is, as described in this book, a third generation East End villain and as such is a man bearing the title of 'what you see is what you get'.

Billy missed growing up like most of us and became a man almost before reaching adolescence and you would think that after all his experiences he would be destined for the doldrums or prison or both.

He has spent his whole life living by the old East End code of practice, brought up amongst some of the 'hardest bastards' in the game and in some instances, going toe to toe with them, on the cobbles. He has witnessed massive beatings, torture and even death.

Billy is a Gentleman, a comic, someone who you would want to watch your back in a situation, a diamond geezer of the first degree and most of all, someone you would be very proud to call your friend.

This story will keep you hanging on to every written word and when you have finished this tale, you may just have a different angle on the yesteryear East End Villains we have all read about.

Chapter One

In reality, the sound made when you remove someone's eye from its socket is not the expected 'squish' 'pop' that you would expect, thanks to TV and the movies but it is more of a slight suction noise that is only exaggerated by the wet, moist noise of bodily fluids that slurp around behind the eyeball. If anything, the sound of the tip of a fountain pen being jabbed into the Cornea and through to the iris gets to you more. However, the sound that would chill you to the bone after witnessing something like that is not the scream of realisation from the victim but the sound of chuckling coming from the owner of the fountain pen.

There are those that believe that violence is the language of the mindless thug, used to terrorise, intimidate and brutalise. Unthinking, random acts that seem to serve no other purpose than to amuse the attacker and humiliate the victim. But those who have seen the dark corners of life can tell you that there are cold and calculating beasts in this world that are cerebral in the way they use their ability to inflict pain and suffering on others without care or remorse. They do not all sport tattoos and shaven heads; they do not belong to cults or use religion, colour or creed to justify their actions, these people have no gender restrictions or unusual sexual preferences. They are everyday citizens who, at this present moment in time, could be living right next door to you and you haven't even given them a second glance. It could be the butcher, the baker or even the candlestick maker. They happily walk and work amongst us, friendly smiles on their faces and springs in their steps, all the while thinking what they want from you and how to get it. This is the story of such an individual and the bloodline that pumps through the roots of his family tree.

He could be laughing and joking with you non-stop, all day long and in a split second he could turn against you, reach inside his tailor made jacket for his platinum cased fountain pen and have your eyeball speared on the end of it before you even realise you said something that offended him. After all that he has done and seen over the years, he would not see anything wrong with that course of action. His perception of what is right and wrong has become so blurred that he sleeps as soundly as an angel no matter what line in the sand he crossed that day. He has already guaranteed that he will not be standing in front of St Pete and the Pearly Gates when he finally leaves this mortal coil. The emotion of remorse is but a faint memory and guilt is a concept that has since eluded him, he has no conscience when it comes to inflicting pain and suffering. He is unforgiving; he is judge, jury and executioner, he is the person you hate to love, he is Billy Michaels and this is his story.

Billy Michaels' lineage is that of East End royalty, 3rd generation villain and is as cerebral as they come. He has worked in the entertainment security business for over a decade, he has been hurting people whether it has been physically, mentally or emotionally for thirty odd years of his life, the worst part is, he is only thirty-seven. To look at him you would not think he was anything special, but as most guys out there have been told, 'Size isn't important, it's what you can do with what you've got that counts'.

Billy was born in Whitechapel, East London, within earshot of the chimes of the old Bow Bells, which used to ring out from Cheapside. He was born a cockney and is proud of it; he was also born a natural survivor. After his Mum Paula, who had endured and panted through forty-three hours of labour, could not take any more, ten pound Billy had to be suctioned out of her womb. Not knowing what damage this may have caused, Billy spent the first twelve weeks of his life in a touch and go situation, enclosed in an incubator. If you do not fight for life, what is the point of living it? After getting the all clear and a stream of sighs of relief, his folks were finally allowed to bring him home to their small one bedroom flat in Hoxton. It did not take long before they were seeking to get a transfer to a new council estate.

Billy spent the first five years of his life living in a high-rise tower block on Chingford Hall Estate. There were three high rise blocks, all named after saints. There was St Frances, St Fabians and the one he lived in, St Albans. There were also a mass of unfinished maisonette complexes that were named after trees, Spruce, Sycamore, Yew and Pine. If you looked down on them from a birds eye view, you would see that the design and layout of them spelt the word "Fish". The whole council estate was like an island, with only a small area of grassland, that had to endure every kid playing football on it, and the rest was all grey concrete walls and buildings. A sea of roads surrounded it and the mazes of under ground car parks were like Aladdin's caves and one of the make out areas for sexually enquiring youths that inhabited the manor.

Despite being a large residential area, there were only two roads in and out of the estate, something that helped young Billy and the horde he would later run with, the "Red Ribbon" gang, with some cheeky exploits. The estate was your typical sixties set up, purposely built to house ex cons, the unemployed, drunks and our brothers and sisters from across the waters. It had a real friendly atmosphere and there are no sarcastic undertones to read into that. Everyone knew everyone, it may sound clichéd but for a place that was rife with villains and the hard done by, you would feel safe enough to leave your door open all day and night. Everyone was either Auntie or Uncle and all the kids ate in each other's houses. It was a much simpler time.

Four years on the sixteenth floor of St Albans tower block that overlooked the attractive pleasures of the tar paved North Circular Road was marked by the arrival of Billy's new baby brother, Vaughan. Vaughan was instantly thrown in to share a bedroom with Billy, much to his annoyance, all because their Dad did not want a waking baby in the same bedroom as himself during the night. He was a man with a real parental flair for bringing up children, *now that is sarcasm.*

Their Mum was brought up an army brat, her father, Billy's Grandad, Charlie, was in the Irish Guard, and so she was forever being moved around, never really making any friends. As a typical teenager, she rebelled in the form of running off and marrying Billy's biological father, a total waste of space that went by the name of Geoff. He was one of those offspring's that all the good, worthwhile family genetic traits skipped, not only was he an embarrassment to his own wife and kids, he was also a constant disappointment to his own father, Billy's other Grandad, big Freddie White.

Freddie was a known villain out of Hoxton, a loveable rogue who when he wasn't selling his import / export goods that he was stealing from the ships down on the docks, ran a fruit and veg stall along the market in Walthamstow High Street. He was a father of eight, four boys, three girls and Geoff, who was not one or the other.

Freddie used to run with a guy, who was a few years younger than him, called Harry Crow. Harry or Hoxton Harry as he was known was the eldest of three brothers. His twin siblings, Tommy and Teddy, were two of the most feared men in the London area throughout the sixties. They reigned supreme until both were convicted of murder and sentenced to thirty years imprisonment back in sixty-nine, the year after Billy was born. Out of respect for Freddie, Hoxton Harry stood as Godfather to him. This, for Billy, meant that he was untouchable in the criminal inner circle, after all who wanted the 'aggro of having Freddie, Harry and the Crow brothers' legacy on their case.

It opened many doors for Billy as he got older which in turn opened up a world that most people should never walk through. It's that path that made him the man he is today. Freddie believed that a man should be a real man, someone who could handle himself, whether it was in a fight, in the detainment of the old bill or in life. Geoff just did not fit that role; he was gutless and paranoid and didn't live by Freddie's golden rules.

Rule 1: Never (ever) hit a woman, there is just no excuse for it. If one is on your case or in your face that much that you felt she needed to be frightened, then and only then could you either shake her or scream at her, only in extreme cases of hysteria, you could slap her.

Rule 2: Respect your elders and those who commanded it and not demanded it. You can always tell someone of importance because they won't act important. (Knowing those kind of people who are somebody and don't need to shout about it, is one of the key elements in surviving the more high profile life on the street).

Rule 3: Always be able to pay your way in life. That means doing whatever you have to do. Always have money in your pocket and never be slow on the draw to put your hand in it.

Rule 4: Never shit on your own doorstep, if you do then be prepared for the consequences. Never complain about it.

(And finally)

Rule 5: Never backchat your mother.

He also said never be a grass, but that just goes without

5

saying and does not need to be a stated rule.

You can only assume that Geoff resented the fact that Freddie did not see him in the same light that he saw his other children in and as a result decided that being lord and master of his own domain would compensate for it. Which looking back, you have to wonder if it was really worth ruling, his domain was a crappy little flat that was just like any other in the tower block and was furnished with the same things everyone else had back in those days. There was a mega large side-unit that housed the record player, which in turn had a six-inch nail as a stylus, psychedelic wallpaper and a white sheepskin rug. It didn't help that he also suffered from short guy syndrome, after all, how can you take the sire seriously when he only stood five foot seven tall and had lost most of his hair before the ripe old age of twenty.

He was always in the pub, so when he was generous enough to grant his family with his presence, he was usually in a drunken state and in the mood to lay down the law. So he would send Billy to his bedroom, which he shared with his brother Vaughan, who although was four years younger than Billy, had the tell tale signs that he was going to be a naturally stocky kid and would one day grow up to be a very big man. While they were out of view, Geoff would then beat up his ever-loving wife. Paula would then burst into tears and shut herself in the bathroom trying frantically to cover up the swelling and bruises before letting the kids see her again. Now as a young child of five you wouldn't think that Billy could fully understand what was going on, but you would be wrong, dead wrong and so was Geoff.

It was on a Sunday afternoon in March; Paula was doing her best to keep the roast from drying out because Geoff was running late, yet again. Young Billy was playing in his room while little Vaughan was having his afternoon nap. It was after five when the sound of the key scratching the lock could be heard, Geoff finally stumbled through the door (it's amazing how a few pints can affect people in different ways, but then considering his constitution it was no surprise he couldn't handle his drink). Without a smile or hello, he started shouting at Paula, going on about not having his dinner on the table. 'Bang' a left hook to her face, causing her to lose her footing. As she regained her balance and stood back up, 'bang' a right to her sternum, she buckled and fell to her knees. All the while, he was shouting at her and insulting her and in all his rage and barrage of belittlement, he just did not acknowledge that Billy had wandered into the front room and was standing there between them. The tears were rolling down his cheeks, as he repeatedly said "Leave her alone, stop hurting Mummy" but his crying seemed to put a mute button on his vocal cords, he knew he was saying the words but no one could hear them.

He saw his Mum hurt, crying, pleading for Geoff to stop. Her words, just like Billy's were falling on deaf ears; Geoff just kept it all coming, never letting up for an instant. Billy could not take it any more; he went into the kitchen, pulled a chair over to the counter, climbed up and grabbed the carving knife that was lying next to the gravy bowl. He clenched the handle as tight as he could, staring at it, mesmerised. He climbed back down and rushed into the front room full steam and without pausing, drove the knife straight into Geoff's left thigh, making his shouting turn to screaming. The pain made him fall backwards. As he lay on the floor wriggling about and trying to reach for the impaled knife, young Billy was pushing all his three and a half stone of weight down on it, yelling at his wounded father that he would kill him if he ever touched his Mum again. Paula had came over and put her arms around him to try and calm her son down, she kept telling him that everything was alright now, that she was safe. He eased up on the knife and hugged her; in return she squeezed him tightly, kissing his cheek, soothing Billy's fury away. By the time he was himself again the Ambulance guys were wheeling Geoff out the door on a stretcher. When Billy saw him again, a few days later, Geoff was sporting a limp and a black eye, he had returned to pack a bag and left the three of them forever. Good riddance Billy thought.

You would think that an incident like that, full of emotion and lost purity, would bring a mother and son closer together but Paula and Billy never really saw eye to eye after that traumatic event, even today their relationship is still a little strained. They never spoke about that day, for whatever reason, and as the years would roll on resentment and a loss of connection between the pair would set in. Deep down Paula always felt guilty for letting the chain of events escalate that far and as a result she witnessed first hand the loss of her five year old sons' innocence. Whereas Billy grew up resenting the fact she had been so weak that she took all that abuse for however long she did and that's all there is to say about that.

A week later Freddie came round to the flat to check in on Paula and the kids. He was gutted that his own son had treated his own family so bad that a five-year-old had to plunge a knife into him and threaten to end his life before he woke up and smelled the coffee. Freddie had a few choice words to say to Geoff when he saw him a couple of days later after he was released from hospital. The conversation ended with Geoff sparked out on the pavement and Freddie standing over him waiting for him to regain consciousness so he could knock him out again. Blood may be thicker than water but scum is scum no matter what it has flowing through its veins.

That was how Freddie was, he did not care who you were as long as you belonged to the male population, if you angered him he would lay you out cold. It was how he was raised to be, a stand up guy who dealt with things like men should, on the cobbles and face to face. That was the East End heritage that flowed through him, British pride, pie and mash, jellied eels, God Save the Queen and anything else you can think of when stereotyping a cockney barrow boy. Freddie was a geezer, a diamond, a name that got said with respect, he was a father, a husband and most of all to Billy, he was a role model.

Billy would hang onto every word that came out of Freddie's mouth; his eyes would light up as Freddie regaled him with stories of the war and the scrapes he and Harry would get into as youngsters. He pleaded with his Mum on so many occasions to stay up and listen to Freddie talk about the old days and the characters that he knew. Paula always thought that Freddie was a bad influence on Billy but she knew, after all that had happened, trying to take away something that Billy loved so much would put that final nail into the coffin. Besides, she thought, Freddie was a few months shy of turning fifty, he was getting on a bit…let him tell his stories, what's the worst that can happen, Billy would go to bed late, again. No big deal. Listening to how his Grandad grew up in the East End, his escapades during the war and how he settled down with the love of his life, Elsie, was not so bad. It was just the emphasis he put on living up to the proud East End bloodline.

"You know boy, battles are won from learning from history…every event that has taken place has given us something to learn from, from building houses to making bread, from winning wars to treating illness. Knowing the history of where you come from is how you'll grow up to beat the bastards that will one day stand in your way. Being from the East End is a privilege, we are known for being survivors, duckers and divers. The bloodline of the East End has held fast for centuries, it rose from nothing to now hold a prominent place in English heritage. It was 500 years ago; when the old East End was no more than green fields as far as the eye could see. An old Roman road from Colchester to the City of London passed through the heart of it and the surrounding landscape was dominated by the old Roman wall and the Norman St. Paul's Cathedral, which was 200 feet taller than the one that's there now".

"It was in the early 1600s that the unpleasant, smelly and dirty trades were being established and I'm not talking about the naughty one's either; although they were popping up in the Dock areas like no one's business. No, I'm talking about the slaughter houses, fish farms, breweries and factories. These all set up home on the east side of London because the dominant west winds kept the smells away from what was to become the rich, fashionable and aristocratic West End".

"It was the Jews, who started the multi cultural flavour of the East End. It was the mid 1600's when the waves of immigrants arriving off the boats in London's docks began. The French who settled there from the late 1600's were Huguenot silk weavers, these were followed by the Pole's, Romanian's and Russian's who fled to England to escape their own crappy lives in their depressing crappy countries. By 1930, the Jews had established themselves in the communities of Stepney, Whitechapel and Hackney. It was amongst these people that the areas of cabinet making, the fur trade and tailoring flourished".

"Commitment, however, is not something that is recognised by the Jewish people. They feel that they do not have to honour debts as the year passes and they were all too quick to forget about the area that gave them hope and reprieve from their own countries, because the Jewish East End has since gone: it moved out to the lusher suburbs of North London. In time the kosher butchers became halal butchers. The synagogues had minarets added to them and became mosques. Ugandan Asians, Bangladeshis and Somalis have taken their place, adding their culture to the area. The loyalty went and once again turned the East End into a surrogate mother to new creeds and colours".

"With the London Docks taking shape in a small area between London Bridge and the Tower of London, you would think that good times were ahead for all those who would benefit from the opportunities that would arise with it. But the expansion of trade and empire in the late 1700's made the

docks grow in size and naturally, so did the labour force required to service the demand. The newly built housing, however soon became overcrowded and deteriorated into slum conditions and poverty took hold instead of the riches that the land promised. Of course, it is during these kinds of times when people lived in squalor against a backdrop of immorality, drunkenness, crime and violence that true colours begin to shine. Robbery and assault were commonplace and the streets were ruled by gangs".

"The streets were the most unpleasant places to be, the alleyways were unlit at night and prostitutes and brothels soon became common place and with them came those who lurked in the shadows to empty the purses of those too weak to defend themselves. It was in an attempt to overcome these problems that a stand up gent by the name of William Booth, founded the Salvation Army, whose head quarters were set up in Whitechapel. The Sally army, as it soon became known helped to act as a beacon to those who had lost their way and actually wanted to change. Booth's and the Salvation's army's success was at best limited, it was only 50 years later that a yank author whose name was, ironically, Jack London went on to describe the East End as an `outcast London'. Then in 1889, George Gissing in the `The Nether World' described it as `the city of the damned', a bit overkill for my taste but people like to sensationalise to draw attention".

Billy looked up at his Grandad, his eyes told Freddie that he didn't understand about eighty percent of what he had been told but just the fact of spending time with him, listening to his voice while resting his head on Freddie's chest, breathing in rhythm with the beating of his heart was enough to keep young Billy enthralled and eager to listen to more. Freddie looked back at him and smiled, took a sip of his tea that Paula had made him (to escape the history lesson) and continued with his story of the birth of the East End...

"Now the tradition of London's and when I say London's, I mean the real London, the East End, Pearly Kings

11

and Queens began in Victorian times when a young orphan boy called Henry Croft, decided that since he shared his birthday with Queen Victoria he thought that he might share some of her glory too. The Royal family would parade in all their finery in the London parks on Sundays so that the common people could appreciate their grandeur. This gesture was not always seen with the same intention by those who didn't live in palaces or wear crowns. It wasn't as though the Queen stopped the carriage, jumped out and had a chat with those that had come out to catch a glimpse of her. So Henry became the royalty for the common man and made his mark in the Music Halls betraying the Pearly King persona and it was from there that it snowballed, giving the East End it's own taste of a down to earth monarchy. A Tradition that still stands the test of time even now".

"However, with every light side to life there is a dark, evil underbelly that can't always be swept under the rug. The Whitechapel Murders in the late 1800's and the siege of Sydney Street created a vision of darkest London with criminals and the East End becoming synonymous. Pre-war detective novels by such authors as Edgar Wallace and the fictitious character of Sherlock Holmes created by Dr. Arthur Conan Doyle did nothing to change this image. Gangland territories and criminal masterminds were made larger than life because of the tales told in their books and with the benchmark set, Villainy started to take on a life of it's own with notorious, high profile figure heads slowly becoming household names".

"The 'Siege of Sidney Street' in the E1 area on the third of Jan, nineteen eleven was one of the most famous incidents in East End criminal history. The robbery of Harris's Jewellery Shop in Houndsditch was undertaken by a Russian Anarchist group intending to raise funds for their cause, went seriously wrong and before they knew it...the Bobbies on the beat, started blowing their whistles and sealing off escape routes. The gang ran and forced their way into some of the *houses in the surrounding streets, one of which was Hundred Sidney Street. Two of the gang members, Fritz Svaars and his colleague `Josef` died in the house when it burned down in the much publicised shoot out with the police and military. A third member of the gang called Peter Piatkov, nicknamed `Peter the Painter' miraculously escaped. Even the best laid plans can be cocked up by the smallest incident and what did Peter get out of it? Nothing but a life on the run, no ill gotten gains and dead friends, learning from history will help win more battles rather than enduring the same losses, remember that young `un".*

"Before the Second World War that ya old Grandad was a part of, the East End was an area of great financial hardship and social deprivation. Housing remained a major problem, the whole area was overcrowded with families living in slum conditions and unemployment was rife. The Docks and City areas were severely bombed during the Second World War destroying much of the old Victorian London. Ship containerisation caused the docks to close in 1969 causing very high unemployment. It was during these 25 years that the East End and most of London saw the rise of criminal activities and witnessed the birth of true villains, such as Harry and his brother's. Teddy and Tommy became known as the notorious Crow twins, who controlled the East End underworld rather like feudal lords, ruling their `manor' with an iron fist against those who tried to take from them whilst protecting the families that lived in their neighbourhoods".

Paula stepped in to end the history lesson before Freddie got carried away and told tales that the young, impressionable youth would try and emulate. "There will be no need for you to continue with those kinds of stories, the less Billy has to listen to the misadventures of what you and Harry and his brothers used to get up to, the better. Besides, it's his bed time...say goodnight to your Grandad Billy" She reached out her hand to escort Billy to his bed, he took hold of it and turned to his larger than life Grandad.

"Night Grandad, love you"

"I love you too kiddo…I'll see ya soon, okay?"

"Okay…give my love to grandma"

Freddie showed himself out and headed home, all the time thinking that Billy had something special about him that he had seen only a handful of times in his lifetime…he didn't know whether to be proud or scared. The same feelings and thoughts ran through Paula's mind as she watched her son fall asleep. It wasn't that long ago that this little boy stood up to a grown man to protect his loved one, showing that violence does have a place in the family home when focused in the right direction. Yet it was the lack of remorse in Billy's eyes that troubled her the most and knew that although Freddie was acting as the Alpha male role for him, it was a temporary solution that needed to be fixed. It was time for all of them to move on with their lives and start with a fresh slate.

Chapter Two

Paula, Billy and Vaughan lived on their own for about a year when Paula started dating a fella who had been born and raised the Hoxton way, a chappy that went by the name of Bob Michaels. Visually, you would think all she did was replace one short, balding fella for another, but there was a world of difference between them. Bob used to specialise in holding up Arctic Lorries and Post Offices, which had led to him doing a spate of bird in his heyday, overall, he was a sound geezer, a diamond, one hundred percent. He too came from a well-known villainous family and had three brothers and one sister, all of whom were into something dodgy. His wife had passed away a few years previous of cancer and so it fell to him to bring up his three sons, Stuart (ten), Mikey (six) and Gary (four).

Gary, who was used to being the baby of the bunch, suddenly had to play second fiddle to Vaughan and become a middle child. Mikey had his own problems, after all, his entire name was Michael Michaels, he was a year older than Billy and Stuart was five years his senior, but they all had birthdays in August and only a few days apart of each other. Just like the Brady Bunch, only without the girls, they tried their best to all get along despite sibling rivalries and the shared attention.

Despite having different bloodlines, Mikey and Billy actually looked like brothers, similar features and all that kind of thing, they were inseparable, always getting into mischief, "a right pair of Herbert's" Bob used to call them and he wasn't lying. The two of them were trouble with a capital T.

Eight months later, Bob and Paula tied the knot, Vaughan and Billy changed their surname from White to Michaels, and they became a very large typical East End family unit. From that point on, both Billy and Vaughan referred to Bob as Dad and they have never seen him as anything but. He was and still is a man who deserves respect.

Ten more months after that, the final addition to the Michaels family was born, Craig, the one who cemented the family bond between the Whites' and the Michaels'. Being the youngest, he got all the attention and was resented by all of his brothers, except Stuart, who had just become a teenager, he just resented everyone.

Due to the rapid expansion, the family was moved to one of the new houses that had just been built on the estate, a three-bedroom terraced, with a garden. This was like paradise to the children after living cramped up in a two bed flat with nothing but the A406 to admire. Mind you, they were still cramped but at least it was three to a room and not six.

Growing up was tough for the boys, no money, no luxuries and hand me down clothes for many years of their lives. They got the basics and were told straight off the bat, "You want more, go out and earn it yourself". So they did. Stuart did things the right way; he got himself a little Saturday job working in the local VG super market, stacking shelves. Mikey and Billy were too young for that, so they turned to crime. The two of them used to shoplift sweets and fizzy pop from the corner shop and sell them to their little friends who got pocket money. They were also breaking open the collection boxes on the washing machines and dryers in the launderette; there were always a few pounds to be had there. The pair of them nicked this and they boosted that, they did everything young children were not meant to do. Gary got dragged along sometimes to act as a look out or a distraction, he was just happy to hang out with his older brothers.

One day little Gary, who had been tagging behind Billy, was out playing over Burwood, the adventure playground. It was advertised as an "adventure" playground but in the loosest of terms, it was one of those places that had a tyre on the end of a rope, a wooden climbing frame and lots of dangerous and unsupervised contraptions. Standing next to it was St Albans Tower, the tower block where the turning point in Billy's life had taken place and lived six to a room before the family moved into their new house. Under the podium ran the car park and it was on this day where Billy stumbled upon a cardboard box full of torn up pieces of red fabric, which he and Gary started to tie around their heads, as kids do. That was the start of the "Red Ribbon" gang, every kid that ran with the young Michaels clan wore one, either somewhere on their person or on their bikes.

The "Red Ribbon" gang was about thirty strong and they would use the launderette as their meet up place and block the pavement outside with their bikes. Even though they were just young children in the eyes of adults, these little tearaways knew they had strength in numbers, although they never abused it, well almost never. That summer saw the start of the ice cream wars on their concrete jungle estate; Mr. Whippy verses Tony's ices. Both would use a different road in, do a circle of the estate and go out the same road. There was an opportunity to exploit there and despite only being eight years old, Billy knew just what needed exploiting and by who.

Tony of Tony's ices was a kid friendly type of guy, he always put on extra nuts, hundreds and thousands and syrup on the ice cream cones, and he seemed the logical vendor to approach. The set up was simple, Billy and his gang would seal off the road Mr. Whippy would use with their bikes and Tony would have the estate's sole business, in return all the little gang leaders would get free "Witches Hats" (Ice cream cones with an ice lolly stuck in upside down). That way they doubled their bounty and got free lollies to dish out to some of the others members. Lush.

The time arrived for Mr. Whippy to drive down Westward Road, which led into the estate and as promised, thirty kids on bikes aimlessly blocked up the road.

"Oi, get out the road you little bastards!" Mr. Whippy yelled, whilst leaning out of the driver's window of his mobile place of business.

"Fuck off!" Came the reply from those sweet, innocent children. A few of them cycled over to talk to him.

"You're not welcome on this estate mister, reverse up and don't come back."

"You fucking cheeky sod, get your bikes off the road before I tell you parents."

With that they cycled over and circled the van, just like the Native American Indians did to the wagon trains in the old Wild West. They started kicking the ice cream truck and calling the irate driver all kind of names, he attempted to get out of his truck, for whatever reason, but they pushed the door shut. Anyone watching this would be thinking that they are only kids, but there were a lot of kids. While Mr. Whippy was yelling at them and they were replying by swearing at him, someone had stuck matchsticks in his wheel valves and let down his tyres. He and his van were now stuck there in the middle of the road, Mr. Whippy was whipped, and he was just too scared to leave this precious ice cream truck. The destructive little tykes just laughed at him and his pathetic attitude to the situation. Billy rode over to the drivers' window and calmly told him.

"If we see you on this estate again mister we're gonna set fire to your petrol tank and burn your van, while you're in it."

They never had Mr. Whippy on their council estate again.

Tony held up his end of the bargain, for about a week, then he decided that Billy and his crew had all the free ice cream they were gonna get from him. Needless to say, after two weeks of aggro' from the disgruntled youngsters, he never came back either. The Red Ribbon gang was large and in charge and the word was out to all vendors not to piss them off. However, the price they paid for becoming infamous that summer was that they never got any more ice cream from the ice cream man, so you would have to weigh up whether or not you can honestly say that was a worthwhile victory for them.

For Billy, growing up on the estate as a latch key kid with his brothers and the Red Ribbon gang, brought up many little scrapes and adventures for him and his extended family. It was experiences like these that made his childhood worth living and remembering and he would never forget or change those carefree times, it just added to the layers that made Billy the man he is today.

On this particular Thursday afternoon back in seventy eight, a ten year old Billy was playing over Burwood when some kid next to him pointed upwards and started babbling about something or other, so as you do, Billy tilted his neck and looked up to see what this kid was going on about. There on the eighteenth floor of the St. Albans tower block was some old dear that had had enough of the world and was sitting on her window ledge. In a blink of an eye, she leant forward and fell towards the ground. It seemed like she was panicking, waving her arms about, as if she was trying to reverse her decision and swim back up to her window sill. Gravity was having none of it and so the old woman hit the ground, followed by an explanation mark in the form of a sound that's beyond description.

The movies have it all wrong, people do not hit the ground and a slight trickle of blood appears while the person's face and body stays intact. Quite the contrary in fact because this one hit the ground and blood splattered up the side of the tower block, reaching the fourth floor. Her faded floral nightgown became soaked, the gravel on the floor cut her a thousand times over and Billy never forgot the thud sound that came from the impact. Nice imagery for a child to see, if life didn't screw you up enough, witnessing that moment in time would have played a healthy part towards it. Billy seemed to take the experience in his stride and thought little of it, he thought to himself that you either want to live or you do not, black and white, it is just that simple.

The stains on the wall stayed there until the late nineties when the council finally pulled down all the maisonette's and tower blocks on the estate. The buildings did not need to be there for the long and happy memories to remain with Billy and the rest of the clan.

You can't be a part of a big family and not be known; those from a certain walk of life knew the Michael's boys old man, so the whole bunch of them were always given fifty pence here, a pound there from the old lags that lived on the estate. They were like mini celebrities and so the other kids started to look up to them, especially the dynamic duo, Mikey and Billy.

To add to their newfound notoriety, the original Michael's clan also got the pleasure of having big Freddie White as family and all the respect that comes with that. Freddie loved having so many more ears to listen to his tales of the East End, the war and the naughty things he and Harry used to get up to. It was even more pleasurable for Harry to tell a tale because Bob used to work for his brothers, Tommy and Teddy. So whenever he told a story from yesteryear, he would always make a point of catching Bobbie's eye and give a little, knowing grin. Now that is not to say that Bob didn't have tales of his own to tell, knowing the kind of men both Freddie and Harry were, he knew he wouldn't be out of order to share with his new expanded family his memories and experiences. All out of hear shot of Paula and the youngest members of the brood of course.

One of Billy's favourite tales told by Bob was one of him debt collecting for Harry's brothers:

Bob and his partner in crime at the time, a big guy from

Sweden, called Fynn, had to retrieve an outstanding debt of a few hundred pounds (keeping in mind this was the mid sixties) from some toe rag who thought he could Welch on his commitments to Tommy and Teddy.

Bob and Fynn turned up on this guy's doorstep and pounded on the door. They could see there was movement happening from the other side of the front door from the spy hole that doors used to have. Fynn gave the door a firm kick and that forced it open but the door had a security chain on it and so only opened about five inches. Bob pushed his arm in to try and grab the guy behind the door and for his troubles got pinned to the doorframe by a six-inch knife. The fella in question had stabbed him right through his bicep. Fynn gave another kick to the door and this time the chain gave way, allowing Fynn to start hitting his intended victim. Bob took hold of the knife's handle and slowly pulled it out of his arm and once free, joined in administering a little payback. Needless to say they got the money both in cash and goods, and on their way back to the twins' house, Bob stopped at a pharmacy, bought some Germoline and attended to his wound, using nothing else, and still till this day you can still see the marks where the knife entered and exited his arm.

When questioned "Why?" he said it was because Hospitals asked too many questions and so recommended that you learn to endure pain and learn first aid, he acted as an inspiration to all his children.

By the time he was eleven, Billy had already been shown how to drive a car by David Marsh, the older brother of Billy's very good friend called Stevie Marsh. Davey used to go out nicking cars and then bring them back to the estate to drive around the car parks. Stevie, Billy and his older brother, Mikey, used to get their turn behind the wheel after Davey had smashed them up a bit. They took it in turns to smash them up a little more, it took ages before they could even get the cars to go in a straight line, mainly because their height wouldn't allow them to work the peddles and see over the steering wheel at the same time. They all had to rely on the secondary instructions of each other, which as you can imagine are not that reliable coming from adrenaline filled minors. It took a while but they all eventually got the hang of it and it was not long before the trio could drive around the car park area without hitting anything, well at least nothing important.

Big brothers are a great source of information, wisdom and guidance. Stevie's brother had passed down the knowledge and hands on experience to the younger generations on how to drive, Mikey and Billy's older brother Stuart, taught them level headedness and their good friend Adrian's older brother, Lynton, taught them the difference between an eight and a ten pound bag of weed.

Adrian was the kind of kid you chose first when picking a football team; he was a strong runner and loved sports. His only downfall, from a ten year old's point of view, was his Sunday trips to church; his Mum was a big Jamaican woman, who would always remind you of that baggy stocking wearing cartoon character from Tom and Jerry, she would drag Adrian along each and every week. She believed that if you had Jesus in your life, you would walk a path right and true, and whenever Adrian would question her thinking, she would use Lynton as an example. Lynton had already spent a few years in prison for aggravated assault and since his release, set himself up as the local drug dealer, supplying weed and hash to all the smokers on the estate. Adrian, like any kid brother, looked up to his older brother Lynton and saw someone who was cool, intimidating and financially endowed, and he achieved all this without going to church. He had attended the school of hard knocks and was all the better off for it or so Adrian thought, but their parents disagreed. They wanted something better for Adrian and were determined to provide it. They thought that their wisdom and guidance would benefit him more than Lynton's advice would. If you were to see and talk to Adrian now, you may think they had been right because Adrian is now a man of the cloth and in his parish, he is the man you look up to.

It is funny how people turn out, because when these young tearaways all ran together as a tour de force, they were delinquents, rascals and rebel rousers. They were like the musketeers, all for one and one for all and nobody would mess with them, but if you were to bump in to some of those old faces today, most have put that way of thinking behind them, hiding their past from their own kids, renouncing their trouble making ways. They quickly forgot about the code they all swore by, whether by choice or through responsibility but there are those that did not forget, who remember their childhood, their rebellious days and the gangs they used to be in. There was a handful of Billy's crowd that stuck tight together. Many a finger and thumb was sliced open to do the old blood brother pact. It was the start of his extended family and its scary just how big that family had become.

Billy and his peers had just started secondary school at Sir William Fitt, in Walthamstow. Many members of the Red Ribbon gang were splitting up to go to different schools but the blood oaths were holding true. Mikey was already at William Fitt with a few others from the estate, making the transition with Billy was Stevie Marsh, Colin Dunn, Jason Moors and Tony Bracknell. It was those particular five that the teachers referred to as the clique.

It is a big step in a Childs life, changing schools, even more so for the clique. At the primary school on the estate, they all knew each other; every one who went there lived on the estate, no outsiders at all. This new school was three times the size and had people from all over the Waltham Forest area. Those who were from Chingford Hall estate were categorised as working class scum and were only matched by those residents of Priory Court estate in Walthamstow. Priory Court estate was the nearest rival estate and that was three miles away from Chingford Hall. Estate kids have an understanding, even if you don't like each other, because you and your family didn't live on an estate out of choice, it was just a product of circumstance.

After running in a crowd of thirty plus, being the upholders of law and order of their old school and knowing nothing different, made them all think that was the only way the world operated. It was a reality shock for them going to William Fitt, because it introduced them to the real world. It emphasised that in the grander scheme of things you really are insignificant. There were groups of kids that were just like Billy and his little group, all with their own friends and it was put across to them, very quickly, that they were small fish in a big pond. Billy didn't like that feeling so he went about making sure he never felt like that again.

If that wake up call was not bad enough, then the next one just made him sick to his stomach, because the scholars of Sir William Fitt also introduced those from Chingford Hall to something else, something they had never really encountered before, Racism.

Growing up on the estate, you did not think twice about someone's ethnic background that is not to say they didn't know any different. After all, the differences in skin colour obviously gave it away, but as pointed out before, you did not live on a council estate just for the fun of it. Their parents were all in the same boat and the kids just got on with it. It did not matter that you were West Indian, Asian, Chinese or even a Martian. What mattered was, you were a kid and you enjoyed yourself. That was not the case here and that started some very serious fights between the Chingford Hall clique and the uneducated, Nazi wannabe's.

Tony Bracknell had been Billy's friend since he arrived on the estate back in nineteen seventy-six. He was a very athletic lad and Billy always made sure that when it was his turn to choose teams, he would always pick Tony for his side whenever they played team games like football or run-outs. After all, only losers actually believe that it is the taking part and not the winning that makes a game. Their Dad's used to play dominoes together on a Sunday afternoon in the local pub, in fact it was Billy's Dad that got Bernie (Tony's Dad) a job working along side him at the Steel Tube Mills in Edmonton. As a result, they were always hanging around each other's houses and being left outside the Greyhound pub, which was the local on the estate, with a bottle of pop each and a packet of crisps. The only difference between Tony and Billy was the fact that Tony sported a better tan, other than that he was a regular kid. Therefore, the minute he was described as a "coon" and a "wog", you would find Billy right by his side punching the tar out of the idiots that said it. This in turn made Billy a "Nigger Lover" and he would not have had it any other way.

Mikey had already been at William Fitt for a school year and he had made himself known to all those who thought they were someone special. Mikey loved to fight and had already gained a bit of a rep in the schoolyard. So being his younger brother worked both for and against Billy because all those that wanted to be in Mikey's good books gave Billy an easy time and all those he had beaten up wanted to see if Billy was an easy mark to extract some revenge on. That first year of secondary school was tough on young Billy but that all changed by the second year.

Between fighting the racists and Mikey's enemies, Billy was trying to establish himself with the newfound wealth of girls that did not live on his estate. He was never one of those boys who thought girls were yucky when he was younger; kiss chase was one of his favourite pass times, when he was not hanging around in the gang and getting into mischief. The only trouble was, being from a council estate, fighting all the time and being a genuine bad apple, the stigma that hounded him made sure that not too many of the girlies would give him the time of day, much to Mikey's amusement.

Billy's Mum, Paula, was on his case to use this change of school to start buckling down and get a proper education, this basically broke down to "Stop getting into trouble and use your brain instead of your Brawn". School was not really Billy's thing but to get her off his back he started to earn some honest money by taking an after school job at the estates' local VG Supermarket. His eldest brother Stuart used to work there a couple of years previous, so he had put in a good word for Billy with the owner.

Billy used to pack potatoes from the big fifty-kilo bags into the smaller one-kilo bags. He was housed into the supermarkets' storage shed under the car park and would pack these bags for two and half-hours a night, straight after school Monday to Friday and then help out for a few hours on a Saturday morning. For all this work he was paid a total of twenty pounds a week, not bad for an eleven-year-old, especially seeing as it was nineteen seventy nine at the time. Along side him, in this shed, was crates upon crates of fizzy pop, boxes of crisps, frozen lollies, toiletries and of course, potatoes. So it didn't take long before the word got out and young Billy was being propositioned by kids and parents alike. After a month of towing the honesty line, Billy the entrepreneur, was back in to the wheeling and dealing and started making a bit of extra cash selling the stuff out the back door.

He lasted another two months there before he was let go, on good terms I should add, the reason was due to poor turnover. It was not a poor turnover for Billy mind you but that is the realism of business for you.

Every penny Billy earned, he saved, he had a little under five hundred pounds by the time he was let go from the VG and compared to the other kids this made him a millionaire. It was at this point that Billy fell in love with the idea of having money and he wanted to make more. He went to his Uncle Tony, who is one of his Dad's brothers. Tony was a bus driver at the time and would get hold of books of free bus tickets, which in turn he passed on to Billy. Then, as any businessmen would, he then sold them at half the ticket price to all his friends that had to catch the bus to get to their new secondary schools. The savings to the buyers meant an extra ten pence to spend a day, still keeping in mind they were only eleven and it was the seventies. Those were the days of four sweets for a penny, a Curly-Wurly bar was three pence and the Beano comic was tuppence, so ten pence went a long way. However, for Billy, earning only five pence a pop was not making him the kind of coinage he desired. It also did not give him much of a profit to split with his brothers, so to include his siblings with a worthwhile slice, another business opportunity was needed. Big money comes with big risks in the criminal world, but just how big was yet to reveal its self to Billy and his family.

The Michaels boys all understood the importance of money from an early age, their Dad, Bob, was trying to set the right example by going straight and away from a life of crime, working all the hours God sent, although deep down they all suspected that he resented it. He knew he could make a few phone calls, get involved with some blag and set the family up on easy street for the rest of the year but he made a promise to his wife and credit where credit is due he stuck by it. After all, men are bastards and the only three things they have to hold true are their word, their pride and their sense of honour. He was trying to show his kids that by giving your word you were declaring your whole being to something, no matter what the sacrifices.

When Bob would take his extended offspring over to the park for a kick about, he would regale them with stories of this poor background and his tough childhood. How his father used to hit him with a belt and the choices he had made and lived with.

In his younger days, Bob and his brothers ran with a crew that worked for Teddy and Tommy Crow, debt collecting mainly, as well as other things. So they had a certain lifestyle they enjoyed, tailor made suits, new cars and every night out on the town. After the twins were sentenced for their thirty-year stretch, every one who didn't go down with them had to fend for themselves and this meant that Bob and his brothers turned their hand to Bouncing at the "Royale" in Tottenham. Bouncing is a lifestyle all on its own.

Although in awe of his tales of the twins and his involvement with them, the young Michaels boys were too young to understand about sacrifices but they were old enough to know they all wanted a touch of that lifestyle. After hearing the stories of how the twins would demand protection money from those who were too weak to defend themselves, Billy and Mikey saw yet another source of income the two of them could cash in on. However, instead of seeking out the weak, they sought the strong. They would beat the crap out of all those who were bullies in school, even the kids that were a couple of years older than them. Once these so called tough bullies knew the Michaels brothers could beat on them any time they liked, they soon saw the sense of paying the pair to leave them alone so they could keep their bully boy reputation, although it was all in name only. It seemed like a good deal to Billy and Mikey, in return they would let the bullies save face and boost their self esteem by letting them publicly act tough in front of them and slag them off without the brothers retaliating. This brainchild racked the two of them in about fifty pounds a week, they could have gotten more but the second rule of business is never get greedy. Why squeeze everything you can straight off and then have it produce no more when you can milk it forever by only squeezing a little at a time.

I'll tell you right now, where you have money and power, you'll find the power to attract the opposite sex. All the girls that would not give Billy the time of day a year earlier suddenly had a change of tune. Billy, Mikey and the crew from the estate were gaining the same celebrity status they were getting as young kids, only this time it was not a case of others just wanting to hang around with them; it was more like a case of those who wanted to hang off them. You had the 'A' crowd, the 'B' crowd, the meatheads and the zero geeks and then you had the clique, the 'A+' crowd. All the crowds invited them to all the parties, and they went to all of them. They did not care if you were one of the popular kids or one of the nerds, a party was a party and they would all show up to all of them. Not that these parties were wild orgies or anything but they were a step up from the jelly and ice cream affairs they used to go to. Better games too, postman's knock and murder in the dark, were two of Billy's favourites, any excuse to cop a snog.

With Stuart off doing his own thing and Mikey and Billy doing their thing, Gary and Vaughan were attempting to live the same kind of life their older brothers did on the estate. Mirroring practically everything they used to do and being just as lucky, they also begrudged looking after the youngest, Craig, when their folks went out for their monthly "Get away from the kids night". After a while their parents let both Gary and Vaughan go to sleepovers at their little friends' houses and their Mum would hire a babysitter to look after Craig. Her name was Kim Davies, she was fifteen and like most teenage babysitters abused the telephone, the fridge and invited her friends over. Whenever Mikey and Billy walked in she would try and tease them about one thing or another, they would make a remark and a little insult session would start. That is how it went for a few months, until one time Billy actually came home early from something that did not go the way he had planned and Kim thought this was her chance to put him in his place, especially while Mikey was not around to have his back.

She started going on about how Billy thought he was a real lady-killer when it was just little girls he was trying to impress and a real woman would not give him a second glance. So he asked how she would know, not being a real women and all that. This got her goat and she threatened to show him what a real woman she was, this started a game of

29

bluff. They both mouthed off trying to make the other one back down, until it went from Kim kissing him, Billy touching her breasts, her undoing his trousers to them having sex. He went from being a twelve and a half-year-old kid to being a man in less than six minutes. You can imagine that it wasn't the greatest experience of their young lives, but it was a stepping-stone no one Billy knew had taken and that made him the 'man'.

It was a confidence booster that winning all the fights in the world couldn't match. Billy would sit back and listen to those who reckoned they had done the deed only to put them straight with some very basic home truths. Once word was out that he had lost his virginity, it was like moths to a flame, baby! Not only was he the man to have at their parties but he also became the man to have, if you catch the drift. Mikey was seething because now Billy set the standard that he had to follow and not the other way round like it had been for all these years. Brotherly love is a beautiful thing to see in action.

Their Mum and Dad got rid of Kim as Craig's babysitter because it turned out she was helping herself to the Prudential money that they kept on top of the fridge. They replaced her with some old biddy from a few doors up so any chance of a repeat encounter was firmly out the window for Billy. Although she didn't last too long either, too much to handle too late in life, Mikey and Billy may have been brought up to respect their elders but boys will still be boys.

It became apparent that it was time for Mikey and Billy to grow up and start taking responsibility for not only themselves, but their younger siblings as well. The journey into adulthood was upon them; the need to be the guiding light for their younger brothers was at hand, but did anyone really want the impressionable youngsters to follow in their older brothers footsteps? They were bad and the pair of them was only just starting out. They were growing up to be criminals, gaining violent tendencies and blurring the distinction between right and wrong. They were not nice people and they were on a downward spiral. The innocence of youth had completely passed them by, and the worst part of it was Billy and his older brother, Mikey, seemed to love every passing minute of it.

Chapter Three

There came a point when Billy's eldest brother, Stuart, had to act like the man of the house when their Mum, Paula, decided that she should go to work to do her share of bringing in an income, especially now that Craig had turned five. This meant that both their folks worked full time and they were all left to fend for themselves.

Craig had just started school, Vaughan was two years above him and Gary was two years above Vaughan. Both Mikey and Billy had moved on to secondary school and Stuart had already said farewell to school, not bothering to sit any exams and got a job in a carpet warehouse. He started early in the morning so he could finish early enough to pick up Craig from school. He would help Vaughan and Gary with their homework and help out around the house, doing housework etc, to make things a little easier on their Mum, so she didn't have too much to do when she came home from work. At the time, Billy thought he was a right Muppet, after all, he was no longer in school and he was out making money. Why turn your attentions to spending your spare time as a wet nurse? Stuart should be out living his own life and saying goodbye to those cramped living conditions and make a stamp on the world. The short sightedness of youth can be a joyful thing to experience, wouldn't you agree?

Stuart used to keep twenty pounds of his wages every week and would put the remaining eighty pounds in the kitty, as keep. His younger siblings could never understand how he could live off of twenty pounds a week, "Christ", Billy thought, "I was earning that when I was eleven years old". But somehow he managed and relieved some financial pressure off the household to boot.

It was just the way he was, selfless and it was only until those same said younger siblings were older, that they would come to fully appreciate just how much he gave up for all of them. Although unbeknown to him, his Mum was actually putting half his contributions in a savings account, the plan behind it was to buy him his first car or something, a reward for his kind heart.

Stuart had always been the level headed one out of all of them, and to this day, Billy would look up to him and commend him for the sacrifices he made early on in life to help support the family, even if at the time he didn't see it.

With the extra money coming in, the Michaels family were treated to a holiday and not a week at Canvey Island either, an honest to god, two-week holiday in the Costa Brava, Spain. It was the first time on a plane for any of the kids and it was a holiday of first times for some of them in other areas too. For Billy it was where he experienced his first Blowjob and it stuck in his mind a lot longer than when the time he had experienced his first kiss.

They stayed in a villa that was within an ex-pat community and as normal the duo of Mikey and Billy attracted a small group of followers, one of whom was a thirteen-year-old kid called, Christian or Chris for short. He was a bit of a Mummy's boy, skinny with no fire in his eyes and by looking at his Mum you could see who had extinguished it. They felt sorry for him, so they tried to include him in on stuff, one of the things being a party that was being held by a couple of sisters, whose parents moved out there that year. Being the experienced Casanova young Billy was, his first thought was to get hold of some condoms, which proved a mini adventure all on its own.

Once that mission had been accomplished they shared them out, one each between Mikey, Chris and Billy. You still got three in a pack in those days from the vending machines; these days the suppliers must know you don't really get that lucky.

Billy started telling Chris the story about him losing his virginity and how he felt afterwards. Chris, with an angelic look on his face asked if it hurt, Billy was a little shocked by his question and pointed out he had sex with a woman not a bramble bush. Chris was getting nervous about the whole concept and so Mikey, ever the joker told him that if he did get lucky that night he should go straight home and have a hot bath with baby oil in it. He said it would loosen all his body up and make his little winkle look bigger, guaranteed. Chris fell for it hook, line and sinker.

The party got under way; the girls' parents let the reveller's have some shandy's and a drop of wine. Which was also accompanied by some smuggled out whiskey from someone's parents drinks cabinet. Being young teenagers and whiskey being so foul tasting, all that participated got a little tipsy within the first hour, and this helped Chris and his confidence problem. Everyone was pairing off and having some cheap thrills while snogging in hidden corners of the girls garden. The ever manly Billy was taken to a sandpit where one of the sisters' performed oral on him, god it felt good, he thought, right up until the bit where grains of sand started to get involved. Ouch!

This was when Mikey experienced his first time, his first time of losing a fight. The young lady he paired off with didn't tell him she had a boyfriend, an older boyfriend at that, who discovered them in their hiding place and proceeded to punch the crap out of him. Some you win some you don't.

That was the brother's tales of that night but they did not see Chris until the following night, he was sporting a bigger black eye than Mikey. They went up and asked him what had happened, thinking another jealous boyfriend or something. He then turned round and relayed the story of the night before. After getting his first time out of the way, he had skipped back to his villa with a smile on his face and a spring in his step, and went straight in to have his hot bath with baby oil. He took his bath and still being tipsy and his confidence levels high, got out and strolled by his Mum, naked. She looked at him and then pointed towards his groin area asking, "What's that?" Chris turned to her and answered "That's my cock, ain't you seen one before?" and then she said the weirdest thing a Mum can say to her son "Not one down at someone's knees". Chris was a little confused by that comment and proceeded to look down at his groin. For whatever reason the condom had got caught on his bunched up foreskin and what with the oil from the bath and weighted down with shot sperm, looked like an extension of his boyhood. It was due to this, that his Mum started to hit him for being a dirty, dirty boy and hence the black eye. He was not allowed to mix with the Michaels boys after that for the rest of their stay but Billy thought that is the price you pay for knowing us.

The group tried to go on family holidays like that every year, but like everything else, it is the first time that you remember the most.

Back home the Falklands conflict was the talking point of every conversation; it occupied the news and created a whole generation of jokes about corned beef. It also made the topic of war and fighting very in vogue, and went to fuel anger and aggression, well that was Billy's excuse for Mikey and him getting into as much trouble and fights as they did.

It was at this stage that Mikey and Billy were really starting to go off the rails and their Mum and Dad knew it. They were too young to be forced into the army and too old for an old fashion arse whopping to do any good. Therefore, the next best thing, according to their Dad, was to be sent to Billy's Godfathers gym in Roman Road and learn the noble art of boxing. The discipline a fighter must show when staying in control of his or her own emotions in the heat of battle, was to teach them a valuable lesson about life and how you live it. What it did do was help lay the foundations that they would later raise a stronghold of power on. Boxing was an escape, it was in their blood, Freddie was a boxer, Bob was a boxer, Harry and his brothers were boxers and the list went on.

Harry loved the idea that the terrible twosome took up the noble art, even more so that they trained at his gym. It reminded him of the old days when he and Freddie would spar and Tommy and Teddy would push themselves to the limit in preparation for their up and coming bouts. A lot of would be fighters and hard men alike would travel miles just to claim that they trained at Hoxton Harry's gym, his reputation proceeded him and people just wanted to own their own thin slice of the fame pie. Freddie would venture up to see them in action, spending countless hours punching the heavy bag and dancing around the ring. Despite being small and young, the older guy's never gave them stick or tried to bully them around; the consequences weren't worth the aggravation. It was during the after hour chats that Harry's life story came about, his own demons and the long shadow that his brothers casted all over London. And the knowledge as to why people just didn't want to mess with him or Freddie for that matter.

Harry Crow, or Hoxton Harry as he later became known as, was by no means a gangster. He liked the quiet life and would sooner talk his way out of trouble than have a fight although he could have it big time if the occasion called for it. Young Harry was born in nineteen twenty six into an East End that was hit hard by the Depression. His Dad's passion was for boxing and when he was not down the pub he took Harry to boxing matches.

Young Harry was brought up on stories about fighting and boxing, and often dreamt of winning the Lonsdale Belt as Champion of the world. Fighting was a way of life in the East

End. It ran in the family so it was inevitable that Harry would keep up the tradition.

He was seven when his baby brothers were born on the twenty-forth of October nineteen thirty three; Teddy Crow was first followed ten minutes later by his identical twin Tommy.

Everybody would fuss over them and ask if they could take them for a walk. Harry too would take them out in their pram and he felt so proud when people would lean over and admire them. Harry loved the twins but he was to see himself being pushed more and more into the background. He did not mind he knew his family loved him.

The Twins caught Diphtheria when they were mere infants and were taken to hospital. Teddy recovered quite quickly but Tommy nearly died. His mother thought that he should be taken home from hospital where she could look after him better. She was also of the mind that being separated from his brother Teddy slowed down his recuperation. She took him home and Tommy was soon on the road to recovery.

They lived in Hoxton, until nineteen thirty nine, when they moved to Vallance Road, Bethnal Green. It was around this time, at the start of the Second World War, that their old man Johnny Crow was conscripted into the Army. Old Johnny was a 'pesterer' a man who liked to go on the 'Knocker', roaming the country buying and selling Silver, Gold and Clothing. This nomadic existence suited Johnny but deprived the boys of a stable relationship with their father. Whenever Johnny came home it was a time of excitement, like Christmas, party time and presents. The best tablecloth and crockery would be spread on the table something that was usually only reserved for Sundays and special occasions.

Although Johnny was away quite a lot he earned enough money for the boy's mother, Rose, to be able to stay at home and look after the children.

37

He was a man who did not like to be tied down and joining the Army just did not fit into his plans. It was not that he was a coward, he came from a family of boxers and enjoyed a good fight, but he had better things to do than getting shot by some German in a foreign land.

Johnny was now on the run, a deserter from the British Army. The Police and the Military were always calling at the house looking for him, sometimes in the middle of the night, waking the whole family.

The homecomings became less frequent, with the Authorities calling more times than Johnny. Although on many occasions Johnny was in the house when it was searched by the Police but they failed to find him.

Harry acted as a substitute father to the twins while their own father was on the run from the authorities and tried his best to control his younger brothers. And it was probably his role as father figure that alienated him to some extent, from the twins in later life. The twins would never involve Harry in their activities unless they had to, for fear of arguments or reprimands and they became very secretive to keep things from their Mum and him.

The Twins began to associate their father's absence with the Authorities which instilled in them a deep hatred and resentment for anyone in a uniform.

It was a hard life for Rose Crow with Johnny working away and then on the run but she held the family together. She had time for everyone. She was always singing and laughing, she had a great voice. Softly spoken but with great willpower and perseverance. She never criticized or complained about anything. Her one ambition in life was to bring up her children the best she could. The boys were always well dressed despite the apparent poverty of the local community. She taught them the value of prayer and to treat people less fortunate than them with the respect that they deserved.

In nineteen forty Harry, the twins and their Mum were

evacuated to Hadleigh, a little village in Suffolk which they grew to love. After about a year away from home, Rose began to miss her friends and family and decided to take the boys back home to London. They were devastated and on returning back to the smoke, young Harry soon took up boxing again.

Boxing began to play a bigger part in his life. He trained in the local gyms and his Grandad set up a punch bag in the top back room of their house. It was here that Freddie would venture round to spar with Harry and fine tune their skills.

After a spell of rheumatic fever, Harry joined the Naval Cadets, not far behind him was his best friend Freddie and the pair of them continued training seriously. They then joined the Navy where their boxing careers really took off. Harry boxed for the Navy as a Welterweight whilst Freddie was a light heavy weight. It was during this time that Harry started to get terrible headaches and it was not long before he was discharged unfit from the Navy, on medical grounds, due to chronic migraine. Once his best friend had left the Navy, Freddie followed in the footsteps of Johnny Crow and went AWOL. Freddie trusted no one other than Harry to watch his back and was not going to face the enemy without him.

Harry helped Freddie hide from the law and the pair found it a lot easier to work along side Harry's old man as a 'Knocker' whilst carrying on their training as professional fighters.

The twins by this time had also been making a name for themselves in the ring and on one occasion all three brothers appeared on the same bill. Unfortunately, Harry lost his fight, the last professional fight he ever fought.

The Twins, Tommy and Teddy, loved the attention they received as young kids growing up. They came to expect it and when it was not forthcoming, it was demanded. Their dark eyes seemed to lack that childlike innocence. It was as if each boy knew more than he ought. The mental and physical relationship between them was intense.

Teddy always liked the company of others, while Tommy was more of a loner. He loved nothing better than going off on his own, searching the bomb sites to see what he could find.

School days were happy times for the twins; they got on with the Teachers as well as the other kids. Tommy's best subject was general knowledge and Teddy's was English. Their Dad used to take them to the Robert Browning Youth club, in South London for boxing lessons three times a week. From there they went on to join other clubs including the Repton Boys Club, which years later was to be the scene of a famous murder mystery.

London was still being bombed and at nights, the family would make their way to the air raid shelter, which was in the Railway Arches across the road. They showed no fear at the events taking place around them. The Twins would just hold hands and shut their eyes. The old Music Hall entertainers would cheer all the people in the Arches with their tricks, singing or reciting. It was party time. Teddy gained a great love for the theatre through these wartime theatrical evenings.

The houses and factories left derelict by Hitler's bombs were their playground and pieces of shrapnel their treasure. They would push each other around the cobbled streets in a homemade go-cart, with a spike at the front to do damage to any rival cart that happened to crash into them.

Aged ten they would hire a horse and cart, take it to where the old tar roadblocks were being taken up, buy it by the sack full for a few shillings and then sell it for firewood around the houses. Even at a very young age, they knew how to make a few bob. When they were twelve, they had their first real brush with the law. They were put on probation for firing an air rifle in a public place it was the start of a regular occurrence.

By the time they were fifteen, the Twins were boxing at an amateur level, helped by Harry who first introduced them into the squared circle. Once a fairground came to Bethnal

Green with its Dodgems, Roller coaster and Boxing Booth, in those days the audience were invited to fight any of the fairground fighters for a cash prize. If they could last three rounds they won a pound. During the interval the crowd were invited to fight each other for cash. Teddy and Tommy stepped into the ring and proceeded to batter hell out of each other. They collected seven shillings and sixpence between them for the fight and ran home to tell the family. They considered themselves as paid fighters. Although the Twins were very close, they would often fight each other toe to toe.

By this time the local papers were writing about his brother's exploits in the ring. In nineteen forty-eight Teddy was the Schoolboy Champion of Hackney and went on to win the London Schoolboy Boxing Championships as well as being a finalist for the Great Britain Schoolboys Championship. In nineteen forty nine, he became the South Eastern Divisional Youth Club Champion and the London ATC Champion. Tommy was also the Schoolboy Champion of Hackney and won the London Junior Championships, and a London ATC title.

Harry said that as boxers, the twins were quite different from each other: Teddy was the cool, cautious one, with all the skills of a potential champion and importantly, he always listened to advice. Tommy was a good boxer too, and very brave. However, he would never listen to advice. He was a very determined boy with a mind of his own. If he made up his mind to do something, he would do it, no matter what, and unlike Teddy, he would never hold back. He would go on and on until he dropped. These same characteristics shown in the ring were to be seen later on in their business activities to devastating effects.

By the age of sixteen, Tommy and Teddy were becoming notorious in the East End. They had their own gang and caused mayhem in the surrounding areas. They were barred from most of the cinemas and dance halls in the area. There were always gang fights in the East End so it was commonsense to have a weapon at hand or be able to get one pretty quick. The Twins usually carried a knife but could call on almost any weapon from their arsenal underneath their bed at home. They were just as happy to use a weapon as use their fists and they would not stop until their opponents were completely subdued. Needless to say it wasn't long before they were arrested and charged with Grievous Bodily Harm for an attack on a rival gang outside a dance hall in Hackney. The local reverend stood as a character witness for the twins. He ran a small youth club in the area and the boys would run errands for him. This association really paid off. They were acquitted of all charges due to lack of evidence. Talk about putting proof to the old saying 'It's not what you know, it's who you know'. When they were seventeen, the Twins were in trouble again. They were standing outside a cafe in Bethnal Green Road with some friends when a policeman told them to move on and he pushed Teddy in the back. Tommy did not let anyone push him around, he hit the policeman and they all ran off. Later when the police tried to arrest Tommy, Teddy got involved and they were both arrested and charged with assault. But thanks again to the Reverend they received probation.

By now, they were boxing professionally; Tommy had six fights under his belt, won four of them and lost two. Teddy, however, had seven fights and won them all. They could have made a career out of boxing had they not been called up into the Army a few months later.

At eighteen years of age, the Twins were called up to do their National Service. It was not something they wanted to do but thought that if the Army were to let them be Physical Training Instructors then they would suffer it. This was not to be and just like Johnny and Freddie before them they spent the next two years on the run. While avoiding the MP's they ended up in court again for assaulting a policeman. This time they were given a month in Wormwood Scrubs and on release they were sent to Canterbury barracks to be court-martialled.

They escaped before they reached their destination but were captured twenty-four hours later. They spent the rest of their National Service in the glasshouse at Shepton Mallet. It was here that the Twins first met Frankie Richards, who, in later years became their gangland rival.

Boxing, like his mentor's before him, occupied Billy's life for six years, fighting in the Amateur Boxing Association or A.B.A's for short. Out of the twenty-three fights he had, one was a loss, three were draws and a whole host were wins, eleven by either KO or TKO. He only ever had his nose broken once while boxing, which his corner man fixed back into place in between rounds. Billy's eyes were streaming as he stood back up for that final round, his vision was blurry and he could feel the bridge of his nose starting to swell. He was fighting on pure grit and determination, acting on everything his Dad had instilled in him about living with the pain and doing what needs to be done, no matter what the cost. When the fight was over and the adrenaline had left his body, Billy almost crumpled to the floor. That was pain he had no intention of wanting to feel again and so he developed a different fighting style just to protect his nose. Because of that night Billy sports one nostril bigger than the other but he, along with many others thinks it looks better than that flat nose look that most fighters have, including his kid brother Gary, who as always made a half arsed attempt to follow in his footsteps.

Mikey and Billy were on the same program for a fight night that was taking place south of the water. The A.B.A fights were always on first, they were just something to warm up the crowd with while they waited for the venue to fill up. The amateur fights were only three rounds and you wore headgear, these were followed by the Semi's, they went on for six rounds and no headgear and then came the pros, and in those days some of the fights would go on for fifteen rounds. It was after Billy had won his bout, showered, changed and joined his Godfather, Harry, in the stands that he was first

43

introduced to a promising fighter and an even more promising villain, Dave Love.

Dave was in his early twenties; short cropped hair and sported a stripe mark down the right hand side of his face. Rumour had it that it was the only injury he had sustained when he was jumped by six fella's down an alley one night. They weren't pleased with the fact that he had won his bout and so decided to get a little pay back. They pulled out knives and he pulled out his fists, an even trade. He done a lot more damage to them then they did to him. That was the kind of guy he was, he didn't give a fuck about the odds, if you were foolish enough to stand toe to toe with him then be prepared to end up on your arse. But make sure to thank god if you were still in a position to get up and walk away on your own accord.

Even then Dave was someone you knew you had to admire; he had a certain aura about him, a presence. He had it written all over him that he was gonna become someone special. And that's just what he became; he grew to become a dominant force in London's gangland arena. He once held a strangle hold on all the nightclubs in the West End and its neighbouring areas, he was Mister Big Time. But like most people who are at the top of their game, the only direction to go is down and in Billy's opinion, that's what happened to him as the years rolled on.

At the time, Billy saw Dave as a grown man and he was just some pup kid but Dave always gave Billy the time of day whenever he was in his company, a show of class. As Billy got older though and started to make a name for himself, Billy was no longer seen as a kid, but as possible competition. It was many years later that Dave and Billy started to see things differently, he was South and Billy was East and never the twain should meet, well in a business sense anyway.

Billy was thirteen when he started boxing; he had severed a lot of his ties with friends because they were travelling in different circles. His day consisted of waking up at five am, eating breakfast and going to work, he had gotten a morning job picking up golf balls at the local golf range before he had to make his way to school. After school he was straight on the bus and heading for Harry's gym and spent 3 hours a night there before heading home and doing homework. The only people he kept in close contact with were Stevie, Jason, Colin and Tony and that was only because they all boxed and trained together.

Mikey was in a different weight class and a different league to Billy. He loved to fight and had a natural aptitude for the sport. It was like poetry in motion watching him dance around the ring. He could have gone on to be a contender but some things weren't meant to be.

Everything was going fine until one morning Billy decided that something was holding him back and that thing was school. When he turned fourteen and moved up to senior school, attending classes was not for Billy but he did not need the 'agg from his folks about ditching school. They moaned enough when Stuart did it, even though it was to help them. So he gave up the golf range and worked for his Uncle Allie instead.

Freddie passed away in eighty-three; it was a loss that affected Billy deeply. One of his mentors had passed away and he knew he would never get any more words of wisdom from this great man. Freddie's younger brother Allen (Allie) took over his market stall and offered Billy a full time job working with him. The plan was to get to the stall by six am, set it up and do some early morning serving to customers. Then Billy would rush to school, get his attendance mark and slip back out to the market stall. Work until lunch time and rush back to get his afternoon attendance mark, attend the afternoon classes that were deemed important at the time, like Math's and English, and then go to Harry's. That's the way Billy's life went for the next couple of years.

The Michaels' three bedroom terraced house was starting to show the strain of all of them living there. Mikey was almost on the verge of leaving school, Billy had been recently expelled for severe truancy and poor old Stuart was in retrospect a grown man still sharing a room with his two younger brothers. Something had to give and it was the three eldest that gave.

Billy and Mikey made Stuart their front man and had him get a mortgage on a four-bedroom house in Walthamstow. Their Mum and Dad gave Stuart his secret savings that they had been putting away unbeknownst to him and the terrible twosome supplied a vast chunk of coinage of their own. The house was almost bought out right. Billy remembered the monthly payment being something like a hundred and thirty pounds. The three of them moved in, which alleviated the pressure at home. Gary and Vaughan still shared a room but they suffered it with the promise that when the chance came up, they could move in with their older brothers.

Living away from his parents could not have come at a better time for Billy, he had been seeing a young girl from the estate called Michelle Taylor on and off for almost a year. It wasn't love or anything, just regular sex with the odd bit of ear bashing thrown in for good measure but to a fifteen year old who didn't know too much about the responsibilities of life the idea of consequences doesn't come into play. So to those on the outside looking in it didn't come as a big surprise when Michelle mentioned those three little words that every young man doesn't need to hear…"I am pregnant". The shock waves of this revelation rocked the very foundation of Billy's world and actually left him speechless. Countless conversations then ensued that always seemed to go into the early hours of the morning, all of which normally ended in Michelle crying and asking what she was going to tell her parents.

Michelle came from one of the few honest families that lived on the estate and did not mix with the unsavoury kind so having long discussions with Billy's folks was never an issue. They did not even know who they were but as soon as

Michelle broke the news to them, they literally camped out on Billy's doorstep hounding him for answers as to how this could happen and what was he going to do about it. The word 'marriage' was banded around a few too many times for Billy's liking and when he put his point across the term 'Shotgun Wedding' came into play. This was never going to be an option; The Michaels brothers would drop this irate father and bury him before their sibling would be made to do something he did not want to do. A message that they made sure he understood with no room for misunderstanding, which solved the problem of him camping out on their doorstep. He became weary about going near the house alone and eventually just gave up coming round all together. The brothers put a serious scare into him which aided his desire to move out of London and leave this situation all together.

Michelle gave birth to a healthy baby girl in May of eighty-four, Billy was present at the birth and suggested the name Adele, to which a semi conscious Michelle agreed with. Although Michelle's family had upped and moved away taking her with them, Billy stayed in touch with regular visits and also got to see in Adele's first Christmas. It was just after that first Christmas that Michelle's father made it quite clear to Billy that keeping an involvement with the two of them would have a negative affect unless he was willing to settle down and make a life with them away from his brothers and the lifestyle that he was presently living. It was a conversation that Billy took on board and gave up all his ties to the pair so they could get on with their lives several months later. Adele had just turned one when Billy walked away, some saw it as an act of cowardice other's saw that it was the most decent thing he had ever done but other peoples opinions didn't matter, it was how Billy saw the situation and he never let on to his side of the story.

Billy was still earning money and getting his own rep as being a half-descent fighter, no longer classed as someone who had to be in a gang to hold his own. As individuals, the old gang were all capable of doing damage and holding their own in a confrontation but together, they were deadly, and that is how people saw them. They may have still been seen as children by any passing adult that didn't know any better but they were a strong unit, filled with loyalty and admiration for each other. Billy still had an eye for the ladies and the gang were still attending parties at the weekend but now you had a group of boxers turning up at these parties and it was well known that it was best to avoid causing trouble with any of them. With that kind of reputation glowing above their heads they made the perfect runners for Lynton's operations, they were known by those who they would do business with and the consequences that would befall on those who tried their luck against them. Lynton wanted Billy's crew to deliver his wares around the estate and a few other areas and collecting any outstanding monies. They jumped at the chance and started running out the seed to all those who wanted it, after all it was only smoked for medicinal purposes. Wasn't it?

Lynton had set himself up in his flat in Yew Court; he had added a few extra security measures to his front door and windows and only dealt on his doorstep through his letterbox. His logic on this matter was simple, if no one can see him dealing then he could never be caught and charged for it, on paper this may seem to work but in the real world, it may be short of reality. All Billy knew was, they would turn up with outstanding debts and orders, push them through the letterbox, Lynton would then post it back out to them through the slot with his list of people to see. He was a very paranoid young man, too much dipping into his own profits (if you catch my meaning). He would always ask about his younger brother Adrian and Billy would tell him what they knew and lied about the rest. Adrian had reached an age where he exercised his free will to make up his own mind about his feelings towards his drug-dealing brother. He no longer saw him as the cool gangst'a but as the scourge of the estate, preying on the weak and exploiting their dependencies. If you took a step back from it all, you could see that must have been Adrian's turning point, from being a no-hoper, following in his brother's footsteps to setting his sights on becoming a preacher man, the messenger of God's word and wrath. Billy just felt that Lynton didn't need to know about his kid brother's resentment towards him or how he chose to earn his money, after all he was their meal ticket, why rock the boat and have him second guess his way of life. Was Billy being selfish, damm straight he was, it wasn't nothing personal, it was just survival. He was giving them a way to put extra coinage in their pockets, fuck him and his family problems, fuck Adrian and his condemning views, and fuck anyone who thinks this was the wrong way to see it.

Whilst doing their runs, Billy and the gang would short change the bags, a pinch here, a pinch there and make up their own ten pound wraps and sell them at the parties they attended. They went like hot cakes and that's when their status got kicked up a notch because it wasn't long before they were being approached by a whole new group of customers who wouldn't necessarily have known Lynton or knew how to do business with him.

Making their own bags by short-changing other people's stash was out of the question, the demand was too much, and so they bought larger quantities from Lynton and divided it up themselves. They had now become mini dealers, earning a better slice of the pie.

Everyone stuck close to Mikey and Billy and everyone saw the sense of not going mad and blowing their earnings. Between the little group they had saved up over the years, about two thousand-pound and were in a nice position to further things. They bought three mobile phones, which at the time, were not the Motorola bricks these were mini houses. They were big, black, briefcase style things and the batteries looked like car batteries and weighed the same as one too. They thought they were the mutt's nuts.

49

On the weed front, they bought in bulk and bagged it themselves. They were making three time's what they were spending and their biggest problem was what to do with the money. So they organised the next step and hired their own runners while they took a back seat, the only difference was they paid them a lot more than Lynton had paid them for the simple reason of not being greedy. After all if Lynton hadn't have been greedy Billy's crew wouldn't have been short changing his deliveries to make a little extra for themselves and eventually branched out on their own.

To make life a little easier they left Lynton with the black buyers and they supplied the whites, so their interests never crossed and no animosity could become of it. Lynton was paranoid enough, without him thinking they were out to take away all his business. It even reached the point where they were making the pick ups from Lynton's main supplying source which got them known by those who would not normally get known by such youth's.

Opportunity creates opportunity, so Billy with the agreement of his partners seized the opportunity to go into business for themselves, and Lynton seized the opportunity to smoke away his own body weight. The problem was for every spliff he smoked; someone was going without a payment. Lynton had to answer to those above him and not in a religious sense. His North London Yardie supplier was getting the run around more and more each month, until it reached the point where an example had to be made. A team was sent round to Lynton's flat, carrying a couple of machetes, they opened up the same letterbox that Lynton used as his security shield from being seen as a dealer. They used a chainsaw to cut the door from side to side, giving it an old horse stable door kind of look. Lynton had forgotten about the bottom half of the door when installing his extra locks, so it swung open with ease. He had smoked so much stash that he could not even muster the strength to put up a fight and defend himself. They went to work on him, hacking at his arms, aimlessly striking him with no real direction.

The bluntness of the blades made the whole process a bloody affair, no clean cuts just continuous chopping. Little bits of flesh and tissue were flying off with each upward movement before the next forcing downward blow was struck. Lynton was attempting to move, but his brain was running at speeds his body could not even begin to keep up with. As they tried to chop and dice his arms and hands; blood was gushing out with the same amount of pressure as a fire hose. It was becoming a scene from an over the top slasher flick.

Tony and Billy had arrived at Lynton's place to pick up some more gear when all this commotion was going on; they heard some noise but could not see what was going on in the kitchen. So they ventured in without a moment's thought and caught the massacre in mid flow. The other tenants that lived on that landing were ignoring the noise, knowing not to get involved and not to call the police, the boy's however were not that lucky.

They stood there frozen, witnessing the carnage taking place, looking at the tiny pieces of Lynton that were decorating the walls, floor and ceiling, stuck solid to the threadbare carpet with a mixture of fear and curiosity. The fatigue was setting into the faces of those cold blooded butchers, which was more than evident as they turned and looked in their direction. They were looking straight at them; it stood to reason that they were next, after all who wants eyewitnesses to something like this. The big fella that was half-way through hacking Lynton's leg in half stared at them.

"Yes bredrin', you and the white boy not bothered by this? What'ja gonna do when it's your turn?" His deep West Indian accent seemed to boom, as though someone had added a bass box to his vocal cords. Billy could see Tony's cheeks starting to puff out, which in turn made his stomach begin to churn. They both knew they were going to chuck up their last meal and so did their audience.

"Yer this bloodclarts' pussies ain't ya?" The assailants huddled together and started to whisper about the two witnesses, Billy didn't know if they were giving them a chance to escape or what. One of them walked off to make a phone call. Time seemed to stand still while waiting for this guy to return from the other room, the others were looming over them, blood coated machetes in their hands. He finally returned and glared at Tony and Billy, they were as good as dead, when he handed Tony a piece of paper.

"Call this number tomorrow, instead of dying you can carry on earning, we'll do business together, now get out of here". It must have been a black thing; he directed every word towards Tony and not Billy. He often thought that if Tony weren't with him, would he still be around today? If Billy, a lone white boy had walked in, would his limbs be getting mixed up with Lynton's? They got up and left, a strong desire to wash their hands consumed them both but the need to bring up five years worth of dinners took priority and they both spent twenty minutes vomiting downstairs in the car park.

For the first time in his life, Billy knew what fear was and yet didn't shy away from it. Was it natural not to be too fazed by the sight of a drug dealer being cut up by machetes, especially when the voyeur was only sixteen years old? Tony didn't seem too fazed by it either, Billy knew they puked their guts out but that seemed like just a slight reaction in comparison. If he was like that then what kind of ghoul was he going to grow up to be? How far would he feel was far enough, when having to set an example to someone that tries to cross him in business? If this was any indication, it did not bear thinking about.

The next day Tony phoned the number he was given, there was a good amount of business to be had out of their council estate and this supplier knew it. He faced the 'agg of bringing in and setting up his own guy's, hoping to retain the network Lynton already had or pass on the business to Billy and his crew, who knew the people and the drops. It made good business to go with Billy, plus they knew first hand what would happen if they tried to cheat the main supplier. It was a step up for all of those involved, and an opportunity to make a shit load of money and a real name for themselves.

Chapter Four

When you move up the ladder like Billy's crew did the contacts and suppliers you deal with are also from the next rung. For their little crew that meant they now had to deal with a couple of high level distributor's named Eric and his associate, Rod. Rod was a big built fella who was in his late thirties and the eagerness to be in your face had since left him. Although he never came across as someone to take the piss out of, he had a laid back approach that made him easy to get on with and joke about stuff.

Eric on the other hand was a firecracker, he was quick tempered and suspicious of everyone. He was in his mid twenties and had a very lean but muscular build; you could see how this team worked. Rod was the muscle with the age and wisdom and Eric was the cautious one keeping his eye on the ball. They both lived in the Edmonton end of Tottenham and where business was concerned, they did not have a problem with colour, which was handy for this eager bunch of young white boys.

Eric and Rod answered to a big time dealer, simply called "T". T ran his weed business from his top floor flat or penthouse as he used to call it, on the Broadwater Farm estate. It was like any other run down council estate in a run down area. It was tucked away between Tottenham High Road and Wood Green and only seemed to house families of ethnic backgrounds. I think that is the most polite way I can put it. Plus that description may help to set the mood, so you will understand just how uneasy our young, fresh faced heroes felt going on to this particular estate whenever they had to deal with T. It was not because Billy or any of the gang questioned their feelings, but racism and prejudice works both ways and you see it more so in this day and age than you did back in that day. It took a few months to feel at ease when entering the Farm but eventually they felt accepted and left alone to go about their business.

T's flat was in the first block and his balcony overlooked the communal area in the middle, which was handy for seeing if any marked vehicles were driving around full of angry YTS policemen. All the unmarked cars were spotted by the ground floor hordes of kids that hung around down there; they would point out and blow the cover of any plod that was looking to make a bust.

The more deals Billy's crew did with this group the better they got on with them. It reached a point where they would go out socially with Eric and Rod, gate crashing a few house parties in their neck of the woods and showing them the same courtesy back on the Chingford Hall estate.

The end of August marked the coming and going of Billy's seventeenth birthday and he had lied to get on the birthday mailing list of a grand old nightclub in the Tottenham area called the "Ritzy". It was the same club his old man, Bob and his brothers had worked at years ago when it was called the "Royale". To help Billy celebrate, Rod and Eric joined him for a night out at the Ritzy and made use of the free birthday passes he had received.

The evening was starting off as a good laugh; they all had an eye for the ladies but Eric and Rod had their hearts set on some white girls and more power to them for it. But when Eric tried his luck with a couple of girls sitting all alone at a table, it all went pear shaped. Rod was at the bar getting in a round and Billy was watching Eric try his luck from a

55

distance. Now from Billy's point of view the girls were responding quite well to Eric's chat up lines, you could see them smiling and chatting back to him, five more minutes and he would have been in there, but he did not get five more minutes.

Out of nowhere came a knuckle dragging pack that obviously left their KKK uniforms at home that night. That's when Billy moved in to see how this scene was gonna play out.

"What you doing talking to my bird?" This guy was a typical yob who wore designer labels and held his beer bottle in a way that the label showed.

"I'm sorry, these beautiful young ladies didn't mention they had boyfriends and now I can see why" The tension was getting thick.

"My bird ain't wog's meat, boy, so fuck off!" 'Whack' Eric let off a wild right to this guys' sternum, as he dipped, his KKK buddies started to come steaming in, which sparked Billy off and so he came running in swinging his experienced fists.

Before Rod could even put the drinks back down on the bar and join in on the fray, the bouncers were coming at the entire group involved from three different directions, hard and heavy. Two doormen cut across the dance floor to reach the fracas but Rod clotheslined one of them before hitting the other one to the ground. Now Eric and Billy had their hands full fending off the doormen while still trying to get in some digs on the idiots that started it all off. Then big Rod came over and started laying into anyone who is not the defiant ones. From that point, they were just throwing out wild punches and kicks just to try and get some distance between them and everyone else but now they were up against nine seasoned bouncers and eventually they had their arses handed to them on a silver platter. To top it off they are then bundled out of a fire exit and left as a pile of battered bodies out the back of the club. Billy had bruised ribs for quite some time after that but it was an experience to look back on. This was definitely helping to sow the seed in Billy's head about being a doorman and following in the footsteps of his mentors before him.

Billy spent the next six weeks healing and licking his wounds, business was good and he had cemented a strong relationship with the Broadwater Farm crew. He couldn't see any reason why things wouldn't stay this way but the world didn't dance to just his tune and bigger and more important factors can occur, like they did on the day of October the sixteenth, nineteen eighty five.

Billy and Mikey had got to T's flat at about four in the afternoon, there was a buzz flying around the estate that was a little unnerving, it wasn't the same atmosphere that had been there before.

"Yo man, roll some smoke and take a space on the balcony, there's gonna be fireworks" If you were to describe a stereotypical Rasta, you would have T, tea bag vest, 'locks and unkempt facial hair, the whole shebang.

"What's going on down there?" Mikey asked.

"You'll see"

A crowd was forming and getting loud, chanting something or other, all the kids that would normally be riding their bikes downstairs were now scurrying on the rooftops on all the tower blocks. The crowd got bigger and louder and as soon as a police van arrived it got mobbed and the officers were attacked. Seriously, you knew that this was going to turn real ugly before the night was up. Within the next hour, the riot police turned up and they were out for blood but they were outnumbered by a community that wanted more than just blood, they were after justice, street style.

Bricks were pelted down from the rooftops, petrol bombs were being thrown and the people were attacking with knifes, bats and machetes. It was a war zone and the carnage that came with it was not going to end.

The brothers were watching it unfold before their very eyes; it was like watching a documentary on a big screen TV.

Bricks and petrol bombs were being thrown from just a few feet away from their heads, down to the police below. It kicked up a notch when the sound of gunfire rang out through the concrete corridors causing even more heightened tension.

T told Billy how this whole situation came about after one of the residents collapsed and died from heart failure the day before. A bunch of heavy-handed plod had come round for her son, on some petty offence, something to do with a dodgy tax disc or something and went over the top with their questioning of her. The presence of these protectors of the peace was just too much for the community and this lady to take and it resulted in her death. The son in question was a chancer, who had given a wrong name when he had been tugged for something. Not really viable reasons for four officers to come round to your doorstep and check someone's address and look over a tax disc. Nevertheless, that is apparently what happened and this was the repercussion of it.

It was when the police and fire brigade turned up to put out a newsagent's that was on fire that the next major tragedy struck. A copper, later named on the news as PC Blakelock, got out of his car to try and create a clearing so the fire truck could get through. He was surrounded by a gang of masked attackers that literally hacked him to death; there was even talk that they had placed his decapitated head on a pole just like in the medieval days. Now Billy had his own opinion about the police force, but even he thought that was one-step too far and when viewing the reaction of the crowd, when word was spread about the slaying of this police officer, so did they. It is one thing to hit one or get one over on them but cop killing isn't gonna get you nothing but trouble.

As the rain started to fall that night, doing its bit to help put out the fires that were scattered around thanks to the petrol bombs, you could feel it washing away the old, making way for the new. Coming on to the estate to do business in the future was not even worth thinking about. Billy and

Mikey were still getting a supply and were still making a living but it was a nowhere venture and they could see nothing but hard times ahead. That is when they thought about cutting their losses and getting out of the smoke game. The money aspect was no longer worth the risk that this line of business carried.

Most of the crew walked away from it but Tony and Stevie stayed in and to their credit still provided the rest of the team with a cut of their profits. But getting free money isn't that satisfying when you're used to earning it, so Billy thought he would take a break from all the ugliness of their way of life and try something completely different. A cleansing of the palette, something he could actually tell his grandkids about but he just could not think what to do. Then one day it came to him, a crazy notion bolted through his head. Why not try to do some modelling. His ego had been going through the roof as of late and his idea of his own level of sex appeal was in a much better shape than his actual punched up looks gave credit to. Billy was just one of those people you would never class as good looking, he is confident and cheeky, but he is no looker. Billy knew his limitations but if you don't try something then you can't comment about it so he went along to a place called Davies Modelling agency, it was a little first floor office whose entrance was sandwiched between a pub and a newsagents opposite Leyton Bus garage.

The set up in the office was a single desk at the top of the stairs, a self built changing area and a curtained off section where the photographer worked his magic. It was run by a husband and wife team who came across friendly enough, Billy could remember standing there all suited and booted, trying to make a good impression. The husband came in and started to look him up and down.

"Good height" He looked Billy over again.

"Modelled before?" Billy was just about to answer him when he said, "You've got a fat chin." Great people skills this guy had.

"Walk up and down" Billy was starting to wonder if there was any point going on any further if he had such a "fat chin".

Billy strutted his stuff down this little make believe catwalk, he slipped off his jacket and twirled it over his shoulder, stopping briefly to give a smouldering look and then walked back again.

"He's got confidence" he told his wife.

"Let's do some head shots". Now this is the point where everyone gets stung. Billy was expected to pay one hundred pounds for his portfolio and a listing in their casting book. To combat the layout, the wife then filled Billy's head with stories about how much money their other models had made. All the TV programs they supplied people for and special advertising deals they got commissioned for. Keeping in mind this was a shitty little office based in Leyton but Billy thought, "Fuck it, it's only a hundred quid" and signed up for the year.

They were having him clench his back teeth and only slightly smiling while taking his head shots, which was just as well because smiling wasn't really one of Billy's strong points. He's po faced by nature and the only smiles he felt comfortable giving were sly ones. The plan with the teeth clenching was to try and bring out his jaw line to help potential clients overlook his "fat chin". If the guy taking the photos kept bringing that up, Billy was gonna chin him, phat style.

What was in Billy's favour was the fact his body was tight, defined and well toned. He had abs in those days that you could grate carrots on and the healthy complexion you got from eating them. But even that obviously wasn't enough because throughout the year, His two biggest claims to fame in the modelling industry was appearing in Kay's catalogue, letting his size twelve feet model socks, both formal and sports. Plus a photo story in a girl's teenage magazine called "Blue Jeans". Billy earnt five hundred pounds that year through modelling. Fabio, eat your heart out.

It was one of those things that he did in his life that he could look back on and laugh about, everyone else does and he still gets teased about it today. At least he gave it a go and that is what life is all about, living for the moment. Billy did not take it seriously; it was just one of those things. After the things he had seen, the things he had done and the pain he had inflicted, taking time out away from it all could have been the make or break of him being mentally strong enough to carry on living the life that he led.

Billy had had his fun and now it was time to turn his attention back to doing the things he loved best, breaking bones and making bread. His life may seem like a chain of events leading him down the path to oblivion, but until you walk it yourself, how can any of us ever comment.

Chapter Five

With his renewed lease on life and the feelings of the last few years deeply repressed in the back of his mind another needed example of real independence was required and it got Billy thinking about getting his driver's licence, He had been taught to drive years before, so he figured it would be a piece of cake. He sent off for his provisional licence and booked a few lessons and a test. His instructor turned up and asked if Billy had driven before, he played like a choir boy and said "No". So the instructor went through the basics and explained what to look for in the five point check, Seatbelt, neutral, Handbrake, Mirror's and Ignition. Pull out slowly and feed the steering wheel through your hands. What a load of crap, with the exception of old people that can barely see over the steering wheel and newly passed drivers, who steers by feeding the wheel through their hands? That technique is up there in la la land with the "Handbrake, Neutral" manoeuvre, when stationary at the traffic lights, what a total waste of time. How many times have you been behind one of those people at the lights who still follow that advice? It's annoying because it takes them the same length of time to put it into gear and drive off as it does for the lights to turn red again. Anyhow, the instructor took Billy through the manoeuvres that he would have to complete in order to pass his test and handed him a copy of the Highway Code.

The day of Billy's test finally arrived and off he went

with the examiner to the car park where the car was parked. They got in and he told Billy which way to turn once on the road. The test went on for nearly an hour, Billy did the three point turn, emergency stop, hill start and reversing around a corner. There was no parallel parking requirement back in those days. All was a-okay until they returned back to the car park where they started from. Billy indicated to turn into it, stopped in the correct manner before turning, and waited for the all clear. Then a group of teenagers emerged, looked at him waiting to turn and then stopped and stood on the curb and waited to walk across the car park entrance. One of them even waved Billy on to proceed, so he did and as he drove forward one of the idiots walked out right in front of him, "Bang" Billy hit him and he's stunned on the bonnet. On that note, Billy jumped out of the car and started mouthing off to all of them not paying one bit of attention or showing any concern for the injured youth.

"Get that fucking idiot off the motor, and watch where you're going from now on!" Billy then got back in the car and looked at the examiner.

"There'll be no need to go through the Highway Code questions, I'm afraid you've failed". Was this guy fucking shitting me, Billy thought, didn't he see what happened? With that Billy jumped back out of the car and walked up to the toe rag that he ran over.

"Are you okay?"

"Yeah, I'm fine thanks" On hearing that piece of good news, Billy then proceeded to hit him a few times.

"Are you okay now?" asked Billy, he waited for his answer because he was all geared up and eager to hit him a few more times.

"No" Good, Billy thought and walked off. He was gutted he didn't pass, but you know the old saying "If at first you don't succeed" and so he applied to take another test a month later.

Although Billy's ability to gain his drivers license

seemed a little off, his natural ability to turn a profit from any given situation was not. The Michaels brothers had this big old house, which was in some dire need of furniture, and a large crowd of friends. So after being talked into the idea by Billy and seconded by Mikey, they decided to use the house as a party zone, every month they threw a bash, charging three-pound on the door and had a bring your own bottle policy. They forked out to pay a lump they knew to stand guard on the stairs, if anyone tried to go upstairs, he was to stop them unless they were selected VIP's. The upstairs were off bounds, the boys used the fourth bedroom as a storage room for the stolen goods they had stashed up there plus they had a spare downstairs toilet, so there was no real need to go up there.

The house would fill up by eleven thirty and when I say fill up I mean around two hundred guests. The house was a couple of hundred yards from a pub, so this worked out just right. Those who could get served would stay there till closing time and those who couldn't; would just arrive at that time to make it look like they were in a pub.

They only had two reception rooms, a separate kitchen, and a conservatory that housed the DJ. The summer parties were better as the warm night air allowed the guests to revel in the garden, it also allowed the brothers to cram an extra eighty to a hundred people in.

Each room had its own look and feel; one was a chill out area. The lights had a red filter over them with a disco ball going in the corner. This room was filled with those big arse beanbag chairs that they got a bulk load of, paid for with a five fingered discount. Billy knew that it was the little touches that made the difference so he made a point of supplying numerous ashtrays, courtesy of the local fast food place, packets of different sized Rizla and bowls of fun size chocolate bars. Stevie and Tony used to attend and supply whatever ingredients were missing from the mix. The other room was strobe light city, all blacked out with strips of UV lights on the walls. If you were wearing white or had dandruff, this was the room that was gonna make it stand out.

Synthesised music was starting to come on the scene and the Miami vice look was all the rage back then, Pastel colours and espadrilles for the fella's and as little as possible for the girls. A far cry from the Hackney house parties they attended on a Saturday night. The brothers just catered for the masses that would not be caught dead in an area like Hackney let alone a jam groove, lover's rock house party.

The parties were a success thanks mainly to word of mouth. People would knock on their door asking for the next date, they would hand them fliers to dish out and it just escalated from there. The constant drawback to them was the arrival of the police and environmental health every time they opened their doors. The police would want to come in and check the place out while the environmental health would get out their decibel reader to tell them to lower the noise. Noise pollution charges and arresting someone because they are smoking a joint is not going to get you promoted, the older coppers knew it and gave cautions but the younger YTS ones were just job-worth's. Mikey always gave the old bill 'agg on the door, some nights he got away with it, others nights he did not and the place would be raided ensuring that the usual suspects would be carted off down the cells. Now, Billy understood they had a job to do but to crush the party vibe was to crush his profits and those operating in the chill out room didn't need the attention either but that's the game they played. It was at these events that Billy and Mikey were getting a taste for door work, vetting the people, taking the money, dealing with gatecrashers and drunken idiots and of course keeping the fuzz out. It seemed to come as natural as boxing did and was just as much fun; this was the route to take and they knew it.

The date of Billy's second attempt to pass his driving test had arrived and it coincided with a little delivery job he had to do, which took priority. Billy got into the car with the examiner and peeled it out of the car park.

"Slow down Mr Michaels, I want you to turn left once we are out on the road" The problem with that was Billy had to go the other way and so that is the way he went.

"I said left, now pull in over to the curb for me"

"No can do, I have to be somewhere" and without a care in the world Billy just carried on driving, breaking the speed limit and not feeding the steering wheel through his hands. The examiner then attempted to take control of the vehicle by using the dual pedals.

"If you do that again, I'm gonna drag you out of this car and drive over you a few times". Billy shot the examiner a look that told him that he wasn't joking, to which he said nothing, so off Billy went with a smile on his face to do his thing and made his delivery. Needless to say, he failed that time also. So he applied again and it was a case of third time's a charm, because Billy finally had passed his test without using violence, threats or running people over and was allowed to legally drive on the roads.

The parties were covering the mortgage and putting food in the cupboard and their own side thing was paying for the next thing. Tony and Stevie were still kicking back a little green, out of loyalty mind you. The brothers did not ask, expect or demand it was just their way of saying thanks for all the help and support. In fact Mikey would go one step further and say it was respect. Everything was going at a nice steady pace; they weren't being greedy or anything and were keeping a low profile so not to get the attention of the plod. Although they had their cards marked, they were friendly with it. They would always get a tug while walking about, a flippant comment here, an innuendo there. The Michaels clan all knew the score but they were never blatant with their ill-gotten gains and they knew how far they could go when chatting back to the constables in question. It all seemed too good to be true and just like most fairy tales an evil monster was lurking in the woods, waiting for the right moment to strike.

August was always a party month for the three eldest, it was nineteen eighty-six and Billy had just turned eighteen, Mikey had just turned nineteen and Stuart had just turned twenty-two. Their big birthday bash for that year was only one week away. This was the party that they footed the bill for everything, drink, food and smoke all free, all night.

The weekend before had them having their own family affair birthday drink in a club they went to quite a bit, called Flappers, next to the Hackney Eastway. They went here for many reasons but the main one was because the owner Pete used to turn a blind eye to their ages including Gary's and Vaughan's. This made their family drinks that little bit more special. Their routine when at Flappers, or 'Slappers', as it became fondly named, was to occupy a booth at the back of the DJ stand, flirt with Albert, the gay bar manager, for free drinks and pulling the girlies into the booth and suggesting naughty behaviour. Most of who took them up on their offers, hence the name 'Slappers'.

There is nothing like having grown women giving your kid brothers' blowjobs to have them feel like part of the grown ups table. They used to love coming out with their older brothers, especially Vaughan, who was only fourteen at the time. They had the woman on a turnstile and the fun just would not stop.

The club closed at two am and from there, they went on to the nearest house party. You needed balls of steel to be white and walk into a Hackney house party, the first few Billy ever went to he was on tenterhooks. He would be stared at and deliberately made to feel uncomfortable until he either left on his own accord or was beaten up and then thrown out. If, like the clan, you kept on showing up at these things, your face gets known and you're left alone. As long as you paid your money on the door and could "Water pump", you would not get any hassles. On this particular night, someone obviously could not dance or tried to cheat the door because right there on the pavement a couple of fella's were getting a beating like no ones business.

The Michaels family had been drinking and were in a loutish mood so they were jeering on the lumps that were dishing the gravy to these spuds, not thinking anything about it. It's all part of a Saturday night after all. Then 'Bang', the sound of a thirty-eight went off and just like in the movies you could hear the stylus on the record player scratch across the record before a deathly silence fell over the house.

People suddenly scattered out of every possible exit from the house and ran off in various directions. Billy could not help but look over the body; the guy who had been shot was still moving or at least twitching. A slight suction noise was coming from his chest area and at the time, Billy could not work out why. He was wheezing and coughing up blood. Billy was so engrossed with his guy that he didn't realise that his own name was being called out until he felt these firm hands grip his arms to pull him away.

"Billy, walk away, just walk away". Billy turned his head to see who had grabbed him; it was his big brother Stuart, acting all level headed as usual. It was then Billy saw the shooter. He looked the person straight in the face only to see that it was his dear friend Tony, little Tony Bracknell, who was standing there, wisps of smoke still escaping from the barrel of the gun that he held in his hand.

"We have got to get out of here and fast." Stuart ushered them down the road to where he had parked his car. The sound of police sirens was echoing through the residential area. He bundled them all, including Tony into his Hillman Hunter and drove off. Needless to say, it put a downer on the evening.

When they finally got back to their house, because Stuart did not want to take any chances and took the long route round, Billy could not help but feel Tony owed them all an explanation. It turned out that the guy in question was a runner for Tony's half of the operation and had been smoking the gear himself, faulting on deliveries and payment. It had come to the point that Tony had to do something to save face but it had to be something that showed people that despite his age he was man enough to deal with his in-house problems. So armed with a gun that was bigger than him, this eighteen year old had took it upon himself, for the sake of proving something to someone else, to become Judge, Jury and Executioner. They had all grown up too fast and everything had come to them all way too easily, now in their own way they were paying the piper.

The Michaels birthday bash was rammed, they had gone about business as usual, but their hearts were not in it. It is not as though they knew the guy and in all fairness they weren't really giving him a second thought, they were all more concerned about the line Tony had crossed and how it affected him. He had become withdrawn and developed a compulsive need to keep washing his hands. He would use a nailbrush and just kept scrubbing them until his skin turned red raw.

Billy was hoping that the party would take his mind off of things, even for a few hours, which at one point it seemed to do. Tony was laughing and chatting to the ladies, having a few beers. Finally showing the strength, the rest of them all knew he had. He even became the life and soul at one point and everything seemed like old times.

That was the only party they ever let the police enter without giving them attitude, because at three forty seven am Tony was found dead in the upstairs bathroom. He had scrubbed his hands for the last time and then took apart Stuart's old-fashioned razor and sliced his wrist. (I describe it by saying sliced and not slit because it looked like his hand was literally coming away from his arm.) Tony had crossed a line that he was not strong enough to handle. Guilt, regret, remorse, these are just some of the things that can effect you. They play with your mind until you either snap or learn to deal with it.

Det. Sarg Brian Gallowhawk was a policeman that Billy

actually had time for; he was as straight as a die but never treated him like scum. Over the years, he would always knock on their door just to chat, no information being seeked, just a chat. In fact, he even went round their folk's house for Sunday lunch on a few occasions. He would tell you to your face what he thought about you and for that, Billy gave him respect. He had attended Tony's funeral because he had known the whole crew since they were nippers and was genuinely sorry for his parent's loss. Deep down Billy always thought that the Sarg was hoping they would all see the error of their ways and change their direction in life.

It was just after Tony's funeral when Stevie decided to call it a day on the weed dealing. He passed the torch to a couple of young bloods and the remaining members of the crew all agreed that they did not want to earn a penny from it. Out of respect for Tony, they did not want to touch any more of the money that put him in that situation. It was the end of a venture and it was one they were glad to see the back of.

Jason and Colin had always been as thick as thieves, ever since they were ragamuffin children. Both had filled out over the years, Colin a little more so as he got older. The whole group used to be so health conscious back when they started boxing but somewhere along the way, Colin started to take up smoking the cancer sticks and developing a taste for the fry ups. You could see him as a plumber or a builder of some sort; he was becoming your typical manual worker, ill-fitting t-shirts, and dirty jeans with the ever-impressive bum cleavage on display. He was also going a little thin up top, a case of baldielocks and the three hairs, and all at such a young age, too much, too fast. He stood in at five foot ten and was still sporting his highlights, even though they were growing out, looking more like coloured tips than anything else. He had it done a year or so ago back when it was fashionable and never kept them up or cut them out. This guy had a lazy streak that would put the London transport division to shame; Jason on the other hand was the complete opposite. He had maintained his looks, hair and physique, not to mention his passion for fighting. Jason was a little taller than Colin was; he had a solid frame and had an Arian look about him, blonde hair and blue eyes but thankfully did not agree with their views. In Billy's opinion Jason was the one he could count on the most in a pinch, that's not to say Colin wouldn't be there, but out of the two Jason was the one he wanted to back him up.

The pair of them loved cars and consequently got into the mechanics game in a big way; this led them to start on an apprenticeship in a chop shop run by a North London family called the Liverton's. They were a tight family, with all the right teachings and scruples. Billy knew this first hand, because lo and behold somewhere along the family tree, he was related to them.

You cannot be part of one the largest family in the UK and not find out that you are related to someone, no matter what the connection, but the story behind this branch was a scream.

Freddie's eldest daughter, Joan, was dating Ollie Liverton back in the sixties. Now there was this whole "Stick to your own" type of thing back then and I am talking districts not colour. Ollie's family was from North London and obviously, Freddie's clan was from East London. The Liverton's were a family of villains that were starting to make their mark on their side of town. The thought of a union between them and the White's would only strengthen their standing, with the added bonus of being in with the Crow family.

Freddie saw it that a test would have to be passed before he made his mind about giving his blessing for Ollie to have Joan's hand in marriage. So he asked Ollie to look after a hatbox for him, not to open it, just keep it safe. How hard can that be, Ollie thought.

Freddie turned up on Ollie's manor with Harry in tow to deliver the hatbox. All he had to do was hold on to it for three weeks and someone else would come and collect it. No problem.

Like a cat, curiosity got the better of him and so he decided to look in the box. Ollie untied the string that was holding the lid on and slowly lifted the top off, only to be greeted by soil. Sticking out of this moist, black soil was some polythene. Ollie brushed away the top layer of soil to reveal even more polythene; he reached in and pulled out whatever it was wrapped up in this plastic. Ollie just froze, his jaw dropped open and he did not even have the strength to close it again. He just stared at the contents and all the while the contents stared straight back at him. It was the head of Knobby Cooke, some dirty whistle blower that grassed on the wrong set of brothers.

Ollie was now starting to panic; he hurriedly wrapped the head back up and put it back into the soil. Sealed up the box; tied it and then rushed it out to the greenhouse. When his Dad came home, Ollie told him what had happened.

"Get that fucking thing out my house!" Came his reply, but now they had the problem of what to do with it because Freddie was going send someone to collect it. So they paid some low life to hold on to it for them while they waited to be told when it was going to be picked up.

The weeks went past and eventually Lumpy Harris knocked on the door and collected the neatly ribboned hatbox.

"Have you looked in 'ere?" Asked Lumpy, a monster of a man who worked for Freddie doing certain odd jobs.

"No". Ollie replied, a short and sweet answer, a blatant lie. Lumpy placed the retrieved hatbox in the boot of his car and drove off.

The next time Freddie saw Ollie, he asked him if he still wanted to marry Joan. He thought long and hard about the question and said, "Yes". So Freddie gave his blessing, knowing that he had made his point, get out of your pram at any time and someone could be looking after a hatbox with your head in it.

You have to admire the class of the man that Billy simply knew as Grandad; he was a real king amongst men and would forever be a role model to Billy, his children and his children's children.

Chapter Six

Colin asked Stevie if he wanted to earn a little bit of crust now that he was out of the weed business. They needed someone to nick cars and bring them in to be chopped up. Stevie, whose brother Davey, who was doing a ten stretch for smuggling at that time, had showed him every trick in the book and so turned round and said "Yeah" and set about blowing the dust off his older brother's slim Jim. Jason showed him a few new tools and tricks and told him what cars they were after, giving Stevie a shopping list or chopping list, depending on your view of it. He then set out to make a dent in it, the list not the cars. All was great for a while, Billy was driving legal cars, and Stevie was still driving stolen cars, everything was settling down and the memories of Tony's suicide were being stored in the back of everyone's brain.

Colin and Jason were starting to make some good coinage out of the spare part, cut and shunt game. Stevie was proving a viable addition to the operation and the Liverton's were happy with what was going on. Everything was kept low profile, the cars were all coming from different regions so there was no distinct pattern to the thefts. Everyone of the original crew was taught not to be greedy in business, this was a no-brainer piece of advice handed down by Freddie and reinforced by Harry. Harry always said that part of the downfall of his brother's was greed, it was a sin that did not need to be enjoyed. With greed came sloppiness and that's

74

when mistakes would be made, every wannabe gangster out there wanted to emulate Tommy and Teddy and it was because of this that very few made the notoriety, too few contenders learnt from the Crows mistakes but would rather make the same ones. The Liverton's were such pretenders to the throne, forgetting about their limitations for being real dangerous men, a lesson that Freddie had highlighted in their bloodline many years before and didn't have the same opinion as Colin, Jason and Stevie. They saw that a lot more money could be made if the three of them upped their game and brought in more cars more frequently. This was something that went against the grain for the boys in question and so things would get very heated between them and the Liverton family.

Colin and Jason wanted to set up their own shop and run business in a way that was tried and tested, employing all the values that had been instilled in them whilst hanging around the boxing club after hours listening to the stories Harry and Freddie would tell. They had always made money without getting into too much trouble and knew that they had very loyal friends to call upon if things got out of hand or if back up was needed. To make this dream a reality, they were all aware that additional funds would need to go in the kitty if they were to brake the strangle hold the Liverton's had over them. It also meant that upping their operations would also need to be done, which made the Liverton's think that they had won the battle of wills.

With a goal in mind, Stevie set out to find more cars that hit the profile and Jason made the contacts to out the motors. The plan was that for every three cars stolen and put out on the streets, the Liverton's would only get a piece of two of them, They didn't know any different and it allowed the boys to make some side money to fund their own business plan. The problem with upping the need for the vehicles that Stevie had to steal meant that he had to work three times as hard to find the cars in areas that were out of their manor.

This led to him becoming lazy and he practically nicked off his own doorstep, doing naughties too close to home was another business no-no and was spotted by the local plod that knew him and knew for a fact that the name that came up on their vehicle check against the licence plate wasn't his. So, Stevie, after a twenty-minute chase, was caught, bang to rights. Detainment, Charged, and two months later sentenced. Stevie, who had already gained a few misdemeanours to his name over the years, qualified for a spate of bird this time round. He got twenty-four months, which should have been seen as an omen because he was caught in the twenty forth car he had stolen.

Now Stevie could handle prison but it was something else he could not get to grips with and that was the smack, H, Brown that was freely on offer to all that wanted it. All those years running and dealing weed out in the open and yet it was only until he went inside that he became a junkie. That is the prison system for you; no wonder the British justice system is such a joke.

Billy went up and saw him a few times and each time he did Stevie looked worse. Each time he would keep recalling the first ten days inside. Going down to the cells after being sentenced, awaiting the paddy wagon to take him away. Being processed and having to spend the whole time running up and down those wrought iron stairs in his Sunday best shoes. They don't give you prison issue or put you on the wing until after your first week. This is so the screws can see if you are going to hack it on the inside or find out if they have to put you in the observation section. You should always keep in mind that if you are ever in the dock looking at doing time, wear trainers on you feet and dark coloured underwear because that's what you're going to be living in for the next fortnight. Word to the wise.

To speed up the days and nights, Stevie was shooting up while running up a little debt to the suppliers. The trouble with H is once it hooks you, especially in a place like that; it owns you just like the people that deal it to you. Stevie would ask the boys who visited to do a few favours on the outside to square him up on the inside. He was one of their dearest friends so there was no reason why they would not assume responsibility for his debts.

One of these jobs was to collect some money from an old colleague of some friend of a friend who had escaped paying back his debt due to the fact the guy that he owed went down for six years. It was one of those sob stories that didn't make any sense or have any real point, it was just another way for someone to look like a big man in front of their easily impressed friends; Billy didn't care who was owed or who owed him. He just wanted to do his friend a favour, to help him out and if that meant roughing up some lowlife that ducked out of paying some other lowlife, then so be it. Just give the guy's name, a few details about who he does business with and where to find him.

Loyalty is a funny thing, with Stevie doing time the consensus from the Michaels crew was to distance themselves from him in case the old bill was hoping for a double whammy or something. It went against everything Billy and Mikey were brought up to believe in and they could not do that. Billy had to choose carefully who to ask for help on this job. It was Jason who stepped up to the plate, he figured he owed Stevie for keeping quiet about the chop shop racket and the added bonus was he was always up for anything that meant his knuckles would get a work out.

Now the full SP on this job was that the fella owed about fifteen grand but with interest, it was now around the eighteen mark. The person owed was not expecting the full amount to be paid up but wanted to make sure, for Stevie's sake, that at least nine grand was collected and hand delivered to his contact on the outside, who happened to be his other half. This way he made sure that his missus was going to receive something or Stevie was not getting out in one piece. Worst case scenario, Billy would dip his hand in his own pocket and assume the debt and because it was Stevie, would write it off as an expensive gesture.

The guy in question was Danny Martin or Dino for short. Dino thought of himself as a suave Dean Martin rather than the dinosaur dog from the Flintstones. He was, in fact, some dink who was acting like a Billy Big Spud because he thought he had got off paying his debt to some two bit scumbag who was threatening to do some damage to a defenceless, smack head who happened to be like family to Billy Michaels. The welcher had no such luck. He had moved to some bed-sit in Reading from the address that they were originally given but he still visited the same old haunts to keep up appearances.

Now Reading was a far cry from the manor that the boys knew, they didn't know anybody out that way and had no resources. They were staying in a B 'n' B while waiting for Dino to surface and were using a car from the garage Jason worked at. They would frequently pop into the preferred pubs and clubs of this stain on society, posing as buyers who had been told to look this guy up. Eventually he was pointed out to them by some lowlife who actually believed that this Dino was a real somebody in the grand scheme of things. Straight away from the way he acted from the second they introduced themselves to him, it was obvious he wouldn't pay up directly, so a different angle was needed to be put into play.

Jason, forever the party animal, was carrying a wrap of cocaine on him and thought of the hook to reel their little fishy in with. Jason and Billy introduced themselves, selling him the story that they were holding a kilo of Charlie from a bust that went down in London and wanted shot of it ASAP. To help the sell they gave him a sample. The way Dino saw it was he had a couple of young cockney tearaways who were out of their league trying to out some white. This was his area; he was a grown and known man and thought he could take advantage. Therefore, he offered to take the kilo off them for thirteen grand. The actual cost price of a kilo of Coke, in those days, was around forty thousand pounds; today it is worth about twenty-eight, if you are lucky. They ummed and arred and then eventually agreed; after all there was no Coke and they wanted to come across as naive bumpkins from the smoky. Just two no-bodies who wanted to make a quick score but in reality, they just wanted to make sure that the price would be low enough that he would have some money on him for the taking.

They set up a meet for the following week at a destination chosen by Dino, just to add to the illusion that he was in control. To show what a Muppet he was, he chose a service station on the M4. It was all too easy. The boys arrived with a kilo weight of mixed powder, mainly consisting of soldering flux, just to add that bitter taste. They acted nervous when he approached them with an even bigger Muppet in tow, saying they did not want to do the deal because it had the trappings of a set up. He reassured them by opening up a Mitre sport's bag filled with the folding stuff. Jason agreed to still do the deal as long as his "minder" went back to the car. Dino, smiled a 'I'm in control of this' grin and promptly ushered him away, acting like he was a don or something. As soon as the lump reached his car, Dino found himself on the wrong end of a couple of coshes and bleeding from his head profusely. Billy worked on his head and back as he started to crumble while Jason kept whacking his arm to get him to let go of the bag. By now the ever-alert "minder", said in the loosest of terms, had looked over and saw what was going on and started to slide himself out of the car.

Jason, who now had the bag, jumped in the motor they were using and started her up while the great ape came running over. To this day, Billy is the first to admit that he would never be able to make that same shot again. Billy let fly his cosh like a ninja death star or something and it clocked the fella right between the eyes, forcing his head back. With the momentum, he went arse over tit, allowing Billy to join Jason and they sped off unharmed.

Once they were many safe miles away they counted out the nine grand to be delivered to the wife of the owed and figured the remaining cash covered their expenses. Stevie's score had been settled and all was happy in the world, at least for a short time.

Christmas was fast approaching and that year they had all planned to do something a little different. So the Michaels clan booked a handful of seats on the "Magic Bus" to Amsterdam. Billy remembered all of them spending what seemed like an eternity on this bus, as it drove across to the land of smoke and sex.

There is nothing like being stuck on a bus with your nearest and dearest, laughing non-stop, while trying to piss into empty beer bottles and suffering a severe case of the munchies after a nine bar of Hash. Mikey was trying to shag some stoned chick that was travelling with her fella; who was out cold at the time and her wanton lust levels were going through the roof. So Mikey being the gent that he is, catered to them and after fingering her, while making sure they all got a whiff of it, prompted to mount her as she laid next to her passed out boyfriend. That was the "Magic Bus"; the journey was actually more fun than the actual two days they spent in the 'Dam. They had just as many laughs coming home too. Billy will never forget that trip or that Christmas because it was the last time all the gang ever got together to celebrate. From that year onwards they just never seemed to connect like the family unit they used to be. The cracks were starting to show, it had been a good run but too many things were starting to go wrong. It served as a sign of the times, that past year had affected all of them and they were all dealing with it in their own way.

Stuart had just started seeing someone and had thought that it could be true love. Mikey was starting to get in with a South London team that was starting to come up the ladder, while Billy was still trying to recapture the good old days. Their kid brother Gary had left school and was trying to make his mark on the big wide world and Vaughan was left to finish school on his own. The only one who felt no change was the youngest of the litter, Craig; he was now eleven and the apple of their Mum's eye. Life had not even started for him yet.

Tony was gone, Stevie was doing time, and Jason and Colin were doing their own thing. The old gang was drifting apart and the time had come for Billy to re-evaluate his life, it is true what they say, you cannot turn back the clock. Boxing was losing its appeal; he had shagged almost every bird that hung out at the places the gang frequented and the money schemes were going through a dry spell.

It was one of those points in one's life when you just have to ask yourself "Can it get any worse?" Christmas had come and gone but Billy got the greatest present of all, news that Stevie's sentence had been reduced and was getting out of stir early for good behaviour. On all accounts, Billy thought nineteen eighty-seven was going to be starting on a good note and the plan was to just push the envelope a little further. However, it is said that how the New Year starts is how the year will run.

January was the month that started the downward spiral, Stuart being the man that he was decided it was time to have his own space, yet felt it was Billy and Mikey that should move out, they of course disagreed.

The real reasoning behind this sudden view on life was because Stuart's girlfriend, Kelly, had been bending his ear about them moving in together but rather than getting their own place, overtaking the brother's four-bedroom house seemed like the better solution. Well it would to a dirty, money grabbing skank. The twosome however, saw it differently and was putting up a fight, Mikey and Billy owned more of the house than Stuart did. However, the drawback being the house was in his name, what with neither of them being old enough at the time when they bought it to have it in a joint name.

Why is it, that women can affect men so easily? The amount of attitudes that you can see change in a blink of an eye all because of a woman's influence is astonishing. It's like everything on the outside of the relationship doesn't warrant your attention any more. You cut your family and friends off; you adopt your newfound partners' routines although they will not adapt to yours. Billy was always amazed by his big brother's change, Billy had a lot of sex with a lot of different women over the years and he just thought that you need a better excuse than you're getting it on a regular basis to justify the change. Especially when you knew that after about six months, you are not getting that much anymore and as far as blowjobs go, forget about it.

The atmosphere in the house was becoming unbearable, especially on the nights Kelly invited herself back. She was turning their older, level-headed brother against them and was causing a rift that would not mend if the direction of things did not change. Billy didn't believe in hitting women but this one deserved a crack in the jaw, and he felt himself come close on more than one occasion to doing just that to her. Just being in her presence would start him off; they would row all the time, which in turn made Stuart, step in and straight away take her side in it all. One night Mikey came home to see her in one of his favourite shirts that Stuart had just let her wear forgetting all about personal privacy and decency, because she got something down her own top. It was the wrong night at the wrong time because Mikey just flew into one and demanded it back. Stuart was telling him to calm down while he was trying to rip it off her back. At that point, Billy walked in on the situation, trying to catch up on what had happened to have these two brothers at each other's throats. That was when she opened her big old trap, Billy told her to keep out of it Stuart took her side. This proved to be one time too many, Stuart now started to get into Billy's face and push himself up on him, Billy wasn't having any of it so he pushed Stuart away. So, as to create a space of arm's length, but Stuart lost his balance and started to fall backwards. He found his footing and started to come back at Billy with a determined look on his face, and that is when Billy hit him. The look on Stuarts face was one of hurt, Billy did not know if it was the punch or the fact that he had hit him that put it there, but it had happened and that was that. Mikey always remembered the disappointment in Stuart's eyes and the smile on that slag's face. Billy had let her get to the better of a situation with her constant interfering and now he had fucked up in the biggest way. He did not play it smart and Billy not only lost the battle of wills but his big brother as well. To save their sibling ties from furthering even more Mikey and Billy decided to move out. Which in turn lead to their own brotherly partnership dissolving as well, Mikey accepted the offer of a place to crash from his newfound friends, over in Camberwell, while Billy rented a flat above a chemist along Walthamstow market.

So now, it was the end of January and Billy had found himself living on his own for the first time in his life. There was bad blood between Stuart and himself which seeing as they now lived a stone's throw away from each other was making stepping out the front door awkward.

Mikey was doing his own thing and after a time rarely called. The elders of the clan all moved on, Gary was waiting for the invite to move in with Billy and so was Vaughan, who had reached an age where he was tired of sharing and wanted a bedroom all to himself. Nevertheless, this was the first time Billy had ever been on his own, without the safety net of his brothers to fall back on and fancied trying it out for a while. So he told Gary to hang in there and just give him a couple of months space, then after he turned eighteen he could move in and start hosting some parties. Gary agreed but there was something in his eyes that showed he was tired of being treated like a second-class citizen by his older brothers, especially by one who was not even blood. The foundations of resentment were setting in, slowly but it was setting in. The tell tale signs were there but Billy chose to ignore them.

Stevie got his release from stir near the end of February, and a bona fide reason, as if Billy ever needed one, to paint the town red was presented. Colin and Jason agreed to come up with Billy to meet Stevie at the gates and bring him back to the fold, which was handy because they supplied the car. It was a lovely looking motor, it was a big flashy Merc', just to give him a bit of luxury after his holiday, courtesy of her majesty's convenience. They drove up to Brixton prison to collect him, now in all honesty because of the 'agg going on with Stuart and his Girlfriend, Billy had failed to keep up the visits to him for the past few months. They drove past three times before they realised that the facially drawn stick figure standing on the corner of the street was Stevie. He went in weighing a good sixteen stone and now he was thinner than a supermodel.

"What the fuck happened to you? You look anorexic." Colin, the king of tact, must have held back the urge to ask that question for all of ten seconds after Stevie got in the car. He tried to smile but the guy was just too weak, he had dark circles under his eyes and his skin appeared wafer thin. This was not the same Stevie Marsh that they were knocking around with just over fourteen months ago; this was his shadow, a mere reflection of a once great man and one of Billy's best friends.

He did not want to come back and stay at Billy's place, he just asked Colin to drop him off at his Mums house. Apparently, they had this big heart to heart while he was inside and agreed that it would be best to stay with her while he sorted out which direction he wanted his life to go. Sally, Stevie's Mum, had known Billy and the rest of the boys since he was five years old when he and Stevie went to primary school together. Billy referred to her as Auntie Sal and always showed her respect and despite his way of life, she never held it against him. She never saw any of them as a bad influence, if anything she used to say she was grateful they all looked out for him as much as they did.

To help Stevie settle back in, she gave Billy a key to her house, saying he could come in and make himself at home at any time. Stevie's Dad had walked out on them years ago and Davey had joined the army after his release and was doing his bit in Northern Ireland. She just wanted as much help as possible. Therefore, every day Billy used to walk in, without knocking, raided the fridge and teased Stevie. Just like old times, only this time round the need for a fix was interfering. He was Billy's friend, his family and he needed help, not to quit but to score. Billy felt guilty that he was considering hooking him up with people who dealt in that sort of class A, but it came down to loyalty.

To ease his own guilt, Billy invited Stevie to a party where he knew this type of business went down. That way instead of bringing him face to face with a dealer, it could be by chance that he would meet someone to help feed his Frankenstein. Billy put some money in his pocket with the "Until you get on your feet" speech and let him loose to mingle. This way if he scored, then he scored making his own connections, Billy was kicking himself really but he knew that if he did not do something, someone else would.

The next morning Stevie was up, smiling, looking happy and eating breakfast. His Mum was thanking Billy for getting him out of the house and getting him back into the swing of things. Billy felt sick to the pit of his stomach, he had betrayed her trust, and deep down he knew he helped put another nail in Stevie's coffin. He felt like scum…

Chapter Seven

Billy and Stevie seemed very different from the young boisterous youths they used to be. Growing up never seemed this tough; the biggest decision they had to make was where to hide the Brussel sprouts from their Sunday lunch. Stevie was the first kid to ever talk to Billy when he started Primary school. Living on the sixteenth floor of St Albans, Billy was never really allowed out to play downstairs and after that incident with Geoff, he was not really allowed out full stop. So starting school was a great escape from the confines of the tower block of doom and his mother.

On Billy's first day, he was partnered with some snot nose, called Mark. It was known as the buddy system and it was designed to help kids adjust to school, but Mark was not Billy's bottle of milk and so he spent most of his first day on his own. It was just after lunch when Mark came over and tried to do some colouring with him, Billy turned to him and told him he didn't want to do it and then proceeded to tell him to go away. Mark then started to cry and shout for the teacher, with that Stevie walked over and punched him in the belly, took his crayons and sat down next to Billy and started drawing. Billy looked at him, he looked at Billy, and they both started sniggering, and that's how it was all through their lives together. They would find the most stupidest of things funny; they both had a very dry sense of humour and the same view of things. As they got older their taste in clothes and women were the same, which in turn resulted in them, having a few arguments. They were the closest of close and often referred to each other as brother. They had always watched each other's back and had shown up just in time to help the other out. Stevie never had to ask for Billy's help or had to say thanks for it, but he always did and Billy did the same. However, this new thing was way out of their control, and deep down they both knew it.

Stevie was getting in with a new crowd, his kind of crowd. The only time Billy saw him was when he tried to ponce some money for his next journey down to smacksville. At first Billy was being naïve and seeing him alright but then one time he just turned around and said "No". Stevie started going into one.

"You wanker, I thought we were mates, I thought we were brothers. I need that money; you have no idea how good it makes me feel. It's entirely your fault!!!" Deep down Billy knew it wasn't him talking, He was hurting and Billy wouldn't help supply the cure. It did not change the fact he was right, if Billy had not hooked him up in the first place, he could have been off it by now. Or at least starting to get to grips with going cold turkey, but no, Billy stepped in thinking he was helping him and now he was turning his back on him; leaving him hanging. Killing him even worst than the H would of, Billy just had to walk away from him. Give him time to calm down and maybe realise, that he did honestly care about him. Billy was on his high horse and believed he was doing the right thing by turning his back on his oldest and dearest friend when he needed him the most.

Nevertheless, it was not all about him, was it? What about Billy? Billy felt he needed some TLC. He always had a string of lovelies on stand by and it was time to call one up. The lucky filly on this occasion was Jessica, a nice Jewish girl from Highams Park. Jessie was a sweet little thing, a lot of love to give but that was all. She was new to the whole "Billy Michaels" thing, if you did not put out in the first week you were history. Billy gave her her due, she tried but he needed dirtiness and she was too fresh and too scared. The truth of it was, he was venting his own failings out on her and she did not deserve it, but then what was he going to do, admit that to her, not in this lifetime. Billy had an image to uphold; a rep to maintain, he was Billy Michaels, and lord of all he surveyed. He was a total dick.

Billy had sent her home crying by the end of the week, he was not a welcomed guest in her parent's house and her older brother Jamie, wanted a crack at his title. Billy did not think he would have gotten anywhere but he was in the right to defend his sister's honour. Still it did cause bad blood between them and consequently had to scratch Jessie's name out of his little black book. Her family had a bit of dough to their name and her brother Jamie was tipped for better things. Better things being a nightclub owner, come promoter, for the venue based in Kings Cross, called the Crucifix. His uncle owned the building originally but he turned it over to Jamie in the late nineties and it was here that he would make his mark and have their paths cross once more.

A week had passed and Billy had managed to upset and piss off two people. One he loved as a brother and one who just wanted the chance to love him. He only had himself to blame but for some reason the world has its own sense of humour and sees fit that everything comes in three's. So now, he was just waiting to see who the third person that he was going to trample on was going to be, and he did not have to wait long.

When Billy next saw Sally, she was sporting a tasty little shiner on her left eye, she had tried to conceal it but she was a rank amateur. Billy had witnessed his own Mother for year's cover up her own marks and bruises with such expertise; you would have forgotten she had any but Sally hadn't had the experience, and it still showed.

"What happened to your eye?" Again being naïve, Billy actually thought some lager lout had tried it on with her and she paid the price. Then the look in her eyes said it all, there was a look of disbelief, which only comes from being hurt by the ones you love. She told me what had happened. Stevie had punched her in the face and robbed her of her handbag for some money to buy his shit with. Billy blamed himself, it was like, he had hit her himself because if he had given Stevie the money when he asked he would not have resorted to this. It is all about chain reactions, a number of incidents that all inter-link with one another. Billy no longer knew the person that was once his best friend; it was time to tell him how it was and get him to stop taking the drugs. He either would learn the easy way or be taught the hard way, whichever route he wanted to take, he would be educated. Billy caught up with Stevie back at his house some hours later, he was on his high, all grins and I love you's.

"We have to talk" Now professionals call it an intervention, Billy called it a solid left to the gut, far more effective. He did not have to say anything, Stevie was on his knees, sucking in air and coughing. Amongst it all, he started to cry, remorse for hitting his Mum or just the realisation of the past year or so, Billy could not tell why but he did know he asked for help followed by forgiveness. Billy told him he was there for him and they would get through this together, he just looked up at him with tear-filled eyes and smiled.

Chapter Eight

April was meant to be a happy time; it was the month of Easter and Vaughan's birthday. Surely, things were going to start looking up. Billy was giving Sally some money every week to help out with the bills and Stevie was actually showing signs of improvement. Billy figured that spring was cleaning away the bad and making way for the good but in fact, it was just clearing the obstacles that had been slowing down his own journey on the path to destruction.

It was April seventh, nineteen eighty seven when Billy ventured round to Stevie's house, it was one of those rare days in Britain when the sun was actually out and the weather was warm. Birds were chirping and everyone was smiling, you were just waiting for someone to break out in song and everyone to start dancing. It was a good day.

Before he even put the key in the front door of Stevie's house he could feel that something was wrong, it was like a dark rain cloud was looming overhead and lightening was about to strike. The house had an open plan living room so as you walked through the door everything could be seen, except for today, because Billy could not see the families Television set or the stereo system. He instantly thought the house had been robbed, Billy slowly walked in; fist's cocked just in case the burglars were still in the house. The downstairs was clear, so he slowly crept his way up the stairs to the landing; he could see someone lying on the floor, looking under the bed in Stevie's bedroom. Billy tiptoed in, praying a loose floorboard would not give way and alert his prey that he was practically on top of him. Reaching out and grabbing a handful of shirt, he lifted the burglars head already to throw a left hook on his chin.

"Gotcha you bastard". However, what Billy initially got was the smell of puke, followed by the aroma of someone's rotten arse, if his sense of smell wasn't being put to the test enough then his sense of sight would be. There was Stevie lying on the floor, his arm still tied off, a syringe hanging out of a vein. Vomit all around by his head and the evidence of him soiling himself. Tell tale signs of function meltdown, body convolutions, and taking the last ride. Stevie had overdosed on a drug he promised he would never take again and Billy was stupid enough to believe him. He sat him up and held him close to his chest; he squeezed him tight, just like Billy's Mum had done to him when he was five. That reassuring hug that was meant to tell you everything was going to be all right without using any words. Billy bowed his head, kissed Stevie's sick covered hair, and stayed in that position until his Mum, Sally, came home and found them.

Billy put on a brave face and managed to stay strong for the rest of that day. He was fine when the police were questioning him, he was fine when Colin had come round when he heard the news, and he was even fine on the drive back to his own flat in Walthamstow. It was at home that the signs became evident that Billy wasn't fine, feeling's that you can only assume were guilt had started to set in, followed by the pain of realisation. Billy's Dad, Bob, had always said never to let yourself feel pain, block it out at all costs, do whatever it is you need to do to block and survive.

Billy was in a desperate need of a drink; his mouth felt dry and white bits of dried saliva formed on the corners of his mouth. He needed a drink, a strong drink, so he cracked the seal on a bottle of tequila that started to stare at him from the liquor cabinet and started to hit back the shots, ignoring the etiquette of the salt and lime. He never remembered stopping.

Billy missed Stevie's funeral and he wasn't around for Vaughan's birthday celebrations, he just spent every waking moment in any establishment that would serve him what he needed to block out the pain and when they would close, he choose to brown bag it.

Billy starting to camp outside pubs and off licenses and was basically sleeping rough; he hardly spent any time in his flat anymore. He shut himself off from everyone he knew and the painful truth was he needed them more than ever. As the days turned into weeks and then months Billy sank lower and lower with no regard to himself or others. He stayed in a drunken state because once the Stevie situation was forgotten he then carried on drinking to dull the pain about everything else that had happened over the years. Geoff, Lynton, Tony, that guy outside the house party, the way he had treated the women in his life, the strained relationship he had with his own Mum, even the people he had ever stolen from or made an unknown profit off of. Every skeleton and ghost he had sealed away in the darkest region of his mind were bursting through the cracks and seams. He was losing it, searching for answers at the bottom of a bottle, when in reality, the only answer you will find there is usually an expiry date.

For Billy the months of May, June, and July were just blurs, the few times he was sober were just to withdraw money, which was slowly disappearing from his once healthy bank account. His rent was paid by direct debit along with the rest of his bills, but now he was not earning so he was not putting any additional money in, just taking it out and as no well is bottomless it was not long before it was all gone.

However, for others, these months were turning points, opportunities were arising and being taken and with that, attitudes were changing and people's real personalities were starting to show. One individual in particular to seize the day was the clan's younger brother Gary, who was finally tired of lurking in their shadows, staying quiet and under the radar. It was during this time when other people's attentions were turned elsewhere he publicly struck out on his own. Gary displayed a cold heartedness that at any other time would have brought a smile to the faces of the crew and a swelling in their dark hearts. Rather than being concerned with his older brother's welfare, Gary had taken it upon himself to move in to his flat and become the lord and master of all his belongings.

The first thing he did was to move all of Billy's stuff out of the master bedroom and move his own gear in, followed by organising a party that he planned on hosting at the flat, now that's a prime example of true brotherly love for you.

Being that little bit younger, Gary ran with a different crowd, one of his closest friends was Lee Small, a trainee chippy he met while undergoing his builders' degree. They talked a better game than they could play or at least that was the general perception and it came across that they were trying to live off the reputation set by Mikey, Billy and the rest of the crew and in all fairness to them, they were getting away with it too. Nevertheless, they were always looked upon as being small time in comparison.

Gary was the shortest out of all the Michaels brothers; he only stood in at five foot seven and had a completely different look about him. It pained them all to say it but he could quite easily have been the milkman's child, if you catch the drift. He was always one and a half steps behind his older siblings as they grew up, he was always included in some of the things they got up to but he was always seen as the annoying little brother that chased behind them like a lost puppy. Billy was sure that if the boys looked back on it now, Stuart probably thought the same thing about Mikey and in turn Mikey could have thought the same thing about Billy. Although despite the age difference between Mikey and Billy, they were always involved in the same things together, where Gary and Vaughan were too far behind and just ended up trialling in their dust. This obviously created some secret resentment in the two of them, as this current situation highlighted where Gary was concerned.

Between the time that lapsed from Tony's suicide and Stevie's passing it was never mentioned that the two young guns that took over the weed business on the old estate was Lee and another would be by the name of Gus, both of whom were introduced by Gary. With the only two men who could shine some light on to why it was never pointed out that were both dead, it was for others to draw their own speculations as to why it was kept on the hush-hush. Those in the know thought it was because they knew what trouble it may have caused, Billy and Mikey were the first to get out of that racket and knowing first hand that their little brother was now getting involved would have caused waves in the water. Others believed that Stevie was trying to play both sides of the fence, hoping for a little monthly reward for keeping the secret. Either way the real reasoning will now never be known. There was no one to set the record straight regarding the gossip that started to go around.

Gary and Lee were using their new found, accumulated drug money to set themselves up as the new generation of house party organisers, the only problem was, when you're one and a half steps behind the times you are getting into the scene just as it already has one foot in the grave. Therefore, the kind of partygoer they were attracting were the complete morons who would rather trash your house than just have a good, mellow time. Of course the biggest problem Little Gary had, although at the time he never saw it as a problem, was that the stuff they were trashing was Billy's and the thought that he would need to replace it before Billy sobered up and got back into the swing of things never crossed his mind.

Gary was not making anything worthwhile on the money side of things from the parties; he should have paid more attention to his older brother's example, because everything they did was designed to make the coinage.

However, this was something that seemed to elude all their younger siblings because as each and every one of them tried their hand at something dodgy, they seemed to get all the grief and none of the dough. You just cannot tell youngsters anything that they feel they do not already know.

The up side for them was that they may not have been making the folding stuff they were expecting but they were making some useful contacts, but contacts didn't pay for the things they wanted so Gary and Lee set about to earn a bit of scratch to supplement their desired spending spree, by doing of all things, security work. Now the only time these two could stand tall is if they stood on each other's shoulders, but their hearts were in the right place, so they entered the field of door work.

Their first night was working as stewards at some music event at the Astoria, in Tottenham Court Road. This went okay but their second night was at the Astoria II, which was running a gay night. These two little cute boys did not stand a chance; all the punters were over the top camp queens that teased them both silly. That was enough to scare off Lee from the field of Bouncing for many years, but Gary went on to do the odd night here and there.

Gary staying in the world of penguin suits and face busting opened up a whole new audience for his wares and for the first time ever was actually getting in at the ground level before his brothers on a whole new craze, Ecstasy. It was not long before they too were knocking the seed and weed on the head, leaving Gus to run the whole shebang while they ploughed all their money into buying the 'Little Fella's' bulk. Gary would turn a blind eye to Lee's full pockets as he entered the club while providing cover for him if any other bouncer tried to out him. Gary was not the first doorman to think of this and naturally stepped on a few toes but it wasn't long before the pair of them clicked that it made more sense to sell it to the masses before they went into the club than competing with every Tom, Dick and Harry in the club. So as the queues formed outside, Lee would walk up and down the pavement declaring, ever so discretely what he had to sell at fifteen pound a go.

They did not hold any more house parties but started to attend them instead, taking their happy pills with them and this aided to lay the foundations for some hardcore escapades later on in their lives.

August had come around and our hapless hero, Billy, had been living in the same clothes for over seven weeks. He absolutely stank. He had alienated most of his family and friends and just existed for the amusement of those that frequented the pubs he was spending and wasting his life in. Although his memory of that time was hazy, there was one incident stuck in his mind for when the day would come that he would get his act together again. One day Billy found himself penniless in the Dog and Duck pub in Walthamstow; he was gagging for a drink and was going around the tables supping down the left over dregs before the potman was collecting them up to put in the dishwasher. It was here that he came across a table full of regulars to that particular establishment, they beckoned him over and basically ridiculed him, but luckily for them but unfortunate for Billy he wasn't coherent enough to care.

There was a dead pint on the table, it must been sitting there for a hour but was never collected so Billy asked the group of revellers if he could have it. They were laughing while dishing out subtle insults at him while making it sound funny, then one of them told him that they would pay him five-pounds if Billy drank it all up in one go. A fiver for downing a pint, sounded like easy money but that is when another one of them chirped in and added that he would add another fiver to the pot if Billy drank it with the added contents of an ashtray. A tenner for the sake of some ash and fag butts, bring it on Billy thought. A few more started in but then, like in everything, there was one who wanted to take it to the extreme, he placed a score on the table top and then proceeded to hock a mouthful of spit and phlegm into the glass, and just raised his head and smiled at Billy.

Billy picked up the glass and knocked it all back; every gulp was a different taste, until it was all gone. He put the glass down and picked the money up. He left that pub to head for somewhere else but about three yards down the road he stopped and threw his guts up. He did not know if it was the dodgy beer or the fact he sold the last shred of his Cockney pride for forty quid that made him ill. Whatever it was, he could not sink any lower or could he? If he did, he never remembered it.

Vaughan had obviously had enough of watching Gary carry on in Billy's flat whilst their brother needed help and so took it upon himself to call in re-enforcement's and rescue Billy before he became a picture in the post office. Although, later on in life, it was asked why it took him until October before reaching his decision to become his brother's saviour.

Billy was sleeping on a bench when a familiar voice called his name; he was being slightly shaken by this firm hand. His head stirred and movement caused him to puke all down himself, this was followed by Billy then pissing himself. Loving the warm feeling of his golden fluid running down his leg, a little smile crept across his face. His eyes tried to focus on the person who had woken him and caused the chain reaction that took place but he could not make out the face, he just knew he had heard this voice before. It was Mikey and he had come to take Billy home.

Vaughan had called Mikey to let him know how Billy was doing and Mikey thought it was time to intervene. His idea of intervention was a little different from Billy's where Stevie was concerned. Mikey and Vaughan dragged his drunken, piss smelling self home and the pair of them threw him into the bathtub and proceeded to fill it with cold water, obviously hoping for a shock treatment or something. It definitely caught Billy's attention. He was then force fed coffee and chunky soup, which he just kept bringing back up, before being thrown back into the bathtub, only this time it was warm water that was in it. Mikey had Vaughan shampoo his hair while Mikey gathered his pass their sell by date clothes and put them in the rubbish bin. Once Billy had settled down a little bit, Mikey set about shaving his overgrown and patchy whiskers from his dirty encrusted face. It was a few hours more, before Lisa came round; she was a hairdresser they all knew and was one of many that had passed the "Billy Michaels" week test.

They sat Billy down and he tried to focus on the lengthy lectures that were being given by everyone and their mother. Lisa cut his hair while all the time joined in by ragging on his case. Mikey threatened to smack him around and Vaughan just wanted to make him continuous amounts of soup. Billy however just wanted to sleep; Lisa helped him to his newly acquired master bedroom and laid him down on the bed. It felt good being in a real bed again Billy thought. Lisa got in with him and just stroked his newly cut hair until he fell asleep.

When Billy finally woke up, almost sixteen hours later, all he wanted was a drink. Gary, who had finally returned back to his new abode and was a little disappointed that Billy had returned and reclaimed his castle done his bit while hiding his true feelings on the matter and had preceded to get rid of every bottle in the flat and was instructed not to let Billy venture outside the front door. Billy knew deep down inside that he was just trying to help his big brother but that did not stop him mouthing off to Gary and swearing like a trooper. However, he did return to his bed, not pushing the cause any further, but truth be known, Billy just didn't fancy his chances in the weakened state that he was in taking his little brother on in a fight.

Billy often considered changing his views on commitment and relationships during those on and off again sober moments, but memories of how his Mum and Geoff were, or even how Stuart and his skank of a bird were, just put him off of doing it himself. If he ever did settle down, Lisa would have been someone he would have like to have tried it with. She was a couple of years younger than he was, and was only five foot two, not that Billy was taking anything away from short people. She had a pretty face and a well-proportioned body, and being a hairdresser, always had immaculate hair. The most important thing about Lisa that always stayed in Billy's mind, even to this day was how good she smelt. He always found that a turn on with women, many women wear a perfume that does not complement their natural scent; they just go with what they know. Nevertheless, there are some that took the time to find the right perfume and when you kissed the back of their necks and you took in a whiff of them, it's captivating.

The reason he never tried to settle down with her was that he felt she was too good for him at the time. Billy was drifting from scam to scam and enjoying everything that came with the journey, he would not have been able to give her the attention she deserved and Lisa was definitely someone who deserved better. As the years rolled on and their friendship drifted apart he always hoped that she would find someone who made her feel special.

Billy had not left the flat once in those following months. He did not trust himself; he was scared and embarrassed and could not look people in the eye, even complete strangers who did not know any different. His confidence was shot to pieces and he was relying way too much on Lisa for company. These were the kind of times when your family and friends stood up and are counted. He loved them all and probably would not be here now if it were not for them saving him from himself.

December finally came round and Billy had not touched a drop of alcohol for nine weeks. To celebrate the Christmas holidays, Mikey and Gary had arranged a party at the flat, a non-alcoholic themed party. People Billy had abused and ignored rallied round to wish him Christmas cheer and well-being. Any other time, this bunch of sentimental hogwash would have made him sick to his stomach, but for this particular time, he thanked them all and enjoyed the moment.

Fruit juice and fizzy pop was the order of the day, and everyone was telling Billy to forget the past year and get back out there in the real world. He knew they were right and arranged to catch up with all of them in the New Year.

Like any gathering the brothers threw, there was always a little scuffle. Some friend of a friend, who thought the idea of a non-alcoholic party was a joke and brought along with him a six-pack of Bud, caused the one that happened that night. Mikey just looked at him and said "You cunt" and then proceeded to knock the crap out of him, helped by Gary, then Jason, followed by Colin and Vaughan. As they threw him out the front door, they just missed the fella walking in. It was Stuart, Billy looked over at him, and he raised his head in recognition sporting a forgiving smile. Perhaps next year would turn out to be Billy's year after all.

After everyone had left, probably in a desperate need of a real drink after spending the evening with a recovering drunken bum like the man of the hour, it was only the Michaels brothers left in the flat. They just sat back and talked; laughing about the scrapes they got into, the things they had done over the years and clinked a glass to those that were unable to join them. It seemed like old times and although they knew, it was never going to be like it was, for that evening they were a tight knitted family again.

Chapter Nine

The start of nineteen eighty-eight was a time of choices, which paths to walk down and what direction to take. After the previous year, making the right choices was paramount. Billy's first decision was to get back into the gym and get back into shape. Harry's gym had since been closed down and the crew had moved their training disciplines to "Pumps" gym in Walthamstow. Billy had been boxing less and less over the years and so when the opportunity to turn pro came up he turned it down. It was one of those paths that he did not want to walk anymore. He was still putting on the gloves and hitting the heavy bag but he only ever got back in the ring to spar. That is the way he liked it and so that is the way it was going to be.

Billy had not been involved in anything too illegal for some time and was pondering if he should start getting his face about again. He had seen so many close friends of his be affected by that way of life that maybe it was time to follow Stuart's example and get a proper job and settle down with someone who made you think that you were happy. It sounded foreign to him but Stuart was happy, even if he was still seeing that Kelly bird. Therefore, there must be something to it, a method to the madness so to speak.

The problem with being a male slag is that all the girls in your life already know what you are like. So finding one that would take you serious enough about settling down is like looking for that needle in the haystack and as for the ones that would want you to settle down with them, what does that say about those psycho bitches?

While waiting for Miss Right to come along, Billy concentrated on his training, pushing the weights around and building up the strength he lost while learning first hand the negative affects that drinking yourself into a drunken nirvana and over staying your welcome. A few months went by before he was starting to feel like his old self. Billy was looking good and feeling better and he thought it was about time to demonstrate that his old will and knack to knock someone on their arse was back by setting out to settle some old scores. His first stop was for retribution at the establishment that held the clearest of memories, the Dog and Duck pub.

Sitting, in a large group in the sofa section, were the same regulars from the year before, the one's who felt justified to humiliate someone down on their luck by paying for the pleasure of watching someone degrade themselves even further. Instead of recognising someone in need of help and giving them a lifeline. They all seemed to still be doing the same old thing that they were doing previously, sitting around, drinking and making fun of others. If anyone needed a lesson of how short life can be, it was this lot, perhaps then they would learn to savour each and every minute. After all, if they already knew that, they would have been somewhere else on this particular day and out of harms way.

Billy walked through the doors and headed towards the bar, staying in clear view of anyone that wished to spy him and as intended, he caught the eye of one of them, who alerted his group and they in turn started to turn up the volume on their voice boxes.

"'Ere, 'ere it's Jack Daniel's"

"No mate don't you mean Jim Bean". They all started to chirp in with one remark or another and were all raising their glasses at Billy with a 'Cheers' gesture. They actually thought they were being clever with their humour.

"Come over here." One called out, directing his comment to Billy who responded by walking over to the group, all the while finding it very hard to bite his tongue.

"Hello fella's, still hanging around this old haunt then, that kind of behaviour could be classed as being predictable". Billy gave a sly smile; his remark went right over their heads.

"What happened to you? We hardly recognised you standing straight and smelling clean. Drunk anymore ashtrays lately?" They started to laugh again while not even bothering to hide the malice in their tone. Billy approached their table still smiling his sly smile; anyone in the know would have been ready for something. Positioned themselves differently so they could keep themselves at arms length or at least have pulled their chair's back to give themselves an easy escape route but these guys were amateurs, who only acted on instinct after the fact. This was a pack mentality, which was going to be their downfall in this situation. Billy reached into his pocket, pulled out a handful of pound notes, looked at the crumpled wad, let out a menacing chuckle, and then threw the money across the table. The group of lads went through a mixed bag of emotions, which their facial expressions reflected. Billy bent down and picked up an empty bottle from their table and let out a little chuckle once more. "Smash!!!" shards of splintered glass scattered in the air as Billy put the bottle straight across the skull of the nearest member of this all male smorgasbord of hapless victims. As their demeanour and approach to life gave away, they acted on instinct after the fact, by all moving back in their chairs. "Smash!!!" This time Billy broke a pint glass across the face of another, the impact still allowed a follow on attack on a third person because the base of the glass stayed intact in Billy's grip. The jagged edge tore into the flesh of his face causing blood to gush forth and exposed bone.

"What the fuck!" Screamed one of the not yet harmed group. "Smack" a left cross caught him with his jaw still open from yelling his sentence, knocking his jaw bone loose. This was followed by a right uppercut on another chinless wonder. Billy was going garrarty and hitting everyone who was stupid enough to manoeuvre themselves into his path.

"Come on you fucker's, laugh now, go on, fucking laugh!!!" Blood started to shoot over the other patrons that had not moved far enough out of the way through either being frozen with fear or just plain morbid fascination. Women were starting to scream and cry, fella's were ushering themselves out of the pub. All signs of gallantry and chivalry went out the door faster then they were and those idiots, who had absolutely no idea who they took advantage of for their own amusement only a few months earlier, were now begging Billy for mercy while sobbing and asking for the intervention of a being, that to Billy, just didn't exist.

During the one-sided onslaught, the manager of the pub slowly made his way up behind Billy with the intention to give him a blow to the back of his head with the bat that he kept behind the bar. A typical lowlife sucker punch, then a lump of a man called Simon Hussein, who resided on the Priory Court estate that was but a stones throw away, stopped him by grabbing hold of the bat that was already in the position to be brought down on Billy's skull out of the manager's hand. Simon was a tall bloke, about six foot four. His dark Mediterranean looks gave away the fact his parents were not from the British Isles. He was a couple of years older than Billy but had attended the same school as him. Simon was in his final year at William Fitt by the time Billy had come up from Chingford Hall. Billy never crossed paths with Simon back then so he could not place the face but Simon remembered the stunts Mikey, Billy and the rest of the crew used to pull and knew what side his bread was buttered on. Simon was street smart enough to know that it was better to be owed a favour from a family like the Michaels clan than become a statistic like the forsaken crew that was lying bloodied and battered at the feet of this particular member of said family.

As the ruckus died down and Billy was left standing there, adrenaline pumping, fists tightly clenched waiting for one of the injured idiots in front of him to make a move or at least give an excuse to be wailed on some more. Billy still had his back to Simon and the manager that had planned on hitting him from behind, and was a little surprised when a voice behind him said "Come on, we need to get you out of here." And with that Simon cleared a path, pushing the manager and the last few onlookers to one side, escorted Billy out of the Dog and Duck pub and told him to jump in the passenger's seat of his car that was parked outside.

"You handle yourself pretty well, how do you fair when there aren't any bottles or glasses to hand?" By now Simon was driving down a collection of side roads to add a little randomness to their getaway journey, sirens that can be heard in the background, slowly faded away the further Simon drove into the heart of Walthamstow.

"I do okay but you should see me with a chain and padlock". The tension eased as they both let out a laugh and heartbeats slowed down.

"How'd you fancy a few nights work?"

It turned out that Simon worked as a bouncer at some nightclub on the High Road in Tottenham and was looking for someone to fill in for a few nights as his regular guy was taking some time off while he healed.

"Heals from what?" Billy asked.

"From the big kick off we had the other night." This got Billy's immediate interest. "It's a tenner an hour and all the birds you want, you up for it?" The pay was right and the work suited his temperament, thought Billy, so he decided to give it a go and help out his new found friend, after all, Simon had already demonstrated that he was willing to watch his back, why not return the favour.

It seemed only fitting that destiny would offer Billy his first real introduction to door work at the same nightclub, a few years previous, he had sustained a right royal kicking.

This was on top of the fact it was the venue his own Dad had worked at many years before that.

The Ritzy was a large venue, if you were playing by the books; its capacity was meant to be around two thousand punters. Over the years, Billy would see it reach nearly three thousand on the special occasion nights, Christmas Eve etc. Where were the Health and Safety officers that used to bring down Billy's house parties when you needed them?

Billy was stoked; the idea of door work seemed to appeal to him in the same way boxing did when he was younger, it just seemed like an aspect of evolution; the next stepping-stone on the path of life. All the greats had done it that way, first the boxing, then the enforcement and the big time crime. It worked that way for Freddie and Harry, it worked that way for Tommy and Teddy, it even worked that way for his Dad, Bob, and his brothers. What is it they say about a leopard not being able to change its spots? It doesn't relate so much to an individual but more of the footsteps one takes when brought up in a certain way of life. It was, and is, seen as the right thing to do. To follow in your parent's footsteps when they themselves are in a profession, be it Doctor, Lawyer, businessperson or criminal. It is just in some people's eyes some professions are not acknowledged as being the right footsteps to follow in but then the same could be said about becoming a Lawyer.

Billy told a few people what he was going to be doing, just so people knew where to start looking if something went tits up and he was never heard from again. It also helped to take his mind off of recent events, his undying craving for a good drink and the need to stay active. What better place to take your mind off of booze and death than a booze-filled nightclub full of dick heads all screaming for a kicking?

Now at this point in time, the uniform for the Ritzy was still the stereotypical dress for bouncers, black bow tie, white shirt and black suit. This was handy for Billy because he needed the excuse to wear shoulder pads. Compared to him, the other guys were monsters, talk about your weakest link. At this stage in his life, Billy was still a slim built fella due to years of exercising for stamina rather than mass and only now he had started to grow taller; his Mum put it down to him being a late bloomer. If only she knew the truth.

Billy's first night of work was on a Thursday, the doors opened at nine and he got there at twenty past eight. He was so hyper about it all; he was soaking in everything Simon was telling him. Noting where the fire exits were, where the toilets were, what the call signs from the DJ meant and most importantly, where the video cameras were positioned. This was the one thing he had to keep in mind, so not to get caught on tape doing something he shouldn't be doing. Simon then demonstrated the basic pat down system when searching punters on the door and what to do with confiscated drugs (basically, give them to Simon).

Simon was the Head Doorman and another lump, by the name of Baz, was his second. Simon introduced Billy to the rest of the team, who showed about as much enthusiasm to having a new guy, let alone a small new guy, in the team, as Billy would show to male gay porn. None at all!!!

Thursday nights started off quiet, it was a good night to learn the ropes. Being green to the world of entertainment security, Billy was given all the lackey jobs, the searching, the food runs, etc. But he didn't care, while they were laughing at him behind his back; Billy was watching everything that was going on. He was seeing how the set up worked and what the angles were, it was never the magic tricks he paid attention to but how they were done, slight of hand, objects on wires. He would always be watching the hand that the magician would be doing their utmost to stop you from seeing.

The front door set up was a basic numbers game, Simon was number one, and he had the say over the door, reception area, and box office. Baz was number two and overlooked the entrance and controlled the flow of punters to be searched, then there were three others on the steps, vetting, and depending on how busy it was, two to three guys on crowd control, as the people queued up along the High Road.

In those days, the actual club manager left the security to run the front of house while he concentrated on the bars and VIP area. No one could undermine Simon on any decision he made but he could undermine you. You could have as many guests as you liked, within reason and the difference between a slow night and a busy night was that you could personally pocket the entrance fee on every fifth person instead of every third person. This was divided up at the end of the shift. A percentage of the bungs on the door for queue jumping or VIP treatment went to Simon and Baz, while any gratuities were your own. The inside dealing was an operation that involved the managers blind eye, so he got a few kick backs from that kind of thing, as well as every managers side line, the bar takings.

The night seemed to fly by with only a handful of minor incidents, not much to write home about. Once the building was clear, the door team would call it a night but not before Simon did the rounds with his guys, paying out from the nights earnings. Being a temp Billy wasn't expecting anything but showing the class he had Simon cut him in for a share.

"So what did you think of your first night?" Billy looked at Simon, wondering what kind of response he was waiting for; Billy thought it might be wise to play it down a little.

"Yeah it was okay, a little quiet for me but okay." Simon just smiled.

"I suppose any night must seem quiet if you're not cutting up people's faces with bottles." Now it was Billy's turn to smile.

Billy said his farewells and jumped into his car, which also got him snide remarks from his so-called co-workers. The other doormen were still lingering outside in the car park, all standing around their BMW's and Ford Granada's. Acting like their shit did not stink. "Nice Car". This little remark seemed to start them off. Billy was not going to let some idiots who were suffering size-a-phobia put him off going back for a second night. Billy just ignored them and got into his little Datsun Cherry 100A that cost him fifty pounds. It was a two door red hatchback that when the accelerator was pushed all the way down, it could do a tonne. It got him from A to B and the back seat had seen enough action to last a lifetime. Billy never wanted to be judged by the car he drove and he had nothing to compensate for. His brother Gary was always quick to point that one out to those who felt it necessary to pay tens of thousands of pounds for big, flashy fast cars. You know what is said about what a big car compensates for; he would just shut them all up and drive off in his Mini.

Billy got home about four thirty in the morning still feeling the buzz, he got a taste of just how much a well organised door could make by the end of a night; this could well be a life he could enjoy living Money and violence, what could be better? He knew he had to start exercising, just to burn off the energy. He started doing knuckle push-ups to the point where he just could not push himself back up from the floor. It was now coming up for six in the morning and for Billy it was time for bed.

Billy did not wake up until gone two that Friday afternoon and feeling refreshed for it. He hit the shower and stood under the water, letting it rain down on him. His chest and arms was a little stiff from the extra workout he put himself through to tire himself out, every water droplet felt like a whip sting as it hit his body. He loved it.

He took it easy for the rest of the day; Billy just waited for when it was time to set out for work. He parked his Cherry 100A in the little car park beside the club and went in through the side entrance. The attitude shown by experienced doorman when one is new to the game is that of distrust and you're shut out of the circle. That is what this lot were doing to Billy; they looked him up and down with a hint of disgust. They obviously all wanted their old team member back and to have things return to normal. They did not say much to him while they were all hanging round, waiting for the doors to open. They were chatting amongst themselves and every now and then, Billy would get the distinct feeling that he was the topic of conversation. Each to their own he thought, he was there to do a job and that was all that mattered.

Friday night was a hectic night compared to Thursdays; the queue started to form early and Billy's first point of call was to get on crowd control. He had them move in closer to the wall, standing in pairs, giving a bit of his cheeky, cockney patter to the masses. He personally could not see a problem with gelling with the punters, trying to put a lighter side to things but this one idiot, a fellow member of the team who thought Billy should never have been asked to fill his friend's shoes, thought that there was one. His problem came from the fact that one particular group of people were not standing in pairs but was in a little huddle, giggling and thanking god that it was Friday.

"Fuck me, if you can't do this simple job then do us all a favour and fuck off home before some real work needs to be done." Billy stopped in his tracks, what was this moron's problem? Billy looked him in the eye and said "Whatever" Before turning around and continuing with his crowd control duties.

He did not like to have someone turn his or her back to him and so the disgruntled co-worker started going into one even more, 'F'ing and blinding all the while. Billy had listened to enough; he was putting people like him in their place for years. He did not need to hear any more. "Thud", "Thud", "Whack" a three-punch combo. A straight left to just below his Adams apple, a right cross to the side of his jaw followed by a thunderous left cross to his temple. The guy's legs turned to jelly and then his arse hit the floor, the crowd went quiet and the rest of the door team came running over. Billy took a step back, got himself at arms distance just in case they were looking for retribution.

"Fuck me Bill, what did you do?" Simon was standing there; mouth open knowing that he had been placed in an awkward situation. He had to back his team and defend them but at the same time it was him that brought Billy into the fold.

"Fucking twat wouldn't get off my case, so I smacked him a couple of times."

"Shit, you're meant to hit the punters not the other bouncers."

"I'll hit whoever gets in my face." There it was the comeback answer that said it all. They picked mouthy off the floor and helped him back to the front door. Simon walked up to Billy, put his arm around his shoulder, and walked him back in the direction of the car park.

"I think we better call it a night, don't you. I'll pay you a full night's money but I think it would be best that you went home." Billy was gutted and felt a little sorry for letting Simon down, he just nodded in agreement. "But I don't want to see this kind of thing tomorrow night; it's bad for our image." He wanted me back? Billy thought he had heard him wrong but he did not. Billy had proved what needed to be proved. He was not one to take shit from anybody and he was not scared to have it, no matter what the size of his opponent.

Billy was feeling a little nervous during his drive into work the next night; he parked up and went in the club. Mouthy was there, standing with some others, he saw Billy come in and walked over to him. Billy was watching everyone's movements, making sure he wasn't getting pinned in, he saw Baz nudge Simon to get his attention while they surveyed the situation and wondered how the outcome was going to play out. Mouthy was sporting a bruise on his cheek, which he was rubbing as he walked towards him.

"I was wrong about you; I shouldn't have busted your balls." He held out his hand and Billy shook it. He made some comment about not wanting to be on the receiving end of something like that again. They understood each other and that ended the doubts. The team knew Billy could do some damage and felt a bit safer about him having their backs and doing his share if it were to kick off. Which it did, seven times that night, Billy loved it.

The end of the night arrived and Billy was invited to sit in on a staff drink; only this time he was not teased about drinking soft drinks, well not much anyway. The team hung around, chatting for a couple of hours; Simon paid Billy for his three nights work, and asked if he would be interested in filling in for anybody else when they were off. Of course, Billy said, "Yes".

Chapter Ten

Over the following months, Simon threw Billy the odd night of work at the Ritzy, it was fun but it was not regular work. Billy's bank balance had taken a mega hit during his hazy days and this limited income was not doing much to rectify it. Gary was a permanent fixture in the flat and was paying his way. He was working as an apprentice for a painter and decorator that Uncle Allie had lined up for him, anything to keep prying eyes from uncovering how he was making his real money. Allie had given up the market stall, passing the business on to his sons. Gary was making a little scratch doing the old rag rolling; it was becoming all the rage in the homes of the middle class sector. It also gave him an excuse to case the homes of the upwardly mobile and pass on the info to his own little crew that Lee was now heading up. It was evident that this motley lot were dipping into their own stash because they were acting like desperate junkies. Why knock someone's house over for a VCR and a handful of knick-knacks when the money they were making from selling the little fella's was enough not to have to draw extra attention to themselves for petty thievery. They came across as small time villains playing at being big time gangsters, Billy saw them as an embarrassment to not only the family name but to those who had spent years giving them advice and their expertise so they could avoid the pitfalls that came with this way of life.

Harry used to tell us all, during our late night chats, that when he and his brothers were growing up, Tommy and Teddy had made a vow that they would be either boxers or villains. Being called up into the Army ended their boxing career and put them firmly on the road to infamy as Britain's best-known Gangsters. For all the good the National Service was meant to do for them, teach them discipline etc...all it did was serve as the fuel that drove them on the path they took. When they came out of the Army, they did various odd jobs including protection and bouncing for some minor villains but they did not want to work for anyone but themselves. The turning point for them came when they bought a seedy snooker club in Bethnal Green. It was the type of club that always had trouble, fights all the time, getting smashed up on a regular basis, no self respecting person would ever set foot inside it. They approached the leaseholder who said "Okay, if you think you can sort the club out then the lease is yours". They called it the Majestic. In no time at all the club was turned around, the fighting had stopped and the clientele had improved. Later on it was discovered that they were responsible for all the trouble in the first place, Harry arranged wave after wave of louts and thugs to bust the place up and the twins just had to step foot in the place for the trouble to stop.

The Twins loved to drink, they could drink day and night and not get over drunk, a skill they inherited from their father, who was always in the pub. Their favourite tipple was a gin and tonic. So it was a natural sort of progression for them to acquire clubs where they could continue to drink at their leisure. Tommy and Teddy started using a club called The Vienna Rooms, off Edgware Road. The club was frequented by two of the Twins heroes, Jack Sprat, who was nicknamed so because of his slender build while it was evident that his other half certainly didn't eat any lean and Willy two-tone, who between them ran the whole of London. The twins would sit for hours with them listening and learning everything they could.

They worked for Jack Sprat for a while at the racecourses providing protection for the Bookmakers. Jack Sprat would provide bucket boys to wash the chalk off the boards and the minders would make sure that the Bookmakers did not get any trouble from irate punters or rival gangs. They had learnt well from their brief time with Jack and Willy but it was time to move on. Now the Twins' reputation went before them, they were into every scam you could think of. They hi-jacked Lorries laden with everything from furniture to cigarettes, they dealt in National Service exemption certificates, and Dockers Tickets which allowed men to work on the docks for short hours and massive amounts of pay and anything else they could get their hands on.

While Tommy was doing a three-year stretch for GBH, Teddy opened up another club in Bow and called it The Double T. Harry, who was usually kept in the background away from any wheeling and dealing, put some money up for the club, for which he was given a percentage of the takings. The club flourished. Teddy acquired many clubs that had previously been mysteriously firebombed. The Crow Empire was gradually being built. The twins, along with silent partners Harry and Freddie owned or had a stake in more than thirty clubs and bars.

The business seemed to operate a lot more smoothly without Tommy's interference. The problem with the Crow 'Firm' as it came to be known was that there was not one Boss. Tommy and Teddy argued constantly about what they were doing and how they handled the proceeds. Tommy, being the dominant twin usually won the arguments, sometimes at a cost to the business. Although Tommy could be vicious and unforgiving, there was another side to his nature. He would always help people down on their luck. He was regarded as a soft touch for those in real need, especially people coming out of prison. He would open up the till in one of their clubs and take out what ever was in there and give it to some deserving cause. Although very commendable, it was not good for business. This caused constant rows with his brothers, but Tommy did not care, they needed it and he gave it to them. The thing about Tommy was that once he had his mind made up to do something, he would do it, good or bad, regardless of the consequences. It was probably this part of his personality, coupled with his oncoming schizophrenic tendencies that made the Crows as feared as they were. Therefore, when Tommy was imprisoned it was inevitable that it would reflect favourably in their business dealings.

Tommy was diagnosed as a paranoid schizophrenic whilst serving time in Winchester Prison. His health slowly deteriorated. Teddy put this down to the different drugs they were giving Tommy and decided to get him out of prison. As luck would have it they moved Tommy to Long Grove mental hospital giving them a better chance of freeing him. The idea was to get Tommy out and keep him out long enough for an independent psychiatrist to assess his state of mind. If the doctor found him to be sane then the authorities would have to re-assess him when he was captured or returned to the hospital.

Teddy visited Tommy and simply changed places with him. Tommy walked out of the hospital and away. Teddy sat reading a paper and then asked where 'Teddy' had gone because he was away so long. The hospital orderlies assumed that the man sitting in the chair was Tommy. When thy realised what had happened it was too late. Tommy had long gone. In addition, they had to let Teddy out as well. Tommy remained on the run for five months.

However, it was not too long before they realised what a dreadful mistake they had made. Tommy really was ill. There were times when he did not recognise members of his own family. He had to be returned to hospital for his own sake. One night when he secretly returned to the family home, the police raided the house and he was arrested. He was re-assessed and returned to prison where he remained until his release in spring nineteen fifty nine.

When he came out he had terrible mood swings and it was clear that he was still ill. He was uncontrollable, he would rant and rave, pace up and down, and thought that everyone was plotting against him. The family took him to hospital to get him the help he so desperately needed. Part of this help meant that he would have to take drugs and injections for the rest of his life. He not only had a mental illness but the treatment that was to keep him calm and subdued affected him physically. He put on weight, his speech was slow and he walked laboriously. He was not the man he used to be. Although there were times when Tommy looked and felt like his old self. What had gone on before was just a taste of things to come.

Unfortunately, for Tommy when he needed his twin brother the most, Teddy was arrested for demanding money with menaces. He was sentenced to eighteen months in prison even though the victim retracted the allegation under oath. He was sent to Wandsworth prison where he first met Jack Browne and 'The Mad Slasher' Mitchell Cleaver, two men who were to play a major part in the twin's final downfall.

At the start of the sixties all the brothers were together again, Tommy was getting back to his old self, the Firm had truly established itself, business was good and they were making inroads into the West End gambling and club scene. Their first toehold in this area was an upmarket gaming club called Felicia's. It was fronted by Lord Hoar, the sixth Earl of Hoar. He was paid by the Crows to welcome the customers as they entered the club. They also invested a lot of their own money in a seaside development in a place called Enugu in Nigeria. It was set up by their business manager Jackie Locke. In the end, the project collapsed and the money disappeared. Later, Jackie was to die under very strange circumstances and another person who was involved disappeared never to be seen again.

The Crows were mixing with some very influential

people and, it was thought by some, that they were getting too powerful. They were being watched constantly by the Authorities but they didn't care, they welcomed the attention.

One of the reasons for their eventual downfall was their love of publicity. Tommy in particular loved being photographed with celebrities and sports stars, he wanted to display himself as the stereotypical American Gangster as portrayed by James Cagney and George Raft in the American films of the fifties and sixties. The difference between The Crows and their real life, American counterparts, the Mafia, is that they kept a low profile and let others do their dirty work. Tommy and Teddy were now forging links with the Mafia. They went to America for a week and met their top men. Although they made some very useful connections on their trip, they did not do as much business as they thought they would. They did however, provide protection, on behalf of the Mafia, for many American celebrities visiting or performing in England. Moreover, protected their gambling interests in the West End as well as entertaining them when they came to London.

The Crows shared control of London with the Richards gang from South London. The main body of the Richards gang consisted of brothers, Frankie and Shaw, 'Crazy' Charlie Smith and Vinnie Cornwall. They were already entrenched in the West End, supplying most of the clubs with one-armed bandits, and the Crows wanted in.

In March nineteen sixty-six a gun battle took place in a club called Mr Smiths in Rushey Green. It has been said that The Richards gang went there with the intentions of wiping out the Crows. There was only one member of the Crow gang present. He was shot dead. Charlie Smith was shot in the hip and Shaw Richards was shot in the backside. They were taken to hospital and on their release; they were charged with affray and sentenced to five years in prison. Charlie Smith was originally charged with the murder of Derek Hart but was found not guilty.

It has also been said that it was Vinnie Cornwall who actually killed Derek Hart but managed to escape before the police arrived, and that was one of the reasons why, in April nineteen sixty-six, Tommy Crow walked into the Blind Beggar public house and shot him in the head.

Some time after the killing of Vinnie Cornwall, the Twins were arrested and put on an identification parade. The witnesses failed to pick them out and they were duly released. At the end of sixty-six, the Twins hatched a plot to free Mitchell Cleaver, 'The Mad Slasher'. They had both met him on previous occasions in Wandsworth prison. He was serving a short term in prison when he escaped and broke into an old couple's house and held them hostage with a meat cleaver that he found. He was recaptured and sentenced to life without any release date.

It was decided that they would break him out of prison and keep him out long enough for the newspapers to run the story with the promise of his case being investigated. He would then give himself up and return to prison. He was sprung from Dartmoor by two of the Crow Firm. Mitchell Cleaver was subsequently killed in a shoot out with the police. Teddy cried when he heard the news of Mitchell's death, he was heartbroken. He went into a deep depression for months. He was drinking all the time and was crazy with grief. It was through this very traumatic period in his life that he killed Jack Browne. Tommy was always boasting about what he did to Cornwall and it has been suggested by some, that he goaded Teddy into killing Browne. Teddy later denied that his brother influenced him in any way but this was totally out of character for Teddy, who under normal circumstances was always in control of his actions.

Jack Browne worked for the Twins doing small little jobs, nothing for him to lay claim as being part of the Firm. He was a dangerous man. He was not afraid of the Twins in any way and was often heard slagging them off. He was a drunkard, took drugs and beat up women. It was rumoured that he was paid to kill Jackie Locke, the Twins one time business manager, and that he took the money and never fulfilled the contract. He had been warned by Reg on numerous occasions about his attitude but to no avail. Jack was lured to a party in Stoke Newington, where he was stabbed to death by Teddy.

This last action proved to be the end of the Crows and the Firm. While the authorities let them get on with it in the past, they had now gone 'beyond the accepted parameters' and had to be stopped at all costs. In May nineteen sixty-eight the Crow Twins were arrested. Two of the many charges they had to answer to were the murders of Vinnie Cornwall and Jack Browne. Their arrest and continued confinement before their trial loosened the grip of fear they had on the community and it was not too long until the East End code of silence had been broken. Within the next few months, with the help of some of the most respected members of the Firm, the police had made more arrests.

In January nineteen sixty-nine the trial started and lasted about six weeks. The ten men who stood in the Dock were all convicted of various charges. Tommy and Teddy were sentenced to Life imprisonment with a recommendation to serve at least thirty years.

Harry and Freddie always managed to escape any involvement with the law but continued to run the more profitable nightclubs whilst selling off the others to financially support the twins while inside. They also used the money to fund other operations that surviving gang members pulled off while funding the new up and coming gangsters in their ventures. They always stayed out of the limelight but still enjoyed all the trappings that came with that life. They both had the same survival instinct to stay one-step ahead of the rest. All of them were born fighters, all had their tales to tell but the similarities between Harry, Tommy and Teddy's and Billy's and Mikey's life were too numerous to mention. Harry always laughed at this with Freddie but they were always serious when pointing out the mistakes made by others, "Don't do as I do but do as I say", a lesson that Gary never seemed to take on board.

The caring parents of the Michaels brothers always had conflicting views about their futures although both agreed it should be in something legal. Their Mum was always going on about getting an education, as if they were all going to become Doctors or something. Their Dad, however, always believed a man should learn a trade. Well the elder brothers never really had time for school, maybe getting a real job and learning a trade was the answer.

There was a vacancy, which Billy's friend Mark let him know about in the Engineering plant based in Fulbourne Road, Walthamstow. Mark worked there himself and figured it would be a laugh having Billy there, working along side him. Billy phoned up and got an interview for the Thursday afternoon of that week. It was the first bit of work he was going for where he did not just walk in and start straight away. This interviewing malarkey was all new to him…shit; they can only say no to him, couldn't they?

Billy turned up at Siddelely Hawks for the interview, in his Sunday best and was taking every effort to watch his P's and Q's. The position itself was for a coil-winders mate, or dog's body, for the ill-informed. They were looking for someone to fetch tools and materials, make tea and do general labouring. Billy personally thought that he was above all that, being the snob that he was but then they said that it would be an easier way to get on an Engineers training program than going to college and coming in on an apprenticeship. He told them he was more than interested in that side of things and to learn a trade and liked to be considered for the role. To which they replied, "We'll let you know."

Billy walked out thinking that was the end of that one; he was obviously not dog's body material. He had not even made it out of the yard before the charge hand came running up behind him.

121

"Can you start Monday?" and that's where it all started. It turned out that Billy was dog's body material after all.

"Sure" He said, and away he went thinking how proud his folks will be now that he was part of the working masses and not some rebel lawbreaker anymore.

This normal, everyday job was to be Billy's chance to go straight. Live a normal life, settle down and live the hum drum existence that a majority of the people spent their whole lives wanting out of. He never saw or thought anything was wrong with the criminal way the people he knew lived their lives, in fact he thought that ducking and diving was on par with that of a top trader in the Stock Exchange. The same drive and lack of weakness was paramount to becoming the best and surviving the stress. That was normal to him, breaking the law, getting into fights, killing; maiming, watching riots evolve before his very eyes. That was all he ever seemed to know, it was this new way of life that he was attempting. Experiencing all that was wrong and dangerous. Nevertheless, Billy had always said, you cannot comment on something you have never experienced. This was his stab at living a mundane and ordinary life.

Billy had to start his new career on shift work and Monday, being his first day, was the start of the early shift. He had to be there for six am and clock in, my god what was all this clocking in business? He thought. He introduced himself to the team he would be running and fetching for; there were three of them, all Grade one Engineer's. There was Cookie, who saw the job as a means to an end; there was Elliot, the self-opinionated one, who had a lot of old fashioned views he would like to air, even though no one ever wanted to hear them. Elliot's brother Pete worked there as well but on the normal Monday to Friday, eight till five shift, he didn't voice out as much as Elliot, at least not to any others. He had a habit of arguing with himself, which got a little disturbing as time went on.

Finally there was little Mickey B, who was a dead ringer

for a young Bill Oddie. Billy's first impression of Mikey was he was one of his own, always had an angle working and always had a scheme. Billy liked Mickey B straight off the bat, he was good people.

"Get the kettle on, son. Feeling a little parched here." And that was it for the first hour of the morning, the full extent of the conversations that took place between the Engineers and their new dog's body. All Billy did was make tea for the three of them and do the grunts work. It was once the machines were turned on and the work actually began, that the real excitement of the role became apparent. Billy was stationed behind this huge, lathe like machine that acted as a device that sent you to sleep by its hypnotic yet slow rotation, hidden from the rest of the shop floor. Every now and then lending a hand to one of the Engineer's he had been assigned to. The priority of the shift was to make sure that the refreshments had been made for the start of their tea breaks, and that was it. By the end of the week Billy was thinking of jacking it in and trying something else but Mickey B, who Billy had confided in and told him what he was thinking, advised him to wait just one more week and then decide. Billy could not see what the difference would be but "Okay" he said; "I'll wait another week".

The following week saw the late shift of two 'til ten begin; with the exception of getting up later for work Billy didn't see the difference. He was still making the tea and still having to sit behind the machines. It all felt the same until five o'clock came round and the normal Monday to Friday working stiffs clocked out. Then from nowhere, the three amigos threw their machines into overdrive, producing half a day's work within an hour. Six o'clock saw the evening tea break and by seven, the whole factory was empty with the exception of those three and Billy.

That is when it all became clear why Mickey B had told Billy to hang on for one more week because from seven o'clock they all went off to do their own thing. Cookie worked on something he was making for his home, Elliot sat down and lit a fag and read the paper and Mickey B went and got his car, drove it in the loading bay and proceeded to work on the engine.

It was all about Ying and Yang. On one shift, you had to look busy and on the other shift, you were paid to do your own thing. Billy just needed to find his own thing and take advantage of the relaxed shift. That thing was working out; the whole place was loaded with scraps of copper and steel blocks. He set up a little work out area, lifting, squatting, pressing, it was great. Billy even made up a heavy bag and raised it up on the overhead crane to use as a punch bag. Although it was not Pumps gym, because of the innovations that went behind designing how to use the objects at hand and designing a method to use them to hit the desired muscle group, it added a new found interest for Billy and allowed him to be paid to train.

Billy's routine was setting in. On the early shifts he would finish at two and head straight for Pumps gym, work out and spar a little with the new up and coming boxers that were training there. Hit the showers, head home to change clothes and by eight o'clock be out socialising in either the "Chequers" pub or the "Rose and Crown".

On the late shift, he would be paid to work out, using the factory's changing facilities and finish at ten. Billy would then go straight to the Dog and Duck pub that had had a change in management and was just down the road to Siddelely Hawks. Simon was in there most nights, although that little group of regulars that were taught that very valuable lesson had never ventured back there. Billy knew that for a recovering drunk he seemed to spend a lot of time in pubs, but where else do you go? It was him that gave up drinking not his family and friends and it acted as a good test of character for him. Besides everyone else knew the score and they all looked out for him, making sure he only drank soft drinks. Billy was just lucky to have such a strong support group, there are many people out there that do not.

As Billy got to know more people at Siddelely Hawks, the more he was called upon to help out. Mostly it was just to stand behind someone's machine; making out they were working while really just having a time consuming chinwag. It is also, where he got to know Michael (another one). Michael was a black guy who was whiter than he was. He spoke with excellent grammar and pronunciation; he did not come across as your typical black guy at all. He was the kind of fella your granny would like; despite the fact, he was a darkie.

The thing both Michael and Billy had in common was their healthy interest in well toned, sweaty men in their underwear grappling each other in the United Union Wrestling Entertainment circuit (Or Double-U. W. E for short), it was formerly known as the United Union Wrestling Federation (Or Double-U. W. F) but due to Prince big nose and the wildlife fund he represented they had to incur a costly name change. It is good to see that the out dated concept of a monarchy is still putting itself to good use. Moreover, there is nothing gay about watching grown men fighting each other in their underwear at least that is what Billy told people. The two main icons at the time were Henry Hogan, who was a *hulk* of a man and the Ultimate Warmonger, who was a true *warrior* in the ring, and this is where their opinions and loyalty differed. Billy was a Hogan-maniac and Michael was a Warmonger fan. They would argue about who was the better wrestler and talk trash to each other from across the shop floor, all done in the best possible taste of course. It reached the point where they were described as the Siddelely Hawks Tag Team Champs. Yes, they were both aware that the outcomes were pre-determined and for part it was 'fake' but you have got to give it up to anyone who can lift a five hundred pound lump above their heads or walk the top rope while being almost seven foot tall and tipping the scales at three hundred odd pounds.

In Billy's eyes, Michael was always a good guy; he lived a somewhat sheltered life and never spent much money. Billy remembers he used to have unopened wage packets in his drawer because he hadn't spent his whole wage from five weeks previous. Billy thought he had to do something and get this guy out on the town.

Whenever Billy was on an early shift, he would get Michael to come out with him and his little gang, introducing Michael to the delights of the outside world. Michael used to drive a mark two Escort and he was always volunteered as the designated driver whenever they went to Southend for the night. On one near fatal night after yet another wild night at Tots, they were all coming back in the early hours of the morning, the car was full; they had four on the back seat, Billy in the passenger's seat and Michael driving. It was about five in the morning and fatigue was starting to set in, so naturally, they all started to fall asleep, leaving Michael to drive alone, big mistake.

Billy stirred from his alcohol-fuelled slumber and looked over at the back seat, all four were slumped over each other and out for the count. He gave a little laugh to himself and turned to Michael to see if he had seen them all cramped up and snoring. He had not; in fact, he had not seen anything because he was asleep at the wheel. Jesus Christ. "Wakey, Wakey Mickey". He awoke with a start and started to swerve, which in turn woke the snoring foursome up in the back. Panic set in as they went from side to side on the A one two seven. Someone from the cheap seats started shouting out that they were shitting their pants while another let out a fart that actually smelt as if he had shit himself. For a brief moment, it all felt too real, that this could be it, wiped out because of the need for sleep. It took a while for Michael to get control of the car again but as soon as he did, he pulled on to the hard shoulder. The entire gang all jumped out of the car "Fuck me that was close". To this day Billy does not know what troubles him more, the fact they could have been killed that night or the fact Michael drove better asleep than he did when he was awake. Needless to say, they all made a pact to stay awake on the journey's home from then on, especially if Michael was driving.

Another time that stuck out during those days of clubbing in Southend, and stayed in Billy's mind as an all time favourite memory, was when a young guy by the name of Carl had just started working at Siddelely Hawks. The guys had nicknamed Carl "Virg", short for virgin. He was a spotty fella, a bit on the plump side and he had flicking movement going on whenever he walked. For some reason, he would flick out his left leg, as though he was emphasising the fact he was placing his foot on the ground. It was hard to explain and needless to say, meant that this guy had nothing going on for him. What made it worse, there was nothing wrong with his leg the affliction was all psychological. His Mum walked with a defect and he had just imitated her while learning to walk as a young child. Some role model, she did not even have him try to rectify it.

It was no secret that Billy and some of the others teased Carl at work but overall they liked him and not out of sympathy either, he was a genuine person that had been dealt a crappy hand. So when he was about to turn eighteen they decided to take him up to Southend for the night out and celebrate in style. Well with as much style that Southend could offer.

Carl's parents however decided he should spend this special birthday, locked in their flat while they went away for the weekend. They actually locked him in, now it may be just me but I do not care who you are, that is cruelty and Billy thought along the very same lines. It made him wonder just how caring Carl's folks had been to him when he was younger. Their flat was on the ground floor so getting him in and out of the flat wasn't going to be a real problem but talking him in to leaving was. After about forty minutes, he climbed out of the window and into the waiting car.

There were a few of the Siddelely Hawks gang going, so Dean, who was working with them at the time as a coil winders mate, just like Billy, brought his van along to ferry the others in. They drove down to the sea front and parked up. The plan was to hit the arcades for a while, hit a few pubs as they went along and then go clubbing. The evening was working out great until they all tried to get into a club. Any doorman will tell you that an all male group is going to be turned away ninety percent of the time, especially if you're a little tanked and not from the area. Asking if you are local is a question that most sea side doormen asked you if you looked like you may be trouble.

They walked through the town until they came across this little place called 'Waves'; the club was desperate for punters so this all male group were shown straight in. It was one of those places that you had to drink hard to get double vision, so you thought the place was full. The half cut gang approached the bar and decided to invent a cocktail just for Virg. It consisted of every optic on display with a dash of blackcurrant cordial and a slice of lemon. It filled up a pint glass and could have stripped paint off of a barge but Virg drank it and that was all she wrote. By the time, he had drunk the last drop; he had gone from timid Carl the virgin to super cool ladies man. He thought every girl in the joint wanted him and so took it upon himself to hit the dance floor and cruise for chicks. Thankfully, Billy was stone cold sober and had his back, because he was pissing off a lot of boyfriends.

In the end, the call of nature came a knocking for Carl and off he went to the toilet. Billy watched him go in and luckily for Carl, Billy clocked him getting followed by a couple of the boyfriends he had pissed off earlier. So Billy went in after him. Virg had gone into a cubicle to take a piss and the two idiots were waiting for him outside.

"Why don't you two go back outside to your girlfriends before I make sure you never go outside again!" They turned around, a little taken back and looked Billy up and down, weighing up their chances; they must have thought it was in his favour because they left the WC without saying a word. Sensible lads unlike Virg, he stumbled out of the cubicle, all smiles. Billy had noticed something he obviously did not; his light grey trousers were only light grey on one side. The fronts of his trousers were dark grey, caused by the fact they were wet from where he had pissed himself. "I wanna dance"; Billy was laughing too much to stop him.

He went back out doing his Travolta impression thinking he was as cool as the Fonz or something. Billy went over to the others and pointed out their disco diva and his pissed on trousers; they just could not control themselves. If Billy had laughed any harder, he thought he might have pissed himself as well.

Once the laughter had died down and the pity factor kicked in, they thought it was time to leave the club before anything nasty took place. So they dragged Virg off the dance floor and walked out. As soon as the fresh air hit Virg full on, he was off. He just turned and ran through the shopping centre. The guys chased after him as he was running along counting aloud the pavement slabs that he was stepping on when he just collapsed on the ground, totally incoherent.

The rest of them just stood around him, laughing, when a group of girls that had come out of another club walked up to them to poke their noses in on what a group of blokes were laughing at.

"Is your mate alright?" One of the tipsy girls asked, the lads began to relay the nights events and the concerned female, after hearing Carl's tale of woe took pity on him and on the reason behind the nickname Virg.

"You mean he's never had sex? Poor bastard lets have a look at his cock." And with that she started to take off his urine covered trousers and yanked down his pants, exposing yet another reason why he didn't have much going for him. This prompted a few Kodak moments that were taken advantage of by one of the gang who brought a throw away camera with him to capture the moments. Dean walked off to bring his van round while the rest stood around chatting to the delightful Essex girls.

While they were all waiting around, the same girl who exposed Carls' knob was now tugging on it to arouse it, she was determined. Just like Virg, the life ebb had flowed from his penis and so that is how far his first sexual experience went and he was not even conscious. Dean finally came back and they lifted him into the back of the van, his trousers still round his ankles. The lads said their goodbyes to the girls and started driving back home, making sure to stay awake on the journey.

When the convoy reached back to Carl's prison or in other words his parents' flat, they had to break in and get him, in his drunken state, through the window. After yet another fit of laughter from the very mature group of men, they were all in, Virg who was starting to come around thought he needed a bath and so locked himself in the bathroom while the rest raided the kitchen cupboards and started cooking a fry up.

That is when Dean needed a piss and so banged on the bathroom door to get Virg to open up, but the door was unlocked and when Dean opened the door wider, he came back into front room where the rest were tucking into the aromatic fry up that had just been cooked.

"You had better come see this". They all jumped up and raced to the bathroom and looked on the bathroom floor; there were Virg's trousers and pants in a heap with a pile of shit in them. To make matters worst, it looked like he had got it on his hands because there were smear marks all over the sink, the walls, the bath taps and a separate little pile in the bath. It was time to leave.

The next Monday at work, the curious mob enquired how he got on with his parents. He told them that he woke up in time to clean up the mess and got everything in order but was busted when they went to have something to eat because the fridge was bare. Nevertheless, he lived to drink another day and it was a night to remember, even if he did not.

While Billy was working on his nine to five way of life, Mikey was getting in deeper with a South London firm that was headed by Tony Eves of the infamous Eves family. The Eves family originated out of Islington, north London but due to watchful eyes was finding a niche in the south London territory. They were heavy into the ecstasy thing and their operation highlighted just how small time Gary and his mini crew were. In fact, it was the Eves who supplied Gary with their wares and they were happy to do so because if Gary did anything silly, like try to avoid payment or grassed them up if caught by plod, it was Mikey who would pay the price. This put Mikey on tender hooks because his faith in Gary wasn't as strong as it would have been if it was Billy doing the business but luckily for the time being all was running smoothly so he didn't have to be too concerned about walking down any dark alleys.

As big and dangerous as the Eves family were, they like any other high ranking firm, didn't make a move unless somewhere along the way it was confirmed that the top man of the manor was getting a slice. The top man in question was Dave Love, who had developed a strangle hold on all major criminal activity in south London. Both Billy and Mikey had recognised the future potential of this individual many years previous but Dave had arrived in glorious style and added a dash of pizzazz to being a real gangster. That was not to say that Tony Eves and his brothers were lightweights, far from it, the horror stories that surrounded their claims to fame could make your short and curlies go straight.

Any member of the Eves crew would be a prize-winner on the rosette board of the local constabulary bulletin wall. At this level of the food chain there was no room for error, the fuzz were already salivating at the thought of seizing a high-level executive of one of the biggest operating organisations in the United Kingdom. You could bet your life that at some point there was a camera taking pictures, CCTV following their every move and at least one tape-recorded conversation doing the rounds in Scotland Yard.

Ecstasy, although becoming a major player on the recreational drugs top ten list, the actual manufacturing side of them was still being handled abroad, in a cosy little hanger near the coastline of Bremen, Germany. This was a perfect location because it would allow a little, fly under the radar, tug boat to sail towards England, bypass Dover and docked practically on Margate beach. This was where Mikey and his team would drive down to and make the rendezvous with the over friendly kraut sailor that was captaining the drug run.

There was a lot of trust needed in these kinds of ventures due to the distance between the parties involved; this trust is not built up through written correspondence, gaining the friendship of a pen pal. No this is built with severe demonstrations of commitment, acts of strength like the one Tony and his brothers showed when first making an impression with their European connections. On their first encounter, the Eves went to the beach a little heavy handed, not knowing what to expect and one of the hired muscle thought it was a good idea to not pay for the imported merchandise and have it away on his toes. The sea captain was now put on edge by the commotion that was transpiring in front of his eyes, Andy, Tony's younger brother, started to get into a verbal with their own hired goon who was making an otherwise simple transaction into more than it should be. Sensing that this could easily become a one time deal if something was not sorted out quickly, proceeded to withdraw the 38 he kept tucked in the small of his back and happily put two in the head of the mouthy piece of muscle. Andy then asked the captain if he wanted to take the carcass back with him as a trophy to present to his employers. The captain must have been dipping into the merchandise because he seemed euphoric with the notion of having a stiff on the

132

deck for the journey back. Each to their own I suppose, but the message was sent and business carried on with no further disruption on either end.

These were the type of guys that Mikey was working directly for so he was under no illusions about what would happen if he fucked up. Needless to say Mikey become a real stickler for details and was always weary if things didn't run to schedule. He had a lot riding on his shoulders and in return was given the burden of having a status that put him firmly on the plods must have Christmas gift list.

Having a nine to five life was not sounding so bad.

Chapter Eleven

Billy was told he was being too loud at work by his supervisor and the only way to quieten him down was to give him some responsibility. Therefore, they made him a trainee Engineer. The idea behind the promotion was to keep him from walking around and wasting time talking to the other Engineers and dogs bodies but all that happened was the other Engineers and dogs bodies used to walk and talk to him. Still, it got Billy on the fast track to learning a trade.

With Billy promoted a space had opened up for a new coil winders mate on his old shift; this opened the door for a fresh faced, red haired kid called Alan to join the fray. He thought he was the ginger version of George Michael and if you thought about it after meeting him, he could well have grown up to have been, in every sense possible. Chocolate bar anyone?

Although Billy did not know Alan, Billy had in fact grown up with his stepbrother John (who was also a George Michael wannabe but from the "Faith" period only) and his cousin Paul, who was part of another large family, the Jeffrey's. They too used to live on the estate and they all went to the same schools, all the way up until Senior's. They would bump into each other over the years but never really stayed in touch. All this came to light after talking to Alan for about a week and so knowing he came from good stock Billy insisted that everyone started to include him on their nights out.

Being the enigmatic person he was, Billy was starting to get a bit of a following at work, he was taking his usual position in life and was setting himself up as the Don and Mickey B, who was the department's union shop steward, loved it. The country was going through a real bad recession and people's jobs were on the line, which I'm sure anyone over the age of thirty will remember. So whenever there was talk of downsizing or revoking certain privileges, the union would rally the troops to air the situation and would want to take action by going out on strike. All those that did not want to strike got the evil eye (and more) from Billy and his new, eager to please, sidekicks. This bunch of tearaways would do anything from pouring sugar in petrol tanks, to slashing tyres to physically getting in your face and make it clear that in no uncertain terms that failing to go on strike was going to be very unhealthy on them and their nearest and dearest. It was a real tense time but at least no one lost their job or their life, in fact in Billy's department, they got to hire extra staff.

Siddelely Hawks had its own social club, which used to serve cheap drinks and on a Sunday, it used to lay out a finger food buffet. It was a real working mans club, where only real men were allowed, twelve pints or more had to be drunk and the rooms had to be filled with smoke. The décor was dated, the pool table was always crowded and the club grub wasn't quite up to standards, in fact it was a real dive and it soon became a meeting place for Billy's ever-expanding numbers before going on to party the night away.

It had been less than a year, that Billy was a slurring, guilt filled drunk. He still felt the urge to drink but never gave in although it was difficult because of everywhere his social life took him; and now Billy's twentieth birthday was upon him and people wanted to celebrate it with him, wild style.

The party crew started at the social club, where Billy had put money behind the bar. The plan was for everyone to take advantage of the free booze and get them to pass that "Go on have a drink, it's your birthday" phase. The plan worked pretty well and when the time had come to move on to the next place, it helped to separate the sheaf from the wheat. By the time, the party-party people reached Billy's flat, it was a good crowd that was left and it ended the evening off well. 'It was better than the year before' thought Billy 'but not as good as the year before that'. For his twenty-first, Billy vowed that he was going to do something different and special and he had a year to figure out what.

All Billy did all day at work was eat, which coupled with the weight training he was doing, he soon found himself to be a big, old pup in the making. The need to meet a certain weight class was gone and so Billy was now pushing weights around for size and not just for strength, before he knew it he was up to seventeen stone and feeling a little monstrous. On a six foot two frame, Billy was looking even more appealing to the ladies. It was a lush feeling...

Billy was always well known by the regulars at Pumps gym but with the newfound mass that was being packed on, it was not long before he was acting like a magnet and drawing a certain type of individual to himself, the nocturnal creature, Thugerous Bouncerous. Billy was always being approached and asked if he fancied doing a little door work. He in turn used to relay his Ritzy adventures with Simon, which acted as a good reference. Most of the enquiring face punchers knew Simon and so they would call him up to see if he would vouch for Billy. Billy used to decline the offers because he did not see the need to take up any extra work but it was nice to know that the offers were still out there.

Along with his newfound size, Billy found his arrogance was growing, women were playthings, and he could not be touched in the ring. Billy was standing alone, not a brother in sight. Stuart was still all loved up, Mikey had disappeared off the face of the planet and Gary was staying out on-site with his P 'n' Din' buddies or so he thought. Billy was shagging everything that stood still long enough to be caught and was never short of company. Alan, the new boy, had his eye on this one filly, Tracey, that Billy used go with every other week or so. Alan asked if Billy could introduce him to her and follow it up by putting in a good word for him. Who was Billy to refuse to help a friend? she meant nothing to him, and she was just a name on a list for booty calls. Billy told Tracey that Alan was a little smitten with her and that he was a nice person, but then, what woman actually wants a nice person?

Alan and Tracey got on like a house on fire and it was not long before they were calling each other boyfriend and girlfriend. The problem with Alan, and it could still be true today, was that he was one of those guys who fell in love too easily. You know the type, talks about getting engaged once he's stolen his first kiss, talks about marriage after his first blow job and so on. Wishy-washy is one way to describe him, total Muppet is another.

Tracey had always been part of Billy's new crowd and even though she now had a steady boyfriend, still hung out with them. This suited Alan because it allowed him to still come out with the gang as well. One night in particular, they were out on a social at the Dog and Duck, when at the end of the evening, Tracey offered Billy and a few select peeps, nightcaps at her Mum's flat, where she was staying for a while, awaiting to move into her new place. There were four of them, Tracey, Alan, Karen, and the main man himself, Billy.

Karen was one of those girls that would get drunk and flounce around the pub, waiting for her turn to slide down on Billy's pole. Billy would have to give her her dues; she was clued up enough only to try it on, if for some reason he had not scored with anyone else that night. This was one of those nights.

They eventually reached Tracey's Mum's, after stopping every ten feet to get a bit of tongue action and were given quite a warm welcome by her Mum, Lisa. She was a P.E. teacher at a primary school, a very firm, very blonde, well-rounded woman who was extremely athletic. She showed the late night visitors into her living room and set about dishing out the drinks. "What's your poison?" She asked Billy, as a silence fell on the room.

"Tea would be fine." He replied with a smile on his face and a chirpy tone in his voice hoping to quickly ease the building tension.

"Is this one having a laugh?" she came back with, but Tracey pointed out that Billy was the one she used to talk about. Billy thought it was reassuring that some girl he knobbed gave a blow by blow account to her Mum but in this case, it paid off.

"Oh" She said, "This is that Billy."

An hour or so into the night and Karen had dropped off asleep on the living room floor. Billy could not say if the booze had caught up with her or if she just wanted to escape the snide remarks that Tracey's Mum had been shooting her the whole time. Either way she was out for the count and he was not going to get any. Therefore, Billy decided to catch some zee's himself and asked where he could crash, "Kip anywhere stud" came the answer from Lisa's luscious lips. So he went up the stairs, found the Mum's room, got naked and jumped under the covers.

Ten minutes had passed and Billy was just getting comfortable, the blankets were getting warm and the pillows had been shaped just right when the Lisa walked in.

"And who's that sleeping in my bed?" You could tell she was a teacher just by the authority in her voice. "If you're gonna be staying in my bed you'll have to move over and put up with the light being on, I was planning to read." 'Read my arse' Billy was thinking, a deaf, blind mute could have read the signs she had been dishing out. He rolled over and threw back the duvet to let her in while at the same time exposing enough so she knew he was stark bollock naked. She stripped down to her matching black set; and got into the bed. She had these little round reading glasses that just made her look prim and proper, a real school teacher. Just the thought of that was getting Billy aroused; she had her nose in her book, but was obviously trying to tease him. Billy turned to lie on his side so she could feel the state of play against her thigh and she smiled.

"Well some one's being a naughty boy" And proceeded to put down her book and take off her glasses.

"No, leave them on." Billy said, "Leave them on."

Now all Billy could say about that night is that, the good thing about teachers is that if you do something wrong, they make you do it again and again until you get it right. Smiley faces all round.

The next morning was a bit slap dash; Lisa's boyfriend was coming round to take her and her younger daughters out for a picnic. Alan had to race out of Tracey's room before her sisters came in and Billy had to make himself scarce, so not to offend Karen by rubbing the situation in her face. It was all a bit of a farce really, like a bad sketch from the Benny Hill show or something but fun never the less.

To put the cherry on the cake of that family affair, not only had Billy now done the Mum and Daughter but also the Nan, wait for it, she used to be his primary school teacher back in Chingford Hall. Talk about keeping it in the family.

A week later, Tracey moved into her new flat above a Wimpy bar in Enfield. She held a little flat warming party and all concerned thought she seemed to have settled in all right, but they were wrong. To get to her front door you had to go down an alley, which of a night time was pitch black, no street lamps at all, and it was round the back of the parade of shops. Some strange looking guy had been stopping her and telling her that he was going hurt her. She phoned the police but after three nights of patrolling the area and finding nothing, they lost interest but this guy was still showing up. Alan was still working shifts and was unable to get round there and sort the matter out himself and was getting desperate to have it resolved. So he asked Billy for help.

Alan paid for Billy's cab fares and takeaway bills, to go round to Tracey's and make sure this idiot didn't hurt her, It was Billy's pleasure, in every sense of the word. The first night Billy was in there, he played it by the book, Tracey and Billy sat up late talking, and every time there was a noise outside, he would go and check it out. When she went to bed, he stayed awake just in case this guy attempted to break in.

On the second night, Billy figured it would be wise to install one of those security lights that are on a motion sensor; at least it would let them know if someone was outside. Billy was drilling and hammering out on the doorstep, getting all sweaty and was catching Lisa's eye. Therefore, when he had finished the manual work he asked Tracey if it was all right to make use of her bath, to which she replied, "It was the least she could do". She even ran it for him, bubbles and everything; she even laid on a few aromatic candles. This was a tough assignment but someone had to do it.

Billy was just about to step into the bubbly water when Tracey knocked on the door "Is it all right to come in?" She had seen him naked before so he thought, why not? He had not got into the tub when she entered the room; he just stood there with all on show, she tried to look away but dirty thoughts were already filling her head. Billy stepped into the tub and sat down, letting the warm water lap over his body.

"I think about you some times." Tracey confessed.
"Well you shouldn't, you're practically a married woman now, and what would Alan say?" She looked him dead in the eye and said, "Well Alan isn't here to say anything, is he." And with that reached into the bath water and started to play with Billy's built in rubber ducky. See women do not like nice guys. From that night onwards, Alan was literally paying Billy to go round and fuck his missus, which he did royally. As for the stalker, he never came back; it was though he only existed in Tracey's mind but women would not pull strokes like that to get attention, would they?

The cheating carried on for a while; they were even doing it when Alan was in the same flat. He used to go out to get some food or take a nap and they jumped at the chance to go at it. There was even one time, during a party, that they were caught doing it in her cupboard, which wasn't very wide and called upon all their contortionist abilities to seal the deal. Billy's old weed supplier pal, Eric, who Billy kept in touch with, had opened the door when he thought he heard knocking coming from the cupboard, all this while Alan was downstairs dancing.

That was the outlook Billy had when it came to women, sex and friendship. If you are a woman, he is going to fuck you. If you are a woman seeing a friend of his and he likes you, he is going to be fucking you, if you are a friend stupid enough to let him get that close to your bird, he is going to fuck you over. It was that simple, sex was sex and notch's on the bedpost is what it is all about. Or so he thought, Billy had never really had a real relationship, he had never really cared about someone, never had someone special in his life and perhaps that was the reason why, he was the way he was. The closest he felt anything special to a female was to his daughter Adele, who he had not seen for nearly four years but thought about all the time. She would be five by now and starting school...he wondered what she looked like but knew that dredging up the past was not the smartest move.

Now, not all the women in Billy's life have been degraded and abused by him. In fact there were three in particular that he worked with over the years at Siddelely Hawks. They were all attractive women in their own right, even if they did want to be Engineers, and he did not sleep with any of them. The first he met when he had just started there, was Nicky, who when he was first introduced to her, was standing in at five foot seven and weighing in at nineteen stone. She was married to this abusive, pleb of a man (using the term loosely) who would not know how to compliment a lady if his life depended on it. She was very standoffish at first, probably because Billy came across as one of those spiteful people that teased her at school because of her size.

She used to speak to Michael a lot and so eventually, she was forced to have Billy join in on the conversations, because Michael was one of Billy's best buddies and there wasn't that many times when these two weren't propping up a wall chin wagging. After a while, she came to realise that Billy was a unique guy and fun to talk to, plus the fact he was a bit of a stud muffin helped.

Nicky then started to initiate conversations with Billy on the rare occasions he was not chatting to Michael. They would talk about training and working out, and she would ask for tips on dieting and the best way to lose weight. Billy wrote her out a program to follow and she would follow it to the letter, with the results showing through every time he saw her. It was obvious that she was developing a crush on him, as she would tell Billy about her home life, her non-existent sex life and relay her sexual fantasies to him, always a dead giveaway. Billy played on this, as motivation for her, for every stone she lost, he promised to take her out for lunch or maybe steal a few kisses with her, little things that made her feel wanted and like a woman. Over a two-year period Nicky had lost seven stone and toned up all the loose bits, it was incredible. During that time, she also lost her deadbeat husband, by kicking him out and filing for a divorce. She had been reminded what it was to feel desirable and gained self-respect and independence, it was an absolute pleasure watching her evolve into a woman. Billy could see she had something special inside her and not just see the fat bird that everyone else saw. He never took things beyond the odd kissing session with her and he always felt glad he left it like that. She had worked so hard to reach her goals that even he thought he would have been too much of a bastard if he spoilt it by using her like every other woman he knew. Billy can only hope that she has been rewarded in life for the sacrifices she made so early on.

Christmas was fast approaching, Michael and Billy decided to play Santa and buy everyone they worked with a token pressie. Billy then came in dressed as old Saint Nick himself and dished them all out. They had a good working atmosphere going at Siddelely Hawks, despite management's interference. It was almost Christmas and no one was going to spoil his mojo because Billy had a bet to win.

Billy was still popping down to the Dog and Duck in the evenings taking up half the pub with his group. Same old faces, same old stories when out of nowhere these two women showed up, after a little reconnaissance mission the boys found out one was called Nikki and the other was her best friend at the time, Joanne. They had never seen them in there before, so they stood out straight away. Joanne seemed at ease with the environment but Nikki seemed a little intimidated. Billy just saw her as fresh meat.

Nikki caught the eye of all of the lads. She stood five foot two and had wild, bleached blonde hair (all the rage in the late eighties), big brown eyes and a set of lips that most women today pay about three hundred pound for. Three hundred pound to have fat from a cow's arse injected into your lips just does not seem right to me. Nikki used a bright pink lipstick, which made them stand out even more.

She was an avid ice skater and her body was living proof, a tight little waist that made her thirty-four C bust appear bigger, and a backside that could put Kylie's to shame.

Now being the lady-killer Billy was he knew straight off the bat that Joanne was the easy mark. She had a dirty look about her, which took his fancy, long dark hair and a quick tongue, judging by her comebacks. It was as plain as the nose on your face that this one knew her way around the boudoir while Nikki was just stand offish, probably due to the fact she was shy. All the lads in his group tried it on with Nikki, but they were all shot down one by one. Moreover, it was one by one that they were all finally realising Billy had the right idea all along and instead took it in turns to do her friend Joanne.

It was leading up to Christmas when Michael put the bet on the table, cop hold of Nikki by New Years Eve or pay up.

The prize in question was a twelve-year-old bottle of single malt scotch given to Billy by Harry on his eighteenth birthday. What did Billy want in return? He wanted Michael's Signed photo of Henry Hogan that he had won in some phone-in competition off the radio. The bet was on.

Billy played the charm card on Nikki every time he saw her; he even got her a little crimbo present. She was slowly letting her guard down and coming round to his projected way of thinking. She told Billy all about how strict her father was. What it was like having a Greek Cypriot upbringing and how she was not allowed to see boys, especially English guys. When she was Nineteen, it had become evident that she had had enough of her fathers rules and decided to rebel by dating a black guy who lived in the same street as her and her parents. Up until that point, she had to be in by ten p.m. and was not allowed to go into pubs. However, these guidelines were revoked once she started dating this fella. In fact her parents raised her curfew 'til eleven during the week and if given prior permission she could stay out until two in the morning on weekends, just to get her away from this guy and his skin colour. Now to Billy, it sounded like our sweet little Nikki was a cold-hearted bitch and just used this guy to get something that helped her escape but you draw your own conclusions.

The year was running out and so was Billy's time limit, he was cutting it fine but on New Years Eve they all went to a party round Johns' (Alan's stepbrother) gaff. Billy and Nikki danced, the pair laughed and before the stroke of midnight, they were in Lip-lock City and it was at this point that they became boyfriend and girlfriend.

Billy was not too sure, why he thought Nikki was the one to settle down with, it could have been because everyone took a crack at her and was shot down and he was not. It could have been because she had only known him for a short while and did not know his rep with the ladies and so didn't judge him because of it. Billy personally thought he settled down with her because of the novelty factor of going steady, it was something he had not done with a woman before and he was all about new experiences. Whatever the initial reason was Billy really could not say, but there came a time when his feelings turned to love or at least he thought it was love and thought that was reason enough to stay with her.

Staying with her would go on to prove that she either became Billy's greatest salvation or his worst excuse for destruction.

Michael always saw it as he won the bet because Billy was meant to have humped her then dumped her and at the time, Billy could not be bothered to argue, so he paid up. Michael later told Billy how sweet that scotch tasted going down his throat.

It was nineteen eighty-nine and for the first time in Billy's twenty years on the planet, he was going steady with a woman he felt he loved. Although it was the being faithful side of things that were getting to him, the love birds used to make out but whenever it started getting heavy Nikki would cool things down and rush off home. Which considering she was only allowed out to eleven anyway meant, for Billy, that half the evening was wasted.

They would go ice-skating and to the pictures, once a month they went clubbing, all typical couple stuff, all the while still hanging around with the gang. It took three months before Billy got any how's your father from her but it took four months before she even admitted to her parents that he existed. It was hard to believe that she had recently turned twenty-two.

Being new to the dating game, Billy was finding it hard having a girlfriend who was on such a short leash. He needed a break from it all, so on his twenty-first, a lads holiday on an eighteen to thirties package deal to Lloret De Mar was booked. These holidays live up to their reputation.

Billy was now living a somewhat normal life and so this holiday was to be a normal boy's holiday. He wanted no trouble, just plenty of laughs. He made a promise to himself that he would not spoil it, and it was a promise that he intended to keep. There were three of them that went from their large group; there was Michael, Billy and a chappy by the name of Matt. Matt used to go out with one of the girls in their group, Annette, but had been dumped a few weeks previous and needed a few laughs to help get over his broken heart.

Vaughan, who was now a school leaver, was going to go with them, but Billy had got him a job at Siddelely Hawks and his first day was on the Monday, the day after they flew out. Therefore, he had to endure two weeks of standing behind machines and making tea before the joys of working along side his big brother would start for him.

Chapter Twelve

After a delayed flight and a long coach ride, the three amigos arrived at their hotel and were given the eighteen to thirties welcome. Hello, welcome, now cough up your dough by booking your places on all our excursions. The boys only booked half of them and were snarled at by the commission-fuelled reps. Fuck, it was my holiday, Billy thought and I will pay for what I want to do what some rep wants me to do.

Their room was on the ground level, right next to the bar, plus a pool table and a table football machine were right outside on the patio and the swimming pool was just down a couple of steps. It is true what they say; "It's all about location, location, location."

Their first excursion was that night; it was a Mexican themed event at some restaurant, where the food was greasy and the cheap vino was free. The object was to finish the plonk, raise the bottle in the air, and get a refill. It was the kind of holiday where drinking was expected and Billy did not want to feel left out. He was cutting the wine with lemonade and was sipping as opposed to knocking them back like the other animals that go on these kinds of holidays.

On Billy's section of the large table that they were sat at was two guys from Wrexham, Keith and Paul, they were staying at the same hotel as Billy and co and were up for the crack. Also representing their hotel was a group of Essex birds that all lived around the Southend area, Sonja, Jackie,

Katie and Michelle. Jackie had her eye on Keith right from the start, but the others were up for grabs.

This liquid meal carried on throughout the night while outside in the courtyard a live mariachi band was playing, the moving and a grooving was taking place amongst the somewhat alcohol fuelled crowd. They were all sitting around the table and Billy had to admit that after two spritzer's and an eighteen-month dry spell, he was starting to feel mighty tipsy. The others mind you were totally lagging, Billy had never seen Michael so out of it before, and it was quite a funny spectacle.

Now this Paul from Wrexham was a total ponce, he was trying to steal everything that was not nailed down and was helping himself to everybody's cigarettes, three at a time. Billy thought Paul was getting leeway because everyone was feeling generous but Paul soon got his comeuppance.

Billy's table was on the first floor of the restaurant and they had to walk down a flight of stairs that ran along the side of the building. As they all left to go outside and join in on the festivities, Paul went arse over tit, straight down the stairs and broke his arm in the process. The cheapskate did not even bother to get insurance and so told his parents back home that he had been mugged and needed money to replace what was stolen. He went on to spend the whole night in the hospital while Keith, his best mate, came back to finish the evening at the lads hotel room, along with the Essex girls.

The bar next door had closed and the place seemed deserted, the only yobs that were making noise and disturbing the rest of the complex, was Billy and the drunken revellers that were partying on in his room. With their patio door wide open, they were letting out the tunes from their cassette radio and playing table football very loudly. The odd "Shut up!" came crying out across the still Spanish air by other holiday makers but this was an eighteen to thirties holiday, if you were too square, you shouldn't be there. But put boys and girls together, throw in some alcohol and you just know that flirting and sexual comments are coming into play.

Sonja was the mouthy one out of the girls, she thought she was all that and a bag of chips but to her credit, she was a bit on the tasty side. Essex may breed them dumb but they also breed them fine. She was going on about how Billy thought he was a big man because of his thick, muscular size and bet him that he could not pick her up. So being up for the challenge, Billy took that bet, picked her up, fireman carry style, leapt down the steps and promptly dumped her into the freezing cold pool. "Splash" the still night air seemed to carry the sound all across Lloret De Mar, "You bastard!" she was screaming "Get here".

Billy had already run back to the room, joining the others in a chorus of laughter. Sonja stood outside on the patio and started to strip down to her underwear, ringing out each piece of clothing as she took it off. She slicked her long, blonde hair back and just stood there, looking good enough to eat. Her nipples were rock hard from the cold water, which just went on to complement her ample bosom. Now, supposedly as an involved man, Billy was not meant to be tempted by this, his new girlfriend, Nikki was meant to be enough for him. Yeah right. He was a soon to be a twenty-one year old, red-blooded male who was thousands of miles from home with a near naked, vision of a woman in front of him and he was meant to be faithful. Ain't going to happen.

"Throw her in again, let's see what else she's gonna take off." There is nothing like a drunken group of horny people on holiday, all inhibitions pushed aside and no regrets in the morning. Billy rushed out and scooped her up again, just to find what would happen if he dunked her again. 'Splash' in she went again, all the way under the water. After emerging from her watery blanket she stood there in the pool, shivering, she reached behind her back and undid her bra.

"You want something else to come off, you better come in and take it off yourself." 'Splash' Billy jumped in and started kissing her. They waded over to the side of the pool and Billy started to claim his prize, he reached down and slowly pulled her bottoms aside. As Billy was feeling her, she was no longer shivering; it turned into more of a tremble. No amount of cold water was going to stop the hard-on he was getting from reaching its full potential. It was not long before they were making the water splish-splash around them. That was his first twenty-four hours in Lloret De Mar.

The next morning Billy was actually feeling pangs of guilt, more for drinking than cheating on Nikki. He was awake by six in the morning but you were not allowed to swim in the pool before eight, but he needed to exercise and purge himself. Billy slowly got into the water, bearing the cold. He felt a little smile go across his face as he thought about the night before and started to swim laps.

Was he in the wrong? Billy was on holiday after all. Shouldn't he be enjoying himself? He just kept on swimming, faster, and faster, until his arms were too tired to do any more. His lungs felt like they were gonna explode and he was short of breath. Billy got out and walked back to his room that guilty feeling had not gone away.

Billy needed to do a good deed so he thought he would get brekkie ready for the two lazy bums still snoring their heads off. He set off to the nearest store for some supplies but just like the pool, nothing opened until eight. Billy thought he would kill some time by walking around and catching some of the sights. There were still people on the roads only just coming home from their night out. What it is too be young and abroad.

The shops finally opened and he grabbed some sausage, bacon, eggs, milk, bread, two crates of lager, and a selection of munchies and set off back to the hotel. By the time he got back, cooked up the food, and placed it on the breakfast table with a couple of cups of tea, it was just after nine in the morning and those two were still in slumber land. Billy tucked into his breakfast and figured worst case scenario, he would eat three brekkies, but that was when the knocking at the door started. Billy opened the door only to be greeted by Paul, with his arm in a cast and Keith. These two then took it upon themselves to barge in and start tucking into the cooked grub on the table, washing it all down with a couple of bottles of beer that they both happily helped themselves to out of their fridge. Now back home, if someone disrespected Billy's home and him like these two were doing, he would have smacked the shit out of them but he let it slide this time, based purely for the fact he was on holiday.

The boisterous laughter coming from these three members of the breakfast club was starting to make the other two stir from their pits but the icing on the cake came when the next knock on the door was the Essex girls from the night before. These four gave new meaning to the term 'Girls aloud', total ladettes. They went into the room Michael and Matt were sharing and pulled their blankets off them both, "Oi, Oi, savaloy" Came the cry. Michael may have acted white but he was still all black, if you catch my drift, especially when being compared too little Matty, who was trying hard to cover his shortcomings. You've never seen a girl's eyes get so big before, Michael, not having Billy's "in you face" attitude where the ladies were concerned, started to blush (although it was hard to tell) and grabbed the blankets back to cover himself up, "Spoilsport" They cried and left to bug the other males in the room. As normal Billy's place was the place to be and become hanging out central, in every sense of the word.

The plan was for these rowdy holidaymakers to just hang around the pool that day, acclimatising to the weather and recovering from the night before. Sonja kept giving signs for an afternoon romp but the sun felt too good as it beat down on Billy's lotion covered body and besides he was relaxing. It even reached the point where this nymph of a girl came over, knelt beside his sun-lounger and started to rub his groin area through his brightly covered sun shorts.

"Come up to my room and fuck me" She whispered in

his ear. There was definitely something sexy about a woman talking coarse and dirty in your ear to get one aroused.

"Well if you gonna put it that way" And off they went, Billy couldn't get off the lounger quick enough. It was a dirty job but someone had to do it.

Back at Sonja's room the action was deep in play; Billy was giving it large with the old three, two stroke whilst she was in the doggie position, when her roommate Katie walked in. She was standing in the doorway watching, licking her lips, and caressing her hips and waist.

"You gonna watch all day or are you joining in?" Billy cried out in-between breathes. Hey, if you don't ask you don't get.

"Maybe another time" Katie replied and gave a sly smile before walking back out. I will hold her to that Billy thought.

That night was an excursion free night, so they all got dressed up and hit the bars and clubs. Billy promised himself that he wouldn't drink that night and he was holding true to that commitment. In fact, Billy became the designated sensible person that night, and as the rest of the gang got louder; the more he found himself covering his face with his hands while shaking it in disbelief to their drunken antics. They must of hit at least nine bars, all of which were doing some deal or other on drinks, when the vote was to hit a club. They arrived at some club at about eleven thirty, there was a queue stretching around the block and it was putting them off wanting to go in and was starting to put a dampener on the evening. When Billy looked over at the door and caught the eye of the doorman, who returned the look and gave the universal flick of the head in acknowledgement. It says 'alright' and 'come over here' all in one gesture. Billy walked over to him to see what was happening.

"You a doorman?" He asked Billy, it was strange to hear a London accent from a Spanish bouncer.

"Yeah, back home". Billy answered with a hint of weariness in his voice.

"Call your mates; you can jump the queue if you wanna come in." Yet another benefit of working in the field of entertainment security.

"Nice of ya". Billy beckoned the rest over and once the velvet rope was held open, they walked straight in. It was like being in this worldwide secret club; that even had its own greeting. It was a sure fire way to impress the girlies.

Once inside, with the music cranked up, the first question screamed at Billy was "Did you know him?" This was accompanied with a pointing gesture towards the front door "No" he yelled back. The second question came from Katie, who got closer to his ear to ask, "Do you want me to suck on your knob?" "Yes" He whispered back and with that, he grabbed her arse and walked back outside with her. As Billy passed his newfound friend on the door he palmed the guy a few thousand peseta's to reward his generosity and said "thanks". The fumbling couple managed to make it a few hundred yards before Katie just fell to her knees and unzipped Billy's trousers, all the while the odd passer-by trying to get an eyeful as her head bobbed backwards and forwards. This is what club eighteen to thirties holidays are all about, come to think of it, this is what life should be about.

By the time they made it back to Billy's hotel room he was up for a second innings and so set about giving it to her, wild style. A few hours passed and the two of them were snuggled up in bed when the door suddenly flew open and in marched the rest of the troops, all pissed up and falling about. Sonja barged in and saw the dirty deed couple in bed together "I see" She said, and then just turned around and started to flirt with the other males in the group. Billy should have told her that jealousy was lost on him.

That was Billy's second day, if it carried on like this he could see himself going home a mere shadow of his former self. Viagra was just too far away from being invented.

Come the next morning their room was still filled with the boozed soaked, deep sleeping, loud snoring house crashers, Billy left them to it and sat outside on the patio waiting for the sun to rise, the warm breeze that blew through was just enough to take the chill away from the morning air. Billy was totally lost in thought when Sonja came out to join him; she brought out two cups of tea and handed one over. Billy checked it for spit bubbles.

"Did you two have fun last night?" She coyly asked. What kind of answer was she expecting?

"Can't complain" Trying to play it down so not to cause a scene, "you?"

"I really liked you…" She started. Billy thought 'here we go, I'm the bad guy now who everyone's gonna rag on just because I've shunned her affections'. "…But if it's just sex you're after then I can handle that, just make sure I get another turn." She smiled at him as he breathed a sigh of relief and they just waited for the sun together, drinking their tea and both getting lost in thought.

By the time the rest were up for anything other than moving at a snails pace and tuning in the English radio stations, the day had come and gone. The Lloret gang all decided to have a quiet one that night, maybe hold a cookout and share a few beers. It was that idea that sat with the rest best, everyone piled back down into the party room that night, Michael threw open the patio doors, cranked the cassette player up and started the party. Everyone from the bar next-door and the other eighteen to thirty holidaymakers in their hotel were hanging around and having fun. It was a real good atmosphere and a good way to get to meet more people, and by people, in the case of the lads, this meant girls. Need to share the wealth as they say. The night went on, the volume on the ghetto blaster slowly got turned down and people started to drift back up to their rooms. Billy saw Michael and Matt had both scored that night, so he decided to just chill out on the patio, sitting in the same chair he started the day in. Billy threw his blanket over him and just waited for the sun to rise. There are just times when you want that little bit of personal space and reflect about life, this for Billy was one of those times.

As the sun rose and the light danced across Billy's face, the realisation of going without sex for a day made him rampant, so rampant in fact he woke up, still in his chair, out on the patio sporting a raging hard-on. Billy was a fire sign and the sun was recharging his manly batteries. He felt relaxed, rejuvenated, and longed for a good session but being the only one up and about this early in the morning he opted for a few laps in the cold water instead.

Billy was hitting the front stroke, stretching his awakening muscles and getting that lethargic feeling out of his system, he looked up at the hotel only to see Sonja and Katie on their balcony, standing there in their bathrobes, looking back at him. Billy stopped mid stroke and started to tread water for a while, he could see them whispering to each other and giggling, what a boost to a man's ego he thought and went back to swimming his laps.

The sight of Billy, with beads of water slowly dripping down his semi-tanned torso while warm sunrays lit up the pool area, was obviously enough to have dirty thoughts run through the girl's minds. Katie shouted down that she needed his help in opening a bottle of wine because their corkscrew had broken off in the cork. Billy threw a towel around his waist, went into his room and got a corkscrew and then proceeded to run it up to Katie who for whatever reason was having vino for breakfast.

While they were standing around in her room Katie actually handed him a bottle of wine with cork that looked as though it had been chewed by mice and had the screw half of a corkscrew imbedded in it. Did he get the vibes wrong, was it just wishful thinking, did she only want him to get the cork out? Billy masterfully navigated the damaged cork out of the bottle and handed it back to her. Katie took it from him and promptly put it on the table

"Now that's done, wanna shag?" You have to admire

forward women. The pair started kissing, a little on the heavy side when all of a sudden; Billy felt Katie's hands on his crotch, which was an amazing feat considering he could also feel both her hands on his butt too. He turned his head to see Sonja smiling back at him, a very sly smile indeed. Every man's fantasy three in the bed and the little one said. It was wild.

If Billy had been judged solely on his performance on the first time round, he would have been ridiculed. Billy came so swiftly it would have made the guy who is faster than a speeding bullet feel crippled. It could have made the whole thing a complete waste of time if it wasn't for the fact that watching two attractive, fit women touch each other in the flesh, made Billy's one eyed snake go straight back up to look at his new hat. Lush.

It was a regular porno movie, all three of them licking and sucking, probing and fucking, this position, that position. It could so spoil a man. And to think if Billy had acted like a proper boyfriend and stayed faithful to Nikki, he wouldn't have been going hammer and tongs with two fit sorts in a ménage-a-trois. Would you convict him for grabbing life by the nipples and riding the journey for all it is worth?

I would like to able to tell all you sexually depraved or even blessed that Sonja, Katie and Billy carried on like that throughout the rest of their stay but they did not. It was such a great night that to try and recreate it would have been greedy and if it wasn't up to the same standard, would have sullied the memory. In fact, that was the last sexual encounter Billy actually had with either one of them for the rest of that holiday. They all still hung around together but it was agreed by all concerned that there were other fish to fry and left it like that.

Just like the holiday abroad he went on with his entire family many years before, this also was a holiday of first times and so it stuck out in his memory more than others did. Not that the threesome wasn't memorable but something more meaningful happened on this trip, it was the first time Billy met Denny Walnuts, the man the police said was a nut too hard to crack.

Billy and his two travelling companions, Michael and Matt, were spending a quiet night in the town, doing a little bar crawl and eyeing up the talent when they stumbled across a union Jack decorated tavern called 'Apples and Pears'. It was run by an old lag who sold up in England back in the early eighties and who had been living the dream ever since. His place seemed like a shrine to everything British but mainly the criminal element. He had photo's on the wall of him in his hey day standing along side some the most notorious people of yester year. One photo in particular stood out from the others, it was a black and white picture of Tommy, Teddy, Hoxton Harry and Billy's very own Grandad, Freddie White all standing outside the Royale club on its opening night under its new management. It was the sight of this photo that prompted Billy to highlight that Freddie was his deceased relative to the owner of the bar, which in turn caught the attention of the gentleman that was sharing a drink with the owner at the time. He stood up and walked over to Billy, his eyes told the tale that his slender, forty five year old frame didn't, that he was not averse to inflicting pain when an occasion called for it. Denny stood in at five foot ten inches, dark curly hair in a seventies porn star style accessorised with a matching 'tache. From his appearance, you were just waiting for a scouse accent to leave his lips as he was a dead ringer of the stereotypical character immortalised by Harry Enfield but it was not the case. Denny was a Londoner whose loyalties were neither East nor South, he was an unbiased villain who danced the dance on both sides of the water.

"Who'd you say was your blood?" His question was more direct than enquiring; Billy raised his arm and tapped the glass frame indicating which person he was referring to.

"Freddie was my Grandad, Harry is my godfather. Did

you know 'em?" Billy asked to which Denny smiled a big Cheshire cat smile and replied.

"Oh yeah I know 'em, in fact there are few people we have in common. If Freddie was your blood and if the stories I am told are on the money that would mean your step dad is Bobbie M and that would make Mikey M your step brother." Billy was a little taken back by this stranger's in-depth knowledge of his extended family tree.

"That's right, how'd you know about my family mister?" Billy then went on the defensive; the fact that Denny had that violent twinkle in his eye was not going to be a factor if he was going to go down the road of disrespecting his family in any way. Billy changed his stance to line Denny up for an on the button left hook, he waited eagerly for this yet to be introduced stranger to answer him.

"Have you ever heard the expression that 'it's a small world'? Well just to give you some idea on how small it is, you have just walked into a bar that is tucked away off the beaten track in Spain, hundreds of miles from home to find on the wall a photo of your blood. In that same bar, a man you have never met before comes up to you and mentions your Dad and brothers' names and points out he also knew the people in the photo. You have no idea how I know them or why the owner of the bar took the initiative to lock the front door while I kept you and your mates distracted..." Billy spun his head round to see if that was the case, it was. This was going to get real hairy real fast, Michael and Matt were good guys but not used to this kind of set up, it wasn't just himself that he had to defend but his two combatant free friends. Billy turned his head back to look Denny in the eye, he was too confident; he hadn't moved and was still lined up for the left hook. 'Bang' Billy let it fly, knocking Denny backwards into the wall, he went in to land a right when Denny threw his hands up to keep Billy at arms distance and began to talk with laughter in his voice.

"Easy big fella, Christ you are of the same ilk as Freddie

and your step brother for that matter." And continued to chuckle. "I didn't mean to spook ya, it's just I'm on the run and if we were going be talking about people, then I can't afford for someone to walk in and overhear stuff." The room settled down, Michael and Matt joined the owner over at the bar while Billy and Denny sat down at a separate table to continue their conversation.

Denny was always a logical villain, although he could have it and would always stand his ground while backing you in a fight, he saw and enjoyed the easier side of things. In truth Denny was a chancer, a confidence man, a smooth talking, ideas beyond feasibility, bastard who took more satisfaction in taking someone's money with cunning than violence. Like most people of this generation who walked the walk, Denny crossed paths with both the East London gang run by Tommy and Teddy Crow and the South London crew headed by their counterparts Frankie and Shaw Richards. Because Denny wasn't a full paying member of either clubhouse during the gang wars, he happily flittered between the two areas, chancing his arm, making friends and connections and not getting seen as an enemy in the midst by anyone. It was during these times that he made the acquaintance of Freddie and Harry and got involved in a few jobs that a young Bobbie Michaels was a part of.

In fact, it was with the help of Freddie and Harry that Denny set up one of his most famous stings that was so well thought out that no one ever figured that it was a scam.

Back in sixty-nine after the twins were sent down for their thirty-year all-inclusive holiday, courtesy of her majesty. Harry and Freddie had an entire nightclub empire to run, some made money and others did not. It was the one's that were dying a death that were sold off for a sizable profit and the money was used to fund certain high return jobs, one involved an armoured truck; another involved one point five million from an airport and there was a prison breakout of a certain high profile *family* man. The pair practically funded every major crime for over a decade in the UK, Europe and a couple over in International waters. It felt like they funded everything except that job that involved the Mini Coopers in Italy. Some were publicised because those who pulled the jobs were caught and others made the papers because those who pulled the jobs, got away, but the job involving Denny Walnuts that the moneymen had funded made the papers for all the wrong reasons, or right reasons depending on who was reading the story.

The decade of love was making way for the decade of art and Denny had come up with an idea to get in on the action. Being the entrepreneur that he was, Denny had set up two limited companies, one in Jersey and one in Greece. It was through the Jersey Company that he made contact with a certain high brow art museum in England offering to loan them a very rare sculpture by the Greek artist Praxiteles that had been found in Athens. The piece in question dated back 340 BC and had been identified to be his last known sculpture that depicted woman in her natural beauty. The priceless magnum opus had been authenticated by the Greek museum of historical heritage, and produced the paperwork to confirm this for the British Art museum in question. Needless to say the Greek museum of historical heritage was the name of Denny's other company. The company in Jersey was to arrange the shipping of this masterpiece and had insured it for a total of one million pound based on the paperwork from the Greek side and the backing of this particular British museum. The sculpture was to arrive over the weekend and would be transferred to said museum first thing Monday morning.

You can only imagine the look of horror on the curators face when the delivered crate was opened only to reveal the sculpture had been smashed in transit. All hell broke loose as the press got wind of this and made it front-page news. This in turn caused uproar from Greece who without actually knowing the full story was blaming England for destroying its heritage and those shockwaves had the insurance company paying out double quick time without dotting I's or crossing T's in hopes of preventing a full scale breakdown in European relations.

While Europe was trying its utmost not to go to war, Denny was in Rio visiting an old friend that was now residing out there with three quarters of a million pound in his pocket. Not a bad mark up for a sting that only cost forty two grand to set up, forty two grand that didn't actually come out of his pocket and it was an easy score for Freddie and Harry who got a cool two hundred thou for their investment. You had to admire the balls and brains of this guy. The downside of this tale was many of the old faces Freddie and Harry included had vices coming out of their arses, drinking, gambling, womanising and in Denny's case, drugs. Not that he was a heavy user but he was a sucker for the profit that could be earned on them. It was this reason that years after that admirable caper was pulled, Denny now found himself on the run over a drugs deal he got involved in along with the Eves family and Billy's brother Mikey that went tits up when the police set up their own sting.

Billy hadn't heard from Mikey in a while so panic started to set in upon hearing this section of Denny's life story, had Mikey been pinched or worse?

"How's my brother, did something happen to him?" Billy was on the verge of knocking Denny around again if his answers didn't come fast enough.

"Calm down kid, your brother is fine, your brother is a fucking hero, let me tell ya. A true credit to his bloodline…" Denny then proceeded to relay the story of that eventful night on Margate beach.

It was the usual set up, the same one that had been used every third week for god knows how long. Only this time the strange kraut captain had already been taken down by the coast guard, the German connection had been raided and the police were hoping to catch the UK connection red handed, building sand castles while waiting for their delivery. Tony, his brother Andy, Denny, Mikey and a few others were waiting on the coastline with their flashlights waiting to guide the tugboat in. By this stage in the game, Tony and Andy would not normally be there, but they turned up once in a while to show their crew that they could still roll up their tailored made shirt sleeves and get their hands dirty. It helps the morale amongst the men to demonstrate once in a while that you haven't forgotten your roots. It was a style of management that was about to prove a very bad business decision for all concerned. Denny had been fronting some investment deals on the family's behalf, after all who better than to put in a face to face with your bank manager than a smooth talking bar steward like Den? His bonus was to be cut in on a slice of the E action and this being his first beach landing was reason enough for him to want to be there. This put Mikey on edge, there were too many variables, and the whole evening just was not sitting right with him. The air smelt different as though there was an out of place odour being blown in by the night time breeze. Mikey had learnt not to leave things to chance so he changed the position of the men to further down the beach, guided the tug boat in but a little down a ways, pushing the meet away from the vehicles and allowed a little breathing room. Tony asked why Mikey was altering the routine that they had been using since the word dot. Mikey aired his concerns; there were too many things that did not seem right this night. New faces, his bosses were here and the boat was late, it felt different so he would try something different.

It was another thirty minutes before the boat flashed it's spotlight in acknowledgement of the torch lights from the beach front. Mikey watched the approach of the tugboat captained by his very peculiar kraut, the same captain that had made this run time and time again. He could have landed on this beach with his eyes closed, there was no need for the guide lights, they were just a formality and yet he was following them in, further down from their original spot without any hesitation. This guy was off the weirdometer, he was loud and proud, and why isn't he shouting at us? Why isn't he questioning the new approach? It just was not right. That is when the direction of the night breeze changed and the faint sound of a small motor engine was carried on it before cutting out. Bollocks, it was a set up.

"Everyone off the beach, it's the filth, it's the filth, go, it's a sting!!!" Mikey bellowed out his warning with the volume turned all the way up on his vocal cords, everyone heard it including the rossers in the water. To throw confusion on the matter, the water rats turned on every spotlight they had to daze the scampering crew that was on the sandy shore, megaphones amplified orders of "Lay down with your hands on your head". Some of the hired muscle froze like a dear in headlights, others, like Andy, drew guns and let off shots, hoping to take out the lights. This was welcomed by returning shots, one of which hit Andy in his leg causing him to hit the deck. Tony cried out for his brother as Mikey practically rugby tackled him towards the waiting cars, his right arm wrapped round Tony, his left around Denny. They would have all been caught that night if Mikey hadn't had the tug boat putter in an extra few hundred yards down the coast given them that additional getaway space. Mikey had saved them the same fate as those on the beach and some serious brownie points had been earned. Tony could rustle up alibis for everyone that needed one but his biggest problem was getting help to his kid brother.

That help came at a price from Dave Love who arranged an interception while Andy was in the hospital, who was recovering from the removal of the slug in his leg. Denny posed as a very convincing Doctor in order to do his bit to help the cause and the two had to disappear. Andy was whisked away to parts unknown and Denny had been dropped off on the coast of Costa Brava, where he had the connections to have himself hidden away from prying eyes. This led him to this moment in time, sitting in a bar, across a table with the brother of the man who had saved his life, if there was ever an example to the phrase 'it's a small world' then for these two men, this was it. Billy shook Denny's hand, wished him god speed on his journey and parted company. If today's events proved anything, it was that these two would cross paths again somewhere down the line and so there was no need to drag out their first encounter any longer than it needed to be, besides Billy had a phone call to make to his brother and check on that he was doing okay. So much for the quiet night in town.

The next morning the boys hotel room was loud with things not being said, Michael and Matt did not push the matter of getting answers on the mini adventure of the night before and when the usual gate crashers came in to help themselves to the contents of the fridge, none were given. Something was needed to change the subject and came in the guise of that day's excursion, for that day was the trip to a private beach for a beach party. The entire gang had all signed up for that one and so they had all grabbed their beach bags, stopped at the watering hole for morning supplies and jumped on the waiting coach that was doing the hotel run to gather up the masses of club eighteen to thirty holiday makers.

The sun made the temperature go through the roof inside the coach, the air conditioner wasn't powerful enough to combat it and everyone was getting irritable. To help matters and cool tempers, the rep brought out a few crates of beer and dished them out to everyone; by the time the coach reached the beach most of the rabble were pissed and loud. It is only when you're sober around people like that that you realise what tits they are but chances are, you're a tit just like them when you're pissed.

The reps did their best to get everyone active but it was a lost cause, Billy's onslaught of followers just wanted to catch some rays and they had wandered off further down the beach and had flicked out the towels in preparation of worshipping the sun god. Sun, sea and sand, the three S's but something else was missing but Billy could not quite put his finger on it, oh yes that was right, Sun tan lotion. Jackie, Michelle, Paul and Billy were burnt like toast by the end of the day. It hurt to move and they were all red raw. Jackie was burnt so bad she had blisters appear on her chest, arms and legs. The others had found it funny in their semi drunken state not to point the reddening out to any of them as they laid there turning over every half hour like slow cooked rotisserie chickens. As I said, people become rights tits when they have had a few.

The day finally came to an end and the coach had got the lobster crew back to their hotel, Billy hobbled up to Jackie's room for some after sun lotion. He, like the other three was in pain and so, not wanting to move any further than he needed to, crashed out on Michelle's bed. She had gone back to Paul's to rest and that was the start of their holiday romance. Keith rushed to apply lotion on Jackie, which she enjoyed and Billy had his own tender nurses, Sonja and Katie looking after him, laying there like a human lobster, going "Poor baby". In-between their fits of laughter they were kind enough to rub in some lotion. It felt orgasmic when that cool aloe-Vera lotion hit his skin. The fact that these two Essex goddesses were then gently rubbing it into his skin only heightened that feeling. It became evident by the bulge developing in his trunks just how orgasmic it was feeling. Katie reached in and pulled Billy's throbbing tribute to manhood out, and as she held it in place, Sonja turned her attention to it. Slowly moving her mouth towards it, all the while wetting her lips in anticipation of adding required lubrication and just as she got there and Billy could feel her warm breath on it, she pulled away.

"Later" She said, "it may be up for it but you're not". Then they both left, giggling away at their cruel actions to allow Billy to suffer alone.

It took three days before Billy could brave the outdoors and the day's hot sun. A week was nearly up and his sunburn was turning into more of a bronzed tan. He was feeling better and had scores to settle with two particular women. He had missed two of the excursions he had paid for and was determined to make up for it that night. It was bullfighting time and the revellers were all bundled on to the coach once more and were driven to a place in the middle of nowhere. On the way over the rep asked for volunteers and Billy was so bang up for it he waved his arm like an epileptic holding a live electrical wire, all of his troops were cheering for him to be picked, which he eventually was.

All of the one night only Matadors had to stand around in a box as one by one they were called upon to come out. The first one out stood by the gate waiting for the bull to be released from its pen, as the gate opened he legged it to the barrier, only to be laughed at because what came out of the gate was a bull, a football (Geddit?). The next one was now ready, he actually waited for the gate to open and saw something moving towards him before he shot off, it was a calf that came up to his waist. It was becoming obvious that this was the "wind up" corral. After the calf fake-out, came a stuffed bull on wheels and after that came a little piglet. All the matadors, despite never actually seeing bull, were still running straight away for the safety of the barriers. Then it was Billy's turn, feeling confident and looking strong, armed with the knowledge that this was a joke farm, he stood there, looking the part with his brightly coloured cape draped over his shoulder, playing to the crowd, blowing kisses to the ladies and standing with arrogance.

Billy waited eagerly for the gates to be opened, anticipating the let down of yet another fake-out designed to humiliate the obnoxious holiday maker who dared to make a mockery of one of Spain's most recognised sporting events. Slowly the gates opened, Billy just stood there, cape in hand still looking at the crowd. It was the crowd's gasps that caught his attention before the sound of the charging, full sized bull coming hurtling towards him did. Billy just managed to dodge it by twisting himself off to the bull's side. The bull turned to have another go; Billy had two choices, turn and run like all those before him or live in the same vein in which he had been brought up to do and stand his ground and do what he enthusiastically volunteered to do, fight a bull. Billy decided to stand his ground. He was waving his cape around like a true professional, "Torro, torro!" he was shouting, his adrenaline levels were going through the roof and then, just like that the bull charged for him, head on. Billy side stepped and the cape went over its horns, Billy moved back as the bull made another turn to try again. This time Billy did not side step enough, the force of the bull going past him knocked him down, the cape was caught on its horns and it was running blind. Enough bravery, thought Billy, who then jumped to his feet and legged it to the barrier, the crowd started cheering and the wrangler settled down the bull. If there was ever a time when he needed a drink, it was then.

That night, Billy enjoyed one of his most favourite things, a thick, juicy steak, which he hoped was the three hundred pound monster that had earlier charged at him. This was washed down with a few ice cold Fanta Lemons, what more could a guy ask for after such a life defining moment, except maybe the pleasures of the young Spanish lass who had been giving him the eye all through dinner, so he asked and he got. There is truth to that old saying after all.

The next couple of days sort of drifted by for the gang, a week had gone by and it felt like they had exhausted all their options on what to do, it soon became very samey, they sunbathed during the day, went out at night and ate breakfast in Billy's room every morning. He remembered the fun they had at the last party they threw on the patio and said they should do something like that again, so they set about organising it for that Wednesday night. A completely new group of arrivals had shown up and it was a good way for the gang to introduce themselves to them.

The music pumped out, there was dancing going on,

mingling and stories being exchanged, the party was swinging. They were carrying it on into the early hours of the morning when Janice the hotel's on-site rep came over to tell them to start winding it down. Janice was all right, a little older than the other reps, and a lot nicer; she had a look of experience on her face; never a bad thing.

Now they would have ended it there but the party had just reached that "Every one in the pool" stage. It was three am and they were making noise like no ones business, so much in fact the police had been called, and these guys carried guns. The flashing Police lights at the foot of the hotel's boundaries told the locals that the noise was about to stop, one way or another. The party broke up fast and Billy's posse all run back to his ground floor hotel room, dripping wet, being very clever and real sneaky. Matt turned off the lights in the room and shut the door, Billy and some others were peaking through the curtain at the police and their flashlights surveying the area. What Billy and the clever crew forgot about were all the wet footprints leading to their door and the fact the curtain only covered the top half of the all glass door. They were all huddled together being quiet behind the curtain and the police the other side could see all their legs and feet. Busted!

The next day, Billy, Michael and Matt were asked to pack their bags and leave the hotel. The lads stored their prematurely packed luggage in the girl's room and made a point of making sure to pull someone in the evening so they would have somewhere to spend the night. Worst-case scenario, Keith or the girls would let them crash on the floor of their rooms and that is how the three London lads played it for the rest of their stay in Lloret De Mar.

It was on the last night of their holiday and Billy had to go back to the girl's room to use their shower and change his clothes. As he was coming back out of their room fully refreshed, Janice the rep stopped him in his tracks, she said she was sorry about what happened and asked if the boys were all right. Billy told her they had been coping and luckily, there was only one more night to find somewhere to sleep. Billy was really laying it on thick hoping for the sympathy vote. Janice turned to him and said, "Why don't you crash at my place?" And there it was.

Billy had the three of them turn up on Janice's doorstep later that night; she opened the door, looked at them and seemed a little disappointed.

"I thought you'd be on your own" She said sheepishly to Billy once the other two were out of ear shot.

"I couldn't leave my buddies stranded, now could I?" He replied with a cheeky grin on his face.

"Suppose not, come in" Michael thanked her and asked how could the three of them repay her for opening up her home to them on this night. A tonne of beer, four spliff's and a game of strip poker later and Janice seemed full of ideas on how the three of them could repay her. She was well up for it by now and not just from Billy. For the second time this holiday another porno scene erupted with all three of the London lads taking a turn drilling for oil in Janice's patch, followed by a little double action. Billy just knew she had an experienced look about her and he thanked God that he was right.

It was a crying shame for the holiday to come to an end, especially now Billy had to return home and look Nikki in the eye and choose to either lie to her or end it. Moreover, the thought of going back to work was a downer. Still at least Vaughan would be glad to have him return and Billy dreaded to think what had been going on at the flat with Gary left once again un-chaperoned.

At the airport, Paul was good enough to inform all those listening that he had nicked an assortment of things during his two-week vacation. He even nicked the glass ashtrays from the departure lounge; all were going to be gifts for his nearest and dearest. Billy could not resist writing "Cheapskate" on the cast Paul sported from his first night in Lloret. Christ you

169

have to pity the woman who marries this guy. As the norm in these situations, they all exchanged phone numbers and addresses and arranged to hook up for a reunion in a couple of weeks for a birthday get together at Billy's place.

Billy's trips abroad, up until then had always been family orientated, not with his Mum and Dad but with his brothers or members of his extended family. They would always be getting into fights with somebody or other but now he was being an ordinary guy, mixing with people that didn't come from the same walk of life. There were times when Billy could understand why people would look at him and think he was a monster based on his past. He had never really thought what he did was wrong before but being around other normal, everyday people was starting to make him think about living a different life, one not to be ashamed of, with nothing to hide. After all, look how close Mikey nearly came to either a very long chomp on the porridge bowl or becoming maggot food. A boring, full of regrets, kind of life that every honest person Billy had ever met complained about. When it's put like that, you probably feel that there wasn't a tough decision to be made, but from his point of view, there was, and it was becoming evident that he had to make it and soon.

Chapter Thirteen

The trio arrived back home in their neck of the woods late on that Sunday afternoon and after crashing through his door, to find his flat surprisingly empty, Billy just went straight to bed to sleep a thousand sleeps. He finally woke up to the land of norm at around five on Monday morning to see the light flashing on the answering machine; Billy had soundly slept right through the continuous ringing of his telephone. Can you get jet lag flying from Spain to England? There were nine messages waiting to be played back, one was from his Mum, who was making sure he had got back all right and to find out if he had heard from his brother Mikey, One was from Vaughan to check that he had actually returned to England and was still going to be working at Siddelely Hawks. One was from his cousin, Monty who wanted him to call him back regarding some business and six were from Nikki. Billy really didn't need to hear her saying "I love you", "I've missed you" and "Did you miss me?" He figured he would leave that problem for later, he was already feeling depressed, thanks to Vaughan, reminding him about the fact, he had to go back to work that morning.

Billy put on a brave face as he entered the grimy gates of work and adopted the Saturday night fever swagger as he cut a path through the shop floor, sporting a big smile and flashing his tan, re-establishing to the masses that he was the Don, and he was back to rule the roost. Billy gave a heads up to Michael while throwing him one of those knowing grins that say's that they know something everyone else doesn't and then started to look around to try and find his little brother, Vaughan, who was eventually discovered sitting behind a machine looking bored out of his skull. Now to Billy, Vaughan is his little brother, but in all fairness he was now standing in at six foot one and was almost the same size as Billy but he was still naturally growing. Billy called out to him to catch his attention, with that Vaughan jumped up; saw his brother, produced a kid in a sweet shop look upon his face and rushed over to greet him in person.

"Thank god you're back, I've been pissed bored. Tell us about your holiday" Billy got settled at his machine and while toiling away relayed all the gory details to Vaughan, who soaked up the adventures with baited breath. The day flew by, which was good seeing how Billy dreaded even the thought of coming in that morning. Vaughan was well gutted he did not go himself but then there would always be other chances.

The end of Billy's shift seemed to have come around in record time; he even had a skip in his step on his journey home. It was when he reached home however and discovered that Nikki had left yet another message on the old answering machine that his mood went back to the same level to what it was at the start of his day. It was obvious that Billy could not avoid her any longer and called her up to arrange to meet her that night. She sounded so happy on the phone that he just played it cool and told her that he had missed her and looked forward to seeing her and left it at that.

The two newly reunited lovebirds met up in the good old trusty local, the Dog and Duck and spent the first ten minutes visiting lip lock central whilst saying hello. The problem when you stop kissing is that it gives your other half the ability to talk and it didn't take long before she asked how Billy's holiday was and had he been a good boy. For a brief second Billy was trying to work out how to tell her the truth about the escapades that happened in Lloret De Mar and perhaps suggest that they should maybe call it a day, in that split second Billy had the whole conversation worked out in his head. He looked Nikki straight in her big, brown eyes and the words he was thinking about saying were not the words that were finding their way out of his mouth. If fact Billy actually made a mental effort to shut his mind down from thinking just so he could hear the words himself. He was spurting out a complete load of bullshit about how he was tempted but did not act on it. How much he missed her, how he wanted to fly home early, blah, blah, blah. Nikki was lapping it up, "Oh you're so sweet" "I'm so lucky" "I knew I could trust you" and sentences to that affect. Billy was just standing there like a nodding dog, agreeing with her all the way. To make matters worse Nikki then turned around and told Billy how upset she was about not being around for his twenty-first birthday because her Dad had booked a last minute holiday for the family to Cyprus. Here she was pouring her heart felt feelings out to him with genuine concern and all the while, Billy stood there thinking 'Yes, two more weeks without her being around' and planning a wild birthday bash in his head, involving the girls from Essex that he had met on the holiday. For as tough and hard as Billy was he just didn't have the guts to end the relationship despite his initial glee at having this women who was declaring her love and sorrow to him leave the country so he could fool around with some old slapper or slappers. But there it was, Billy had bare faced lied to a woman he was intending to break up with about his holiday exploits, planned an orgy in his head and found himself being commended for it. He did not know why he lied; perhaps he did have real feelings for her. Perhaps he liked the idea of being in a relationship but after the way he acted on holiday, Billy knew deep down he should have done the right thing by her and ended it. Alternatively, he should have at least come clean and let her make up her own mind about what to do with their relationship. Billy had taken that decision away from her and that stayed with him throughout their entire relationship. Men are such bastards.

The delightful Nikki and her unfaithful, lower than a snake's belly boyfriend spent all their remaining free time doing all the things young couples do until it was time for Nikki to go on her family holiday. Billy had been making all the arrangements for his birthday bash all week, he had it lined up as an open house and stocked up on all the essentials. The plan was for Keith and Paul to come up on the Friday evening and get the ball rolling with the girls coming up on the Saturday. It turned out that Paul's holiday romance with Michelle did not carry on after touchdown, so he had pulled out of coming down because he did not want to be confronted by her. He probably stole from her too.

Keith travelled down on his own; he was in the RAF and was living in Marlborough, Wiltshire at the time, sharing a house with three female nurses. Some people have all the luck. Keith came to party, he reached Billy's place at about eight, threw down his bags and the pair hit the town carrying a large can of red paint. Billy took him on a bar crawl and for every bar they left, they had a few extra people tagging along with them, by the time they reached back to Billy's flat they had pied pipered around sixty people. The tunes were cranked up and everyone started the weekend off right. It went on throughout the night and into the early hours of Saturday morning, in fact, it went on so long that Jackie, Sonja and Katie turned up on the doorstep to be greeted by a full house. Michelle had not bothered to turn up for the same reason Paul did not, so they both missed out.

Saturday was more of a chill out day for the remaining guys left in the flat, the girls however wanted to go out shopping. So Billy told them to look over the market that was right outside his window, it ran over a mile long and is still the longest open aired market in Europe. Go knock yourselves out.

The shopaholic's went out on their little spree to buy

whatever it is that women feel they constantly need to have. While the lads just sat about, having a little smoke and basically chatted shit, all throughout the day all you could hear was the call of 'It's open' from the mellow heads as people just kept turning up to join in on the weekends festivities.

"Is it like this all the time?" Keith enquired, he just could not believe the way Billy's flat resembled the comings and goings of Waterloo station.

"Nah, usually it's quite busy." Came the answer, Keith looked around at the other guests that were accumulating, walking in unchallenged, sitting down and generally making themselves at home; they just turned to him and smiled one of those smiles that says more than words ever could. On holiday, Billy kind of told Keith little snippet's about his life back home but Billy thought it was only at that moment Keith realised that he was like no one he had ever known before.

It was seven o'clock when the household all started to get changed to go out, the girls had spent money on new gear and were trying to get dressed without any one barging in on them. Too many guests not enough bathrooms. That is when the doorbell went for the umpteenth time, Billy shouted out to Alan, who had made his way round earlier that day, to answer it for him. Alan came back into the front room with a wry smile on his face.

"Billy, it's for you" Well that was fucking obvious, it was his flat, who else would be for? Thought Billy, pissed off that he had to get out of his chair. He went to the front door only to be confronted by a blast from the past. Her name was Dee and she was someone Billy had not seen for quite some time. She used to live on the estate back in the day, she was five years younger than he was and he had always seen her as an annoying little kid who used to follow him around all the time.

Dee was a gangly girl growing up; she was tall for her age

but with not much body to accompany it. When she was twelve and Billy was fast approaching seventeen, she had become his shadow, so to get her off his case; he kissed her, for Dee it was her first kiss. Billy had introduced her tonguesville and with that the deal was sealed, she was smitten forever. Over the following years their paths took them in different directions but they would always seem to bump into each other every now and then, it had been a couple of years since their last encounter, so this was obviously about time that they bumped into each other once more.

Standing in front of Billy however was not the gangly young girl that he remembered, quite the contrary in fact; standing in front of him this day was a well-developed young woman, an extremely well developed young woman.

"Hey stranger, what brings you to my door?" Billy stood there propping the doorframe up and was starting to give Dee the same kind of looks that he gave his other female victims. When it suddenly clicked in his head that, this was a sixteen-year old girl, and if he were to be honest for once in his life, he would admit that she was someone he called a friend.

"I was in the neighbourhood and word was that a party was happening here tonight." Dee gave a little smile that tried to show she was a woman but emphasised her youth and lack of experience.

"Baby, there's a party here every night" Alan had decided to join Billy at the door, to have another look at this particular guest that would have been let in already if they were anyone else. He figured Billy must have been hiding something so he wanted to get himself into the conversation. Billy shot Alan a look and told him in no uncertain terms.

"Back off from her, this one's protected." To which Alan reacted respectfully replied.

"Say no more boss, I'm gone" Alan then went back into the front room to the others, probably updating them all on what was happening on the doorstep.

"So I'm protected am I, who by, you? Are you my bodyguard?" Dee asked with a very seductive tone in her voice. There was something unnerving to Billy about this young kid talking like a dog on heat.

"Cool your jets and come in, I'll introduce you to everyone" which he did, making sure everyone noted that she was not to be touched. After all Billy's word was law.

That night started off like a repeat of the night before with the only difference being they didn't need to attain a crowd from bar crawling, word was already out and the flat was packed before the stroke of midnight. Now Billy had three girls staying over and he had history with two of them, a young girl giving off enough vibes indicating that she wanted him to make her a women and a flat full of additional women that he had either already slept with or they wanted to sleep with him. Any other guy would be acting like a kid in a sweetie shop but for some reason Billy was shunning all offers. He did not know if it was because of Nikki or because he did not want Dee to get the wrong idea about anything between them. Whatever the reason Billy was on best behaviour and that is how it went for the rest of the night. To prove the point further when Dee came into his room while he was getting some much needed shut eye in those wee early hours, his body resting and easily controlled by certain parts of his anatomy. She got close to his ear; her breath tickled as the gentle warm air danced across his earlobe and whispered 'Are you awake'. She was wearing one of Billy's denim shirts that was unbuttoned to reveal that she wasn't wearing a bra. She took his hand and placed it on her breast, in his half awake, sleep deprived state, he would have been lying if he said he wasn't tempted but the need to do the right thing came over him a lot faster than anything may have came over him if he hadn't pulled his hand away. He turned to her and softly told her "Another time".

He had let Dee stay in his bed as he went to find somewhere else to sleep. The party was still going on in the front room, people were making out all over the place, and the girls had Gary's room. Billy locked himself in the bathroom and fell asleep in the bathtub. Thank god, the flat came with a separate WC or he would have had to keep getting up while it was constantly being used, not an ideal situation for a tired son of a gun.

Being part of an all boy family, and having a limited, emotional relationship with his own Mother, meant Billy's attitude towards women was always a little off. Nevertheless, working a nine to five and actually having a girlfriend was changing him. On paper, he was a regular Joe; he paid his taxes, was thinking about marriage and at rare moments even saw himself becoming the kind of guy who could be a great father despite his previous effort or lack of. Billy was treating Dee, like the little sister he never had, and he refrained from getting his oats from someone other than Nikki. This was not the real Billy, this was not how he had lived his life up until that year, he was feeling ordinary and he was having some seriously mixed feelings on whether or not this was someone he wanted to be.

Billy was woken up hours later by the continuous thumping on the door and loud screaming.

"Get out the fucking bathroom!" Billy did not recognise the voice, so he did not rush to get up. The pounding continued, the guy wasn't taking the hint and so Billy eventually got out of his makeshift bed and opened the door.

"'Bout fucking time" and with that the screaming, pounding fella barged past Billy and started to relieve himself in the sink. Billy had no idea who this guy was, why he wasn't using the WC in the next room or why he was telling Billy, in his own place to get out of his own bathroom and pushing him out the way. Now an ordinary fella would have left the situation as it was, but the Devil on Billy's right shoulder was winning the battle and had talked Billy in to not being ordinary that day.

Billy kicked him at the back of his knees, which caused

this very disrespectful fella to buckle, so Billy used his weight to help the momentum and forced his victim's head to hit the side of the bath. He then grabbed him by his hair and helped his head to hit the bath a few more times. Blood spurted all over the bathroom tiles from this forehead as his flimsy skin started to tear. All the noise that was now coming from the bathroom got the attention of Mr bargies mates.

"Easy mate, leave him alone before we fuck you up!" Billy turned his head to look the Muppets in the eye; he then stood up to his full height, leaving the loud mouth, whose blood was redecorating his bathroom walls, to fall to the ground.

"You'll do what?" Billy quizzed the lead mouthpiece as he lined him up and while an answer was being formulated in the mind of the numbskull who issued the threat, Billy let a left, fly wild and punched him on the bridge of his nose, one of the few sweet spots to hit someone on the face. People that actually knew Billy started rushing over and began to manhandle the rest. A few digs later and they had them all pushed to the front door.

"Now fuck off before I get into a bad mood and use each and every one of you to redecorate my whole place!" Billy squared up to the lot of them, his frame ever expanding as he breathed, pushing the trickles of adrenaline around his fired up system. That is when it sank into their pea-sized brains just who he was and they ran off, dragging their injured mate with them. Billy turned to the others and rather than thanking them for their assistance, he asked.

"Who's for breakfast?"

If you are not used to violence then seeing it first hand, up and close can be a disturbing thing. People around you who you count as friends suddenly become weary of you; some shy away instantly others drift over time, hoping not to hurt your feelings to the point that you exact the same measure of violence on them. Not everyone can stomach it, you need to have very few feelings, if you ever find yourself filled with guilt, wondering how the other guy is doing, then when push comes to shove you're gonna lose. If you let up for an instant, people will see it as an opening to strike and exploit. In a fight, hesitation could be the weak chink in your armour, second guessing and not being willing to go that one step further than your opponent(s), is gonna get you hurt. Billy never wanted to be hurt, if in a confrontation he found himself having to kill someone to stop himself from experiencing any form of suffering, than that is what would happen. He would put you down, keep you there, and not lose a minute's sleep. Billy had lost fights in the past but he had never really been hurt, just bruised, and that is how he was going to keep it.

Billy had truly spoilt the mood that morning and consequently his party guests were gone from sight. The Essex girls had they bags packed and said a hasty goodbye, Billy could not blame them, Keith was not too far behind. Dee on the other hand, stuck around and joined the remaining few of the violence-tolerant guests for breakfast. She was a woman after his heart and as the night before made clear, other parts of him.

"Dee, I take it your Mum knows where you are?" Billy was starting to go into that protector mode, acting like the big brother she did not need or want.

"Yeah, I phoned her yesterday" She replied while looking down at her toast. Billy was not one hundred percent convinced by her answer.

"I think you should phone her again, let her know you're okay"

"Yeah, I'll do it later" Her tone changed to that of a disgruntled youth, Billy should have been listening with more conviction to his inner voice, it was telling him that it was red flag time, but like a typical male, he ignored it. Billy left the rest of his guests to do the washing up while he tackled the mess of sprayed blood that had dried on the bathroom walls and fixtures, after all, his mess his problem.

After Sunday morning's activities, the plan for the rest of the day was to throw on some action flicks and get the old testosterone levels to their maximum peak. There's nothing like sticking on a Van Damme movie with your buddies and hitting each other all the way through it re-enacting the fight scenes in the same triple angled cinematography to get the blood lust flowing. Although hitting Dee in the chest was a lot more fun than hitting either Michael or Vaughan in the same area. With the odd bouts of take away food and mugs of tea, the day just seemed to disappear.

The next morning found the lads having to go into work while Dee was still hanging around Billy's flat with no evident signs that she was leaving anytime soon. Billy thought it would be wise to plant the seed in her head about leaving by reminding her to make sure she turns everything off before leaving and he would catch her another time. The day slowly drew on and when the five o'clock whistle blew, Billy flew out the factory gates and straight into the gym to let out the remains of his pent up adrenaline levels from the weekend. It had just gone seven when he reached back to his empty home; Dee was nowhere to be seen so Billy just assumed that she had gone back to her own place and that their paths would cross again later down the line. You know what they say about assumption. Billy had been home for a total of thirty minutes, after a hard, long day at work and a good session in the gym, which was preceded by a full weekend of partying; his eyes were on the verge of shutting up shop for the evening when out of the blue there was a knock at the door. It was not an ordinary knock, If like Billy, you have had at times given reason for the police to knock at your door, you will understand when I say that they have a distinctive approach to knocking on your door, a knock that you get to know real quick. Billy opened the front door to be greeted by two officers in plain clothes, who obviously had not made their quota for the month if they were clutching at straws by banging on this door. Billy knew that Mikey had been cutting things close these days and that Gary was a dirt bag that was into something not too chicken soup (Kosher). Then he thought they were here because of the idiots he made an example of over the weekend who finally decided to press charges but he was wrong, very, very wrong.

Billy was kindly asked to accompany them to the station for questioning, regarding the disappearance of Dana Fields (Dee). Now at first he thought he was the good guy in all of this but it turned out Billy was suspect number one. There had been no ransom note, so the need for a full-blown kidnapping investigation had not been needed at this point, but answers were still required. Dee's Nan had telephoned the police with the accusations that her granddaughter had been missing for two days and her last known whereabouts, was in Walthamstow to visit the much older than her, Billy Michaels. Now Billy could understand that he wasn't a parent or guardians first choice of a role model, he had done a lot of illegal things in his time that he wasn't actually tugged for by the McGarret squad but it was all still acknowledged through the whispers. Nevertheless, to be put in the frame for something he did not do, that was totally British Telecom, out of order!

Billy waved his right to a solicitor because he figured that since he was actually innocent, he did not need one, plus of course it only delayed the processing time and Billy was already tired and longing for his own mattress and not the wafer thin sports mat that would be awaiting him. He spent the first two hours of his stay in a cell followed by three hours of the same questions in an interview room followed by another hour in the cells. Billy kept telling them that Dee was there for a party and as far as he knew, she went back home that morning. He had witnesses to say that when they left his flat she was unharmed and free to do want she wanted, he could also provide witnesses that could account his movements all day. Over and over again the same questions, like the answers were going to suddenly change or something.

The officers that were questioning him tried every trick in the book to get Billy to 'fess up. Good cop Bad cop, the 'Do yourself a favour' routine. Even the old 'we're on your side in all of this, just kids being kids...Now what did you do with her?!?!?!' The old ploy of 'someone has put you at the scene' was somewhat lost, because after all, of course someone can put him at the scene; the crime supposedly took place in his own flat. Billy even had to put up with them slamming the table, throwing pencils at him, and using continuous threats of prison time where big burly men would love to break in a tough nut like him for kicks. Now this was in the late eighties and the police were just coming off a large ten-year witch-hunt because they were beating answers out of people and forging confessions. So unless these two pigs were throw backs from the seventies, Billy was pretty confident that if they went too far he would be proving just how loud one voice can shout and get itself heard. After several, gruelling hours Billy was finally free to go, with not even a lift back home. Pinky and Perky made sure that he understood that if they had not heard some good news about Dee's whereabouts by the end of play, then Billy would be coming back for further questioning. This was something he really did not want because they do not half lay on a lousy breakfast in the morning accompanied with a weak, arsed cup of Rosie.

Dee's day however had been a little less stressful; it turned out that she had a lovely time watching morning TV followed by a long hot bath. She then danced around the kitchen with the stereo on full blast while helping herself to the contents of Billy's fridge and cupboards. After this eventful morning, she then decided to go out and see if any of her old friends were still knocking around in the area. It was just as the front door slammed shut behind her that she remembered that she did not have a key to get back in. After all this was not Chingford Hall estate, where latch key kids ran wild and doors were never closed. So she found herself locked out and with no knowledge of where Billy worked or how to get hold of him. Dee then decided to waste the day until his return by spending her time visiting her old haunts and doing a spot of shopping.

She met up with a few old girlfriends, chatted for hours and then they thought they would go see a flick on at the cinema. Of course, while she was watching some chick flick, Billy was being carted off by the investigating officers. After the movie, she went back to the flat to see if Billy was back yet, but obviously, he was not, so she went off somewhere else. This time, not being around when the police came to check the place for her or signs of foul play. It was not until little Gary had come home from work and found her sitting on the doorstep that she got back in. Gary spent twenty minutes shooting the breeze with her catching up on her antics since he last saw her on the estate then told her to make herself at home, and assured her that he was certain Billy wouldn't be long from wherever he had gone. But of course Billy was a long time; in fact he was so long it went past Dee's bedtime who acted like Goldilocks and slept in Daddies bed.

Billy got back home at around three in the morning, he had to be up for work in three and half-hours, his eyes were already closed as he stumbled from his front door to his bedroom door. He took off his shoes and jumped into bed. It took him a full ten seconds before realising someone was in there with him, it was Dee. Billy did not know what gave him his second wind more, the shock of having someone already in his bed or the fact that the person in question was the cause of his crappy evening.

"Get the fuck out of my home. Call your Nan, call your Mum, and call a cab. Go home, and never bother me again!" Dee could tell by the frightening look that had been implanted on Billy's face that now was not the time to question why the stern tone. Three phone calls and a twelve-minute wait later, the cab turned up and Billy personally put Dee into it, more for reassurance than anything else. Little girls should not play grown up games.

184

Deep down Billy was not really mad at her but the toll of the situation had to be taken out on someone. He hated not knowing the true answers to the questions that were being thrown at him at the police station and having the old bill looking at him with smug looks on their faces, this really grated his carrots. Billy didn't see or speak to Dee for almost a year after that.

Billy was not in the greatest of moods the next day at work and time just seemed to drag. After the pleasant evening he had spent in the nick, it made him wonder if there was not more to life than this. It was his first brush with the law in an age and despite the reasoning behind it, it was an issue that was easily put to rest but the memory would always linger, but for his brother Mikey however, his rollercoaster ride didn't seem to have an ending in sight.

Although Mikey had escaped any jail time from the caper that went down on Margate Beach, thanks to the cast iron alibi set up by Tony Eves, the police were still taking great pleasure in yanking Mikey off the streets for frequent bouts of questioning. They knew he was there that night but had no evidence to charge him but that did not stop them from harassing him. However, the main reason for continuously bringing in known members of the Eves gang was that they had lost a lot of face by having Andy Eves vanish from the hospital while in their custody. Nabbing Andy red handed at Margate was a dream come true for the boys in blue, the whole family had been targeted by them ever since eighty three when one of the country's key high profile robberies went down at Heathrow Airport. They knew that Andy and his family had been major players during that daring, news making event but despite getting his Uncle on charges they never got him or the rest of them and it wasn't through the lack of trying. Any conviction of any member of the Eves could make an officer's career, instead they broke them.

The robbery in question took place back in late

November of eighty-three; six robbers broke into the Bronx Securitas warehouse at Heathrow Airport. It was supposed to be a relatively easy job, stealing three million in cash with the help of an inside man. That score alone would have been easy money even split seven ways but once they were in that is when it all changed, because instead of finding the three million all neatly stacked for the taking what they found was twenty six million pounds worth of gold bullion.

To all those it concerned, this caper appeared, at first, to be a huge scale operation that had been extraordinarily well planned and not the stroke of fucking unbelievable dumb luck that it turned out to be. In reality, the operation was in fact an extremely detailed job, but the robbers were expecting to find money, not ten tonnes of gold bullion, waiting to be transported to the Far East. The luck of the Irish must have been smiling on these guys, because they had stumbled across a pot of gold that must have belonged to a herd of leprechauns and not a glimmer of a rainbow in sight. It should be pointed out that the twenty six million in gold was not just lying in the warehouse waiting to be stolen. It was locked in a safe, deep inside a secure airport building surrounded by guards, but that did not deter this team of jammy bastards.

Thanks to their inside man, the crack team already had some insight into the layout of the building, the gang burst into the secure area, disabled the guards and tied them up. That allowed them privacy while undertaking the task of cracking the safe, not being prepared for it meant that they failed miserably. Their next approach however was more up their alley, as it became obvious that it would be much easier to force the guards to reveal the combination to the safe, they poured petrol over them and threatened them with lighted matches until the guards gave in and blurted out the sequence.

When the safe was finally opened, they looked in disbelief on a haul of gold bullion that was far beyond any previous 'cash-only' heists they had ever been involved in.

What should have been a five-minute "smash 'n' grab" robbery, ended up becoming a lengthy operation. A few of the gang members had to leave the airport to get some different transport; there was no way their Ford Granada was going to endure the extra weight of this booty and there was no way they were planning on leaving any of the gold behind. The getaway drivers hurriedly returned with their new bigger and better vehicles and nearly two hours after they had entered the building, the gang finally made their getaway, twenty six million pound richer.

The Bronx Securitas robbery was a bold and brash manoeuvre, so it did not take the police very long to trace the core element of the gang from the usual suspects by extracting the sheaf from the wheat. The word on the street was that Nicky McLoughlin and Barry Robson had been scouting for trustworthy recruits, weeks before the robbery, and were only short-listing the best of the best.

Robson was already quite well known to the police and was nicknamed "the Commander" due to his natural ability to lead any villain into battle, no matter what their status on the pecking order was. His partner in crime, Nickey McLoughlin, also had a notorious reputation and was considered to be one of South London's most prolific armed robbers.

The first problem McLoughlin and Robson faced was what to do with twenty six million in gold that they were now in possession of, not exactly the easiest thing in the world to hide. To have any chance of getting away with the job, they would have to arrange for it to be carefully laundered and discreetly transferred into their own pockets. This kind of laundering required a great degree of care and subtlety, both of which theis street gangster team of Robson and McLoughlin lacked. Before the crime of the century went down, they were both living in modest council houses in South London, but only a few weeks after the heist they were living in a very large house in Kent, paid for in cash. It was also rumoured that McLoughlin had bought two Rottweiler dogs to protect his mansion and named them 'Bronx' and 'Securitas'.

Deciding what to do with such a large physical amount of gold would have been extremely difficult for the two main men of this blag. There were not many people in their immediate circle who could have known what to do with such a vast amount of gold. It was concluded that some bigger fish from the London end of the criminal pond had to be reeled in.

The Bronx Securitas gang called upon the services of a criminal figure known only as the Mongoose. The Mongoose was a well-known character in the criminal underworld and had risen to become one of the senior figures in the UK due to associations with many London gangs, particularly the infamous Eves family. Using his contacts, the Mongoose arranged for the gold to be delivered to a variety of different people so it could be smelted down into more manageable forms. The Eves family were happy to oblige, for a small cut of the proceeds. They involved the services of a jeweller named Solly Goldstein, who was willing to sell on the smelted down goods.

The first job for the police was to find out the identity of the gang's insider who worked for Heathrow. It turned out to be a lot easier than they expected. One of the security guards at Heathrow was called Toni White, on the morning of the robbery; he had been late into work and missed the entire heist, a rookie mistake that was duly noted by the police in their preliminary investigations. It did not take much in the way of detective work to discover that White was living with Barry Robson's sister at that time. With a little pressure from the authorities, he confessed to his role in the robbery and began pointing the finger at the rest of the gang who were now living a life of luxury. It seemed like the game was up, but there were still a few more twists in this tale.

After finding out that Toni had committed the ultimate

act of treachery by grassing them all up, McLoughlin wanted to use his substantial wealth as a get out clause from a long-term prison sentence. He figured that he could willingly give the money up to the authorities and hopefully not have to spend his entire middle age in a cell. Therefore, after he was arrested, McLoughlin entrusted his share of the gold with a variety of friends including Barry Naide. It seemed that McLoughlin still believed in the much fabled 'honour amongst thieves' code despite only recently being farmed out to the law, but when he came to claim his temporarily loaned wealth, both the money and gold was nowhere to be found.

To put the icing on the cake for both him and his partner in crime, McLoughlin and Robson, were jailed for Twenty-five years.

As a personal friend and business associate, McLoughlin didn't question the motives of the Mongoose when he told him that it was Naide who had the money and was refusing to part with it. To confound things further, Naide denied this accusation and, despite the fact that the Mongoose was living in even greater wealth than before, McLoughlin still believed it was Naide who had betrayed him.

When Naide was arrested for handling the gold, and all throughout his trial, he received a letter that threatened his life if he didn't give the money back to its rightful owner. The letter pointed out in no uncertain terms that those that were wronged by him wouldn't be in prison forever and that Naide ought to hand over the money now.

Whatever Naide felt about this threat, after spending nine years at Her Majesty's Pleasure, it appeared that he had managed to convince those with grievances against him that he had done nothing wrong to them. On his release from prison, he did not even request any protection, preferring to make no complaint and began living a quiet life; and that is exactly what he did. Naide rebuilt his legitimate taxi business and followed a daily routine that suggested he believed he was living in safety. His enemies eventually caught up with him almost eighteen years to the day of the robbery and royally blew him away with a couple of up and under's.

A final piece in the Bronx Securitas puzzle came to light when it was discovered that Naide had introduced Kevin Nott into the ever-growing circle of Bronx Securitas associates. Nott appeared to have some expertise in the gold smelting trade and had connections with Jack Parker, the owners of a Bristol-based gold dealership. Knott's expertise was used to introduce copper to much of the Bronx Securitas gold during the smelting process. This changed the carat of the metal and made it impossible to trace back to the Heathrow robbery. Despite this apparently foolproof way of distributing the wealth, a lack of subtlety and lack of caution raised suspicion from the McGarret squad.

The first mistake the gang made was withdrawing large amounts of their laundered money from a single branch of a bank in Bristol. This normally wouldn't warrant it being flagged up but the sheer amount of cash that was continually being withdrawn from that particular branch, meant that they had to request additional funds from the Bank of England. This earned the robbers the attention of the Treasury and, unsurprisingly, the police. All of this meant that Nott was placed under heavy police surveillance.

The desire to keep hold of his newly acquired wealth became too much for Kevin and despite being under the close eye of Five-O, cracked when he discovered a stranger, who unbeknown to Kevin was an undercover detective in his garden, a row ensued and the officer in question was stabbed to death with a pair of shears. Nott was subsequently arrested for murder but as much as the prosecutor tried to paint old Kevin in a bad and dangerous light the jury believed the defence case that he acted in self-defence and he was acquitted by a majority decision.

Kevin should have cottoned on that that was the luckiest escape he would ever face and got out of the country, but In nineteen eighty six, Nott was back in court to endure a lengthy eleven-week trial, with his co-defendant Thomas Eves (Andy's Uncle) after eleven bars of un-tampered gold were discovered in his home. It was this second arrest that eventually led to his conviction of conspiracy to handle the Bronx Securitas gold, as well as VAT evasion charges. He was fined a total of seven hundred thousand pounds and given fourteen years in prison. Nott left the jury with the final words: "I hope you all die of cancer".

Although the gold that Nott had hidden was eventually recovered, the Bronx Securitas case was never officially closed because there was still three tonnes of gold that could not be accounted for and its whereabouts was still a mystery to those who are not in the know. The police always figured that villains always bragged to other villains about the jobs they pulled and they were going on this theory when forever pulling in members of the Eves gang. Leads have to come from somewhere, it was just unfortunate for them that the one person who could have supplied all the answers they wanted, with regards to the missing gold, was currently on the run, and besides he was too hard a nut to crack.

Chapter Fourteen

Billy had been back in the country from his little vacation for a couple of weeks now and had allowed his time to be taken up by a lovesick girlfriend, birthday celebrations and kidnapping charges. So he hoped Monty would understand why there was a delay in getting back to him and hoped that he could still be of some help.

Billy came from a large family, branches of the family tree stretched far and wide and each and every one was covered in leaves but out of all the leaves on all the branches, the one leaf that stood out the most, was Monty. His Dad, Mark, was a big Montgomery Clift fan and it was at the screening of the nineteen sixty-one classic 'The Misfits' at the Odeon that he met a pretty young girl by the name of Anne. It was a year later while sitting in the back row of the local picture house whilst supposedly watching 'Freud' that Mark asked Anne for her hand in marriage. In sixty-six, Anne broke the news to Mark that she was pregnant while they were enjoying Montgomery Clift's last ever movie, 'The Defector'. Their first-born was named Russell, after Jane Russell, the connection related more to the evening in which he was conceived than when the news was broken but it was the birth of their second child, that the infant was aptly named Montgomery.

After exhausting every possible apology that Billy could give over the phone, Monty finally agreed to forgive him for the delay in returning his call and promptly told Billy what the story was concerning the favour that was needed.

A hot and trendy nightspot called the 'Riverside Club' was catching the attention of all the brand label wearers and recreational users and with any decent nightclub comes the requirement of decent doormen. This particular team had a known face amongst them, who was simply known as B and it was well documented that he had highly educated hands and on occasion, feet. B had a reputation that meant those in the know would tip their heads in acknowledgement to show a little respect, he could have it with the best of them and he knew it, so an air of arrogance surrounded him and to be honest, rightly so. The problem with arrogance is it can take a person in one of two directions; it can make you likable because of the aura of confidence that surrounds you, making you a presence that people are drawn to or it can make you a bigheaded bully. B unfortunately was the latter and that is what contributed to the incident that happened a few weeks previous.

Young Nathan was your typical flash Harry, eighteen, designer clothes and full of charm. He was always decked out in the finest clobber that was easily paid for by his fathers' wealth. Nathan's Dad was a promoter in the music industry who did a lot of work with Harvey Goldberg the music manager of some of the biggest acts worldwide, so Nathan had grown up never knowing tough times and was always popular thanks to the free concert tickets and backstage passes that he could obtain. His ebony skin glistened with a natural, youthful glow and emphasised his brilliant white smile as he applied his smooth one-liners on the impressionable ladies. Nathan must of weighed in at a buck fifty soaking wet if he was lucky and on a physical level he was no threat to any male or female over the age of twelve. That fact was even more evident when pitted against B who was sent into the dance area to eject Nathan and his group of followers. Nathan and the numerous of hangers on that orbited him like the gas rings of Saturn, were making a dent in the bar. Showing their ignorance by paying forty-five pounds for a bottle of bubbly that was, in fact, cheap pomaigne. When the loudness and constant swaggering gave the DJ reason enough to have the door crew escort this bunch of merry people out the door for the evening.

On response to the DJ's request, B went running into help deal with the problem, Nathan was in a little world of his own, bemused by what was taking place around him, arms out stretched with a bottle in one hand and a champagne flute in the other. B went steaming in and made a beeline for Nathan, dropping a right into his gut. Nathan doubled over and in between trying to regain a normal breathing pattern told B 'You won'. Nathan was beaten, he knew it, anyone else looking in knew it, even the blind man in Mexico knew it, but B thought Nathan still posed a threat and digged him a couple of times in the face for good measure. Once outside, Nathan just looked B in the eye, nodded a knowing nod and walked off without giving any backchat. Nathan knew that something had to be done to balance the scales of justice but was realistic enough to know that it was something he could not do without help from some serious muscle, so who better to call upon then his old school pal, Monty.

Monty was happy to show up and challenge B for his title, what better way of making a name for yourself than taking on the main man of the area but he knew that B didn't work alone and needed someone to watch his back while he called him out. This was the favour he needed from Billy and anyone else he could bring with him, a favour that Billy was more than willing to help out with.

The five-car convoy pulled into the car park of the Riverside Club eleven thirty on a Friday night. This was the perfect time to strike because the crowds were already inside, the doors were closed to any more punters and it was still early enough that crowds of people would not be leaving. B was holding court on the door with his colleagues when

Nathan approached the entrance to call him out.

"Oi! No neck, you remember me?" Nathan stood there waiting for an answer while a couple of his braver friends came up either side of him, the main reason for this was so Monty could approach the door undetected.

"Yeah I 'member ya, what's up, you and your little pals up for a little payback?" B threw in a little chuckle to prove that he thought that their attempt at revenge was nothing short of laughable. However the thing with laughter is it can also mask the fact that fear may be lingering in the system. B had been threatened with the dreaded "I'll be back for you!" on many occasions but this was the first person to actually ever return. Nathan cracked a smile before answering.

"Nah, I wouldn't stand a chance against ya, but he would..." and with that Nathan and his comrades parted like the red sea to reveal this fair haired pretty boy who weighed in at more stoneage than his actual years. Monty's large, bulging biceps stood out from his purposely bought T-shirt that was one size too small. B's jawed dropped so low that it picked up chewing gum from the pavement. The other doormen stood straight and got themselves ready to back their team mate up. That was when Billy, Colin, Jason and young Vaughan showed themselves to the boys in the tuxedos.

"This can either stay a one on one or it can get real messy". Billy made sure to have a look on his face that doubled as an explanation mark to his warning; Monty added his bit just to show this was an even playing field.

"What'dja say champ, willing to step out beyond the velvet ropes for a straightener?" B was in a tricky situation, if he backed down in front of his team mates and the now gathering onlookers he would lose the respect that he had spent years acquiring. If he stepped up but lost to his challenger, then it would be known that he was only hard until harder came along or he could accept and win and hold on to his title. Fear was mixing with adrenaline, his legs shook a little, he stepped side to side to hide it, and just like that decided to go for it, unhooking the rope divider and charged towards Monty. Monty stood fast, waiting for the idiot hard man to reach the mental marker he had set up that told him that was striking distance, then 'bang' a thunderous over hand right, dead centre to B's face putting him on his arse. Monty then followed up with two sharp kicks to his head to seal the deal.

Nathan was ecstatic with the result and tried to lavish a monetary gratuity on all the hired help but Billy, knowing what his Dad did for a living, simply said.

"Keep your money, I'd rather you owe me a favour". With Vaughan outing his creative side by playing rhythm guitar and being the lead singer in a band, being owed a favour by the son of a music promoter seemed like a nice thing to have in the bag. Nathan smiled that big smile of his and replied.

"No worries."

Monty had become the man of the moment and as B lay out cold on the ground, all those that he had bullied before stepped over his deflated ego with a 'good riddance' look on their faces. It was obvious that a change of personnel was needed on the door of the Riverside Club and so Monty was offered to fill the vacant position that B would be creating as soon as he came back from la la land. Monty agreed and the cheers went up from the masses and as the sound echoed around the car park it become obvious to all that the king is dead, long live the king!

The following months seemed very quiet in comparison to those that had just gone by, Billy was making an extra effort to stay in contact with Jason and Colin who both didn't hesitate to help out that night even though Billy hadn't been hanging around with the old crowd any more. The flames of some friendships just need to be fanned from time to time rather than constantly stoked. Vaughan's three man band, Portent, was starting to play a few venues other than Jonas, the bass guitarist's garage. Nothing special mainly warm up play at the local watering holes but it allowed them to find their stage feet and their own sound was being developed. Gary finally gave up his key to Billy's flat; Gary was still doing the business with the recreational side of drugs. He was building up quite the little empire with Lee and Gus; it was almost like they had found their calling in life. Although they still came off as being children playing an adults game, with the money coming in and the contacts made, a good businessman wouldn't take the wild approach that they were still doing. A nasty end was going to befall one of them if they kept it up, but like most kids in a grown up world they knew everything and no one else could understand them. A strong lesson was going to be learnt somewhere down the line but for now they were still doing things their way and that was that. The one that was having second thoughts about choices made was Mikey. The business on the beach was playing on his mind and the constant questioning about Andy's whereabouts was becoming tiring. Mikey needed a change of scenery and the need to re-bond with his brother was the perfect excuse to kill two birds with one stone. It wasn't going to be long before the newly returned door key was going to be handed back out very soon.

Nikki had been yammering on to Billy about the new girl, Kelly, which had started working with her at her place of work, Décor, the laminate wholesalers for weeks now. She went on non-stop about her, how they spent all their lunch times together, telling anecdotes that held no interest to anyone else other than to the two ladies it referred to and the plans they made for the pair of them, Kelly's fiancé and Billy to all go out somewhere, on a double date. Billy was always trying to put it off; double dating sounded like such a couple's thing to do besides he was always weary about meeting new people since settling down. You did not need to be Freud to know that Billy had issues with trust, he knew a thousand people, but Billy only have a handful of real friends.

They were all the friends he felt he needed, although he hadn't kept the contact with them all like the old days, they were still his friends, his back up, his family. They had all gone their separate ways in one form or another but whenever they organised their little reunions, it always felt the same. It always felt like they had only seen each other the day before. Even today, Billy can come across as being ignorant towards people, he does not mean anything nasty by it. Billy can just find it hard to talk to some people despite being the loud, outgoing guy that he is.

Billy also did not trust or like people coming into his home and looking at the things that crime had provided for, always asking questions about what he did for a living and going on about what his childhood was like. If you never had to fight everyday to survive or get what you wanted out of life then you would not understand the logic behind it, you would just be seen as a thug or something, being looked down at by those who felt the need to be superior. Although these people would go on thinking that their life was better than your life. When their time came to say goodbye to the world and all those close to them, who would be laying there with limited memories and a heart full of regret for wasting so much of their life. In addition, who would be telling the endless stories about the little adventures that they had shared or learnt from; the superior feeling, honest law-abiding citizens or the poor, council estate villains who stole every possible moment and took every risk that came their way? You can make your own decision on that one.

It was Décor's Christmas do and Nikki begged Billy to come along and be by her side, because that's what couples are supposed to do, it was also the last time she was going to take 'no' as an answer to mingle with Kelly and her fella. They had to meet in the "Ferries Arms" along Ferry Lane, Walthamstow. The first person Nikki introduced Billy to, was her new best friend and work colleague, Kelly, whose face couldn't hide the look of both surprise and disgust when she looked up to greet Nikki and her faceless other half. It is a small world after all. Then Kelly's fiancé came over from the bar where he had just got in a round of drinks, to introduce himself. Not that there was much need, Billy already knew him, after all he was his older brother Stuart. Kelly was gutted, because now wherever she and Nikki went out somewhere, the two united brothers would be going as well and Billy, with his sadistic sense of humour just could not resist being extra annoying towards Kelly whenever he got the opening.

Stuart was sporting long, hippified hair, a 'peace' style philosophy and an instinctive need to never go twenty minutes without rolling up a spliff. He had lost a lot of his size and was wearing Lennon style bins, he looked different, acted different but he was still Billy's older, wiser brother and they still got on the same.

The pair of them had not really talked since that Christmas party back in eighty-seven; Billy always felt that some wounds take a while to heal. That is why Nikki did not realise who Stuart was whenever Kelly spoke about him. Nikki had met Vaughan and Gary, heard them all bad mouth their youngest brother, Craig, but had never met Stuart or Mikey. Mikey was living his life south of the water and was out of view from all and Billy's relationship with Stuart had never been the same since he hit him when Stuart choose Kelly over his brothers. Billy always felt like such a wanker over that incident, he had replayed it in his head a million times over. He always felt that Stuart deserved better from him; he deserved better from life as a reward for all the sacrifices he had made for the family.

When Stuart's biological Mother lost her battle against cancer, he was only eight. He was old enough to know what was going on but still young enough to feel the pain and sorrow of loss, he knew she had gone to Heaven and he knew he had to be strong. Gary was but a mere baby and Mikey was just starting school, his need for an older brother was paramount. When their Dad met Billy's Mum, some of the pressure was taken from Stuart and deep down it was always thought that he might have resented that. Any one, who has had to encounter an eager stepparent, will tell you how over the top they act just to get you to accept them. It took years for things to start working out within the Michaels new family unit, but then with the birth of Craig, it all went back to square one. Stuart had just entered his teen years and was angry not just at his family but at the world as well. All eight of them were all crammed into that little two bedroom flat, sixteen stories up in the sky and then, even after they were moved to the newly built home in Hazel Way, they were all still crammed in their three-bedroom house. Thank god that there were no sisters in the fold otherwise, someone may have ended up sleeping in the shed. No privacy, no money, no life, and that is what was on offer to all of the siblings and Stuart knew it. Therefore, to make sure the rest of his kin never had to feel that way; he dropped out of school and got a full time job. This was to start bringing into the house an extra wage, to help pay for the things that the Michaels parents were not in a position to buy. He gave up his childhood and went straight to being a man, forsaking his freedom and opportunities to go out into the world on his own. He was like a second father to his younger brothers and the only thanks he got was ridicule. As the years rolled on, Stuart's contributions to the household were priceless and it wasn't until the brothers were all a lot older and making their own way that they truly realised just how much Stuart had given up to help in raising them. Billy knew he would never be able to turn back time and give thanks and recognition to Stuart when he needed it the most. Nor could he take back the incident that lead to their falling out. Billy knew to seize this opportunity to re–bond with him now and thank him for everything he had done and hoped Stuart knew he was sincere.

There is something about a brother's bond that you just

cannot break, you can bend it as much as you like, but it cannot be broken. The two of them would be off in their own little world, pissing off Kelly and Nikki because of the way they were acting so immature whenever they got together. The two brothers would find this even more rewarding when Vaughan used to join in the mix and the three of them would all just act like a bunch a gross, embarrassing pigs. However, women in general are devious bitches and it was not long before Nikki and Kelly had their revenge on Billy and Stuart because once Kelly started talking about marriage and kids; Nikki's topic of conversation was not far behind. 'Do I really need to be walking down the aisle?' Thought Billy, 'That was the beginning of the end, wasn't it?'

Before even entertaining the thought of tying the knot, Billy thought it would be a good idea to live with Nikki first. The recession was in full swing and house prices were at an all time low. It made sense to buy their own place instead of living in the flat, plus Nikki didn't like the idea of people forever knocking at the door at all hours. So the pair of them started house hunting for their dream hideaway, their own little place of residence where they would raise little Billy junior, and be happy for the rest of their natural lives. Nikki's strict, Greek Cypriot father on the other hand wasn't having any of it, he hated the fact that a man was touching his daughter even though the pair denied actually having a physical relationship, what burned him even more was the fact that Billy was English and not someone from their home town of Limassol. In his opinion, Billy should first change his religious beliefs, and then the couple should get married, and then live together as Man and Wife, and then and only then should sex come into the equation. This was his view on the whole matter, Billy did not agree. The two men rowed for an eternity, Nikki's Dad saw Billy as the young lion who had come to take claim on what was his and Billy just wanted to shack up with his daughter. After a couple of months of tearful nights, family pressure and a whole load of

201

compromise, the bull headed old lion finally agreed to allow Nikki to move in with Billy as long as they got engaged, and were blessed by a Greek priest. Nikki was well up for that, a permanent smile seemed to be instantly transplanted on to her face, once again Billy did not agree.

What had the world come to, when two people can not decide how to go about their lives? Religion and politics have never had a place at Billy's table; everyone was allowed to have their points of view and should live their own life to those values. Nevertheless, in this day and age, waves of immigrants, with their own brand of what is right and wrong set sail to the shores of the great English empire. Just so they can experience freedom and choice that these shores hold. Yet when they get here, they suddenly buy into the things they wanted to get away from ten fold. In this case, it was a man who left behind his life and family in Cyprus so his daughters could grow up with wealth and opportunity but held fast his belief that he should dictate how they lived their lives. Talk about wanting your wedding cake and eating it.

It was at this point that out of the blue Mikey turned up on Billy's doorstep wanting a place to crash for a couple of weeks. It felt good to return to his East London surroundings after spending so many years south of the water. He needed to recharge his batteries and see some of the old faces; he also needed a break from all the crap that was going down in his neck of the woods and the increase in questions as to whether or not he had a brother called Gary. It seemed that Gary had been using Mikey's name to open a few doors that would normally be closed to him. Mikey would not have minded so much if he knew in advance but it was turning out that Gary was getting off from getting a few beatings for his attitude because of who he was related to. Mikey put the word out that if Gary showed up anywhere and acted in a way that a beating was called for then give him the beating, no one would face any form of retribution from Mikey or any of his associates. It was on this piece of news that certain individuals were chomping at the bit to run into Gary again. After all pay back is a bitch.

With the return of Mikey to the area and Billy's new found relationship with Stuart, it seemed to call for one of their old fashioned, tried and tested parties. The whole family would get involved and have a true to form East End knees up. It was on this thought that Nikki said that her parents would be happy to hold the get together at their house because it would give them a chance to meet Billy's family and friends, seeing as it was evident that his daughter could one day have children with this man. Hey, if someone else wants the aggravation of having his or her house smashed up, then it was no skin off Billy's nose, plus there was the added bonus of not having to face clean-up duty the next morning. A date was set for the inter-cultural gathering and the days, hours, minutes were counted down with hesitant trepidation. The first major meeting of the clans, what could possibly go wrong?

The onslaught of cars that drove from Chingford, Walthamstow and Enfield towards Leyton was enough to warrant the three minute warning to all those in an immediate vicinity that war was about to be declared on the Greek Cypriots that lived in the area. It was meant to be a friendly gathering of two potential families to put faces to names and to start the tradition of blowing out the other family when invited to nights out in each other's social circles. Because it was a family orientated thing, the evening was to start off fairly early as compared to the late starting shindigs the Michaels were used to. It was a little after seven when every available car parking place within a five minute walk from Belvedere Road was being taken up by either one or the other members of the joining bloodlines.

Upon entering the house, pleasantries were exchanged and the sight of a fairly decent spread was laid out for all to see. A make shift bar had been set up and it was fully stocked with kegs on tap and an assortment of spirits and soft drink mixers. With all this in plain view, early start or not, it had the makings of a good time that was of course until Nikki's Mum asked if anyone wanted tea or coffee to drink while the introductions were still being made. From the outside looking in, that may not have seemed just a weird thing to offer as it was seven thirty and the tone was meant to be civilised. But then also from the outside looking in most people would have thought it very hypocritical that Nikki's Mum was in fact English, an attractive, in her younger days kind of way, blonde haired looker, she looked like Jilly Johnson's not quiet page three material sister. Not bad for a guy who seem to despise Billy for being of the same nationality. However the real reason behind the soft beverages, was that it was deemed impolite to drink alcohol before the priest had entered the room...the priest???

The engagement event was planned, discussed and arranged without Billy's side of the family or himself being involved. This wasn't a gathering of families so introductions could be made, this was an engagement party that was going to be blessed by a Greek priest. It was the set up of all set up's and one could not help but wonder when Jeremy Beadle was going to jump out and tell Billy that he had been framed. Deep down Billy did not care, he was not a churchgoer, this was not going to affect him in anyway, and it was a means to an end. It was just a few hours out of his life; it would get Nikki's parents off his back and Nikki under his roof. Besides, if it were not for the fact it was Billy on the receiving end of the deception he would have found it quite clever and as entertaining as everyone else in the room seemed to be finding it.

It all became so obvious now why they were eager to hold the event in their house, no one could eat or drink before the priest turned up and when he did, he was already a little wasted. Billy wished he were in the same condition. Yet another sign of hypocrisy, you can not eat or drink alcohol in fear of upsetting the priest but he can turn up smelling like a meth' factory, with crumbs in his ZZ top beard. Don't do as I do but do as I say, when Billy had been told that by Freddie and Harry while he was growing up, their advice seemed to have a positive feel about it. They were telling him for a reason but this was just the typical double standard play that Billy had become so accustomed to since dealing with this family of southern Greeks.

Billy and Nikki had to go through with a ceremony of swapping rings and repeating religious phrases in Greek. At least he knew why she wanted to know his ring size. Considering how this night was turning out Billy thought he was now being tricked into marrying Nikki and no one had bothered to tell him. That is your conversion, your engagement and wedding all in one convenient evening, thanks for coming see you when I have to read you your last rights and goodnight.

That was how the night went on, it was a real Greek affair and not a cockle or jellied eel in sight. Billy couldn't wait for it to end, there was nothing worse than being in a room full of people that know that you are a recovering alcoholic and love you too much to turn a blind eye for you to have a few shorts to celebrate. Although it wasn't the desire to celebrate that was feeding Billy's craving for a drink, but the whole sick to his stomach, what have I just done type of desire. He couldn't remember when he had ever had the wind taken out of his sails so easily before, he might as well chop his cock off there and then, hang up his boyhood memories next to the mantel piece, curl up and die. At least it gave Mikey a chance to finally meet Nikki, after Billy introduced the pair; Mikey pulled him to one side and said "I don't like her" and that was that.

After weeks of browsing the housing market, Billy finally put a deposit on a three bedroom terraced house just off Billet road, Walthamstow. It was meant to be Nikki and Billy's dream home and the start of their lives together. The first few months were great, when the newly shacked up love birds were not at work or out with Stuart and Kelly, they were in bed having sex like rabbits. This is what Billy's idea of living with someone was all about, but as the months went on the sex slowly faded out and the arguments set in. At first, it was just the little things like the toilet seat being left up or the lid on the toothpaste was being left off, but as the months turned into years, the reasons got worse.

Even then with all his sexual experience Billy could still be a little naïve where women were concerned. As soon as they moved in together and Nikki was no longer under the watchful eyes of her folks, she just changed and not for the better, it was all down hill from there. Billy was big enough to put his hands up and say it was not all Nikki but the trouble with going downhill is that it is hard to stop and change direction. You just usually wait until you hit the bottom and start again.

Chapter Fifteen

The first half of nineteen ninety was a wash with fuelled emotions about the recession and the newly introduced scheme to replace the council rates charge, the Poll Tax, yet another Thatcher idea. Billy could never understand the logic behind the Poll Tax; it was based on how many people lived in your house and worked out a lot more than the cost of what the rates were although the government service levels remained the same, at a piss poor average. Anyone who thought the Thatcher era was a breath of fresh air from a political point of view was obviously not from the working class. Yes she made it possible for people to buy their council properties but then she also turned round and charged them extra for the privilege. The gripe here was the actual Poll Tax concept and the enforcement of payment and not Thatcher's mark on the country.

The cost of the Poll Tax for the average family was around five hundred pounds a year, which you had to pay monthly. If you did not pay it you faced a court appearance and the prospect of imprisonment for a sentence of up to a year. So already, the government had spent around two hundred pounds, on court procedures, admin staff and stationary to get back five hundred. If you then went to prison for a year, this would push the cost of getting your payment to around nine thousand pounds of the taxpayer's money. Once you came out of prison, your job prospects were non-existent and you had to sign on the dole. Not only did the government then pay you a fortnightly wage but they also paid your rent and your Poll Tax, as well as your previous outstanding payments. The government then wondered why there was a huge deficit in the country's financial resources and a recession happening. To combat this bit of thinking, they then raised the Poll Tax to cover the loss of income from all the non-payers the financial year before, while still chasing up payment from all those same said non-payers. When they finally got a previous non-payer to settle their account, was there a refund to all those that paid extra to cover it? Hell no. Therefore, what followed were the infamous Poll Tax riots.

The Poll Tax demonstrations took place in literally every council borough throughout the country but none was more news worthy than the one that turned into a riot, which took place in Whitechapel in March of that year. There was violence, fires and carnage it was almost like another version of the Broadwater farm incident, and once again the establishment caused it all. Although where the protestors in Brixton were concerned, when the riots broke out there, just the revenue lost to looters alone, equalled what was owed in that entire borough. Well that is how Billy saw the situation, if the common person was causing a scene then ask the common person why and not those who are not directly affected. That was one of Billy's opinions and until they find a way to outlaw free speech, he will keep having them.

While all the craziness throughout the country was being voiced by all those willing to stand up and fight the power. The inevitable changing of the calendar months continued and the month of April was upon the world and it was this particular month that saw Billy's baby brother Vaughan turn eighteen.

Like most people, the tradition of reaching adult hood, is met with yet another excuse to get totally out of ones head and abuse every law that was once illegal to them. Although

Billy had never met a person who hadn't at least tried alcohol before turning the legal age to buy it, it was always seen that the very first drink that goes past your lips on this day would stick with you always. Billy wanted to be part of that memory that would always sit with Vaughan until the day he died so he organised a little drink up. They all met up in the social club of Siddelely Hawks, Vaughan accompanied Billy to the bar where Billy bought him a pint of beer and a JD chaser, Billy told him that the world was full of opportunities and possibilities and that he was proud to call him his brother, his blood, his friend. Once the touchy feely moment was over and Vaughan had downed his first legal pint and chaser, they rejoined the other revellers who were more than happy to help Vaughan celebrate this day of days. To help set the tone of the evening and hopefully the rest of Vaughan's life, a little something had been arranged by his work colleagues and as if on cue, much to the surprise of Vaughan and to the delight of everyone else in the bar, a strip-a-gram turned up to do her thing.

She was the embodiment of heavenliness, for she was dressed as a nun and she was rubbing the wrath of the lord in Vaughan's very embarrassed face. She spanked him, whipped him and had him standing in just his boxers. Everyone in the social club thought it was a great laugh but it affected Vaughan in a way that no one was expecting, he was so set back by it, he became withdrawn and a reclusive for almost a year and his song writing took on a complete new turn. He would go on to be the complete opposite to what he had been all his life up until that point. It didn't seem that long ago that he was a pimple faced kid getting sucked off by some old slag in a nightclub or joining his brother on a tear up with scum that deserved a beating. Why did this incident affect him mentally? Billy could only feel that it was because it was in front of people that were not family. Vaughan had been put on the spot and Billy almost felt a little bit guilty for putting him in that position. Then he thought otherwise and just continued to tease him along with the others about it for the next few months. After all that's what being a big brother is all about.

The disaster of April's birthday bash had passed and May was now upon the land, spring was in the air. With the coming of a new season came the need to set up another surprise to humiliate someone in the same vein that Vaughan had been. Billy was wondering who had been getting a free ride lately someone who deserved to be set up, and once again, it was at the expense of Alan. He had since been dumped by Tracey for reasons unknown and attached himself to the first shoulder that came along that was tear proof. He was now seeing a red headed bird, by the name of Lisa. Billy had kept in touch with the Essex girls from his holiday to Lloret De Mar. Billy had got them all to finally forgive him for the violent outrage during their last reunion, and they were happy to arrange to meet up with Billy and the brood for an evening out in good old Southend. Alan had taken a real shine to Sonja at the reunion and Billy told Alan that she was interested in him. Billy had been jeering him up all week and by the time the weekend had come around Alan was like a dog on heat.

The motley crew drove down as a big group taking it in turns to speed past, mooning and shouting obscenities at the other cars in their convey just to make the journey a bit more memorable. They all pulled into the car park outside 'Totties', the land mark nightclub in the town and met up with the girls in a pub called 'Dukes' that resided near 'Waves' that a year previous had seen the unmistakable 'Virg' strut his pissed damp trousers on the dance floor. They spent a couple of hours chatting and catching up; all the while Billy was fanning the fire that was burning inside Alan. He was wrestling with his desire to have Sonja and the need to stay faithful to Lisa. While Alan was going through his dilemma Billy had pulled Sonja to one side and asked her for a favour, he got her to agree to French kiss Alan on his signal, no hesitations just plant a wet one on him when she got the nod. Billy then went up to Alan and told him that Sonja had been asking about him, whether he was single etc because she was really up for something from him, Alan was on the verge of exploding.

After a few drinks in the belly the party moved from the beer garden of 'Dukes', and down to the sea front for a go on the arcade machines, to pass the time before hitting a club and have a laugh. The gang were getting all set into the slot machines and making use of the pool tables on offer. Billy made the announcement that he needed to go for a Jimmy to act as an excuse to leave the scene for a brief time without anyone thinking anything strange and proceeded to leg it up to the car park to rendezvous with some late arriving guests. The set up was taking shape.

Billy hurriedly returned to the slot jockeys, everything was in place, Billy gave Sonja the nod, and without missing a beat she grabbed Alan and planted one on his lips. Now even Billy was surprised by Alan's following reaction he thought he was gonna jump back in shock but he didn't, in fact Alan grabbed Sonja and pulled her closer, going full steam, even getting a bulge happening in his trousers. It was when Casanova opened his eyes during mid kiss, just to give that 'who's the man' look to all the on-lookers, that he saw the group of late arrivals, that Billy had rushed off to meet, one of which was Alan's new girlfriend, Lisa. She had travelled down with Nikki and a few others, Lisa just stood there; staring straight at him and it seemed to take a lifetime before he put all the pieces of the puzzle together. When it finally registered that his girlfriend was watching him snog this other girl, he turned pale. He put Sonja down and stormed out, yelling "Fucking Bastards!" Billy was on the floor, his sides splitting and tear's streaming from his eyes. Billy loved it when a plan came together.

Alan spent the rest of the evening apologising to Lisa, who milked it to death because she was in on it from the start.

Although Billy thought the reality of it was not as much fun for her as the idea of it was. Still you reap what you sow.

Work had become a drag for all and sundry, in the summer month of July, a recreation of the club eighteen to thirties holiday Michael and Billy went on was being attempted by Vaughan. If any one needed to get a break and have some fun, it was him. He was trying to reclaim his dignity after that Nun incident and a little of his own self so he organised the trip for his generation of cronies that were now working in the coil winding department. The only problem was the firm had a policy that no more than two operatives from each division could have annual leave at the same time and of course, they all wanted to go. The plan seemed simple, they would combine sick leave with annual leave and jetted off on holiday, youngsters, all hormones and no brains. This left the shop floor devoid of dog's bodies and a few Engineers, the unsettling silence was enough to worry the chain of command and the suits upstairs required answers as to why production had dipped. So without any surprise from all those that remained behind, Billy was pulled in and questioned as to what was going on.

Billy was labelled the ringleader by the management of Siddelely Hawks and they found it hard to believe that anything would go down on the shop floor that he did not know about. Billy was flattered but he explained to them, that if something untoward was going on, being the so-called ringleader wouldn't he have been on the missing list as well? Billy told them they should just chalk it up to coincidence and bear it out, he was sure those who were out on sick leave could walk back through the door at any time. What else could he have said?

Meanwhile back at the bat cave, leaving a recluse to plan a wild holiday was yet another mistake made by these young holidaymakers. Instead of booking a fun filled vacation to Majorca, Vaughan had booked a villa in Minorca. One is for the young at heart who set the pace the other is for those that need pace makers. The only thing wild about Minorca was the local ex-pat bingo hall. Although god bless them they tried to make it worth while by still going out getting drunk but seeing as there were no other youngsters they only had themselves for company. If it wasn't for the fact that there was a beer swigging, football loving female, Angie, amongst the numbers you would actually stop and think that this was a sausage-fest of the gayest order. Billy would have had to laugh at the notion that his baby brother who had busted heads side by side with him on so many occasions would be a driver of the old pink Cadillac cruising up the Bourneville Boulevard. Although they tried to make the best of it, the weeks dragged and they could not wait to get back home to England.

As stated before, Billy worked with three women at Siddelely Hawks that he never slept with; Angie was the second one out of the trio. She was a right geezer bird who loved football and drank pints. She was like the annoying little sister you never wanted. All the male populated Engineers purposely gave her all the dirty jobs around the shop floor. Billy couldn't remember a day going by where he didn't have her covered in some form of lubricant but the memory that sticks the most is when she joined the main gang on a pub crawl and after leaving their third bar to make their way to the Rose and Crown. Angie must have been hit by the fresh Walthamstow air because she went totally para' when a cop car drove past. She was convinced that she was going to get arrested for being drunk whilst walking...pretty face but absolutely no street smarts. She started dating another coil winder's mate called Chris and the last thing Billy could remember was the two lovebirds getting engaged. However, that was some time ago and young love does fade, so who knows what she is up to these days.

Back at work, it was becoming ever so obvious that no one was returning from sick leave, when asked for info everyone just shrugged their shoulders with a 'what ya gonna do, they're kids' attitude. However, there is always a job's worth that just has to chocolate nose to attain those brownie points. In this case, his name was Mark Brock and he was pure slime. He forever tried to include himself in the activities of the others but to no avail. The guy just had narc tattooed to his forehead. Billy even heard that he tried to join the police force when he left Siddelely Hawks, but he was even too slimy for them. Anyhow, he blabbed it loud and proud on how the others were using their time off through either annual or sick leave, which in all honesty confirmed what the management could not prove. The fact they all came back on the same day sporting suntans did not help their stories, no matter how many Doctor's notes they brought in.

To set an example, the management decided to fire Vaughan, who had the least plausible excuse and because he was even more depressed with his choice of holiday destination, he did not even make an effort to blag it. They then suspended Dopey Dave (Another coil winders mate) and reprimanded the others. This outcome did not bow well for Mark the grass, who was sent to Coventry by the whole shop floor. No one spoke to him, even those who he called for to help him with what they were being paid to do. Billy told him to his face that he was going to get hurt one way or another. To which he then grassed that little bit of information to management as well. This guy just didn't learn.

Outside, Vaughan was waiting with a chunky wooden mallet in his hand. He had marched straight out of the manager's office after being fired and straight into the Homebase DIY store that was next door. He bought the first hammer shaped object he could find and was planning on knocking dents in Mark's head and body. Billy could not say if there would have been anyone who would have tried to stop him.

Word got back to the shop floor and the charge-hand decided it might be safer if Mark hung around for a few extra hours, just until it was clear for him to leave unharmed and then advised him that they could get the police involved but saw that as a last resort considering whose brother he was. Billy was then called upon, once again, by management to resolve the issue. Billy told them they should be more careful not to employ people like Mark again, as it made the rest of the department uneasy and it effected the high level of team work they had going. Billy thought that must have been finally sinking in, that like most managers and directors, their importance and levels of power only relate to the confounds of work and not outside its walls. Billy, was a powerful man both inside and outside of work, he was capable of earning respect whereas they had to demand it. In the grand scheme of things, they were nothing but hollow little men who had to hide behind their titles and positions to feel good about themselves, Billy, on the other hand, was not that insecure.

He went out and calmed Vaughan down, telling him to leave it for today and they would give Mr Mark Brock his comeuppance another time. Vaughan was ranting on about doing time for that grass and was determined to have his pound of flesh. Billy told him that if he was hell bent on having his revenge today than he would have to put him on his arse and keep him there until his baby brother saw sense. Billy could see another Stuart incident taking place, but Vaughan saw Billy was serious, took a few deep breaths and agreed to go home and leave it for another day.

Billy went back in to tell management that the coast was clear and it was safe for Mark to go home. Mark held out his hand and went to thank Billy for resolving the issue with no violence, but in front of all the managers, Billy told him to "shove his hand up his Harris and fuck off!" He was a grass and an arse lick and he didn't do it for him, he did it for his brother, because if Vaughan had hit him especially with his mallet, Mark was the kind of lowlife that would have pressed charges and then that's a whole different problem.

Vaughan didn't seem to wait to long to inflict some revenge, the next day, it was reported over the tannoy that a car had been vandalised in the car park. It was Mark's, the tyres had been slashed, all of its windows were smashed in, and there were dents all over the bodywork, the words "Fucking Grass" were spray painted along both sides of the motor. The police were called but they could not do anything, as there were no witnesses, even though it was on company property and the security post was but a stones throw away.

This time Billy was called into the directors' office. There were six of them all seated around this long mahogany table, Billy was asked what it was going to take to end this once and for all. He told them that Mark should go and Vaughan should be allowed back. For everyday that the situation was left how it was, the consequences would only escalate, until it reached a point where someone would get hurt. Billy's point had been made; Mark was going to be asked to leave Siddelely Hawks, although the reinstatement of Vaughan was not going to happen. Order was expected to be resumed with no more incidents like this one to occur again. Billy told them he could not make any promises, and it was left as that.

Before leaving the Directors office Billy was told something that would go on to stick with him for many years to come. The director said that Billy was a mans man with a good head on his shoulders, he had the world in his hands and could go on to do great things but with the compliments came the wisdom:

'It takes but five minutes to gain a bad reputation but it could take a life time to earn a good one'.

Mark was gone by the end of the week, management felt his presence was demoralising the rest of the workers and was therefore deemed detrimental to production. No one was sad to see him go. With Vaughan gone and the open position caused by the departure of Mark, it was time for a reshuffle. They made Alan up to a trainee Engineer and this opened up two dog's body positions. One was filled by a constant bullshitting streak of piss called Stevie Perks and Darren Cole filled the other. He was a real short arse and cheeky because of it and just like most short people, he felt he had something to prove. In fact, give him a busted nose and he could have been Billy's kid brother Gary. Just like Billy, Darren had a liking for gangster movies; "Goodfellas" being at the top of his list and all his life all he ever wanted to be was a gangster. Cue the song, "Rags to Riches".

Darren was a welcome addition to the team and he enjoyed the way Billy and the others had the run of the place, he called them the Siddelely Hawks Mafia. Darren wanted to become Billy's enforcer, collecting the debts that were outstanding. Billy had been running a little loan shark operation throughout the company charging such an exuberant interest rate that it took three times as long to pay back the money. Billy thought Darren was like a pit bull, so he let him run with it, every Friday Darren would do the rounds, seeing who needed to be seen. In those days, people were still paid cash at the end of the week, so there were no excuses and if there were it just meant interest would be added and more money would be coming back to the fold. Darren felt like a wise guy and always wanted to do more, he reminded Billy of himself when he was running with his brothers. Darren's enthusiasm was also re-lighting the passion for Billy to get back into some dodgy business and earn some real coinage. The seed was being sown.

This would also come as good news to his brother Mikey; who had been flitting back and forth to South London, doing a few odd jobs for the Eves family and then disappearing again for a week or two back in Walthamstow while the heat died down. He had taken over the tenancy on Billy's old flat and was trying to get back into his brother's life. Mikey was forever airing his dislike for Nikki and as Billy's relationship dissolved with her, he was more and more agreeing with his brother, although he didn't know why Mikey had such a strong opinion about her. With the way things were going in his world, the idea of having his brother close was a haven, Mikey knew some good money could be made but he needed people he could trust to watch his back, Billy was at the top of that list.

By the time the year nineteen ninety came to an end, most of the fun of home life had been sucked dry for Billy. His relationship with Nikki had taken a severe nosedive after a certain incident. They had been talking about having children ever since the pair moved in together; they both felt it was something that was missing from their family unit and the reason why they were not getting on that well. Billy absolutely loved the idea of children and becoming a father again, only this time he was going to stand up to his responsibilities and see this thru to the end. Being from a big family makes you want to have a big family of your own.
Billy could not wait to start fathering his offspring and Nikki knew how much this meant to him. Therefore, when it turned out that Nikki had fallen pregnant, you would think Billy would have been over the moon but no. To be over the moon, he would have needed to know the news. Nikki had told Kelly about a minute after she found out and Kelly was also the first one to know when Nikki had an abortion. Billy was not told about either until a few weeks later, although Nikki declared to Billy that it was in fact a miscarriage that she suffered.

The trust thing had gone out of the window, he was hurt and felt betrayed, and knowing that Kelly knew before him was adding insult to injury. Things were never the same after that and so their first Christmas together in their new house was just barely a passable event. A New Year was about to start with the knowledge that the good time party was over. You know that period of time when the sun seems to shine twenty-four/seven, birds sing and every love song has meaning to your relationship. Well that had faded for Billy, the real world was coming into focus and it was not a pleasant sight.

Chapter Sixteen

Ninety-one saw the start of a great year for Billy but not for those that were involved in the Gulf war. The troops had been called in to help return independence to the small country of Kuwait. The Iraqi forces, under the leadership of a taller version of Hitler, Saddam Hussein, invaded Kuwait in the month of August the year before. Once the US and our boys and girls got involved, the conflict lasted a little over a month, although the problems with Saddam went on for a lot longer.

Nevertheless, as stated, for Billy it was the start of a very rewarding year. In addition, whenever Billy came into large, financial gains, he was always reminded of the Lessons that Freddie taught him. Where money was concerned, Freddie was forever telling all the siblings this piece of advice and the reasons behind it:

Back in the old days, the British film making industry was practically non-existent. Hollywood was spawning the classics and the genre of movies that captured the attention of all the men were Gangster stories. These black and white flicks had such stars, as George Raft, James Cagney and Edward G Robinson, and were mainly based on the prohibition days of Chicago in the roaring twenties. These actors lit up the screen and the world they portrayed was mesmerising. Organised crime; Al Capone and the whole Mafioso rules of conduct thing were subjects seriously followed by him (Freddie), Harry and his twin brothers, Tommy and Teddy. The lessons they learnt from these idols was how to present to the world who you were while hiding from the world what you have. The characters were always friends of the people; they looked after their own, especially their mothers and always remembered where they came from. They only started to get their comeuppance when they forgot who they were and what their limitations were. And nine times out of ten, they would be gunned down in the street and it was proved to the whole world that they were not immortal or untouchable. Al Capone, who was a real life gangster, who suffered from his own arrogance, put all his earnings on show, rubbing it in the noses of the police and FBI, he was finally arrested and sent to prison for tax evasion. It was from these situations that Freddie knew that there would always be two kinds of villains, those who wish to be high profile and those who wish to remain low profile. He always said it was best to be low profile, never flaunt what you've got, never flash what you have and always play smart. Life is just a game and if you are not winning then you are not cheating.

He would tell Billy that the reason Harry was never seen like his brother's was not because he was not as involved. It was because he remained low profile, in the background and out of the way. It did not make him any less feared, just a little more approachable, and that is how you stay a man of the people. Tommy and Teddy liked being high profile and thought they were untouchable and so paid the price. You can see the same thing in action today; there are villains, who opt for the high profile way, that are household names. Their pictures are in the newspapers, their names are in the news, and there are those that you would not give a second glance to. The police would always be out to get the loud, high profile guy before wasting their time on getting the villain that wouldn't get them in the papers or on the telly. If Freddie felt that that was the way to be, why should Billy think any different? Instead of spending forty grand on a luxury motor for everyone to take notice of, Billy would prefer to use his money wisely. He would rather leave it in a high interest saving's account or in this case, invest it with long-term growth potential.

Billy's neighbour, Pete, who had a sideline of breeding Bull Mastiffs, was having his house repossessed after losing his nine to five. He had a wife and a young child to support and being thrown out on to the street was not an option. Pete was desperate for a way out that suited him and his family so he turned to the one person he knew, that despite the effects of the recession, had the know-how and readies to solve the problem, he turned to Billy for help. Billy told him that he would contact the Bank and offer to buy the place before his family were put out on the street. A quick sale was far better than having a property on the market, not making any money. The bank agreed to the price offered by Billy and set about putting the wheels in motion. The plan was for Billy to buy the house at a very reasonable price and have Pete and his family stay there while having the council, now that he was unemployed, to pay the rent. This seemed like a sound business venture and it gave Billy the perfect excuse to take a second job to raise the additional cash needed for this deal to work. In addition, working all day and then working throughout the night would also act as a way to get him out of the house and away from the nagging pressures of being at home with Nikki.

Billy had stayed in contact with Simon over the years and asked him if there was any work going. Simon told Billy that his call couldn't have come at a better time, a friend of his would soon be opening a wine bar, called 'Scallywags' in Hoe Street, and they had asked him to supply some doormen. Because the soon to be owner was a close friend to Simon, he was worried that the hired help might not do right by him, but knowing that someone like Billy was keeping the peace worked in both their favour. The gig was Billy's if he wanted it and he also got to choose his own backup. It was only a two-man job, four nights a week, cash in hand. Timing is everything and this year would prove to have all the hallmarks of being Billy's year for profit and adventure.

Before Billy had to take on this new role and start to work every weekend, he thought a road trip might be in order to have a blow out to rival all blow outs. So he rounded up Michael, Vaughan and Steve Perks, they agreed to take Steve with them, not out of any real friendship but they figured he would drive the four of them there and back. Steve was so grateful to be included; he insisted that they did not need to give him any petrol money, like Billy was going to pay him anyway. The plan was simple; it was to set out, to go visit Keith, the Wrexham lad Billy and Michael had met on their club eighteen to thirty holiday, who had just returned to England from being called out to do his part for queen and country in the Gulf situation. He was living in a little town called Marlborough, in Wiltshire and shared a house with three female nurses.

The boys drove up early Saturday morning, it took them two hours to get up there and an extra hour driving down these narrow, non signposted country back roads, before finally finding Keith's house. It was situated about a ten-minute walk from the town centre, where every other building was a pub and the locals did not like outsiders.

Keith introduced Billy and his travelling companions to his housemates (hubba hubba). They were good-looking women in their own right but knowing that they all had a nurse's outfit in the wardrobe was the icing on the cake. Moreover, it was a cake that Billy was more than tempted to get his teeth into. They spent the day catching up, Keith was telling the guys, who were listening with an eagerness that a young child in front of the TV gets when his favourite show was about to start, about his time in the Gulf. He then went on to tell them what that cheeky, skinflint Paul had been getting up to and they in turn regaled him with tales of work and the other things they had got up to since last seeing him. Keith had invited a few of his friends from Swindon to come down that evening. The idea was to have a few drinks and then back to his place for a little get together; well that was his idea anyway.

Vaughan and Billy were laying on the old Michaels charm on these pretty nurses and it was working a treat. In fact, the only time they found that they had to start from scratch was after every interruption by Steve Perks and his constant bull shitting. It reached the point where these lovely Florence nightingales told him point blankly to shut up and then went out shopping. This fella seriously cramped their style; Steve had made sure that this, for him, was his one and only road trip with these lads.

As early evening crept in, Keith's friends from Swindon turned up, when asked later down the line about this particular weekend, Billy would like to say he could remember who they were, but he couldn't, they were all forgettable, with the exception of one. Her name was Wanda; she was this huge blob of fat with an air of snobbiness about her, Billy just did not take to her at all. That was his first impression of her but for whoever it was that said first impressions count, was wrong, because over the following years, Wanda became a very dear friend of his and the mother to his Goddaughter Amber.

With the gang now all there, they thought they would start out early and see how the evening went. The delightful nurses stayed behind to get the place ready for the party as the remaining guests walked into town and into the first pub. Billy hadn't had a drop of alcohol for nearly two years, he wasn't finding himself having an ongoing internal battle of good verses evil or anything, but he just didn't trust himself. He did not want to start drinking again on a regular basis but he thought he was strong enough to handle a night on the town. In addition, all the shit he was getting at home was causing a big ball of pent up anger which was starting to boil.

Billy had to find a way to vent or someone was going to die a very serious death, he was being truly pushed to the limit and if a few drinks could help that feeling pass then his lapse should be seen as a medical necessity. Billy told Vaughan and Michael that he was going to have a drink but to stop him, with any means necessary, if he started to go too far, they both knew what he meant. Billy went on the old Brandy and Babychams that night and Vaughan joined him, what a lovely drop of drink that mixture was. The first pub they went into was a quiet little place and it acted as the climate control pit stop. You know when you are out in a crowd that you do not really know and so you just want to knock a couple back to get the party mood started. This was the feeling that Billy had so they spent an hour in that particular place, each little group talking amongst themselves while poor old Keith was the middleman who was trying to get everyone to mingle. By the time they left for the next pub, everyone was warming up to one another, a few jokes were being told and the level of bitchiness was reducing.

Marlborough is a quiet place with not much going on in the evening entertainment area, so the locals go out early. By the time the pub crawling visitors entered the next pub, it was showing signs of being a decent place to hang about in, for it was starting to fill up with all the local lads and lasses. Once inside Billy was making his arrival to this sleepy town known and was talking to everyone who would listen and there were plenty that did. The drawback to not drinking for two years was that no matter how good a boozer you were, you would feel the effects of alcohol kick in early. Billy, who was getting all nice and toasty inside, was inviting the inhabitants of this sleepy burg all back to Keith's house for a party, unbeknown to Keith of course. The proprietor of this particular establishment did not care for loud cockneys in his pub and so Billy and his companions were instructed to move on, which they did but taking half of the landlords clientele with them. This meant that they were now a crowd of thirty as opposed to the eight they started out with and so where else would a group of thirty drinkers going to go but another pub, so that's what they did. The third place was more of the same and it was not long before another twenty people had joined their pub-crawl. The fourth place just flatly refused them entry because they thought they were a coach party, so they took their business and moved on to another drinking establishment.

A couple of more places later, where the landlords were grateful for the business and the locals were more than happy to join the travelling party, they finally ended up in a pub called the "Rising Sun", and there was more than sixty of them by this time and the landlord thought his lottery numbers had come up. His pub was at the far end of town and judging by the look on his face, he never had so much business. Billy had him blow the dust off his CD player and was promptly told to put on some tunes, while they overloaded the bar with orders. By now Billy was in his element, he stood up on a bench and started to hold court, Billy warmed up the crowd like a professional stand up comedian by knocking out one-liners left, right and centre and the crowd loved it. Or at least he thought so, looking back on it, if Billy was in the crowd having to listen to some drunken Londoner, he would probably be thinking 'what a wanker'. Billy spotted a guy in the crowd who had some wild spiky hair standing with his girlfriend, who was soaking in the entertainment.

"Oi mate, you look like a cockatoo!" Billy pointed directly at this poor fella with the outlandish hairdo, which in turn caused his girlfriend to let out a little snigger, Billy couldn't resist.

"I don't know what you're laughing for love. You look like you had a cockatoo before you came out!" Now it was the boyfriends' turn to laugh, and that is how the evening played out, people were literally begging Billy to insult them, even the landlord.

Now surprisingly not everyone seemed to enjoy Billy's loudness or his brand of humour because one guy took offence to the comment he came out with next. You see Marlborough was a stone's throw away from Hungerford, the town where some guy went garrarty with a shot gun back in nineteen eighty eight. Billy's comment was "Seeing as we're near Hungerford, someone shoot over to the bar and get me a drink", which went down a storm but this one guy had to bring a downer on the occasion. He started to moan about how he nearly lost his parents that day and Billy should shut his mouth. Billy looked at him and replied how gutted they must have been not to have succeeded in their plan of getting away from him. Now this off colour remark was out of order and even Billy was expecting some form of retribution. The upset yokel then went to take a swing at Billy and rightly so, but Vaughan came at him from the side and just pushed him using all of his nineteen stone of mass, the guy fell, and his punch, although in full swing missed Billy by a mile. The landlord had a couple of the local rugby boys throw the fella out and the evening continued until the sound of the final bell. It was better to sacrifice the one local than spoil the mood and bar takings by having the cockney thrown out. Once outside, however, the same fella was waiting for Billy to emerge, while holding a broken bottle in his hand. Big mistake for this guy, who should have just made his way home because the people who had never met Billy before this night all started in on the waiting assailant and threw him to one side. Billy was speechless for the first time that night.

All sixty of the crawlers, including the landlord of the Rising Sun, went back to Keith's place armed with free booze, courtesy of everyone's new best friend, the landlord. The house party needed to start where the last pub left off, the place was filled to the rafters, the music was pumping and the festivities were well under way. Billy was mingling with the crowd of his newfound friends when he saw Wanda make a move on his homeboy Michael. What was going through her mind, how was a lean, muscular guy that Billy had taken under his wing ever going to find this beast of a woman attractive enough to get down and take care of business? There was no amount of alcohol out there to make her appealing. Michael even went up to Billy a little later on and asked for help to get her to leave him alone. Billy told him to get a chair and a whip, but he reckoned that could be something she liked, so that idea was soon forgotten about.

Vaughan and Steve were trying their hand with two of Keith's housemates but to no avail, to escape from Steve the bull-shitter, these two nurses insisted they were lesbians and after meeting him were glad they were. That guy was hopeless. In between taking the piss out of this six foot five, welsh sheep shagger called Bob and calming down the rambunctious rugby players, Billy was getting the eye from Julia, the non lesbian nurse out of the three. It turned out that one of these rugby players had been after her for years and was giving her a hard time, say no more Billy thought and made sure that this annoying flanker saw Billy go upstairs with his precious Julia. That way if he followed to interrupt Billy would chin him and if he did not, then he would know that there was just no chance for him. There was a method to the madness.

It went without saying that Julia and Billy got up to naughtiness in her bedroom that night, even more so after he talked her into putting on her uniform. It was during their third go when Vaughan walked in to see if Billy wanted a drink, breather, or just someone to stand in for him. Billy assured him that he had it covered and off Vaughan went.

When Billy came downstairs the next morning, he saw the floor was a sea of strangers all passed out and bottles were scattered all over the place. The biggest shock was seeing Michael in his sleeping bag with Wanda who, judging by the pile of clothes to her right was naked. The mind boggles but hey, it was something to rib him about for the next hundred years. The Londoners showed their respect for their host's house by helping to tidy up, grabbing some brekkie, saying their goodbyes, and driving back to London. If you were about to say goodbye to your weekends then that was the one to go out on.

The grand opening of Scallywags was on a Thursday night, and the resident DJ was Mad JB, who was Alan's stepbrother and Billy's old school chum from the estate. Small world. Billy had gotten Darren in on the action with him to begin with; Billy did not think there was any need to bring in the heavy guns. After all, this place was in Walthamstow and Billy either knew or was known by everyone who came through the door that night. Vaughan, Mikey and Stuart had all turned up to join in on the festivities, so there was no lack of back up just in case it went tits up. The evening was going great; the bar closed the doors to any punters at ten. Darren stood inside to watch the door and to let people out while Billy mingled. It was like being a celebrity; everyone was calling him over, shaking his hand and just generally chatting shit just to say that they had spoken to him. It was like a beehive round the table that the Michaels brothers were sitting at; everyone was buying them drinks and asking if they were ever going start up the house parties again. It was a good evening.

The manager called Billy over and asked who the group at the table were, he told him that they were his brothers and that they were well known faces in the area. Billy even went further to say that if they were to state this was the bar to be seen in, then this place would be packed out every night, especially on the weekends. This caught his attention, you could not buy better publicity than this but he was wrong, everything comes with a price. The deal was that between them, they would ensure that the place filled up every night for a percentage of the takings. Billy figured this was a fair deal seeing as this was a new club and Antonio, the owner, wanted to recuperate his costs as fast as possible, so it was agreed after only ten minutes of 'umming and 'arring. That is how it started, the brothers put the word out that this was a place to use as a meet up point and people started to come in all the time. Billy worked the door with Darren, while his brothers would grace the bar every now and then with their presence. It was a sweet set up and after the first month or so, they were making a grand a week from the place, on top of their wages.

Scallywags was the sweetest thing going, there was never any aggravation, it had a good atmosphere and there was skirt and blouse everywhere you looked. In fact, it was too sweet and after a few months, Billy was starting to feel that was becoming boring. He had the mortgage on his new house sorted and covered, so it was time to use the money the brothers had been making from Scallywags and invest in something else to spice it all up. With their new influx of wealth, the Michaels lads thought they would set up an O-eight-nine-eight business, touting pre-recorded sex talk at a pound fifty a minute. Mikey was only using the flat for his occasional stays so it was only going spare when he was doing what he had to do south of the water. It made sense to use the space as a place of operations; they had ten phone lines coming in all hooked up to their tape player. Billy had a selection of girlies he knew do the recordings, sounding seductive and teasing, as it took them four minutes to finish a complete sentence. Billy being a budding poet wrote out a few scripts, setting up a selection of scenarios to capture the attention of the male orientated callers. There was a little naughty schoolgirl action, a secretary working late with her lecherous boss and the bored housewife using her feminine wiles to pay off the milkman. Each one sounded like a seventies porno flick but if it could keep you on the phone for over twenty minutes then it was good enough. The first month was hectic with calls, the money spent on advertising was well worth it and it was obvious that the recordings and variety had to increase. The lads had got another five girls and two fella's supplying them with their vocal chords. A little something for everyone, Billy didn't care if you were straight, gay, Bi, Saido/Mas' or just plain shy. Money is money and he was willing to collect it any way it came. The spare bedroom was all decked out as a recording studio and the vocal actors recorded their dialogue for the message machines.

The whole thing was basically an answering machine, the phone rang and the machine picked up the call. The greeting kicked in and went on for ages, all the while the caller stayed on the line listening to the message and paying the out of control call charges. The only difference was that unlike a standard answering machine you didn't get to leave a message after the beep. In the early nineties, the sex lines on offer were not so in your face like they are now; it was still being shunned upon. Not to mention that it was a business venture that was only just finding its feet. The best times to get into something is right at the beginning or right at the end, when you just blatantly abuse it. Billy was always looking for an angle and prided himself on being one-step ahead; in addition, it was legal. This one took a huge investment to get off the ground so the first load of returns was reimbursement but it was not too long before the returns were pure profit. All ten lines were ringing off the hook; there were a lot of horny guys and girls out there, running up large phone bills on their company/parent's/mobile phones. Thank god, Britain is such a sexually repressed country full of people looking for an outlet that they can keep private from the rest of the world.

Mikey took his share of the phone line profits and bought a house in Wandsworth as an investment, following the example of his brother Billy. The harassment of the South London police force had died down and Mikey was starting to get back into a full time swing with the Eves family. Tony Eves and his family were now running a security business to get their own doormen into a host of clubs, so their dealers could have a free reign. Mikey was working as a minder to the dealers, if anyone tried to rip them off or another dealer was working their corner, then Mikey would deal with it, using any means necessary. He had become a real cold, sadistic bastard over the years.

Mikey called upon Billy with a proposition to make some serious green, which grabbed his attention straight away. Over the years, Mikey had made a long list of connections and was always being offered little sidelines. Some he took up, some he declined but the one he was just offered was too big to refuse.

The underground rave scene was nearing the end of a successful run; big clubs and promoters were losing out because they were not housing them. Manchester was pushing the music scene while Liverpool was giving chase. It was moving into a new era and as people moved with it, it opened up opportunities to new faces that were only usually offered within the closed ranks.

Mikey had been offered to run the inside security team for a mass blow-out rave being hosted in an abandoned warehouse on an industrial estate in rural Surrey. These things were always going down in country areas, because the local cop shop was usually twenty miles away and the station was closed after seven p.m. All the raver's, who wanted to attend, had to meet at certain locations, usually near a main line train station and await for some one to Chinese whisper the address through the crowd. This stopped the police from being in a position to either raid it or put a stop to it right from the word go. It was quite an impressive set up and even Billy had to admit, that even he would tip his hat to the originators of the whole thing, bravo. Running the security meant that he was also allowed to run the drugs side of things. This is where Billy came in; Mikey needed a financial partner to buy as many of the little fella's as possible, to get the best price, plus he knew that with someone he trusted at his side, there was going to be no need for things to get nasty when it came to dividing the profits. It was to be a once off thing, so to get the best return they involved as few a people as possible. The plan was that the inside security would act as the sellers, cutting out the need for runners. Billy could not refuse such a promising arrangement but he wanted a few conditions met first. Billy wanted in on choosing the inside team, he also wanted to run a watermelon stall and he wanted Mikey to promise he would show his face more often at his house and be nice to Nikki because lord knew Billy had been treating her like crap for the last few months. Mikey agreed.

Running any kind of refreshment stand at these things was an absolute gold mine in itself. For the sake of a paste table and a trip to Covent Garden flower market, in Nine Elms (where they just do not sell flowers), it was a good way to earn. They bought a bulk load of watermelons at a pound each, cut them up in to thin slices, scooped away the seeds and sold each slice for two quid a throw to the pill popping masses. On a good size melon, you could get about thirty slices of mouth refreshing, body cooling goodness. With approximately three thousand people at these things, it did not take a genius to see how much of the dough-ray-me could be made. It's the simple things that work the best.

Billy was out all hours of the day and night, if he wasn't at Siddelely Hawks, he was checking on the phone business, if Billy wasn't there he was at Scallywags, if he wasn't there then he was asleep. Billy was almost staying faithful to Nikki, he was turning down at least ninety eight percent of the offers presenting themselves but he was so money orientated that all the temptations that were on offer took a back seat while he raked in the dosh. Although his home life was suffering, Billy just never let up to take time out to make it up to Nikki. Every penny he made was his and he kept quiet about it all, even pleading poverty at times, just to give himself another reason to be out even more. For a tough guy, Billy was a coward when it came to doing the right thing where Nikki was concerned. Any one on the outside looking in could tell he should have just told Nikki how it was so they could part ways and move on with their lives but instead they played their game. Nikki, although ignored and treated second best to everything else, was still grateful to be away from her over bearing parents and was enjoying living her own life, with no fella to answer to. Billy was out so much that he did not even know that she was going out as much as she was; he also did not know what else she was getting up to.

Billy had sorted out the house next door and he had his eye on buying another property before the end of the year. Billy was winning two ways, the properties were his and his alone, and everything else was a family affair that they all got an equal share from. Billy was putting the Michaels clan on the map and not just in a ten-mile radius of Walthamstow, he was branching out and this Rave deal was the start of the next big thing for the family.

Chapter Seventeen

The night of the rave arrived and Billy had Simon arrange a spot of cover for him and Darren for the evening at Scallywags. Billy had offered Darren a chance to come work the watermelon sideline with him and he took Michael and Alan along too. The four of them went down in one car while Monty and Vaughan rode with Mikey. Billy had dragged his cousin, Monty, along as extra back up. Monty had become a bit of a legend at the Riverside Club after that incident against B and was happy to add more fuel to his explosive CV. The ladies loved Monty, what a specimen, even Billy thought that if he was a woman (or gay) he would be all over Monty like a German's towel on a sun lounger. Monty's older brother Russell was the same, only not as cute looking, it was obvious to all that there was definitely some muscular genes running through that side of the family.

Mikey had a couple of his pals meet him at the secret venue, it was not as though Billy did not trust Mikey's friends but this involved an investment of their family's money. He only wanted either kin or people he trusted enough to call them a part of his extended family working with them, Mikey kept the peace by having his guys patrolling the inside perimeter for the night. Michael and Alan, who had been spending the day cutting up watermelon, had set up the stand near a fire exit, for a quick escape. The DJ equipment was being erected while outside a big back up generator was spluttering away feeding power into the abandoned warehouse that was once a thriving business. The recession was meant to be ending, according to Thatcher and her cabinet, but you could still see a whole host of people out of work, businesses closed down and Hospitals were receiving budget cuts. Although you never hear of these politicians taking a wage cut or going without a bonus to help matters, and they call people like Billy and his family villains.

The outside security team was a North London firm, called Force Security. It was primarily an all black company who took Rockies everywhere with them. Big fucking dogs them Rockies, which would explain the big fucking lumps that were keeping them under control. The headman was a bloke called Joseph; he must have tipped the scales at twenty-four stone, if he was an ounce. He stood in at six foot and sported a shiney shaven head, big shovel like hands, and a serious look that could equal the destruction of the four horsemen of the apocalypse. Billy knew this as fact because Joseph gave him the look just after Billy offered him some watermelon. Looking back on it, Billy thought the idea of this white boy offering watermelon to a big black guy must have come across a little stereotypical. However, Billy had a van load of it all sliced up and he was just trying to be friendly. Billy told him so; Joseph just smiled and patted him on the back, "Maybe later".

Inside, the Michaels brothers set the formation of their distribution team up, including themselves there were eight of them working the crowd; knocking out the Dove's at fifteen pound a pop or two for twenty-five. If you had nice tits, you could have got one free. Billy had put up seventy percent of the capital while Mikey put up the rest, between them they had bought ten thousand of the little fella's at a pound seventy-five a piece and the mark up was out of this world. The venue went beyond capacity and by midnight, there must have been over three and a half thousand people, blowing their whistles and white gloving it in the air. The whole team

235

had dipped into the merchandise and mingled with the crowd with smiles on their faces and a mellow mood on display, it was all good, man. Once the rush of coming up set in, the atmosphere seemed to kick up fifteen notches, every tune felt like an anthem, the bass build up seemed to mirror the feeling of the blood rushing around the punters systems. The love doves were doing their job; the lights took on a life of their own and as the sweat dripped off everybody in the hijacked warehouse, the beat kept them all on the vibe. The greatest thing about the rave scene was that next to the dealer the second most popular person in the room was the one with all the chewing gum. You needed a stick of the wriglies to keep your jaw busy or you may have ended up jawing your face off.

The happy people were enjoying the night; there was not an ounce of trouble. Except the one guy who must have been giving Vaughan some aggro over payment or something because when Billy looked over, he could see Vaughan with his hand on the guys' chest pushing him into a quieter, darker corner presumably about to give him a beating. Vaughan over shadowed the sweaty, shirtless runt whose facial expressions were putting a professional gurner to shame. He did not need back up, Billy did not think it would take much before the guy was on his knees begging Vaughan not to fuck him up.

The watermelons had sold out by one in the morning, so Billy advised that it might prove beneficial if Michael and Alan started to make a move home and take the money from the stand with them. Billy also gave them the money they had earnt from the E's thus far. After all, if you are going to be busted by the fuzz, it is best to keep the money and drugs separate. The dynamic duo gathered up their paste table and carving knives, bundled everything into the back of the van and took off. Being able to trust someone one hundred percent is very important in this game. If Billy had not trusted these two, one hundred percent, they would not have been involved from the start. They understood the relevance of him calling them a part of his extended family and would never do anything to betray that. Billy knew his money was safe.

The remaining six carried on selling the last of their wares, the temperature in the building felt like boiling point and the constant thud, thud bass line of the music was starting to wear thin as the pills wore off. They had flogged a little under nine thousand pills, revellers had necked an average of three a piece just to keep the buzz alive well into the next morning and judging by the glazed look in a few of the team's eyes, a second dip into the merchandise had taken place. No harm, no fail.

It was five thirty in the morning when Mikey got a heads up from one of Joseph's team, sirens were wailing in the distance and that meant evacuation time. The DJ stopped the tunes, bagged his records, and was off, although that didn't seem to stop the masses from continuing to dance. The Michaels crew jumped into their respective motors and spun off, there was no way Billy wanted to get a tug while he was still carrying around fifty grand on him not to mention over a thousand E's sitting in Mikey's glove compartment. As the cars drove up the country lane the filth was just starting to pull in, the lads had to swerve around them to get away and after taking a few back roads and three laps round the roundabout; they all drove off back to Walthamstow. Why three laps? Because if you are being followed by undercover police, then a tail has to brake off to maintain that cover after two circuits of a roundabout.

Billy sprung for breakfast that morning at a little chef, after an initial layout of seventeen and a half thousand pounds for the happy pills, the nights return was a little over a hundred and ten grand, he could afford to splash out on the crew, after all, these places weren't nicknamed little robber for nothing.

Both Billy and Mikey took back their investment money as well as keeping the remaining E's for later distribution.

Billy then gave five grand apiece to Mikey's friends and five grand to Darren. He then rewarded Vaughan and Monty with eight grand apiece, with a twenty-five grand payoff for Mikey for bringing the deal to the table. Billy was happy because not only did he practically triple his money but between Mikey and himself, they would also get the money that would be generated once they sold the twelve hundred E's that they had left over. All in all, a good nights work on the drugs front.

On top of all that, Billy had also pocketed a further fifteen grand return from his two hundred and fifty pound layout on the watermelons from that night. He gave three and a half grand each to Michael and Alan leaving Billy an additional eight grand. Life was good. When all was said and done, Billy was on target for making around sixty grand from that one venture, all cash no tax. Who can really condemn the life he led? Certainly not the people that benefited because of it.

Billy was making money hand over fist that year and he was making sure everyone was getting a share, just so there was not any resentment in the ranks. As well as Darren, Billy had also called in Jason and Colin to out the remaining happy pills. Billy divided them all up, giving only two hundred to Darren and a thousand between the other two and told them he only wanted eight pound a pill in return, whatever they earnt on top of that was theirs. Within the month, they had sold the lot and Billy was another ten grand up. Darren had outed most of his share actually in Scallywags and was happy with his little extra earnings but now Jason and Colin had a taste for it and wanted more. The money to be made from selling these little white, graphic indented tablets was obscene. Billy told them he was not interested in doing it full time but they could see if Mikey would act as their contact to buy them cheaper and run the business on their own. If they bought in bulk then the price per pill was going to be three pound seventy five pence. After all, why not make two quid for every one they bought thought Mikey, business is business after all. The two chop shop mechanics turned pill dealers used the cash they had earnt from selling the pills Billy gave them and went into business for themselves. There is nothing like free enterprise. Billy was happy to help out, but memories of how the last time they were all in the drug business ended, still haunted him. Mikey was happy because he was earning a couple of quid on every one bought. The guys were happy too because they thought they were getting a good deal at three seventy five a pop and their customers were happy because the pills were good quality. It was a win-win situation.

Billy had just turned twenty-three and the year had been a financial godsend. He had used the money he earned from his active year to pay off the outstanding mortgage on the house he had bought from Pete, his neighbour. Billy was getting five hundred pound a month rent money from the social on that place and so he thought now would be a good time to buy another piece of property. Billy figured he could use the rent money from one place to pay extra off on the mortgage of the new place. It was a long-term investment that took long-term vision, something young Billy was always able to see, he knew that one day his number would be up and he may face a bit of scrubs, having a retirement plan this early in life was not the dumbest thing he had thought of.

Billy was still under the illusion that he may get a second chance at fatherhood if he and Nikki worked out their differences but things had changed, they had gone past that lovey-dovey stage where they were at it at every possible moment in every possible place and had entered the twilight zone of couple's hell. He was still getting earache from Nikki about the lack of time he spent with her; Billy told her that he had to work so much to cover the costs of their home and the investment house next door. Billy had never let on to her just how much money he had made over the year, just that, what they both brought into the house didn't cover all the bills.

Billy's time away from home was justified, not that there was much reason to stay home in the evening. He was lucky to get sex once a month, which when you consider they used to be at it two to three times a day is a bit of a let down. Now Billy would not break a relationship down and say that sex is everything in a relationship but it is a good part of it. It makes you feel close and desirable to your partner, it shows you that the passion is still there and your interest has not waned. Although he wouldn't say it out loud or anything, after all he didn't want to sound gay, but he personally believed that it's sex that keeps you in love with someone as opposed to just loving someone, after all you love your parents and siblings and you don't have sex with them (well you shouldn't be). You love the way your favourite restaurant cooks your favourite dish and you do not have sex with that, sex separates the term love with actually being in love.

It went against Billy's up-bringing to wear his feelings on his sleeve like that, none of his brothers were that soppy, perhaps he was in love and it just hadn't registered because of the betrayal he felt over the pregnancy incident a year earlier. Whatever it was, it didn't out weigh the desire to make money and be set in the future and besides, if Billy was going to question anything it would have been if this nine to five lark was really for him. He had earned three times his annual salary in one week (almost); shades of the old Billy Michaels were creeping in.

Chapter Eighteen

The Michaels family reputation had increased ten folds over the last nine months and Scallywags had to turn business away because it was reaching capacity early on in the evenings. The place was busier than it was when the place first opened yet the boys weekly cut was the same, Billy didn't question it, but he was thinking about how much money the place must have been taking in a week. It was food for thought.

It was not just their family name that was getting attention but Billy was also. Simon called Billy up to see if he fancied a change of scenery, there was a position that needed covering up in a West End club and the Michaels name was mentioned to fill it. Now Billy would be the first to admit that his reign of power was mainly centred in Walthamstow, reaching out to North Chingford, Highams Park, Leyton, Seven Sisters, Edmonton and Enfield but he did not think or expect his name to be known in the West End of London, let alone be known enough for someone to ask for him. Billy was a bit sceptical about the whole thing but Simon reassured him that this was on the up and up.

The club was a well-known venue on the corner of Leicester Square, called the Thunderdome. A high profile tourist trap that was deemed the pinnacle of a doorman's career because of who the head doorman was, Big Lenny Shaw. A world-renowned hard bastard and bare-knuckle fighter who held the mantle of 'The Man to Beat', that particular title was no gimmick; Lenny only attained it after years of chasing and fighting the holder of the crown at the time, Roy McLean. Roy was another hard bastard who was no stranger to the world of pain, whether he was inflicting it or taking it. These two gods never liked each other that much although they would show respect to one another when asked about their fighting abilities. It was an underworld rivalry that had been going on since the late seventies.

Lenny Shaw was born in the month of April, nineteen forty nine and grew up in the same era as Billy's father, Bobbie M. By the time Lenny was making a name for himself, the Crow twins had put a strangle hold on anything dodgy and had built up their nightclub empire. It was in one of these nightclubs that Lenny, the future weightlifter and World Heavyweight Bare-knuckle Champion who was constantly referred to as 'the hardest man in Britain' acted as a fill in bouncer at the tender age of seventeen.

Lenny, like practically every one else who would have such an inspirational influence on Billy, was a Cockney born in Hoxton, in the heart of the East End of London. He was viciously abused by his stepfather from the age of five on a regular occurrence, Billy thought about how the way the world worked. Billy's real father was a complete arse who would regularly abuse Billy's mother until the youngster drove a kitchen knife into the leg of this so-called tough man at the age of five and that's when he left his life. When his mother Paula finally remarried, Billy's step Dad was a saint in comparison and Billy was proud to announce that he was his son. Whereas Lenny's real father was the saint and the step father he got at the age of five was the total wank-stain. By the age of ten, young Lenny had had his jaw broken twice and many other bones broken as well, all by the hands of this monster that demanded respect from the shit on his shoe adolescent that he had to refer to as son. But just like Billy, there came a time when Len had to dig in deep and do what had to be done to end the madness, depending how you looked at it, it was lucky for his abuser that Lenny didn't use a knife but his fists to solve his problem. At the age of twelve Lenny stood up to his step father and put the full stop on all the beatings by giving one of his own. His step father never hit him or any of his siblings again.

Riding on that turn of character, Lenny adopted that ability and confidence and put it in the face of every person who fancied their chances against him by turning to street fighting, fuelled with a determination to not be beaten ever again by any man. It was unfortunate for his opponents that this wrecking machine was expending the bottled up rage of his abusive childhood on them with such ferocity that many times it would take three or more people to pull him off his challenger.

During his teen years Lenny found himself on the wrong arm of the law a few times and was arrested for petty crimes which finally got him an all paid vacation for eighteen months at one of her majesty's deluxe rest and relaxation spa's. By the time he was fifteen and back in the land of the living, Lenny had worked a string of short lived jobs to get by on after he was fired from his first legit full time job for beating up his foreman.

At nineteen Lenny thought that with a string of bad work references behind him, an explosive temper that was on a short fuse and a bite out of the porridge bowl that he would never catch a break and turn it all around. That was until he met Val. Val walked into his life and brought the sunshine on his cloudy day, Lenny showing that he wasn't all brawn made the cleverest decision of his life and only after a year of dating asked Val to marry him to which she said yes. It was with this desire to support his new wife and a possible family that it dawned on Lenny that he could make a good living from fighting. He learned that all that pent up aggression from his violent childhood could be channelled into making money and, as a result, began bare-knuckle fighting. It soon became obvious that he had made the right decision. Fight after fight, Lenny had yet to lose. He became the most well-known and feared bare knuckle fighter Britain had ever seen.

After a few years, Lenny turned to unlicensed boxing. To many people, he had always been 'The Man to Beat', but he did not actually earn that title until nineteen seventy-eight. Len had previously suffered a heavy defeat at the hands of unlicensed boxing legend Roy McLean, the fight in question had to be stopped in the third round because of its pure savagery. It was not until September eleventh, of that year, that a rematch would be presenting itself to the public. It was at the Rainbow Theater in Finsbury Park, London that Lenny stopped Roy in a dramatic first round win. A decider was needed to resolve the war once and for all, but sadly it could never be arranged between the two fighters. So their supporters would spend years arguing who would have won and been the deserving fighter to hold the mantle of 'the man to beat'.

Lenny went on to challenge and beat some of the biggest names in the business. He stopped the Irish bare-knuckle heavyweight Shamus Daugherty in the first round and in nineteen eighty six, Big Lenny beat Baz 'Psycho Pikey' Brookes who at the time was undefeated, and again just like McLean and Daugherty, the win was in the first round. Brooke's made the mistake of head-butting Lenny before the bell, which only really served to make Len more determined to win. In fact this bout, once the bell did ring, lasted all of fifty seconds before Lenny had to be stopped from stamping Brooke's skull into the canvas, the footage from this has gone on to be used in many a documentary about violence and hard bastards. Lenny was truly established as being an animal and should not be crossed by anyone, not just in the UK either. Len's reputation was echoing around the globe and it wasn't long before international invitations to step up for a straightener were issued. One in particular was presented by the man mountain from New York, Big Shaun Cormack, who was out to prove that once again the yanks were bigger and better than anyone else. It was in this fight that Lenny hit his opponent Cormack so hard, knocking him clean out; he broke both his own hands. Len also showed that he can call out victims, and issued a challenge to the feather ear ringed tough man turned actor. Who had just picked up the title 'King of the Bouncers' in New York, but the tough man obviously preferred to be an actor than defend the mantle and turned down an offer of £20,000 to fight in London.

Being the most well known figure in the illegal underworld of unlicensed boxing brought with it many fans, as well as enemies for the now nicknamed 'Big Lenny'. Over the next few years he suffered two bullet wounds from separate attacks as well as being stabbed on two different occasions, on all of these attempts on his life, the cowards responsible always came from behind. It was shortly after this that Lenny decided to go into semi-retirement, only having the occasional bare-knuckle fight. He turned his hand to body guarding and also returned to his other profession that he excelled at, bouncing on the doors. With his worldwide fame for knocking people out and generally being one hard bastard, Lenny, rightly so, took the mantle that the previous holder refused to defend and made sure everyone knew he was 'The King of Bouncers'. Lenny used that title to stamp the seal of protection, because it was just the threat of his name that would many times stop the heavy trouble in all clubs and pubs in London that he had a hand in looking after while basing himself at The Thunderdome in Leicester Square.

Roy McLean on the other hand was born a fighter and stayed a fighter and while he didn't take the high profile route that Lenny did, speak to people in the know, and you'll be told the same. That even without the newspaper advertising him, glitzy fights in the states with actors that did not want to know and televised documentaries, Roy was and still is a deadly fucker when it comes to the gladiatorial world of fighting.

Roy was born in nineteen thirty six and grew up in the tough, war torn area of the East End. He, like many others from this gritty land, started boxing at a very early age and was taken to his first boxing gym by his uncle when he was just eleven years of age. Roy ate, drank and slept boxing from then on, training on occasion with Harry and his brothers as well as Billy's grandad and mentor, big Freddie White. Boxing wasn't the only thing that Roy had in common with the lads he boxed with, he had also developed a healthy disrespect for authority and because he stood his ground against the blue Peel's, Roy was forever finding that his training was broken up by regular over night trips to the cells plus a couple of spells in prison. His first experience in the bars and stripes came in the guise of an army glasshouse while doing National Service and the second came when back in civilian life, with a stay at borstal. Roy was not a fan of borstal or the rules it tried to enforce and so it did not take long for this strong willed mass of fury to earn the following of several other inmates while organising a break out. Roy and his loyal associates attacked the borstal doctor one day and stole his car. Roy, once again, just like his old boxing friends had gone against the system and found himself on the run.

It was while having to keep looking over his shoulder, that Roy wanted to make a go of boxing professionally. Under the pseudonym Roy South and with the great Mickey Doyle as his manager, Roy had ten pro fights as a middleweight and won them all, six by KO. However, just as there seemed to be light at the end of the tunnel and a real chance of success thanks to his capable and educated hands, Roy found his lifeline to be short-lived when he found himself in a fight on a club dance floor and was arrested by police. While cooling off in the cells the police realised who Roy South really was and, before he knew it, he was back in borstal serving out the remainder of his time plus a little extra for everything else.

On finally getting out with his reputation of being a hard

bastard and successful boxer in tact. Roy was hit by another knockout blow when he was told loud and clear that he couldn't get his boxing license back due to his criminal background and so just like everyone that he associated with, turned his granite hands to crime to make his money, robbery in particular. It was for just that that Roy's luck once again ran out and when he was caught for using menace to extort funds from some one who didn't want to give generously and consequently found himself sentenced to fifteen years in stir, munching the same bowl of porridge as those before him. By the time he got out, Roy knew a pro career was most certainly out of the question and when someone suggested unlicensed boxing to him, although he was forty-two years of age, it seemed like a good idea.

Roy's first big win was against the King of the Gypsies, Jonny 'The Ox' Bunion. Bunion had a fearsome reputation as a bare-knuckle boxer, so it was something to say the least when Roy knocked him out with a single right-hander that was to become his trademark finisher, before he knew it, Roy McLean had established himself as 'the man to beat'. Roy went on to some truly memorable bouts, defeating Patrick 'howler' Muldoon, then ABA Champion Larry Hemsworth, but it was the bout that followed that was to put Roy on the map, when he defeated Lenny Shaw, in their first bout. This fight was seen by none other than the main man from the movie 'The France concoction', Gene Hickman, who was so impressed by what he'd witnessed that he was key in arranging Roy's next fight, against US heavyweight contender Rob 'The Bruiser' Sander. Needless to say, Sander was out of his league and dropped to the blood stained canvas in the third round.

After his victory against Sander, Roy was to suffer the only loss of his fighting career and that was at the hands of the man who had initially put him on the map earlier that year, Lenny Shaw. If he was going to lose a bout, then this was the man he would be professionally happy to lose to.

Despite the drawbacks Roy soldiered on and went on to defeat Lou 'The Beast' Bates, the hard nut lover from Liverpool and Keith Pollack, the only bloke to ever go the distance with Roy, Keith also fought Lenny and destroyed him. It's all swings and roundabouts, any given Sunday you can either win or lose no matter who you are, it just depends on if you whine about it or get on with it. Roy retired from professional fighting with eleven bouts to his name, having won nine, eight by KO but he still knocked out the odd slag who ever become out or order while in his presence.

Through the years, Billy had both the pleasure and privilege to know them both and he would not even dream of taking anything away from either of them, they just had different outlooks on life, which was reflected in their personalities. Lenny always came across as a loveable uncle, who was always out to hug you and seemed larger than life, whereas Roy came across as someone who lived life and seemed more reserved for it. Saying he had a tough life full of bad fortune and wrong turns would be an understatement, for either of them for that matter, but Roy carried the burdens heavier than most, he did not suffer fools and it was his preferred sense of privacy that came across from the first moment you met him.

Knowing what a formidable man and legend that Lenny was Billy would like to have said to any one asking or listening that Big Lenny Shaw himself had asked for him but alas it wasn't, not to take anything away from the person who did, for he was just as well known and just as deadly. He was a man who had made his mark in that kind of environment the hard way. He boxed, he debt collected, he minded and he dealt in illegal activities, he was a shaven headed South Londoner that made good, he was Dave Love. The same Dave Love that Billy had been introduced to by his Godfather, Hoxton Harry all those years ago, and Billy had always said that Dave was a man to respect, even back then. You could just tell he was going to be a somebody and he didn't disappoint.

Dave either ran or got a share of every major to minor deal that went down in South London and earned a nice little slice by being indebted to by the Eves' family and the different degree's of business that they have been a part of. The eldest son, Tony who always remembered and respected Billy's brother Mikey for getting his fat out of the frying pan when the sting operation went down at Margate, was still heading the Eves. The same sting that got his younger brother Andy shot in the leg but now has the luxury of recuperating from his wound in parts unknown.

Although Mikey was taking occasional time out's from business deals south of the water by returning to his hometown to gain a little breathing space and hopefully get his face and name a little less known by the metro surveillance squad. When he was back in South London, stirring his spoon in that cup of tea, because of his elevated status amongst the Eves family, the need for Mikey to interact face to face with Dave was presented. In fear that conversations were forever being recorded around Dave, everything was in code and to blend this into an audible to and fro, normal topics were discussed between the two and the only common ground they had to talk about was boxing, which brought up the time that they were all in the same arena so many years previous. It was during their coded conversations, that Billy's name would come up and Mikey would report how well he was doing in his own neck of the woods. The last chat they had was just after that profitable rave the Michaels brothers headed up and so Mikey was bigging Billy up on how his mind worked and how he could turn a greater profit from any situation. The thought of a street smart, profit making lump that had been given a proper upbringing in the world of family businesses but wasn't known was reason enough to stay fresh in Dave's mind.

The way the world of door work works is different from the world of crime. With crime, it is all about territories but with door work it does not matter if you are East, South or

North London because the chances are you will all end up in the West End anyway. So with this kind of network of family friends helping other family friends, it wasn't hard for Dave to make contact with Simon who in turn made contact with Billy to find out if he wanted some work up West. Although the Thunderdome was Lenny's baby, Dave had a hold on most clubs in that area and so it was a hand across the water kind of set up. Everyone helped everyone else if they were short of a bit of manpower or back up plus because of the thought of another door war may have taken place. It made a lot of sense to show you were the bigger man by not being afraid to use an opponent's man, especially one who was from the East, recruited through a North London door as a favour to a South London face. Confused?

The fella Billy was filling in for had to disappear from the London scene for a while due to a near death beating he had administered to some Triad wannabe's from around the corner in China Town. They did not want to mess with Lenny and all the rest of the package that came with him and the club. They just wanted this one particular doorman who had gone into hiding. Now Billy had found it hard to believe that he would make a worthwhile replacement for this guy, after all he knew he could handle himself but he was realistic enough to know that he wasn't in these kinds of leagues. Billy was small time compared to Lenny and his hand picked crew, but Lenny had asked Dave to come up with someone who wasn't known in the area but still knew how to play the game. So here, Billy was being invited to join one of the most feared doors in London as an equal (of sorts).

Billy's first night up at the Thunderdome was on a Monday, he had got there early to make a good impression and acquaint himself with the fire exits and such. Dave had come up to meet Billy face to face and formally introduce himself, Billy always looked back on this gesture as a ploy to catch what he looked like just in case he crossed the line or said something to someone he shouldn't have and examples had to be made. Billy knew who Dave was straight away but Dave who was armed with Billy's background thanks to Mikey, wanted to show he was a good guy by making out he actually remembered that teenager from so many years before when he was introduced to them by Harry.

"Fuck me; you've filled out, what's your Mum been feeding you?" Praise from Caesar himself. Dave continued to chat to Billy like they were old running buddies or something, it was mainly small talk about how Mikey was doing and that he had heard good things about Billy and his own family. Dave then began to tell Billy the rules of the house; no hitting anyone unless you get the nod from Lenny, no private scams on the door and always 'know your place'. Billy thought that these seemed like simple rules to follow. Dave then showed Billy through the club, to where Lenny and a couple of others were sitting, the others being other known faces to those in the know.

"This is Billy; he's the replacement I was telling you about". Dave stood there with that cheeky grin that he was always giving on his face; the false niceties echoed around the dance floor as everyone acknowledge everyone else. The fact that Dave was in Lenny's camp, supplying him with soldiers was a moment he wanted to savour. Billy was given the once over by these seasoned professionals that were all seated around the restaurant area; it was like Billy's first night at the Ritzy all over again only this time Billy did not think he was going to get away with knocking one of these guys out to prove himself.

Lenny held out his shovel of a hand, it looked like it could wrap itself round Billy's twice over, the false niceties were still being banded around.

"All right boy, up for a bit of the big time?" Billy was just humbled to be in this great man's presence. Billy did not have an agenda in this whole situation; he was a pawn that was being used in the great chess game of entertainment security. Every emotion he was feeling was genuine and wished for Dave to leave just so these men would get to see Billy for the person he was and not the spy that their biggest competition had brought in.

"Yes Mr. Shaw, whatever you say, will be done" Lenny liked the Mr. Shaw bit, it showed respect and he could tell that Billy was sincere when he said it and not saying it out of fear or sarcasm.

"You're gonna work up front with me, see how it all works". The rest of Len's team sort of chuckled amongst themselves; this really was the Ritzy all over again.

"Okay" Billy replied nervously, training from the master himself, he could not contain himself. Billy was keen, watching and listening to everything that was going on around him, it was like being a newbie all over again. Dave finally left to do the rounds on his own patch of clubs and Lenny escorted Billy to the reception desk and cloakroom.

"Don't say much, do you son". Although Lenny was the same height as Billy, even an inch or so shorter in fact, Billy felt this giant of a man was able to pick him up and use him as a toothpick if he so desired.

"No sir, only when I'm spoken to". Besides what is the point in talking, there was nothing in Billy's life that was going to be considered attention grabbing to this man, or so he thought.

"We're gonna have to speak to you more often then, ain't we". Billy was like a whole different person that night and he couldn't explain why. He was in awe of this giant man of inspiration, he watched as Lenny was polite to everyone who walked through the door and even those who had been ejected for one reason or another. Lenny was truly a prince amongst men.

The biggest surprise of the night was when a couple of suits started shooting their mouth's off because they were refused entry for being too inebriated. They were being abusive towards Lenny, who had taken it upon himself to deal with the situation, and to a point even down right insulting. Billy thought it was only a matter of time before he smacked them silly; Billy stood their, watching how Lenny positioned himself while his fellow team mates moved with grace to watch his back and moved in to inflict damage when the time came. Billy just kept thinking 'Any minute now' but nothing happened. Eventually these suits got bored with arguing and staggered off, still shouting insults and threats towards Lenny. Once the two drunks were out of sight and off bothering another doorman at another club, Lenny turned towards Billy and leant right into his face.

"I bet you would have hit 'em both wouldn't you son?". Lenny's gravely voice was enough to make you tell the truth, better than any polygraph on the market.

"Well you definitely showed more patience than I would of". Lenny eased his face back a bit, to change the tone from enquiry to wisdom and while looking Billy square in the eye he waxed lyrical with a piece of philosophy that would have toppled Socrates.

"If you learn anything from me during your time here, it should be this, 'It's nice to be important but it's important to be nice', you should always remember that". And Billy always did.

Billy had always been lucky to have such great mentors to learn from over the years, like Freddie, Harry and his Dad, Bobbie to name but a few and now, Lenny Shaw. Here was a man who had used his brawn all of his life and had gained a following because of it. Billy did not want to take anything away from him by thinking that; he also did not want to come across as implying that Lenny could not think his way out of a situation. But when you think of Lenny, you think of him as the hard man he was, over three thousand fights, three thousand wins a thousand lifetimes of stories, whether or not they were all true or at least semi fictional is a different story.

In Billy's eyes, this god could stand toe to toe with Godzilla and hold his own; he was a man's man and did not have to take shit from anybody. Nevertheless, there he was, listening to those two supposedly, intellectually superior beings insult him and his chosen profession. Besmirching his capabilities to do anything other than stand on a door like a trained gorilla, turning people away just because he didn't like them. Yet he let them walk away, unharmed and feeling like they were better than him because of the line of work he did. Billy just did not get it.

A little later in the evening, Lenny just started to talk aloud, at first Billy thought he was talking to someone else but it turned out he was aiming the conversation towards him. Billy did not want to reply, he just wanted to hear this man talk and provide him with his words of wisdom.

"Not everyone knows who I am, not everyone walks our path, and therefore those who are insecure about their own inadequacies will always try to put you down. What's important to me is that I know who I am; my family knows I am a loving father and husband and my friends know I can be relied on. Along the path I have chosen, I am known for many things, but no matter what reasons it all comes down to one thing, I am known. I am a somebody to somebody else, and whether it is out of fear, respect or loyalty, certain people will always listen to what I have to say. It is a good feeling knowing you can hold court whenever you want, most people will never experience that yet it is something they wish for. By not hitting them two prat's, I have given them their moment, it's now something they will talk about for years. They will wake up tomorrow and feel big about themselves on how they put a bouncer in his place, they'll feel even more special if they ever realise who I am. It has cost me nothing, I am still the hardest bastard you will ever meet, it has taken nothing away from me, and so I have nothing to prove. Never feel you have to prove something to someone whose opinion will never count, know inside what you are capable of. As long as your nearest and dearest know of your importance, twenty-four seven, then any chance you get, let someone else have a brief moment of importance. It could be the only moment they will

ever have. You won't be thanked and it could take years before they realise what you did, but you'll know and that's all that matters".

Billy stood there, listening to this man, his words had a sense of intelligence connected to them, and he could do nothing but be in awe of him. By Lenny standing there, telling Billy this, he understood that Lenny was giving him, his moment. Lenny was letting Billy feel important by giving him his fullest attention. Billy knew he would never be an equal to Lenny but from that point on, he did not feel so insignificant next to him either.

The team there was twelve strong yet there was eight on the front door, which seemed weird to Billy because there was no searching going on and just four well-placed, experienced doormen would have had it covered. However, this is the way Lenny had it set up so, who was he to question his insight.

Lenny would mainly be in the back, behind the cashier's station in the reception area. The guys up front were the deterrent, the opposing threat; Lenny was the actual nuke that you activated when you just don't have any more options. That was how any trouble on the front door would be handled but inside was a different story. If the call came that there was something going down then the heavy hitters were called into action. They would file in, single file, Lenny up front; Johnny M behind him, behind Johnny was Peter G followed by Johnny B with Paulie N bringing up the rear. They would cut through the crowd, like a snake through the undergrowth, each had one hand on the next mans shoulder. When they were right on top of the situation, they would go full steam, like a locomotive, and hurt everyone involved. It was a thing of beauty.

Now in those days, being a bouncer was a great occupation, because the council had not yet sucked the fun out of it and most club managers left you alone to handle the front door. What made it a great occupation was the violence, the women and the perks. It was because of the perks that the front door was set up the way it was. Billy always thought that the Ritzy team had a nice sideline but the crew at this club were the Don's of organised scams. The Thunderdome held around two, maybe two and a half, thousand people, eighty odd percent of them were passing tourists that were dazzled by the bright lights of London. It had an entrance fee of fifteen pounds and the bar carried price tags like three pound a pint or four fifty for a shot and a splash. On top of that, you were encouraged to put all your belongings into the cloakroom at a pound per item, because that is how the money for the cloakroom staff was generated. Not a place to go for a cheap night out.

Just like the Ritzy, the entrance fee of every third punter went into the pot. The main front of house guys each pocketed the money and walked the punters past the box office, this way Lenny could keep a mental note of how much was due to come back at the end of the night. All the front door crew had a target to reach because at fifteen pound a pop on an average of two thousand people a night, seven nights a week meant that the pot walked away with nearly fifty-six grand a week. Now on top of this, for every large group of tourists that wanted to come in and did not know no different, they would be charged fifty quid a head and still think they were getting a good deal. That generated another four grand a night. Over time, the money that these guys were making made the job too hard to leave. The top six guys were making on average seven grand a week each, cash. That was around half the amount most people made in a year before tax and stamp. And people call these guys mindless thugs. The rest of the money was broken down, with four grand apiece going to the other two front of house team and two and a half grand each to the four inside.

Billy was replacing one of the six; although he did not get a full cut he was still given a target and did his fair share to help the cause. Billy used to walk away with five grand a week with the extra two going to the guy he was replacing, to help the fugitive out while waiting for the heat to die down. Billy was not about to complain.

Despite the money he was earning Billy was still working at Siddelely Hawks. He knew the gig at the Thunderdome was temporary and he did not see the point of giving up a regular job for the sake of a one off opportunity. So he balanced the two, getting minimal sleep, living off of speed and spending even less time at home, which he thought suited the ice queen because it meant he wasn't bending her ear about the lack of sex that wasn't happening.

Billy was living a superman existence, a mild mannered Engineer by day, and a real life hero to the people by night. Well a hero to the people who knew him. Living the life of superman seemed quite fitting as many years later he actually got the nickname of "Superman" given to him after surviving a gun attack while doing some minding work for a certain businessman. However, that is the future and this was now.

On top of the perks, came the added bonus of inflicting damage on people. By the time Saturday came around on Billy's first week, he was pulled in to be part of the heavy hitter's team. They would go in and bring nothing but a world of pain to whoever was foolish enough to kick it off inside. Now when it went off big style, meaning that swarms of fella's were going at it full tilt. You would find that bottles would be smashed over heads, glasses would be broken and jooked into faces, chairs would be used as weapons and a whole lot more. It was their job to resolve the incident, quickly and effectively with just their *cough, cough* bare hands. The police get full riot gear, CS gas, pepper spray, telescopic batons and in some cases, guns but a doorman is expected to go into the same sort of situations with a loud voice and respect for his fellow man. And yet if you defend yourself by knocking someone out, so you know they wont be getting back up and attacking you from behind while you're dealing with someone else, You're the one in the wrong. What is that all about?

Billy was earning his stripes working along side Lenny and as a result was being introduced to all the faces that turned up to say Hi. As well as the new up 'n' coming players, war dogs and rogues, were a few old time lags that were still keeping a toe in the water. It was this generation that really gave Billy a boost in Lenny's estimations; these were the people that he had looked up to while coming up the ranks himself and so respected everything about them, including their advice. Lenny would introduce Billy to them and they would ask 'What's your background?' No sooner had Billy announced that he was Freddie White's grandson would the old stories about Freddie, Harry, and his brothers start to do the rounds. 'This kid's from good stock treat him well Len' would be the advice they would give.

One night an old hand turned up, sporting a tan and an easygoing persona, he had been living in the land of sun, more through need than desire and was back in England on the quiet just to say hello to a few old faces and basically see a man about a golden dog. He had a club he owned in Magaluf that was doing well with the partying tourists and kept him busy during the slow months of winter. His 'tashe was showing the same signs of grey that the side wings in his hair were but that didn't stop his eye from surveying the talent. He was like a medallion man only without the medallion, his top two buttons on his shirt were undone and he just could not stop dancing to the music coming out over the PA system. He and Lenny were shooting the breeze for a while, talking about the old days and how he was over for a visit to see the old faces. Lenny then called Billy over to meet him with a slight twinge of pride in his voice. Billy came over to meet yet another part of criminal history with anticipations of being star struck while they reminisced about the days of the twins, whether it was good or bad, and the level headed Harry and his partner in crime, Freddie White who helped many a villain who found themselves in a jam. However, this was one old lag that did not need to be introduced; the lag in question was none other than Denny Walnuts, the man who was too tough a nut to crack.

"Alright young Michaels, I've said it before and I'll say it again, it's a small world". Billy smiled as he shook Denny's hand, Lenny's face lit up as Denny regaled him with his version of his first encounter with Billy Michaels when he had to leave for Spain.

Denny asked Billy about Mikey and whether or not he had heard about Andy Eves, he then went on and shot the breeze with the pair of them a for a couple of hours. Lenny's face was awash with a youthful glow as he spoke to his old friend about growing up and the chances they took. In that short time, it was also leaked that Lenny was not just about the violence but had turned his hand to a few other things in his youth although nothing to the extent or style of Denny's escapades. Billy was like a kid in a candy shop as he listened to the two icons as they made each other feel like giggling schoolboy's again. Before leaving, Denny jotted down his address out in Magaluf and handed it to Billy.

"Any time you wanna come out, you come and stay with me. I'll give you a bit of work over the holiday season if you want". It was a casual invitation but where Denny was concerned and his small world theory, it seemed as though he knew one day Billy would need to get away from it all and now he knew he had a place to stay and a way to earn a bit of scratch.

"Thanks, I might just take you up on that offer". Billy put the piece of paper in his pocket for filing.

"Make sure you do". Denny said his goodbyes and off he went, slinking into the night like a ninja, blending into the crowds, staying under the radar of the police that patrolled that area.

Billy was only at the Thunderdome for two months before his predecessor was given the all clear to return to work, but he always popped up there to see Lenny and the team whenever he could. The stories that he walked away with would sit with Billy forever and he looked forward to seeing Lenny later on down the line, when the next up and coming was working along side this great man and sitting down and laughing about the time young Billy entered Lenny's life. Billy was looking forward to having his Denny Walnuts moment.

Having Lenny's seal of approval was a feather in Billy's cap for later on in life, not to mention the glowing reference that Dave had got back about him. It opened doors that Billy wouldn't have even thought about entering, it was at these times that Billy would look back on his life and think 'You've lived some life, Billy boy but then he reminded himself of the price tag that came with it and the personal demons he would carry around because of it.

Billy had reached this point in his life after losing his innocence at a young age; he had witnessed death and destruction, being up close and personal to it all. He had found two of his closest friend's dead and he had tried to drink himself into oblivion. He had fathered a child and had turned his back on her and her mother, he has cheated, swindled and lied, he had been a complete bastard to every woman in his life and his appetite for violence seemed to be growing. That was just a fraction of the things Billy had done to that point, but it was all a snowball effect. Every time he did something new, he did not see anything wrong with going that extra step. People draw lines for themselves, which they say they will never cross; some do and set themselves a new line while others just cross the line and carry on until that line is but a faint image in the background. Billy had his own line drawn in the sand, but the thing with the snowball effect is that every thing you do has to be bigger each time around, and that is how it was with him. Everything Billy did, whether it was in business or violence, had to be bigger, he was always out to top his last big moment and there is only so far you can go before there is nothing bigger and with that moment comes the price you must one day pay.

Chapter Nineteen

After returning from a successful stint on a West End door, Scallywags just seemed to be beneath the new wide eyed Billy. Spilling blood with the likes of Lenny and the gang at the Thunderdome for two months and then coming back to the trouble free zone of the wine bar was a real let down. There was never any trouble and the nights just seemed to bore him. This is where the student had yet to surpass the master because it was that kind of thinking that showed how new Billy really was to the game. Work your night hassle free or get paid the same amount but have nothing but 'agg, Tough choice. Still, Billy was hungry for some action and this place was not going to give it to him, so he considered jacking it in.

During Billy's absence the number of punters coming into the bar slacked off a bit and this was reflected in the reduced figure from the normal amount that had been agreed when their deal was set up. Typical, it did not go up when business was booming but it sure as hell went down when it dipped. Billy used this life lesson in the con section part in the weighing up process of whether or not to leave Scallywags behind him and move on to bigger and better. Plus, on top of all this, Darren was also thinking about quitting the door because he found himself at logger heads with the replacement Simon provided while Billy was rubbing shoulders with the rich and infamous. It was on this note that

Billy decided that enough was enough, everything seemed to come in three's, and there were three reasons to move on right in front of him, boredom, reduced pay off's and an unhappy colleague.

Billy told the owner, Antonio in no uncertain terms what he thought about the reduction in his share of the takings, it was a fucking liberty and totally out of order. In addition, if Antonio thought the numbers were easing off now, wait until Billy told the masses to stop coming in altogether. Antonio then started in with how he had been more than generous with Billy right from the start and it wasn't because of his brother's and the word they put out on the street that people came to Scallywags. Billy personally thought Antonio was over estimating the drawing power of his wine bar if he actually thought it got to full capacity based on his bar prices and lively atmosphere. The final nail in the coffin for Antonio was when he had the cheek to turn round and tell Billy to his face that their business arrangement had ended and that him and his family were no longer welcome in his bar. Without any thinking, rhyme or reason, Billy hit him in the mouth, cutting his lip open and stunning him for a few seconds. Antonio put his hand to his mouth and wiped the warm sticky feeling on his lip away, checking just how much blood there was, he then looked at his hand, saw the blood and then looked back at Billy. The look in Antonio's eyes was as if he was mentally calling Billy a cunt for hitting him. Red rag to a bull because Billy then hit him again, then again and again, Antonio would have faired better by actually saying the words rather than shoot Billy that dirty look. The last person you really want to piss off is the hired muscle, especially one who had just done a tour of duty with the one and only Lenny Shaw. For every piece of trouble that Billy had sorted with just his presence rather than violence in his trendy wine bar was being washed away by this explosive display of violent behaviour on the owner.

Eventually Billy stopped and he just stared at Antonio,

curled up on the floor, begging Billy to leave him alone, while tears rolled down his cheeks and the sobbing tones were interrupted by the need to snort back the snot that was running out of his nostrils. Antonio had the physical presence of a five year old who had just been smacked for uttering their first swear word to their parents. Billy had enjoyed hitting him around so much, it actually gave him a hard on, his heart was pumping, and the adrenaline was fading out the pain of his knuckles swelling up. It was like a drug. Billy bent down and whispered in Antonio's ear that he should forget all about this incident, because if the old bill gave him a tug, he was going to come back and really put a beating on him. Antonio was actually crying while finding the ability to reassure Billy by saying.

"I won't say anything, I promise. I won't say anything" Antonio put his hands up to emphasise the point and to act as a feeble defensive move just in case of a further beating.

"Good" Billy snarled and then decided to put Antonio's defensive blocking to the test and started to pound on him some more. With every blow, Antonio would cry out that he would not say anything and tried desperately to cover himself up by turning into a human hedgehog and roll into a ball. When Billy had enough of watching him cry like a reprimanded child, he walked behind the bar and over to the sink and began to wash his hands and face. Getting as much of Antonio's blood off of himself as he could, he then grabbed a bar towel and dried himself off.

"I'm helping myself to what is owed, you don't mind do you?" Billy tried to get a look of approval from Antonio before collecting up all the takings from the tills and stuffing his pockets. Billy stepped over the limp body of the big time owner of Scallywags and walked out of the place for the very last time.

Scallywags closed two and a half months later, the numbers had dropped off so drastically that they were not making any money and so could not afford to pay the DJ or security. Even the regular barfly's went elsewhere when there was no good time ambience anymore. Funny how his business went to pot after Billy and his brothers had no more to do with it, there was a lesson to be learnt there and Billy could only pray that Antonio realised what it was.

After the Antonio incident, Simon had been called in to resolve the vacant doormen spaces by supplying two new guards (for the short time it stayed open). He was also asked to have a quiet word with Billy, to insure that he would not put another beating on Antonio again. Billy reassured Simon that it was all done and dusted as far as he was concerned and that he would turn his growing aggression elsewhere. That is when Simon asked if Billy wanted to turn it somewhere in particular, he had a contact that was always on the lookout for collectors of a certain calibre and was always fair with the wages side of things. Billy told Simon that he was up for that and he should put his name forward, which he did.

Although Billy was starting to question his career choices and contemplated the newfound release for boredom, he still liked being at his day job. He was left alone to get on with things, Billy had his friends around him and he was actually building something with his own hands, because we all know that busy hands are not idle hands itching to give you a smack in the chops. Billy would talk to Michael, Darren, Alan or even Mickey B about all the crooked stuff that had and was going on in his life and have a whole host of normal people to talk about normal everyday things, like TV or the cost of living. He also had the new wave of apprentices coming through the coil winders department for him to torture and upset, and there were plenty. Billy would have them working under the machine so oil; glue and usually his left over tea would get all over them. He would make them lift and carry things that were not needed, not to mention sending them to the stores for things like skyhooks and glass hammers. Billy loved it, he would scare off all those that did not fit in on his day shift; after all, he did not want another

Mark on his hands, and sound out those that managed to hang in there.

One of the brave souls who passed the test to stay on the apprenticeship was the third young lady that worked along side Billy but not in his bed. Just like Nicky and Angie, this one escaped the Billy Michaels treatment because she was lucky enough to actually witness his gentler side, her name was Donna.

Donna was only five foot two but she had a rack on her that just caught your eye no matter how much taller than her you were. In fact the taller you were the better the cleavage shot you got, and the best thing was, she was one hundred percent firm. Nothing bounced, it was solid and she put it all down to playing volleyball. Now it was a known fact that Donna got the hardest time off of Billy because deep down he wanted to give into temptation and give a squeeze to those big, juicy melons and so he would flirt by throwing innuendoes at her every chance he got and she would come straight back with a counter remark. Billy liked her because she could hold her own (ooh 'err missus) in an insult match and she was a very funny person. Billy remembered one time it had come down to a bout of insults that got physical, because she said something that made Michael and him give chase with a pair of scissors. When they caught her, they cut her bra straps and proceeded to parade about with her black, lacy bra waving in the air. This earned her the nickname "Snipper" but she took all of this in her stride when others would have bitched and moaned, she was good people and it was a shame when things come to an end and she moved on to another department as part of her apprenticeship.

Donna had also caught the eye of Steve Perks, who just hounded her from dusk 'til dawn. It reached a point where Billy interfered and set them up on a date, which turned into a thing between them that lasted all of about two weeks. Billy could have also been the cause of the break up, but hand on heart, if you asked him he really didn't know. Would continuous flirting and belittling her new boyfriend really be a cause to dump the lanky streak of piss? Donna used to knock about with the motley crew on some of their more civilised nights out, and Vaughan, Michael, Steve (they needed a driver) and Billy were even asked to act as bouncers at her sister's engagement party.

Donna was a good person to be around, she had had a hard upbringing but she didn't let it get her down and never told you how lucky you were not to have had the same problems. She, like most people in Billy's life, was good people, one of your own who was on the same wavelength. Nowadays of course in the era of political correctness and sexual harassment charges, those kind of day to day shenanigans wouldn't be permitted unless you had a real, independent woman involved rather than one that was a lawsuit waiting to happen.

After walking out of Scallywags that day Billy felt reborn, he had a bundle of spare cash after helping himself from the tills and from working at the Thunderdome, but he had Darren pestering him for a new sideline. They still had a nice little thing going on at Siddelely Hawks with their loan sharking, so Billy thought that he should expand out from the confines of work and take it to the streets, therefore increasing business and giving Darren something more interesting to do. Billy put the word out that he was in a position to lend out money to all those that needed it. Billy tapped on a weekly interest rate of ten percent and set up a scheduled repayment time, every Saturday afternoon in the Chequers pub, between the hours of one and four.

Darren would sit in the pub every weekend to wait and collect from those who had borrowed, anyone who did not show up, had until the following Friday to contact one of them. If they were dumb enough to keep out of the way for two weeks straight, then Darren would take it upon himself to go visit them at their home or their work or wherever, just to prove a point. You missed three weeks and you got hurt.

266

Billy thought it was best to leave this little venture for Darren to run with, he felt it was a little beneath him with the other strokes that he had been pulling recently and besides it made Darren feel like a true gangster running the business like it was his own. As the loan sharking business got bigger, however, Darren started recruiting his own little crew to handle the additional legwork. He was becoming an under boss and Chequers was his Bada Bing, he even had the bar staff play Louie Prima on the CD player every time he went in. There was a pool going by the bar staff on how long it would take before Darren had people queuing to kiss his pinkie ring while he held court in his place of commerce.

Billy liked Darren because he truly believed he thought he was living in a Scorsese movie, all that was missing was De Niro and Pesci. Darren always wanted to be a gangster and knowing Billy allowed that dream to come true, he believed in the Mafiosi code of conduct and he was someone Billy trusted one hundred percent, all in all Darren was a good fella.

Chapter Twenty

Billy met up with Sammy, the fella that Simon had put him on to, who ran a wholesaler's in Waltham Abbey. He supplied cash 'n' carry's and market traders who couldn't get credit from other suppliers. It was the same set up as loan sharking only instead of money it was goods and just like loan sharking, there were people out there that did not like to pay their debts. Hence, why there was so much collecting work on offer from this guy. Due to the nature of the set up and his customers, he was more than willing to forgo the monies owed in exchange for people being injured, a man after my own heart, thought Billy.

Sammy was your typical bad boy made good; he had a big, gold chap's bracelet, weighing down his right wrist and a gold sovereign ring on nearly every finger. He was white trash in the biggest sense and was proud of it. He had gotten to his station in life the hard way, as did ninety nine percent of the people Billy already knew. He used to work the markets selling any and every piece of junk or stolen goods that came his way. Sammy was a bit over the top for Billy's liking, which in turn gave Billy reason to think he could not be trusted when push came to shove. Nevertheless, a job was a job and so Billy listened to what Sammy had to say and agreed to give it a go. Billy was to be Sammy's new hitter, which meant he was the one who hit all those that did not pay up. Billy was teamed up with a caller, named Derek, who handled all the face-to-face approaches. Derek started out as the hitter and got the opportunity to move up a few months previous. The new hitter they got in to replace him was put into hospital on a collecting job that went wrong, so now the word had gone out for a new hitter and Billy stepped up to the challenge.

The procedure was simple, the caller would make contact with the mark (the person who you were collecting from) and remind him or her about the outstanding debt, making arrangements to have a part payment by the end of the week. Come the Friday, if a payment hadn't been made, then the hitter would go round and do some minor damage to their property, i.e. keying their car, a brick through their house window during the middle of the night, etc, etc etc. The damage was minimal so not to arouse suspicion about where the attack had come from. The caller would then make contact again, always being polite and never threatening; if he got the brush off again then the hitter would go in and take it to the next level. I.E. post pictures of their kids outside their school to them; blow up their cars with rags in the petrol tank or shoot their windows out with a 'thirty-eight' snub nose. If by the third time the caller was still being told to fuck off, then the hitter would have to go around and hurt them and nick back any outstanding stock. Only the stubborn and the stupid ever took it to level three and Billy always felt they deserved everything that they got when they did.

The money side of it was worthwhile too; Billy got paid for every visit he had to make as well as a five percent cut if the debt was under ten grand. Billy got ten percent if it was over ten grand and twenty percent if the debt was over twenty five grand. It was easy money and easy work and it all seemed to go without a hitch. Derek would give Billy pointers and tell him about the days he used to be a hitter and just how far he had to go to get the point across. Derek also told Billy that most of them paid up without argument once you involved their loved ones, and that there had only been a handful of times that some of them had called the police. However, because the caller was never threatening or aggressive and was never at the scene of the crime, the police had no real evidence to go on. It was a well thought out system that was all within the legal parameters, well from the callers' part at least. Billy, was always on the outside of the legalities and was always thinking up new ways to hurt people both physically and mentally. He was treating this debt-collecting gig as a way to enhance his personal knowledge of inflicting pain, finding more efficient and productive methods to get the job done if and when it reached the third level. Billy really loved it when someone let things go to level three.

Christmas was looming up and it must have brought a blue moon with it because out of nowhere Mikey phoned Billy up again with another offer of a job. Billy had not spoken to him for a little over a month, not since Billy saw him to update Mikey about working with Lenny thanks to him and Dave Love. Billy had given Mikey a set of keys to his house for the times when Mikey needed a place to crash but he was starting to feel that he was only making the effort to call when he needed something else from Billy.

Mikey wanted to know if Billy fancied working along side him over the Christmas holidays, looking after some dealers during the busy holiday period. Although Billy was a little narked at Mikey for seemingly making an extra effort to avoid him whenever he was in Walthamstow he did always enjoy working with any one of his brothers, especially Mikey so he thought what the heck and told him "yes". However, yet another one off offer, where the whole situation would snowball into a completely different thing all together by the time it was over.

The plan seemed simple enough; the two brothers were meant to pick up a lower end pill dealer and his runners and go do the business in a certain, high profile club in Elephant and Castle. Now it was Christmas, so all the pill suppliers would be supplying in bulk so all the dealers wouldn't keep coming back over Christmas holidays wanting their wares replenished. Because most raver's were now off of school, college or even work for a while they would be out partying all day and all night, meaning the need for chemical substances were in high and constant demand. This meant their particular guy had picked up around twenty thousand of the little fella's with a street value of three hundred thousand pounds to be able to supply and cope with the non stop, partying revellers. He was used to doing small-scale stuff but because the big time dealers were either heavily under surveillance or taking the Christmas off so they could party, he got the chance to move up the ladder.

The problems started on the night that Mikey and Billy were meant to meet with their band of merry men to do their babysitting gig. The dealer in question, who was getting his Rocky moment, you know, an out of the blue chance of reaching the big time, wasn't at the pick up point and neither were his runners. At first, the brothers figured they were just running late and so they waited, and then waited and waited. Then they thought maybe they were at the wrong location and so the Michaels boys tried to call Rocky's mobile, and surprise surprise, no answer. Already something did not smell right, Mikey thought that maybe something came up and the little team made their way straight to the club in question. The brothers went to the club to see if they had used their guest list passes.

They drove down to the side road in Elephant and Castle where this particular venue stood and checked with the guys on the door if any had turned up claiming their place on the list, there was nothing, nada, zilch. It became apparent that the dealer and the runners had had it on their toes with over a quarter of a million pounds worth of drugs. And the Michaels siblings didn't have the foggiest idea on where to start looking for them.

Mikey had to make the call to the people who fronted

the money; it would be an understatement if you were told that they were not pleased. The brother's assignment was instantly changed, now they were charged with the task of finding the absconders and getting either the money or the pills back, but if they could get both then there would be an extra bonus in it for them, by any and all means necessary. Not to mention that a lesson was now needed to be taught to all those involved in double crossing the hand that fed them, this one was going to get very, very ugly.

Mikey and Billy spent the following week chasing up everyone that Mikey knew who was connected to the three absconders and they were getting frustrated because they were getting no-where, because the dealer was small time he was able to operate under the radar, it was time to turn it up a notch. The motivated and angry brothers went back to everyone that they had already questioned; only this time they took pleasure in smacking them silly on their doorsteps in front of their families and friends. Billy who was already filled with ideas on how to get people to part with stuff they really did not want to thanks to his debt collecting career. Billy showed the seriousness of the situation by putting guns to their heads, knives to their throats and hammers to their feet. Billy, who was enjoying putting the explanation mark on his questioning way too much. This acted as the perfect leverage for when Mikey would then inform those concerned that if they had to come back a third time they would do the same thing to anyone who either answered the door or was in a ten-foot radius of their lying arses at the time. Eventually the word 'Liverpool' was mentioned, and now the brothers had a new area of investigation to follow up on and they intended to do it on Boxing Day. Billy would also remember that particular Boxing Day, nineteen ninety one as the day his sexual relationship with Nikki ended, it was the very last time they ever had sex together and the last time he ever felt any closeness to her.

The Michaels made sure to tell a few of their nearest and

dearest where they were headed to and why. Vaughan had been heavily into his band, practising and gigging at local venues. His drummer, Marc and he were forever working on lyrics and rifts for their big discovery. So every spare moment Vaughan had was spent with Marc or practising at the studios in Stratford at all hours of the night with the third member of the band, the bass player, Scuzz. Although Billy gave him the heads up, he was not totally convinced that it was sinking in so he gave Jason and Colin the four one one. These guys were into the pill scene now and were also burning the candle at both ends, while still running their chop shop business. Gary must have been in some serious trouble because no one had heard from him in ages; he was laying low for whatever reason and was therefore unreachable. Mikey told some of his connections but Billy put all his faith into Monty to be there if push came to shove and back up was needed in this deadly situation.

The two of them drove up to Liverpool on the Thursday night, their only plan was to wait outside a different club each night and see if they could catch one of these bastards in the queue or something. It wasn't a great plan but it was the only one they had. The brother's contacts up this way were extremely limited and they could only rely on themselves if the shit hit the fan. They had to keep a low profile and not get their faces noticed, so staying in hotels or B 'n' B's was out of the question, even if there had been any open and vacant.

Now rather than bore you with the sightseeing spiel, because after all you either know how Liverpool was surviving the climax of the recession or you don't but it is only fair to point out that it's a whole different jungle during the clubbing hours as it is in the day time ferrying the Mersey or visiting "The Tavern". The people up there had nothing to lose; most would be better off in prison than existing on the opportunities on offer by the high unemployment and the poor living conditions that the local council estates produced. It was a dog eat dog world, everyone and their sister seemed to have a handgun and drugs were dished out like candy between the kids and parents alike. Fortunately, over the years, the town's conditions have improved and the opportunities on offer equal that of any thriving metropolis. But this was nineteen ninety one and you still had to watch yourself.

Friday night and the town was buzzing, for the amount of punters that went into each club, the brothers on a mission could only fully check one club per night. Liverpool was not only the gun capital of England but it was also rave central; equalled only by Manchester. It was cold that night and they were parked across the way of some club getting a glimpse of everyone who was queuing up to get in. On top of everything else that was going on, they had yet another problem to contend with, Mikey was the only one out of the two of them that knew what these people looked like. He gave Billy a brief description of all three but he still had to put up with him forever saying, "Is that one, is that him, what about them?" Even Billy thought it was annoying and it was him that was forever saying it, mixed with the low temperature and the smell of two grown men and their assortment of bodily odours, it did not make for an enjoyable experience. That Christmas week the clubs were open every night, they must have sat outside each and every one of them. Anywhere you would have been able to sell pills in the quantities that would make the evening worthwhile. The 'New Car' smell air freshener in the car couldn't compete with the rank, beefy smell that was coming off of the stakeout duo, they had been literally living in the car. They walked the streets during the day, sitting in fast food places and making good use of the sample bottles of deodorant and aftershave in Boots. Brushing their teeth and rinsing their mouths out with cold tea in the mornings and generally looking like a couple of bums, minus the shopping trolleys.

It was on New Years Eve that Mikey finally saw one of the runners trying to sell his wares to the anxious masses that were queuing up outside this particular nightclub. The Michaels lads were both tired, angry and Billy, who had been used to being pampered, was in dire need of a hot bath, with bubbles and aromatherapy candles burning to help soothe away and relieve the stress, he loved taking those long baths.

Mikey went running up to the guy who was in the middle of making a transaction and belted him to the pavement. He then picked him back up off the floor using one of his favourite techniques of gripping the top lip and pulling upwards. If you don't stand up, you would be missing half your mouth. Mikey then hit him again and dragged him over to the car where they bundled the fugitive runner into the boot. This bit of commotion caught everyone's attention but in Liverpool, if it wasn't someone they knew then they didn't see anything.

After what seemed an eternity of living the rough life tracking down scum, they finally drove back to London with smiles on their faces, it had been a long week and they were going to take it out on the scared fella in the boot, who if he had not already done so, must have been shitting himself. The journey was long because they were obeying every motoring law known to man because the last thing they wanted was to get pulled over while they had a trussed up person in their boot. Apart from anything else, this was kidnapping and Billy had already been pulled in for that, it was not going to happen again.

On reaching the A1 and heading towards Enfield, Billy gave Jason a call because they wanted to use one of his garages to store the motor while the pair of them got a proper night's sleep in a nice soft bed. Jason said he could supply the garage but the nearest thing he had to a soft bed was his double, foam-padded put me up that was in his office, which the brothers would have to share. It was just as well that we are brothers, thought Billy. The next morning they woke up somewhat refreshed and eager to go. They took it in turns to use Jason's razor to get rid of the weeks growth emerging from their faces and used up all his hot water as they took it in turns to shower a couple of times over. They finished up by getting some homemade brekkie down their necks and slipped into some overalls that Jason gave them to wear in place of their stinking and stained clothes. Once all that was out of the way, it was time to go to work.

The good thing about being in a chop shop garage is the array of tools that are at your disposal, rubber mallets, angle grinders and Billy's personal favourite, cordless drills. They opened the boot to get their guest out and the initial smell that caught their noses was that of an un-cleaned builder's portaloo. This little toe rag had shit and pissed himself and to make matters worse had gone and puked all over the spare tyre. He was not doing himself any favours and was certainly not gracing the brother's good books. They pulled him out, hosed him down and sat him in a chair, bound his elbows and wrists to the armrests, gaffer taped his knees together and taped his ankles to the chair legs. It was starting to resemble a scene from this bootlegged copy of a movie Billy had seen a couple of months back, called Reservoir Dogs. Some new breed of filmmaker, called Quentin Tarentino directed it, and it got rave reviews when he had entered it into the Sundance Film festival back in January of Ninety-one. The scene in question was the one with this uniformed cop bound to a chair and this dark haired fella, who was dancing to the song 'Stuck in the middle with you' pull's out a cut throat blade and slices the cop's ear off. A totally bitching movie!

Mikey started to ask the captive questions about the dealer and where they could find him, what happened to the pill's and how they thought they were every going to get away with it. The captive in question was crying and repeatedly saying that he was sorry, they were getting nowhere fast. Once again it was time to turn it up a notch, so Billy grabbed a cordless drill, puts in the smallest drill bit he could find and tightened up the chuck. It was going to hurt him a lot more than it was going to hurt me, chuckled Billy. Mikey held the bound man's head back while Jason got involved and started pulling down on his chin, causing his mouth to open up, nice and wide. Billy revved the drill a few times to get the wide mouthed bound captives' attention, and it must have worked because he pissed himself again. Christ how big was this guy's bladder? He tried to shake his head back and forth; Billy could see his tongue wagging from side to side as though he was trying to say something. The boy's let him go and he started singing them a song about how the pills were divided up between the three of them and they all went their separate ways. The plan was to sell all that they had and then fly abroad somewhere and live out their days as kings. It sounded like a good plan, too bad it was not working out like that. He then told them that the other runner went to Manchester while the Dealer said he had a contact that was going to buy a bulk share from him but he did not know where he was.

The interrogators believed he was telling them the truth, he even pointed out that he was wearing a money belt under his trousers, where he kept all the cash he had made and had stored the left over pills. The lads thanked him for his co-operation and assured him that he was going to live to see another day. A sigh of relief came from the bodily waste smelling low life, as the tension in his body seemed to fade away, in-between the tears; he even started to smile a little.

"I said you get to live, I didn't say you get to go unpunished!" Mikey grabbed his head again while Jason pulled down on his chin; the guy started to thrash about as Billy pulled his finger down on the trigger of the drill and started to attack the captives' teeth with it. Tooth chips and blood were flying out of his mouth, as Billy bored the drill bit into the guys' molars. He was trying hard to scream but the boy's had a firm grip on his head.

The more he tossed about the worse he was making it for himself, because it was causing Billy to lose his aim and rip into his gums. Billy spent about ten enjoyable minutes acting like the dentist from hell. All the while, he was fantasising on how much pain he must have been inflicting and how much pain his victim must have been feeling. Billy also thought how sexually pleasing he found it to inflict that much hurt and damage to a person.

They finally cut him loose from his restraints, and the recently operated on poster boy for dentistry school just slipped out of the chair and straight to the floor, his mouth making him look like a 'Billy Bob' from the backwater swamps of the Deep South. He tried to touch his mouth but it must have been hurting him as the slightest amount of pressure on it was causing him even more pain. The guy was sobbing his heart out, what did he want, sympathy?

Mikey reached down and scooped him back up and put him back into the boot of the car that the kidnapped, toothless runner had previously used as a toilet. The brothers drove to the original meeting point where they were supposed to meet the three absconders on that particular evening and just left their tortured friend on the side to serve as a warning to every nickel and dime scumbag who fancied their chances. They then had to scrap and crush the car at a breaker's they knew, so not to get any comebacks on the motor.

They did not see the point of driving up to Manchester and staking out the clubs like they did in Liverpool. In addition, they didn't have a lead on the rogue dealer neither but there's an old saying that if you stand still long enough then the whole world will go by you. It was just a matter of waiting and biding their time, this guy would resurface and when he did, they would have him. Besides, the moneymen of the operation were happy that they got a result, no matter how trivial the returned stash compensated for the total loss. It was all about saving face, it showed that no matter where you went, you would be found and dealt with, and that got proven here. It also did not do the Michaels family reputation any harm either and as a result, even more collection work started to come their way. This could become a full time career.

Despite everyone being happy with the result and the rewards and recognition that came with it all, Billy could not help but feel that there was a missing piece to the puzzle that everyone was overlooking. How did three low level snot noses have the foresight to split up and go separate ways, especially up to unknown territories like Liverpool and Manchester? And how did a dealer that was so far down on the ladder have contacts that could buy bulk? If he had that kind of hook up then why was he still doing small-scale business? Something just was not right, someone must have organised this bold and ballsy move, someone who knew that these guys were going to get a chance at the big time; only a handful of people would have known that. If they hadn't gotten a result Mikey could have been held accountable, which meant whoever set this up didn't care about what happened to Billy's brother, which meant that they didn't have a right to live if they ever revealed themselves. That was a promise that Billy would not welch on.

There were times when Billy would look back on his life, when anger and fury were flowing through his veins and to be honest he could not say he was very proud of the things he did, but the scary part is he was not sorry for them either. Billy only hurt those who deserved to be hurt, it was people who existed in his little world, and all knew the penalty that could come their way if they fucked up. You did not like it, then live a normal life, have a cola and a smile and shut the fuck up. Just do not complain when things go bad. That was the law of the land and this jungle cat was happy to enforce it.

Chapter Twenty-One

Billy finally walked through the front door of the home that he shared with Nikki, after spending half of the Christmas holidays sitting in a car with his brother and never phoning her once. She was sitting in the armchair watching TV when he poked his head through the door and said "Hi"; she just nodded back at him in recognition. She did not ask where he had been or how things went, it had become apparent that they stayed together as a means to an end, and that is how the pair of them played it out. Billy thought maybe she was having an affair and deep down he was kind of hoping she was. He felt like he helped her escape one prison for another, but Nikki was a real homebody, she had her things around her, and she was content. While Billy did not have to answer for anything, he did, as far as Nikki was concerned, his money was his own and if he did not get some action from home, and then he would go get some elsewhere. Isn't that how all relationships should be? He could never understand how she could take it all on board and not unleash on him the pent up anger and frustration. Christ she didn't even bat an eyelid to Mikey for letting himself in and making himself at home, all the while knowing that he has never liked her since day one. Nikki was not a doormat despite what those on the outside looking in may have thought; Billy just always figured that her parents were so strict that everything else seemed like a walk in the park; well that's what he figured.

The Christmas shutdown at Siddelely Hawks was over and so it was all back to work for another year of Engineering. Billy knew it must seem weird for someone like him to hold a full time regular job, but he always saw it as the Ying to his Yang, in fact, all the Michaels boys had full time jobs. Stuart was still working at the carpet warehouse, Mikey was a trained plumber, Gary was now a qualified builder and decorator, Vaughan was working in a meat factory and even their little baby brother, Craig, had a job. He was about to turn seventeen that February and had left school with zero qualifications and got a job in Covent Garden market up in Vauxhall. They all led a regular life during the day; it was how they conducted themselves outside of the normality that was seen as the problem.

The beginning of Nineteen ninety two also saw Billy complete his engineering apprenticeship, he was in fact the first person to complete the five year program in only three years and was qualified as a skilled Engineer. Plus, due to his rapport with the new staff, Billy was also made up to supervisor level to help train the new apprentices. Now this should have been a turning point in his life, a job with career prospects, honest money through honest work, but Billy was not destined to live a nine to five existence, it just was not in his blood. What was in his blood was the life he led outside of work, Billy was addicted to the excitement and rushes of adrenaline, the violence and the money, he loved the status he was acquiring and all the trappings that came with it. It was like a drug, you can understand how people become addicted to things and you can also understand how over time, too much of a good thing can affect you. Billy was once told that he was too tough to die and too free to live, but he always saw it the other way round, too tough to live, too free to die. The way he saw it was people made choices about what they did with their lives, some played it safe while others pushed it to the extreme. Yet, no matter what way they chose to live, they all end up at the same point, Death. That is what had to be remembered, life was a journey not a destination, you shouldn't wake up every day waiting for the inevitable, you should be doing whatever it is you want to do. Whether it's being good or being bad, don't live life and regret not doing things, live life and regret the things you did do. Billy has always been somewhat of a philosopher, others just say that he is opinionated, but there are those out there that seek his wisdom and wish to learn from his mistakes and experiences. Billy is always asked if he knows what the meaning of life is and his answer is always the same, the answer is yes. The meaning of life is death, for without it, life has no meaning.

Billy smoked a lot of dope back in those words of infinitive wisdom days.

Business outside was picking up; Billy was being asked to do quite a bit of financial retrieving for those who could not go through the normal channels. He was still working along side Derek, collecting outstanding debts for Sammy, the cash 'n' carry king. Darren was still running the loan sharking side of things and Simon was still putting Billy onto people who may benefit from his area of expertise. Billy was still popping up to see Lenny and the guy's up at the Thunderdome and made it a point to give the odd courtesy call to Dave Love out of respect for who he was and what he had done for him. Life was good.

In fact, the only part of Billy's life that was not on a high was his home life; he had moved his things out of the bedroom he and Nikki shared and into the spare room, where Billy now slept. In reality Billy could have moved out but this house was more his than it was hers and it became a territorial thing for a while. The minute Billy was sleeping in a different bed, he just saw it that their relationship was on a break and started openly dating other women, although he never waved it under Nikki's nose and he never brought it to their doorstep. Nikki would later play it as if she was naive and clueless about that period of their history, but the way Billy saw it, whatever gets you through the day.

When it came to love life's in the Michaels fold, Billy wasn't the only one having relationship problems, Stuart and his young lady, Kelly, who he had discarded his brothers for, was also going through a rough patch. The details of which Stuart never discussed with Billy, but they were definitely heading for splitsville and with good reason. Billy would go out on a limb and say that at least seventy five percent of it was Kelly's fault and that is all he would have to say about that.

One night Vaughan, who actually ventured away from his music and band mates, and Billy went up to the Chequers pub to see if Darren was around and to have a lemonade, what they found going on inside was an arm wrestling tournament going on. It was a pound to enter and it was for amateurs and professionals alike. So being up for the crack, Billy placed down his pound and entered his name into the fray for both divisions. In the amateur's division, he won the first two rounds and was beaten in the finals by someone a lot smaller than him, yet another lesson to be learnt there. And in the professional league Billy was lucky not to have his arm ripped off in the first round, but it was all in good fun. It was in the women's division that a certain contestant caught his attention, she was easy on the eye, with forearms like Popeye's and you could only imagine what the grip on her must have been like. She dominated the few challengers that stepped up and was crowned ladies champ. Billy wondered, what is the worst thing that could happen if he went up and spoke to her? And figured whatever it was, it was worth the risk. The only problem was her boyfriend who had won the evening's professional division. He was a very tall, strong looking fella and quite good-looking, in a non-Homo kind of way. Billy weighed up if it would be worth getting into a confrontation with him for the attention of a woman who may or may not be interested, and eventually decided against it. Billy did not even get her name but she did make an impression on him and destiny was to have them meet again under different circumstances a year later. It was also on this night, that a young fifteen-year-old lad by the name of Gareth first entered Billy's life. Gareth was standing in at six foot six, and must have been the same wide, although in fairness it was mainly all baby fat. The exploits of Gareth, Billy and another young man who went by the nickname of 'Tigger', due to his passion for bouncing, would consume a fair slice of the nineties for the Michaels family but all that was the future and this was now.

Vaughan seemed a little put out that the whole pub was loud and awash with arm wrestlers, Darren wasn't there and Billy had a bit of business to take care of later that evening and wasn't really in a quiet drink and a chat mood. Once Billy had lost both tournaments, and had a few laughs with the regulars he was ready for the off so he could meet up with Derek as they had to take care of some third level stuff. Vaughan sheepishly withdrew from speaking up and saying whatever it was that was on his mind; and said he might as well see if Marc was around to go over to the studio and make some music. Billy could tell something was wrong but was stuck for time, whatever Vaughan's problem was, if he wasn't willing to just come out and say it then it wasn't as important as being late for a friend. They said their goodbyes and went their separate ways.

Billy reached the rendezvous destination and met up with Derek who was sporting a look longer than Vaughan was twenty minutes earlier. It turned out that the visit had been called off for tonight, Sammy had heard from the intended victim and was giving him a little more time to pay up. The late night buzz of busting heads and removing digits was being wasted hanging around with nothing but bad news to keep it company, so Billy parted ways with Derek and thought he would drive over to Vaughan's band practise and see if he still wanted to go somewhere for a quiet drink and a chat.

Billy had visited the studio a few times before to hear his brother sing, Vaughan had a set of pipes on him that made him sound like the lead singer of Pearl Jam. Billy could not wait to cash in on the favour owed to him by Nathan and his music promoting Dad. Portent could be the next big grunge band to enter the music scene and scoop the Kerrang awards, Billy thought it would not be a bad idea to really get behind this trio and invest a bit of capital and time and perhaps see where they could go. Besides the idea of groupies doing anything to get backstage was appealing enough for Billy and his perverted mind.

He entered through the security guards entrance and walked up the stairs to their usual room, he could not hear any music coming out but with all the soundproofing that was not so unusual, Billy quietly opened the door, so not to disturb the musicians at work. He peeked through the black out curtain. He was glad he did not make a noise coming in or he may have interrupted his kid brother shafting some bird from behind. The sly old dog, Billy thought, making use of the female followers before even becoming famous. Vaughan had his long, blonde haired lover bent over the drum kit and was giving it the slow, gentle touch as opposed to his brothers pump and grind method. Billy watched as this girl's long locks gently swayed back and forth like a curtain in the wind, shielding her face from the public's eye. Billy felt somewhat dirty for watching his baby brother get busy but he had to admire the loving technique, even more so when Vaughan dropped his hand for a reach-a-round, only to tug on her erect penis. Penis?

"What the fuck!" Billy stepped out from the curtain to stand face on to Vaughan and his bum buddy. The longhaired lover looked up in shock; the hair cleared his face to reveal that it was the drummer Marc that was enjoying being on the receiving end of the pork sword that was still inserted in his rectum. Vaughan froze while Marc stood up from his bent over position, with Marc standing up and Vaughan not pulling out the connection between them made them both wince in pain, even Billy flinched.

285

Billy was speechless, Vaughan, who was still recovering from the shock to his system, pulled up his strides and started to walk over, muttering words in an attempt to explain. There were just some things that Billy did not want to hear explained and ran out the room, then the building. Billy jumped into his car and made his way home, this was way too much to deal with, he needed to talk to someone and fast, and so he grabbed his mobile phone and called Stuart and told him to meet him at his place. Stuart had always been the level headed one, so if any one was going to calm the situation Billy knew it would be him.

As Billy screeched to a halt outside his house, he could see that Mikey's car was in his parking bay. 'Thank god' Billy thought, the three of them could talk this through and get a game plan together. 'How on earth can their little brother, who has busted heads and enjoyed the ways of a woman, be gay?' the question kept going over time and time again in Billy's head. Of course it's when you weigh up the evidence that it all becomes obvious, the way he acted after the stripagram incident. The funky lyrics to his heart felt songs, the holiday to the most secluded island in Spain with a bunch of lads in tow, even the topless fella at the rave that Vaughan was pushing into the dark corner. Christ it was all becoming clear and it hurt more because it went against the grain of the family.

Billy walked up to the front door and was about to put his key in when through the netted window he could see some blokes naked arse going ten to the dozen, please let that be Mikey with some tart and not another homo affair, pleaded Billy. He rushed in to disturb the normal sex, because his need to talk to his brother preceded anything else going on under his roof. Billy came into the front room and was instantly reminded of that age old proverb that everything bad comes in three's. First his evening of head busting and digit chopping was cancelled, then he found out that his baby brother was batting for the other side thanks to a front row seat and now he came home to find Mikey, naked giving it to some bird in his front room and the bird in question was Nikki.

Mikey had the decency to jump off of her instantly, yet another brother with his cock out trying to explain something. Billy stared at Mikey while Nikki feebly attempted to cover her naked body and tried to blend in with the wallpaper. There had yet to be a word invented that could describe how Billy was feeling at that very moment, a feeling that was amplified when Vaughan, who had given chase once Billy had sped off, came crashing through the front door and into the room. It was a Mexican stand off to end all stand off's, Vaughan looked over at the naked Mikey and saw what the problem between him and Billy was. Mikey looked back and wondered why Vaughan was busting through people's doors and Billy just looked at them both, fists tightly closing, as he got ready to give into the blood lust that was surfacing to the top.

Mikey was trying to calm Billy down, still being naked really didn't help his cause, all the while though Mikey was positioning himself into a fighting stance, whether he was in the wrong or not, there was no way he was going down without a fight, brother or no brother. Vaughan too changed his stance, carefully watching his siblings while not making eye contact with Mikey's member that was now looking at his feet rather than his head. This was going to go only one way, down hill. Nikki was pleading with the three, lined up men to stop before it even started; she was professing her apologies to Billy for cheating on him all this time, 'All this time? How long had this been going on for?' With everyone trying to calm the situation down, all the while giving off the signs that they were ready to attack, the sounds were falling on deaf ears. Billy had been hurt, betrayed and shocked by the people he loved the most. Mikey who had forever declared his dislike for Nikki had been coming round while Billy was out working and giving Nikki the sex that she was denying Billy, obviously through guilt? Vaughan had been living a lie and was spitting on the bloodline by being everything that that the family wasn't, weak and gay.

All the while, the imminent eruption of violence was thick in the air; Mikey was trying one last time to convince Billy that it didn't have to go down this way. Vaughan stepped in to add his piece about how he should be supported in the choices that he made in life, that him being gay was not going to change anything between them, they were still brothers. Vaughan's revelation then prompted Mikey to step in to confirm that what he just heard was right, that Vaughan was a bum bandit.

That was it that was when the little switch in Billy's head flicked and everything went black before it went red.

Chapter Twenty-Two

"Monty, I need to get out of the country right now, you up for a spell in the sun?" The heat was on and Billy needed the space to breathe. Every violent situation that had taken place throughout his entire life had been leading up to that moment. Now, because of it all, Billy was finding himself needing to leave the manor and his nearest and dearest to avoid the staring eyes and pointing fingers. It seemed so natural, it was instinct, it was something he had been born to do, or so it felt at the time. Billy was not saying it was a mistake but it could have gone a different way, perhaps even should have, but what was done was done and there was no turning back, he now had to live with the consequences, the nightmares and the forever lasting memory of that night.

Billy and his cousin met at Gatwick airport, both were loaded with the essentials, passport, money and a destination. They booked the first available flight that day to Magaluf and figured they would go on a spend up buying some suitable sun lounging clothes when they got there. Billy was going to use the time to escape the questions, regroup and maybe experience some of the local culture. Not to mention, have a few drinks and score with some of the senoritas. It sounded like a good enough plan, plus it would help to relieve the weight that was bearing down on his shoulders.

Monty on the other hand knew that something bad must have gone down, there was no time for him to question and pry about whatever it was, Billy needed to disappear and Monty without hesitation would follow him to the ends of the earth to watch his back. As far as Monty was concerned, nothing is more important than the bond of family, after all if you could not rely on family to do right by you, who the hell would? Who indeed.

It was in the month of March that they set foot on the sandy beach of Palma Nova. The tourist season was just starting and the place was gearing itself up ready for the onslaught of holidaymakers. They spent the first few days acclimatising to the heat and getting a base for a golden tan. Pulling the college girls, that were taking a break before their exams, was a piece of cake, especially with Monty the poseur by Billy's side. Monty was a body building fanatic and needless to say was a well developed young man. Everything was tight, in place and was twice the size of an average guy. Thankfully, Billy was above average in every area so he did not look so insignificant next to him. Monty's sunbathing trick was to use oil instead of lotion to capture the rays because this made his skin shiny and his definition stand out.

By the end of their first week on the run, they had slept with the entire collection of college chick's that were staying in their apartment complex and had done the tour of local bars and clubs.

Deep down Billy knew he was just going through the motions, in his mind and in his heart, Billy was not having the amount of fun that he was portraying to the outside world or even to Monty for that matter. Even here in the sunny climate of Spain, with no one around who knew who he was, Billy still needed to get away from it all, but that was the whole reason they had flown to Magaluf.

Billy decided it was time to give Denny a call and tell him that he was in the neighbourhood. Billy had to go through this whole conversation at first just to remind him of who he was, when the penny finally dropped Denny tried to cover himself by saying he was only pulling Billy's leg.

Nevertheless, as time went by, it was evident that Denny's memory left a lot to be desired. Billy and Monty caught a cab to where Denny had his club established and he came out and greeted them at the door of his own place the 'Apples and Pears 2'.

"Welcome to my little establishment fella's, everything is on the house for you both" He then put his arms around their necks to try to imitate a double headlock, it didn't come off. "Nice place Denny must have set you back?" Monty figured he would break the ice with this new face; Billy had vouched for Denny whole heartedly so the guy must have been on the up and up. Monty was still in the dark over what happened to make Billy want and need to skip the country but knew that he had to keep one eye on Billy and the other on every one else.

"Nah, it was a steal" and with that started to laugh, Monty figured some thing's were best left unknown.

"Come on; let me get you both a drink". Now Denny was a proper character, after he somehow wangled the ownership of a club called "Diego's" which he then changed to 'Apples and Pears 2' Denny started using his new found earnings to buy up retirement homes in Spain. This guy was always about making a deal.

"You fella's out here for the season?" Monty looked at Billy with a 'do you fancy a spot of that' gaze in his eyes. Billy figured it couldn't hurt to spend a few months doing a spot of work while hiding from the world, it could help take his mind off of things and keep him away from the hell storm that was happening back home.

"Why, you got some work for us?" Denny looked around his place as some old Abba tune was being kicked out of his sound system and let out a laugh.

"What you wanna do, work the door or the bar?" There's a question, you have a genetic freak that stood in at five foot eleven and there was Billy, weighing over eighteen stone and standing in at six foot two, they both agreed to work the bar. After all how hard could it be if Tom Cruise could do it in the movie "Cocktail"? That and the fact Billy didn't trust himself if he had to start wailing on someone, would he have been able to leave them breathing or just like a drug addict, would he carry on to get that first time feeling back. Billy felt like he was really starting to lose it and he did not seem to care in which way.

Denny said the boys could stay in the flat above the club, so they moved their gear out of the complex where they were staying and set up home in their new gaff at Denny's. Its big balcony doors led out to a roof top patio area where the refugees set up some sun lounger's and bought a kiddie's paddling pool, seeing as they were a bit of a walk from the beach (about ten minutes). That became their castle as well as Billy's fortress of solitude.

Thankfully March and April were not busy months and the boys had a chance to get used to the world of bar work, they paced themselves at first and chatted up the women who wanted to know why the bar staff were bigger built and more menacing than the bouncers on the door. It was a nice and easy time, which gave Billy the breathing space he needed to get his head around the internal struggle he was going through. Then May came and so did the onslaught of tourists.

Denny's place was almost open for twenty-four hours a day; it caught the breakfast crowd, the lunch crowd and the all-nighters. Monty and Billy worked mainly the night times from eight 'til six in the morning, if they had scored, then they were on the job for another hour or so followed by sleep. Normally they would get up around two and catch some rays on their roof top suntrap, eat, exercise and get ready for the next shift. Denny handled the late mornings and early lunch shift, but if he got lucky with either a bored neglected housewife or a young impressionable girlie then he would come wake one of them up to cover the bar. That became their routine and it was a busy routine that Billy was grateful for.

Billy could see that Monty was getting a little worried by the way Billy would sit bolt upright from his sleep, begging for the screaming to stop. Monty would fuss around him all the time, never letting Billy out of his sight. Billy was glad he was with real, close family while he was going through this conflict. If you cannot count on family, who can you count on?

Every now and then, during the evening shift Billy and Monty would have to spring out from the bar and sort out some unruly punters or do money runs through the crowd to the office. Billy loved the power feeling you got from either being in a confrontation or from the possibility of being in one. The blood surges round your body, your heart pumps twice as fast, you get that little tremor running down your spine and you can taste the victory before it even happens. All the things Billy loved about violence seemed to be heightened lately and he could feel he was walking more to the dark side. Billy seemed to be falling into a self-destruct mode, not giving a damn about who he might hurt or what he had done before coming out here.

Denny had came up with a guaranteed moneymaker to capture the Hen night business. He had Monty and Billy stripping off and shaking their thang's in the ladies faces. Hey, if it was good enough for the Chippendales then it was good enough for these two, and besides, you needed fella's who can handle themselves because these women were wild! They were scratched, clawed, grabbed and (wo) manhandled by these liquored up, sexually frustrated, sun charged women. Some of which could have been your Mum's. Now there is food for thought. Billy would sleep with every woman that wanted him, sometimes two or three at a time. He was out of control and loved every minute of it, his path to self-destruction was narrowing and yet he was still proudly walking it.

June flew by with more of the same and then July came and went Billy turned twenty-four that August; it seemed like only yesterday when he and his family and friends were playing as kids on Chingford Hall estate. Time flies and memories become a blur; Billy felt he had done too much too soon and that there was nowhere else for him to go. Billy guessed his recent deeds were making him question his own mortality; would what he done come back ten fold and consume his existence? That was when Billy decided to make a choice, live with guilt and consider ending it all every waking moment or wash away all feelings and emotions from his being. Get on living or get on dying, pros and cons, right and wrong, there was no other reasonable choice to make.

Monty must have sensed that Billy was on the verge of flipping a coin on whether he should continue living or not because he went out and made a call for re-enforcements. Monty figured that family was a strong issue for Billy so he needed his brothers around him, the only problem was Monty did not realise that one brother would not be attending no matter how many times he called him.

Jason had come out to Magaluf on a boy's holiday and brought some of the Michaels clan with him, Monty went to the airport to meet them all to arrange the surprise for his suicidal cousin. He was becoming more concerned when Billy started to mumble to himself about his old childhood friend Tony. Monty feared Billy was going to take the same way out as Tony did and felt that he needed family around him to get him through it all. Monty was right in his findings; Billy was spending more and more time looking over the edge of the mountains that Monty and he would jog along. The amount of times Billy would just stop and look at the drop, picturing what his mangled body would look like if he just stepped off and fell to the ground. Images of that old woman on the estate, falling from her window when he was just a kid, kept springing to mind. Would his blood stain the rocks below like her blood did on that tower block?

On the journey back to the club, Jason was telling Monty about the trouble he had gotten into with the

Livertons, they were not happy that they had to endure not only the old bill breathing down their necks regarding a certain individual bound to a chair but also the cost of setting up a new chop shop. That was Billy's fault; he just had to push the boundaries. Nevertheless, Jason was a good mechanic and an even better body man, so when it eventually all died down for them, Jason said he would pay the costs of the new set up, which Colin threw in with to help out. The police had given up looking and had it as an ongoing investigation.

When the people wagon reached back to the 'Apples and Pears 2', Billy was standing in the doorway to see who Monty had rushed off to meet so eagerly that morning. The first face he saw was Jason who beamed him a big old friendly smile; he then motioned his head to turn Billy's attention to the other passengers. From out of the side door of the seven seater, stepped Stuart, who tried to give the same smile Jason was but the pain and concern would not allow him to carry it off. He was followed out of the vehicle by Vaughan, who bowed his head and looked at the floor in an ashamed kind of way; Vaughan was feeling guilty that Billy's present state of mind was his fault and that he did not help to stop what had happened a few months previous. Then the next brother, who was bringing up the rear, stepped out from side door, Mikey looked Billy dead in the eye and gave that same cheeky that he gives the ladies. The cavalry had arrived and it was time to catch up on all the gossip and to get the feedback of that night.

Mikey had moved up the ladder amongst the Eves family crew and was now in a position to step back and let others get their hands dirty while he took a percentage. However, Mikey being Mikey was getting bored and needed hands on action, so Billy did not see the easy life lasting too long. Mikey also told Billy that Dave Love had been asking after him, and told Mikey to tell him to give him a ring when he got back to England.

Stuart and Kelly were on a time out in their relationship, she tried some of that 'I want half' routine claiming that she was seen as a common-in-law wife, common being the operative word, and deserved compensation. This did not go down well, especially seeing as the house they lived in was also Billy's and Mikey's and not Stuart's alone. After she realised she was not going to get a penny, she sloped off back to her home town of Whoresville while the pair worked out their differences.

Vaughan quit the meat factory, which under the circumstances seemed like a missed opportunity of a constant line of homo jokes, and was filling in for him working along side with Derek and doing some collecting for Sammy. Vaughan felt that since the way that Billy discovered that he was gay and felt that the bloodline of the family had failed, Vaughan wanted to prove that he could still inflict damage and help the honour of the Michaels' name. Besides, he liked the work and wished that it was a bit more regular. When he was not working along side Derek, he would be hanging about with Darren and the two were still handling the loan sharking business out of the Chequers pub in Walthamstow. Although there were signs of it reaching the end of its run, all good things have to end sometime and Billy did not see it being too long before this was one of them. Vaughan then went on to tell Billy that Michael had apparently been nipping up to Swindon to see Wanda, the beached whale from the road trip to Marlborough, on a regular basis. Billy believed love was starting to blossom there between them, but he did not see the attraction.

Then the rest of the news came, their baby brother Craig did not intend to ever leave home and was starting to make a nuisance of himself. Then he was always the one that was shielded by their parents, especially their Mum and therefore did not have to learn the lessons the rest of them did. Consequently, he never attained any real street smarts on how to conduct himself. He was just spoilt and would have to eventually snap out of it. He was taking liberties and answering back, he was breaking the five golden rules that was handed down by Freddie a life time ago, and it became evident that in every family barrel where there were always going to be bad apples, different coloured apples and at times apples that were really oranges in disguise.

As Billy sat there, listening to the tales of home, he felt himself starting to sink again; guilt was starting to win over from the feelings of destruction he was having. Perhaps Tony had the right idea after all; ending it all would balance the scales, set things right and even out the force. Billy looked at the faces of his nearest and dearest and just like that, he was back on top of the world and in a mood to party.

Monty introduced the family clan to Denny, who was ecstatic about meeting them all. He kept having drinks sent over and it was not long before they were pissed up and laughing about everything and absolutely nothing, it was just like old times. That's when Denny threw on the karaoke machine and started to belt out some tune from some singer that they were all way too young to know. Denny was like a man possessed, swinging his hips about like a Tom Jones wannabe, the Michaels brothers thought it was time that they showed him how it was meant to be done.

Both Mikey and Vaughan had been blessed with not only size and strength but with fantastic singing voices, and at the right pitch, even Monty and Jason could sound all right. However, Stuart and Billy could not carry a tune in a suitcase, although it did not stop them from singing. All six of them jumped on stage and selected the tune "Try a little Tenderness" by Otis Redding, Vaughan started it off with Mikey singing every other chunk, Stuart and Billy added short, deep bass bits while the other two harmonised. They could have taken this act on the road, you had your boy bands but these guys were a man's band. They were even drawing in an audience, which in turn prompted an encore, consisting of "Cloud Nine" by The Temptations and "You to me are everything" by the Real Thing. That afternoon turned into a karaoke party that just did not want to end.

The next couple of weeks flew by and everyday was a happy one but it all came to an end and it pained Billy to see the fella's at the airport, waiting for their flight back home. Having his family around made him forget the war that was raging on in his head and heart but now that they were leaving, the fight stepped up a notch and the enemy was winning.

Chapter Twenty-Three

Billy was sitting in the bar one morning, when Denny came over and started to shoot the breeze. Billy had always thought that Denny was a bit of a flake at times, but he had a big heart and good intentions and he never struck Billy as someone who would be astute enough to see an emotional problem. At first Denny asked Billy if he was on drugs, because he felt there must have been a strong reason as to why he had such bad mood swings. Billy was not the same guy he had met years before in Lloret Del Mar nor was he the same pie eyed youth outside the Thunderdome, back in the West End of London. Denny said it was obvious that something was bothering Billy and he should just get it off his chest. He was there to listen and not to judge. Billy did not know where to start, his relationship with Nikki was over and he had quit his day job just as the opportunity to have a promising career presented it self. Billy had made a conscious decision to return to his old ways and live the life he was always destined to live.

It was the telling of the missing piece of the puzzle that followed which changed Billy's life forever.

Seventeenth of March, nineteen ninety two
There they were, standing in Billy's front room, all staring down each other when in his head, Billy could hear the bell ring and the fight was on. He and Mikey went at it as

Vaughan tried to pull them apart, which in turn got Vaughan a few slugs to the gut and face so he then returned the compliment to both his brothers and all three of them were going at it tooth and nail. As Nikki was still in the corner of the room, hiding her modesty and screaming for them to stop, Stuart, who Billy had called earlier on, turned up and walked in to see his three brothers knocking seven bells of shit out of each other. He looked over to Nikki who then pleaded with him to stop them from killing each other and went into the kitchen to fill up a large saucepan with cold water. He then came back in to the war zone and poured the contents all over his siblings. The shock of the cold water gave them a wake up call and they all stopped out of shock, it was at that moment that Nikki, who couldn't contain her bodily movements any longer let out a fart that brought with it the smell of death, it was foul (show me a man who doesn't laugh at toilet humour and I'll show you someone who wasn't in that front room), all four of the boys broke out in laughter and although a few extra digs were given out, the main fighting stopped. Nikki rushed off to use the bathroom and put some clothes on while Mikey himself got dressed, while still amongst his brothers and Vaughan's exploring eyes. That eventful night took place on March the seventeenth and the luck of the Irish was running true that St Patrick's Day. The need for a drink and a civilised airing of their problems was on the cards and the only late night bar they knew of to blow off some steam and enjoy a knee's up was in O'Donnell's bar in Bethnal Green.

It was while the brothers were knocking back a few beers, Billy included, issuing apologies and explanations and begging Vaughan not to go in to too much detail that Mikey went over to the bar to get a round in, when he spotted the runaway dealer from the Christmas incident walking past. Mikey went over to the table to tell Billy who he had just saw, at first, Billy just laughed but Mikey then ran outside and tore off up the street. He swung the fella in question around and low and behold, it was him, the dirty, little double-crosser *who made off with some very important people's drugs. It was a spur of the moment thing because Mikey lifted the fella clean off the ground and hoisted him over his shoulder and started to run back towards the pub where his brothers were now waiting outside to see what was going on.*

"Get the fucking motor started!" Billy ran off to get the car, while the rest of the family didn't know whether to laugh, run to the car with Billy or go back into O'Donnell's and make out they didn't see anything. As the car screeched to a halt along side the curb, the boot was popped; the scumbag was thrown in and the whole clan bundled into the car.

"Where to?" Billy revved the gas pedal waiting for a direction.

"Go to Jason's garage, we'll teach this cunt a lesson" So they went to the same garage where the fella's co-conspirator was introduced to entry-level dentistry 101. It seemed a long old drive from Bethnal Green to Enfield, especially with the fella in the trunk pounding away at anything remotely solid. But they all knew that this was a situation that was going to get out of hand, after all you don't steal three hundred thousand pounds worth of drugs and think you're just going to get your wrist slapped when you're caught. It was a case of either you are in or you are out, no second chances, no one thinking less of you, it is the nature of the business they were all involved in. When the call was made to Jason to get the gates opened and the question was asked, Jason said yes but Colin opted for out, as did Stuart and Vaughan, like it was said, no hard feelings, this wasn't everyone's cup of tea. Billy loved his brothers, and if truth was known he didn't want them to be a part of it anyway, so he went to drop them off outside Stuart's house, when they parked up outside his place Vaughan was refusing to get out.

"Do the right thing and go into the house, V. I'll call you tomorrow" He sat fast but it was for all the wrong reasons.

"I should stay with you, family should stick together."

"If you're concerned about the bond of family, then do as

I ask and call it a night. It's not your problem, now get out the car." Vaughan looked at Billy, lowered his eyes, and reached for the door handle.

"Make sure you call me tomorrow" Vaughan got out and slowly walked up to the front door, while Stuart comforted him.

"Drive Bill, let's get this over with" It must have been truth or dare time because Mikey hadn't called Billy 'Bill' in years and off they drove to meet the moment they knew had to come.

They got to Jason's garage at around three thirty in the morning, Billy reversed the car in and they jumped out. Neither of them saying anything to the other; it was like they were all on automatic pilot or something, they knew what needed to done. Mikey shut the garage doors; Jason got the lights while Billy got the chair. Because of the last incident at the garage, Jason found that he had to throw that other chair out, seemed that the fabric was holding onto the smell of urine. Their small bladdered friend had soiled it so much that new furniture was needed, so Jason and Colin had gone out and hijacked some aluminium garden chairs. They were all right for drinking your mugs of tea and reading the paper in but they were so low compared to the other chair that they thought it might steal from the moment. To make matters worst, there was only a little bit of gaffer tape left, so Jason found himself scrounging around for plastic ties but only managed to find strips of electrical wire.

Mikey pulled the dealer out from the boot, and they started going to work on him. All three of them were kicking him in his gut and back while he was slumped there on the floor. In between administering the hiding, Mikey asked if there was anything left of the pills or the money. This fella insisted that there was not anything left and that they should know that already, had this low life been talking to his old running buddy who had found himself in this very garage a few months earlier?

"Why should we know if you have any thing left?" Billy figured the guy was stalling for time, and would tell you he sucked on the dick of Christ if it stopped him from getting a similar treatment to his friend.

"Because it was your brother, Gary that set the whole thing up, he told me that it would all be cool". This put a fly into the ointment, Gary had always been a loose cannon in comparison to the rest of them but this would mean that not only did he make off with a vast amount of someone's money but he put his own brother in the firing line. Mikey thought back to see if had ever mentioned to Gary about the deal, he couldn't remember. Billy pointed out that anyone could have told him, Gary was in the business himself and had made enough contacts to catch wind of that little whisper. They had to tie up every loose end before word got out that it was open season on the Michaels family. They took a time out and bound this fella to the almost comical garden chair with the electrical wire, using the last piece of gaffer tape on his mouth.

They made up a story that the guys supposedly bulk buyer skanked him and took everything off him for the price of a beating. He had came down to East London to try and earn some money so he could return home to South London and make things right. Mikey made a call to the people the fella had cheated.

"It's me; I got that piece of scum that made off with your stuff. Whatdj'a want me to do with him?" The line went quiet.

"Does he 'ave any of the gear left?"

"No."

"What about some money?"

"Nah, he reckons he was ripped off."

"Who by?"

"Scot's" Now villains from Scotland are in a league of their own, and the decision had to be weighed up whether or not to push that side of the matter further.

"Did he say who?"

"No one I've heard of" The line went quiet again.

"Hurt 'im 'til he passes out, bring 'im round and then hurt 'im again" Mikey waited to hear if that was the end of the sentence.

"Is that it?" The line went quiet for a third time.

"For now, we still want names, see what you can get out of him and then bring him over to us, what he won't tell you we'll make him tell us". And then the line went dead. Mikey walked back over to his brother, he just looked Billy in the eye and he knew what had to be done, Jason had not fully twigged yet. They huddled up and started discussing their options; they were in a very tricky situation.

For Mikey to stay on good, breathable terms with the South London family he run's with, he must make this thing happen here and now. There was no way he could offer this dirt bag up if all he was going to do was serve up Gary and the rest of the Michaels family on being a part of it. At the same time, the powers that be were still expecting to question this guy themselves, either way Mikey was screwed. On top of that, this thing would have to take place there in Jason's garage because they could not chance going elsewhere and getting a tug. This then would put Jason in the frame and the North London family he ran with, who in all fairness were not going to be that forgiving. Plus they had picked the fella up off the street, as he was visiting people in East London and they had no idea who. If that wasn't bad enough, they had their own family involved in the middle of it all, and no matter what, they were lined up to take the fall if it all came on top. This was not going to end pretty.

They decided to pack up all of Jason's files and tools, and chuck them in the car, what didn't fit, did not go. Everything that was left they covered in oil, the logic being that if you wiped the oil away, you would also wipe clean the fingerprints because none of them thought to wear gloves or had the time to deep clean the place. Billy then opened the doors and Mikey drove the car outside while Jason started dousing their tied up friend and the rest of his garage in petrol. The guy was frantically trying to get loose, tears rolled down his cheeks, all hope faded from his eyes, he fucked up and it was all for nothing. Greed is the wrong deadly sin to have in this game, there is enough to go round, and it is only those who get greedy that end up out of the race. That is why the Michaels boys had always stayed below the radar and maintained a low profile. They are all still around while others are either doing time or rolling in a box, it's not about doing good business, it's about doing smart business.

Billy stroked a match and tossed it into the room; it landed in a puddle of petrol. The heat from the flame ignited the foul smelly liquid and the flames that rose started to absorb every drop, as it spread across the room. Billy could not help but watch as the flames started to burn the fella's clothes, the flames went higher and his hair caught alight. The smell of cooking meat started to taint the air, a sudden burst of heat as the oil-covered tools caught alight. Billy could suddenly hear the fella screaming as the flames melted away the gaffer tape that was on his mouth. It was as though his whole face was melting, even the chair he was tied to, couldn't take the heat as it started to give way. The whole place was melting down, as the ceiling became black from the smoke. Billy was mesmerised by it all and it was not until Mikey ran over and dragged him away that he snapped out of it. All three of them got into the car and drove to Mikey's place, they needed to get out of the area, and into one where they were not really known. Jason then unloaded the car and Mikey drove it to the breakers yard so it could be disposed of, they seemed to lose so many cars that way lately.

Billy couldn't sleep until the adrenaline rush had died down, he felt euphoric and invincible, all at the same time, and they were emotions that allowed him to sleep soundly that night. But like any good drug, you soon come down and reality sets in. The sound of their victim screaming and the images of watching him melt into a black tar like substance *haunted Billy's head for many years. Nevertheless, as you do the next bad thing, crossing that next line in the sand, everything else becomes the norm and any thoughts of it are pushed to the back of your mind.*

It was two days later before the newspaper started to run the story about this chargrilled body that was found in this North London garage. The police were investigating everyone they thought could be connected. They pulled in the Livertons and a couple of other little firms but of course, there was nothing to tie them to the scene. Jason had a lot of explaining to do when he showed his face back in that neighbourhood. While Mikey was being treated like a king for helping send a message to all those who thought they could get away with taking the piss, although they wanted the fella alive for questioning, Mikey told them that the guy gave up his desire to live and died from heart failure or something. As for Billy, he just needed to get away.

He felt like a piggy in the middle, on one side someone was getting into trouble when on the other side, someone was getting all the kudos. When in actual fact it was him and him alone who took that person's life, it was Billy that should face the music and it was Billy who should get the glory. But all Billy was getting was mixed emotions on the whole thing. He thought back to when Tony had shot that fella that tried to cheat him, he remembered the look in his eyes, and it was as though he had lost something. Some might say it was his soul, others would say it was his will to go on living, and considering the turn of events, those people could have been right. But Billy was paranoid that the same look was now in his eyes, which would mean the same turn of events could happen to him.

Denny had listened to everything Billy had to say about that night, he never interrupted, and he never said a word. When Billy had finished telling his tale, they both just sat there in silence. Billy wished his Mum were there to hold him like she did that Sunday afternoon, when he was five years old. However, she was not and it was not the first time that she had not been there to reassure him that everything was going to be all right. It was at that moment that Billy knew nothing would ever seem the same again.

The next morning Billy had set out early and started running along the same mountainside where he had contemplated day after day to just step off and pay his penance. He kept running all the way to the top, his lungs felt like they wanted to burst and his legs turned to jelly. Billy stood at the edge, catching his breath and looked down at the ground that seemed to beckon him. Billy knew what had to be done, he raised his head to feel the warmth of the sun on his face once more, there was a slight breeze blowing and for a split instance every thing seemed to be in line with nature, the setting was so tranquil. Billy raised his arms, acting like a human cross, letting the breeze lift him off the ground until he felt like he was floating. Billy took a deep breath, filling his exhausted lungs with every ounce of air they could take. And then, without warning Billy released it all, in the form of a declaration for anyone to hear and for the mountains to echo throughout its caverns.

"I'm Billy Michaels and this is my life, my choices and my way!"

Billy was tired of being a victim of his own decisions; it had to end there and then. He turned around and started to run back down the mountain trail, Billy was still on the path of self-destruction but he decided to travel down it in his own time and his own way. Billy only wanted to regret the things he did not do, not the things he did. The guy was scum, he got what he deserved and Billy was through feeling sorry for his actions. If the images wanted to haunt him in his dreams over the years, then so be it, but Billy still had things to do, place's to go and people to meet. Besides there was unfinished business with his younger brother that needed to be settled, and anything that had taken place already was not going to compete with that meeting. Billy just was not finished living yet and that was the final argument to his dilemma. He would go when it is his time to go and it was not that time, that place or that way.

He is Billy Michaels and this is his life, it can drive you over the edge if you are not strong enough to handle the lines you cross. Emotions will play with your mind until you either snap or learn to deal with it. Tony could not get to grips with the feelings he had inside and decided to end it all, but Billy was stronger than that, it just took a while for him to realise how much stronger he was.

Billy was now looking forward to returning back to England and to the life that he led. Billy wanted to be amongst his family and the business they dealt in.

There was no turning back for Billy and he would not have had it any other way…

Lightning Source UK Ltd.
Milton Keynes UK
30 March 2010

152140UK00001B/17/A